CLUB OLYMPUS

James Morley

C

This book would not be possible without the help and support of so many people.

Thank you to my cousin, Bethan and dad, Lee, who both read early versions and gave great feedback.

Thank you to my partner, Caleb, who gave me the emotional support to keep going when I wanted to give up.

Thank you to my mum, Marie, who let me grow up weird and imaginative.

PART I

One

God, King, Boss

The dappled light of an early morning sun fell through the gap in Zeus' curtains. A soft haze of dust danced in the yellow beam that illuminated the room where the ancient god slept. As the brightness began to pierce through his eyelid, he tossed and turned, fighting the command of his mind to wake. The figure next to him still slept soundly even as Zeus finally opened his eyes and pushed himself to sit on the edge of the bed. The worn brass creaked, and the springs popped as he lifted his weight off the tattered mattress. The soft silk of the sheets fell away from his body revealing the toned physique underneath.

Zeus had always looked older than the other gods. The burden of ruling from the skies had sent him grey before his time, and his messy hair and cropped beard showed only the occasional strands of the dark black he had once had. However, his body had kept its strength. He grabbed the shirt that had been tossed in passion over the back of a chair and pulled it over his broad chest, covering the scruff of grey hair that covered his pectorals and descended towards his mid-rift.

The woman in the bed turned to him and smiled. The deep red lipstick that had drawn Zeus in the night before was now nothing more than a faint smudge. Her hair, that had seemed so inviting, now fell in tangled lumps over her shoulders. The curves of her body were hidden under the billowing silk sheets. Zeus had been entranced the night before, when soft light and a tight dress had made the woman look like the goddesses of old, but in the light of day, laying before him, he saw nothing but another in a long line of mediocre women. He pined for the lost days of queens and goddesses, when beauty beyond words surrounded him. She came towards Zeus, her green eyes sparkling with passion. She ran her hand over him and began to tease the top button of his shirt undone. Zeus grabbed the slender wrist and threw her to the bed. He didn't have time for this. He had an empire to run, and she had served her purpose. He put on the last of his clothes and made his way to leave the room.

"I'll see you at the club tonight then?" the nameless woman asked, deepening her voice into a sultry and seductive purr. Zeus appreciated it but a voice wasn't enough. He turned to her.

"You'll be working at the Oceanid from now on. Don't contact me." He instructed, staring down at her. She looked so small on the bed: weak and used up like the space she laid in. The room was now bright with the light of the morning. It illuminated the spackled walls and grotty corner kitchen. Mismatched furniture filled the rest, and faded green drapes hung limply beside the one window. The place almost seemed to sigh with depression. Thankfully, Zeus only needed this dilapidated studio, with its constant smell of mould and damp, for his trysts. He could return to the luxury he had earned, now he had had his fun. The girl looked up at him, her eyes still wide with desire and eagerness.

He closed the door behind him and walked from the apartment. The elevator rattled as it descended through the grotty floors of rotted hallways and staircases. Between the grates he saw the dregs of society move through their turgid lives. Lesser men, who had had their way with his prostitutes, shuffled, burdened with shame, from the tiny apartments. Drunks, who had sold their life to him for an ounce of whisky, slept beside faded doorways in a stupor. He rolled his eyes as he watched the world of filth swirl around him. Again, he found his mind drifting back to the ancient days, yearning for the time when debauchery was done right. The elevator shuddered to a stop and Zeus walked from the building into the blinding light of day. The mesh over the curtains in the apartment had managed to filter out some of the brightness, but in the streets of New York it blazed in his eyes.

His car sat, still parked, on the side of the road. Its shimmering silver paint glowed, a beacon of decadence and wealth; a diamond buried deep in the grubby bricks of Manhattan apartment blocks. Of all the inventions of the modern humans, Zeus loved cars the most. Propped up against his beloved vehicle he found his son. Apollo reclined against the polished paint job, one leg up, the dirty sole of his shoe threatening to scuff the perfect exterior. His pinstripe suit fit well against his muscular body, the lines of clothing pulling at his frame. His face was shadowed under his trilby, the golden skin and hair almost hidden. He flipped his dime into the air, catching it every time it fell back in a spiral of silver. Zeus wondered how long he must have been waiting that he'd resort to dime flipping and car scuffing to keep himself occupied. It was only when he saw Artemis that his heart truly sank.

"Get the fuck off my car." He bellowed towards the pair of them, causing them to start. Artemis leapt from her reclining position on the bonnet, lowering her slender frame to the ground. The long pleats of her dress ruffled as she descended, beads and pearls clattering together against her chest. Zeus had rarely seen her look so feminine. She usually looked like she had just finished rummaging through someone's garbage. The two of them must have been traversing the speakeasies last night if they looked so elegant. He ran his hand over the curve of the black wheel arch, and then moved his gaze to the long square bonnet and Bentley insignia, checking for any sign of damage. Luckily for his children he found none.

"Alright boss," Apollo began, "Sorry about that, forgot how precious the wheels are to you."

"More precious than you two. I'll happily have Ares riddle you with holes if you touch my ride again. Clear?" Zeus replied, only half joking with his son. "Anyway, why are you two here, and why do you look so well dressed?"

He shot a glance at Artemis as he spoke, taking in her sumptuous outfit, that was ruined by the long mess of tangled brunette that fell from her head.

"We found the punk who's been running the speakeasy on seventh. Thought you might like to pay him a little visit." Apollo said, his azure eyes glinting with glee over a job well done.

"That sounds more like a job for Ares. Go tell him."

"Oh, c'mon boss, when's the last time you enjoyed your job."

"It has its perks" Zeus replied staring up at the window of the apartment he had just fled. Of course, he had never had a problem finding female companionship, but being the most notorious gangster in New York helped his search for carnal conquests.

"Fine." Apollo sighed. "I'll go tell Ares, I hope he's in the mood to crack a few fingers. I did not spend my night resisting every advance that came my way to not have my hard work lead to violence."

"Your sister seems to be able to keep herself away from advances." Zeus scoffed.

"Only because she's a prude with a cunt like a bank vault." He laughed back, the two of them sniggering at Artemis' lack of sexual encounters. Artemis didn't respond. She had endured teasing for a long time now and had become increasingly used to it.

"Just because I follow my senses and not my genitals, doesn't make me a prude. Plus think of all the extra intelligence I have keeping my brain in my head rather than my balls."

She walked forward and grabbed Apollo by the arm, dragging the still chuckling god away to find Ares. Some small part of Zeus wanted to go with them and teach the man muscling in on his territory a lesson, but that was Ares' job. Zeus was the boss and needed to keep his hands as clean as possible.

Once he was in the car the door clicked closed. The sound prompted his driver to throw his paper to the seat beside him and start the engine. As the car moved through the bustling streets of early morning New York, Zeus closed his eyes and listened to the sounds around him. Cars rumbled, the last few horses left working in the city clopped, people yelled, and the city buzzed with life. His head slowly started to throb as Dionysus' special liquor from the night before caught up with him, circulating through his veins. Back in the days of power he had never had a hangover, but as the centuries rolled over him his humanness had started to take over his aging body.

"Sir we've arrived" his driver announced with the melancholy formality of a man who just wanted his task to be over. Zeus raised a grey eyebrow at the back of the man's head as he opened the door and walked out. Olympus hardware was the epitome of nothingness. The worn shop front and dirty windows hid only a dust covered collection of tools scattered through a variety of tubs, buckets, and shelves. A wizened man sat behind the counter reading a worn book through thick spectacles. Age dripped from the man's body, pulling his skin down toward the ground. Every part of him drooped, including the clothes which swamped his feeble frame. He looked at Zeus from the corner of his eyes and moved his hand to the latch under the counter. The wall behind him swung open at the soft clunk, the smell of stale alcohol and cigarette smoke rising to meet him from the darkness of the doorway.

The club at the bottom of the stairs looked so different in the day. The soft light of table lamps was replaced by the harsh ceiling lights, the chairs, usually full of people laughing and gossiping, were upended on top of the tables, the once warm smoke-filled air was now cold now harsh and full of tension. The table closest to the small stage was hosting his family. Hera and Athena sat muttering together, their hushed tones and solemn looks giving Zeus cause for concern.

Two

Thugs

A res pulled his braces over his shoulders, the elasticated material stretching itself taught against his firm body. His shirt fit well, the white material only just tightening around the buttons on his broad chest. Everything about the man was large. His body seemed to shoot like a tree from the ground, his oversized feet rooting him, sturdy to the spot. His arms and legs were as thick as bollards. Every item of clothing he wore was specially tailored to accommodate the girth of the mighty warrior god. His brown slacks matched the bowler hat he placed on top of his cropped hair, and the coarse material rubbed against his calloused skin. He only glanced at himself briefly as he passed the mirror, but he liked what he saw.

Other members of the family like Apollo, Aphrodite, or the insufferable runt Hermes liked to look good. They cared about fashion and beauty. Each one of them spent hours refining their clothing collection and preening themselves in front of gilded mirrors. It was a waste of time in Ares' opinion. He only needed to look intimidating, to be able to terrify the people who saw him with just a glance or a flex of his muscles. He didn't need a bursting wardrobe to be able to do that. His sheer size and the dark holes of his eyes were able to turn the bravest of men into a piss-stained cry-baby.

When Zeus had suggested coming to New York and working in the underground the others had been sceptical, but Ares had jumped at the opportunity. The criminal underbelly of a lurid, decadent city was where he belonged. He had led militias, battalions, rebellions, and riots in his long life walking the earth, but nothing gave him the satisfaction that his current work did. Ares loved being an enforcer. Everywhere he walked people treated him with respect. They nodded or cowered when he came near them. They always had a drink or meal to offer him, to make his duties more bearable. This is what war was for: the attainment of glory, and there was no one more glorious than him on the island of Manhattan. He felt like he should walk around in armour that glistened in the sun, but he settled for his simple outfit as he embarked on his day.

He made his way downtown, the flow of people carrying him with them, like a wild river that moved through the streets, carving a canyon between the sentinel-like buildings rising around him. He rolled his sleeves up revealing burly arms bristling with dark hair, the same thick shag that coated the rest of his body. He saw women look at him, their gazes fixed on his masculinity and strength. He gave them small nods but made no effort to pursue them. It wasn't that Ares had gone off women, he wasn't bed hopping with every man who came along like Hermes, it was just that he found the women of the modern world dull. In his youth the women and goddesses around him had been sinuous, rippling, creatures of strength and determination. Women had fought and hunted and taken down great men and beasts. Now they sprayed themselves with perfume and tittered every time a man said something remotely comical. When Ares could be certain he would find a strong woman of impressive character, he would take her to bed in a second.

As he reached his destination, he moved his focus from women to work. The restaurant he stood in front of was a small Italian place, a coffee house that threw pizzas in an oven more than a real eatery. The window was dark, the venetian blinds pulled low to keep the light of day out. Even the murky glass in the door was covered. Small signs with scrawled, handwritten offers had been stuck to the glass surfaces boasting of coffee that was cheap and food that was good. Ares knew that both of the statements were a lie, but luckily for him he wasn't here to try the food.

He pushed the door open, causing the brass bell above it to ring with a high-pitched excitement at the presence of a customer. The room was dark, the smell of black coffee and garlic almost strangling the air from Ares' lungs. The candles on the table did little to compensate for the lack of light that made it through the blind-covered windows. Smoke surrounded everyone, the gathering of elderly Italian men that were dispersed amongst the tables contributing to the ever-growing cloud with rollup cigarettes, fat cigars, and bent pipes. Each table was covered with a grid work of ivory, the men content to while away their days playing dominos. None looked up from their games to see Ares enter, their concentration locked on which inane move they would make next in their game that did not matter.

Ares walked towards the bar where another elderly man sat reading the New York Post. Some story about the stock market was plastered on the front page, but Ares didn't care, so he simply glanced and ignored it. Guiseppi Bianci was a man so short Ares was sure he must have had his legs cut off at the knee at some point. His age was all over him, turning his skin to leather and forcing his bones to protrude so obviously he might as well have been a xylophone covered in an old handbag. His white hair was nothing more than whisps atop his head, almost blending in with the smoke that was on the air. Once upon a time he had been a player in Manhattan, but that had changed when Ares and his family had set their sights on the island. Now he was just another old Italian with an espresso machine.

"Ares," he said, without looking up from his paper. "Is it that time of the month already?" His thick Italian accent making the words only just discernible.

"I'm afraid so Guiseppi." He replied stretching out his brawny hand to the old man.

"My protection rackets actually got you something." Guiseppi huffed as he reached under the counter and pulled a manilla envelope free, the bulge of dollar bills obvious.

"Your windows aren't smashed and there's not another Italian coffee shop in sight. I'd say you've got plenty." Ares said as he took the envelope, stuffing it into his trouser pocket. The corner stabbed out, but Ares didn't mind. He couldn't imagine anyone would be stupid enough to try and pickpocket him.

"Coffee?"

"Thanks, but I'd rather drink the dishwater."

With that Ares left the building, content to set out on his day of collecting payments. If he was lucky someone would refuse, and he would get to see how many punches it would take to break all their ribs. He was feeling like he might be able to beat his record.

"Well, Arti I owe you ten bucks, I genuinely didn't think he stank enough for you to track him by smell alone but here we are." Apollo said, beaming at his big brother as he bounded forward, the pressed lines of his suit barely moving as he made his way up the pavement. Artemis followed behind him, her eyebrows raised as she took in the scene of the blonde fop trying to lightly tease the hulking mass of muscle and rage that was Ares.

"You're lucky I'm in a good mood today."

"What if I was Hermes?"

"Then you'd have a broken nose." Ares replied, smiling at the idea. Apollo simply laughed, grabbing Ares' hand and pulling him close for an affectionate embrace. As ever, Artemis was content to simply attempt to smile at him. Ares had never liked the twins much, but he didn't hate them, at least. His brother and sister were sarcastic and prone to arrogance, but they worked hard, and in an army hard work matters most.

"So why have you tracked me down and ruined my day?"

"We have a treat for you." Apollo answered, leaning forward and nudging Ares with his elbow. "We've found the bootlegger on seventh and we know where he's about to be. Want to come join us in tracking him down?"

Ares could do nothing but beam at the idea.

The Roxy cinema at night was a shining, illuminated beacon of Manhattan. It was a building covered in colourful bulbs and vivid signs that drew the people of the city in to watch the fantastical movies on display. Silent films, and talkies alike brought in throngs of people that filled the velvet seats. In the day it was less impressive, the matinee shows bringing in only the most desperate film fans. Ares' prey was one such man. A small-time bootlegger, he had been spending too much time taking money from the family. Every red cent spent on other booze was money that they weren't seeing, and Ares' job was to keep them rolling in cash.

Apollo had pointed the man out and Ares had followed. He had wanted to catch him in the lobby, but the guy was petite and meandered through the small gathering of people quicker than Ares, making his way past the usher and into the screen. Ares hated having to buy a ticket. He was never going to watch the film, but it was a better option than causing a scene by beating his way past an employee. Not every person knew who he was or the honour that he deserved. Instead, he paid his dues and made his way into the seating area. Apollo and Artemis re-located the man with ease and Ares made his way over, lowering his massive body into the seat behind. The row of chairs groaned under his weight, but he still sat comfortably, checking around himself, before reaching into his pocket and pulling his gun free. He pressed the cold metal barrel against the man's back, causing him to flinch.

"That's a Luger you can feel against you. Stand up and come with me or I will fire it." Ares whispered into the man's ear. Dutifully, the man stood up, his body rigid with fear. Ares nudged him in the direction he wanted him to go, and the man moved, his legs stiff, feet thudding with every step. It wasn't long before he had returned to the lobby and saw Apollo, who led them off to a room meant only for staff. Signs and rules had come to mean very little to the lot of them during their time in the city.

"So, you think you can set up a bootleg operation in Zeus' city, eh?" Ares asked, his face close to that of the quivering man he had pushed up against a metal shelf full of cleaning products.

"What? No." The man replied, but before he could utter anything else Ares thrust his fist into his gut, sending him into a spluttering heap on the ground.

"We know it was you, now if you give us what you've earned, we might let you live." Apollo said, moving to back up Ares.

"Might!" Ares barked at him.

"I gave it all to Jimmy Short Stack." The man finally managed to gasp. "He said he was passing it onto Zeus. I swear. I thought I was working for you guys."

"Jimmy left town days ago, where's the money from last night?" Apollo asked, his eyes lighting up at the thought of another hunt.

"Wired to his bank in Chicago." The man panted, desperation in his voice. "That's all I know I swear." He began blubbering, tears rolling down his face to meet the snot that had started dripping from his nose. Ares looked down at the pathetic mess huddled by his feet. He gave the man another swift kick to the gut before deciding to leave. Killing him would achieve nothing now.

The three gods left the room, leaving the injured man to fend for himself. Ares seethed, his face turning red as his heart pumped his blood faster than it had ever moved before. He hated being betrayed.

"Kill that motherfucker." He hissed through gritted teeth as he stormed away from the cinema, leaving the twins to plan their next move.

Three

A New Enemy

"If you're worried about the bootlegger on seventh, then I wouldn't be concerned. Artemis and Apollo found the guy. They're getting Ares to pay him a visit." Zeus announced to the room, smiling as he pulled off his Jacket. He walked towards the bar, pouring himself a tumbler of scotch, the last few bottles of imported liquor they had in stock. Zeus supped at the drink and let out a contented sigh. Hair of the dog had always been his philosophy when it came to his hangovers.

"Anyway, I thought I told you to manage the south side clubs" he said as he walked towards the table. "What's my favourite daughter doing here?" To anyone else he would have raised his voice and been irritated by their presence, but ever since Athena had burst forth from his skull, he had been besotted with her. He planted a small kiss on her cheek and pulled up a seat next to her.

She was his most trusted lieutenant, and he knew that if she was here it was for a good reason. She looked up at him and managed a small smile in return, her face still lined with seriousness. He leaned himself closer to his daughter, drawn in by the look of concern. It also helped that he was able to shift himself ever so slightly away from Hera; the last thing he wanted was for her to smell the remnants of perfume on him. He looked across the table into his daughter's blue eyes, their intense and piercing nature hidden beneath her furrowed brows. She let out a deep sigh.

"Last night three of our clubs were attacked." She announced, looking directly at Zeus, her gaze never dropping. Strength radiated from her. Her body was constantly tense and her face a collection of angles and edges. "They burned them all to the ground, father. The Iliad, the Titan, and the Argo are nothing but ash now."

Silence hung over the room, nothing but the soft rustle of broom bristles moving over the sleek wooden floor of the club as cleaners moved debris and detritus from the night before.

"What's more concerning is that all fires seem to be due to one person."

With the final word she rooted in her pocket and pulled out three gold coins. They weren't like any coin used in the city. Modern American coins were perfectly round and flat, and blazoned with the arrogant images of this young country. The coins that Athena had slid to Zeus reminded him of ancient money: misshapen and lumpy, clearly crafted by hand. He picked one up and turned it over in his hand, the only sign was the letter K raised on one side. The silence that filled the room became suffocating.

"Why am I only just hearing about this?" Zeus asked, his voice steady amidst the rage that swelled and churned inside him. "You've had time to investigate and pick through the remnants of my clubs and yet I only find out about it now?" He let his gaze linger on his two family members. They were his closest and most trusted empire builders, and yet they did nothing but disappoint him in this moment.

"We would have told you earlier my dear but it's hard to find you when you spend the night hiding from us with whichever blonde catches your eye." Hera raised a martini to her plump pink lips, taking a sip of the clear liquid and smiling with a smug satisfaction. The millennia living off Olympus had not brought the two any closer, and she delighted in using her words to jab at Zeus, even in his darkest times. Especially in his darkest times. She placed her glass down and shrugged her shoulders back into her fur shawl. She gazed at her husband from the side of her eye. "Maybe if you paid some attention to your empire and to your family rather than what is between your legs you would have found this information earlier."

There was a time when feuds between Zeus and Hera had shook the world around them, but now they were nothing more than a bitter married couple that spoke in snide insults and passive aggressive taunts. In this moment, though, Zeus had to acknowledge that his sister was right.

"The key is finding out who did this, not drinking and sniping dear." Zeus responded, giving his wife only the quickest of glances, and no chance to respond. "I'll make contact with all of our friends in the police department. I've made plenty of them rich so they can do some work for me. Investigating crime scenes is more their bag than mine anyway."

He knew that paying off the officers of Manhattan would have its uses beyond keeping his bars free from raids. He turned to Athena, her eyes that had been shrouded in her furrowed brow were now alive and sparkling with eager anticipation. The goddess hated peace and complacency and he could see the desire for the challenge in her eyes.

"Athena, I want you to reach out to the other crime families. Talk to Frank in Brooklyn, he usually has his ear to ground. Find out what you can."

She nodded silently at his order.

"I'll have Ares increase security at all the other clubs, bring in as many guys as he can. We'll keep better control of the doors." Zeus spoke with the light-hearted zeal of a man with a plan. There hadn't been a turf war in Manhattan since he'd slaughtered his way through the families that had called the island home years ago. If some upstart wanted to try and take him down, then so be it. He'd crush them like he'd crushed all the ones who'd come before him.

"I'll speak to some of the prohibition gals," Hera declared "if there's new speakeasies about those nosey bitches will know about it. I doubt he's destroying clubs without giving the drunks of the city somewhere else to go."

It didn't take long for the gods to disperse after they had been given their jobs. Hera had been the last to saunter away, her elegant fur-trimmed coat trailing behind her as she sipped at the last of her morning cocktail. Silence shrouded Zeus as he sat in isolated contemplation. He didn't know who would do this to them. The family was strong, respected, and it owned every official and authority that mattered. There must be a new gang who dared to challenge him. The soft thud of heavy glass on wood stirred him from his contemplation. A new tumbler had been placed before him, a squat, thick container of sculpted crystal glass. The light danced through it casting a smudged and faded rainbow against the table. Zeus looked up straight into the warm eyes of Dionysus. The god of wine and revelry looked back at him and smiled; a coy smile that tugged only the very corner of his mouth upwards. His eyes seemed golden, shimmering like honey in the setting sun. He sat next to Zeus and began to fill the crystal tumbler with scotch. The liquid lapped at the sides of the glass, coating it and, filling the air with the sickly scent that Zeus adored.

"Father, I think there may be a problem." He stated, running his slender hand through his slick backed hair, somehow not pulling a single black strand loose. It stayed in place against his scalp, accentuating his sharp features.

"Of course, we've got a fucking problem" Zeus retorted "three of my clubs were burned to the ground. Pay attention boy."

"It's worse than that. Those clubs were also stockrooms. All the supplies we brought in last week are gone now. They were due to be distributed around the city today."

The atmosphere that had been surrounding Zeus had been heavy with anticipation and curiosity, but now it started to fizzle with anger. It was as if the very air itself could sense the rage burning within the crime boss. His posture, which had been slumped, strengthened, and became rigid, the muscles in him tensed and contracted. Calmly, Dionysus raised his own glass, and sipped, as the table it had been resting on made its way from the floor to the other side of the room. It seemed to explode on impact, sending chunks and splinters out in a cloud. Chairs and lamps followed, each making their way to a different part of the club, to become nothing more than a mound of shrapnel. Dionysus watched on as Zeus raged, and howled, and panted. The fury left his body with every item that faced its destruction. As soon he was done, his anger abated. Millenia ago Zeus' rage could last for generations, but old age had calmed the storm to a certain degree, making a destroyed room the usual end to one of his tempers.

"Whoever it is must have known. That's not random. If they know where we have storage, then they probably know our supply routes as well."

As Zeus spoke, he realised that his thugs and connections may not be enough. His influence coated the island of Manhattan like a thick fog. It surrounded everyone and everything, penetrating the darkest alleys and slickest boardrooms. It was not unlimited though. Outside of the city he had done little to gain control and he relied on more than just the people and streets of Manhattan to keep his criminal empire stable.

"Dionysus, I need you to go to the farm."

"I was only there last month" Dionysus replied, adequately masking his indignation and annoyance. "Everything was fine and running as planned. Demeter had no concerns and there were no issues with supply."

Dionysus was going to continue but he stopped as Zeus stared at him, eyes still shadowed with anger. Dionysus had always had a good relationship with his father, as good as can be expected amongst Olympians, but he still carried with him that churning fear of the imposing man; it sat in the pit of his stomach; a writhing knot of worry and tension that kept him alert to the sociopathic king of Olympus.

"Whoever attacked our clubs knew what they were doing and knows how our stock system works, if they know that then they probably know about our supply and other business interests. For all we know they know about the candidate too. I will not lose my empire. We check every last corner and protect every possible weakness until we find and punish the bastard who hurt us!"

Zeus' rant had started calmly, but talking about enemies inflamed him, sent that old fire surging through him again. By the end he had been booming, his voice reverberating around the club, flecks of spit flying from his mouth as he enunciated every word, making sure his anger and purpose were clear to his son, who's calm exterior had begun to crack and wither away. Dionysus rose and ran his hands down his suit, smoothing out any crease that had managed to creep onto his perfectly tailored waistcoat. He left the club silently, not daring to speak to Zeus. He had been given his orders, so he left, downing the last of his scotch as he fled into the darkness of the stairwell.

Zeus drank greedily from the bottle. The golden liquid tumbled down his throat, sending warmth through his body in waves. He didn't stop as the door to the club opened, the sound not registering as his entire world became contained in the square bottomed bottle. He didn't even hear his own name spoken in a gruff voice that rattled through the air. He did not see the beaten and limping form come close to him, dirty beard matted with dried blood, and worn clothes torn from contact with hard ground. It was only when a hand composed of broken fingers touched his shoulder that he noticed his brother next to him.

Four

The Night Before

Poseidon loved a shack. He had never enjoyed the structure and stability of brick or stone buildings. Stone was thick and unmoving. It was dead and cold to the touch. When one was inside a stone building one might as well be buried, in his mind. Wood was much more his style. He never felt cut off from the world when he was in a wooden building. The walls breathed, taking in the cold, damp air of the sea and letting it seep out into the room that was enclosed within. The smell was what he loved most, the earthy rich and humid scent that hung in the air around wooden buildings. His shack was no exception. He had built it at the top of one of the dozens of the docks that made up this wharf. All along the edge of the harbour buildings stood strong and to attention; warehouses filled with goods sheltered their contents from the rain, offices held manifests, logs, and records in tight metal containment within their brick walls, and sleeping quarters stood strong against the cold winds that blew off the river, keeping inhabitants warm. Amongst all this sat Poseidon's shack.

The wood was worn and covered with a film of grime both inside and out. Every gust of wind caused it to creak and wobble. The windows barely fit and the glass trembled, threatening to break, even on the stillest of days. The roof dripped and leaked even in the mildest of showers. Not that it mattered. The dark wood and murky windows went unnoticed by those within. People did not come to Poseidon's shack with hopes of grandeur and luxury; they came because he kept the liquor flowing, the women easy, and the rules suspended. The night was still and calm, no rain or wind buffeted the meagre shack, but the sound from within shook the night air around it. Inside no music played but the mood was still light and full of joy and merriment. The sailors inside poured streams of hard bootleg liquor into their mouths and gulped, faces contorting as the liquid burned its way down their body. They roared with laughter and slapped backs as the dirty jokes that men tell each other were yelled above the din. The shack was full of joyous cacophony and in the centre of it all sat Poseidon.

Poseidon had always looked like his younger brother. He had the same mess of grey hair and same grey beard. He had the same piercing blue eyes and muscular frame. He had the same roaring laugh that seemed to punch through the air regardless of any other sound, and he had the same ravenous look in his eye when a beautiful woman walked past him. Poseidon was different though. He rejected the fashionable suit and clean look, his beard and hair were messier, having not seen a pair of scissors for some time. He didn't wear suits but instead favoured loose clothes of sturdy fabric. He sat, reclined in his chair, white shirt undone to show off his thick plume of hair that coated the toned chest underneath. His clothes were spattered with stains where he had let drink slosh and spill onto him, his care for his appearance lost to his merriment. The people that surrounded him looked similar; loose clothes and disregard for personal hygiene evident on all of them.

Each man was enraptured by Poseidon, watching as he spoke. The god gesticulated as he talked, his voice rising and falling in a never-ending crescendo of charismatic wonder. Poseidon had been known for many things throughout his long life but amongst these men, in this shack, he was known for his unparalleled ability to tell filthy jokes. The men leaned in as the punchline approached, anticipation swelling and surging within them.

"Well I'm sorry madam but if your handwriting was better this wouldn't have happened." He finished, slapping his knee as he delivered the final comedic blow.

The group around him exploded into laughter, some slapping knees too, some wiping away tears, and others hoping to remember the joke to tell other friends. Joyous laughter swelled through the room as other jokes and anecdotes received similar reactions from the groups dotted around the shack. Poseidon swallowed the last drop of his liquor in triumph and then moved to the bar.

The shack wasn't part of Zeus' glorious empire, but Poseidon kept it well stocked. The bar was nothing more than some wood, some glasses, and plenty of bottles. The young girl he paid to serve the gathered men smiled as he approached. She bent down to grab a bottle from under the bar, her low-cut dress flashing Poseidon a sight of her smooth, pale cleavage. Brown hair fell over her shoulders obscuring the graceful line of her neck and collarbone. Poseidon smiled back at her when her face reappeared. To many this young thing would have been far too immature for him, but age was a construct that little bothered the gods. As she handed him the bottle, he let his fingers caress her hand.

"Bitch I was here first." A gruff Irish accent sounded across the bar. Poseidon turned to see the speaker. A stocky, round-faced man stood glaring at the two of them. He didn't look old, but his hair was thinning as it receded away from his weathered face. He wore overalls that were tight around his swollen chest. Years of lifting cargo from ships had made his upper body strong and large. "Maybe you can flirt with your grandad after I gets me whisky" he continued, his words slurred.

All the gods had various ways of dealing with those who annoyed them. Zeus had always favoured shouting and breaking things, Hera had loved long and complex machinations that broke spirits. Poseidon was blunter. Without speaking he walked to the man and, with a brawny hand curled tightly into a fist, knocked him to the floor. The man was dazed, clearly expecting a fight to need some form of announcement. He tried to rise but Poseidon kicked him in his broad chest, sending him sprawling once again. Poseidon was funny, charming, and a god men enjoyed their time with, but he was also angry and vengeful. Little Irish fuckers who spoke to him with disrespect learnt that quickly. Poseidon leaned over his quarry and continued to beat him. Blood flowed from a broken nose, and teeth rattled in a beaten mouth. Face blows preceded body blows as Poseidon mercilessly continued his onslaught. No sound escaped him except the occasional grunt as his fist met a solid part of the body. After he was done, he walked back to his table leaving the Irishman's friends to drag him from the shack.

The evening continued as usual after Poseidon's altercation. He returned to his group and soon alcohol fell from glasses and bottles held askew as jokes were told in boisterous voices to be greeted with booming laughs. Men of the sea made merriment their business. Slowly but surely the crowd began to drift away as night became early morning. Sailors left in groups singing old songs. Some left with their arms wrapped round the waists of beautiful women, or beautiful men. Most simply staggered out into the hazy darkness of night in a city that thronged and thrived at any time. Poseidon leaned back in his chair, letting the last drops of bootleg whisky run down his throat. His night of joy had been well deserved. The night before a large Caribbean shipment had come in and, as with anything that came by sea, it was Poseidon's responsibility. Gallons of rum had been moved that night all under his weary and sober supervision. If Poseidon had learned one thing about himself over the millennia he had been on the earth, it was that he should not drink and work at the same time. Which meant he should not work very often.

Just as the girl behind the bar began her saunter towards the god, her hips swaying with each elongated, sultry step, the door to the shack swung open. In the doorway a young man stood panting. He held himself against the frame, desperately gasping for air. He was wearing a suit, clearly cheap and poorly tailored, but was attractive enough to get away with cheap clothing, despite the sweat that was beading down his forehead. His bow tie was loose, and his vest and jacket were flung open. His eyes, the colour indiscernible in the dim light, roamed the inside until they saw Poseidon lounging in a chair, empty bottle sitting on the edge of the table next to him. The young man moved purposefully towards Poseidon.

"The Argo is on fire."

Poseidon did not ask questions, did not delay. He rushed from the shack into the cool air of night. His loose shirt pressed against his taught body as he dashed through the streets of New York. All around him people walked the streets, their figures lit by lamps and the warm glow that cascaded from nearby homes. Poseidon moved with precision, managing to weave between the street walkers without catching a shoulder. He kept pushing forward, making his way through the grid of streets that was Manhattan. Where he could he dashed down back alleys, dodging the trash cans and dumpsters as he went. Every alley he ran through smelled the same; the pungent odour of rotting food and tramp piss entering his nose. One alley had clearly become a popular urinal that night, the smell hitting the back of his throat as he gulped in huge waves of air to fuel his furious dash. It took all his focus to not throw up as the scent, mixed with his intoxication and exertion, hit him in a great wave of nausea.

Soon he had arrived at the Argo. The speakeasy was the family's closest to the water, a small place that usually sat squat and unassuming, buried amongst the other stores that littered every street of the island. Argo's Bait and Tackle was its formal name; the kind of place that always smelled of fish and dirt; a place for the casual fisherman to get his essential supplies. The secret it held was the Argo club: a small and intimate place where the booze was cheap, and the band played non-stop. It had never been much to Poseidon's taste; always hard to tell dirty jokes when a band was filling the room with its distracting cacophony. Now the small shop was consumed by flame. Men and women stood at a distance from the building gawping in astonishment as the fire danced within. Eyes sparkled in the burning orange light as glass blackened and cracked from the heat. Smoke rose in a great column of churning greys. Poseidon looked on in horror. Sirens pierced the air; their shrill wails audible just above the ferocious roar of flames. They would be able to extinguish the fire, but it would be too late to save the club.

The young man who had brought Poseidon the message finally caught up to him, panting, his clothes and hair slick with sweat. He looked at Poseidon, shocked to see that the old man had already recovered from the run.

"How did this happen?" Poseidon asked, not taking his eyes off the ever-growing mass of writhing flames.

"A man came in; he had a gang. They overpowered the bouncers and just torched the place." The man informed between deep breaths.

"What did the man look like?"

"I don't know" came the reply, less breathy and desperate, as the man slowly began to recover.

At his answer Poseidon wrenched his gaze away from the inferno. His eyes glinted with rage as he stared at the young man. The messenger recoiled slightly to the safe shadow of the alleyway.

"He was wearing a mask. A black mask that covered his whole face."

The man planned to continue, scared that any lack of detail would be met by that stare again, but he fell silent as Poseidon walked away from him.

The god of the sea had seen someone suspicious. Every person in the street was enraptured by the burning building; they watched the flames dance into the dark night sky and the soft rain of smouldering embers fall on the street. Except one man, shadowed in the darkness of a nearby alley, who seemed to look straight at Poseidon and his wheezing companion. As Poseidon closed the gap between them the figure moved deeper into the alleyway. Poseidon dashed forward and swung himself around the corner into the alley. The figure was walking just slightly ahead, close to leaving Poseidon's sight.

"Oi!" He bellowed down the dark passage, his voice echoing off the dirty brick walls and containers of garbage. "I don't like being stared at. Who are you?"

The shrouded figure turned silently. In the dimness of the alleyway Poseidon could not make out any of the figure's features. It was only when the figure took a stride forward and a scant pool of light fell around him that Poseidon saw he was wearing a mask. It was made of wood and had been carved to give the impression of a face whilst holding no details. The whole thing had been painted black and the soft gloss of the paint gleamed in the small amount of light they had. The figure was tall and stood with perfect posture, his back straight and large chest pushed out. He was clad in a black suit, with a shirt and shoes of an identical shade. He stood purposeful, defiant towards the god in front of him.

"You must be the fucker who burned our club" Poseidon stated as he strode forward.

He didn't run but took long strides, quickly closing the gap between himself and the fucker he was about to turn into a corpse. It had been a long time since he had had two fights in one night and he could feel his blood pumping through him as the mix of fury and anticipation surged within his body. He launched at the figure and threw a punch directly at the masked face.

The figure moved, quickly darting out of Poseidon's strike. The god wasted no time and turned, making another strike, this time for the figure's ribs. Again, the black clad man dodged out his way. Poseidon could feel the anticipation slipping away to be replaced with more rage. He let out a scream and continued to throw strikes towards his opponent. Each one was gracefully dodged. The figure moved with deliberate, fluid motions keeping himself out of Poseidon's reach.

"Fucking fight me properly" he roared, fist flying angrily at the mask again.

He felt pressure on his wrist. A hand, covered in soft leather, held him. The figure pulled Poseidon forward, not by much, but enough to make it easier to ram a knee into the god's gut. Poseidon recoiled, staggering away in shock. The arsonist was upon him. He moved towards Poseidon with swift grace, throwing punches. Poseidon was able to dodge most but the man was quick. His fists made contact with Poseidon's face and ribs in painful jabs. Poseidon kept his fists up, dodging and deflecting, his rage ebbing away as he fought to keep himself safe.

The figure in black launched forward, but in a singular motion, squatted to the ground and swung his leg around. He caught Poseidon in the ankles, causing him to fall with a great thud to the floor. Poseidon's head landed in a puddle. The odour of piss, dish soap, and rancid garbage water swirled around him as his assailant moved closer. Poseidon rolled away but as he made to stand a foot connected with his chest and sent him crashing into a nearby dumpster. He gasped as the air fled from his lungs. The fighter was upon him.

The gods may be immortal but for a long time now they had felt pain as acutely as any human on earth. Poseidon's body was consumed by agony; it filled his head and chest and arms and legs. The fight had descended into a beating as the aged god failed to defend himself from the onslaught of fists and feet that raged against him. He placed his hand on the ground in the hope of pushing himself up but soon the hard heal of a shoe found them, crushing them, breaking the bones with a sickening crack.

As the beating subsided and darkness swam at the edge of Poseidon's vision, closing in around him, threatening to drag him into unconsciousness he heard the voice of his enemy cut through the wail of sirens, the scream of people, the surge of flames.

"These are the consequences of your actions."

The darkness finally consumed Poseidon as the beating ceased and a coin tumbled beside his head, clattering on the hard ground.

Poseidon opened his eyes to the sight of a vagrant rummaging through his pockets. The man was shrouded in ripped clothes and matted hair, his eyes and lips lost to the limp strands of dirty brown that fell around his face. As he went to probe Poseidon's pocket for a wallet, the god grabbed his wrist and raised his own head. Blood coated Poseidon's face, drying in his beard, turning the distinguished grey to a filthy, rusty brown. The vagrant managed to wriggle free, scurrying away from Poseidon into the main street.

The morning light filled the alleyway around him, bright and full of warmth. Using his one unbroken hand, he pulled himself to stand next to the dumpster. His head swam with pain, alcohol, and shame as he stood swaying on the spot. He began to limp towards the mouth of the alleyway, trying to ignore the pain that was infused within him, knowing only one thing; he must tell Zeus.

Five

What Money Buys You

Zeus couldn't stop his lower jaw from hanging open as he stared across the bar at the battered and bruised form of his brother. Poseidon held a bottle in his hand, the blood-stained fingers trembling slightly as he gulped the liquor in monumental gulps. The other hand was rested in the small and delicate fingers of a slight woman. The nurse was tending to Poseidon's fingers as gently as she could, but he flinched as she moved the broken bones within. It had taken a long time to get his brother to agree to be seen by a nurse. He had insisted on telling Zeus everything that had happened to him the night before. As another young woman tended to the cuts that marked Poseidon's aged face, Zeus could see how hard the fight had been on him. His top lip, only just visible beneath the scraggly grey of his moustache, was split and swollen, both eyes were bruised and puffy, the soft grey of them that shimmered like sea foam in the sun, hidden behind the enlarged lids. It was when he allowed one of the nurses to take his shirt off that the real damage could be seen. Large bruises coated the man's body, the strong, taut muscles blemished by the red marks, some starting to turn purple.

Poseidon didn't make a noise, accepting his nursing with silent winces. The women could only do so much, so he slumped at the bar, dried blood and filth still matted in his shaggy mane. When one imagined a man at sea, they imagined Poseidon, Zeus thought. The man had the air of roughness and wear that marked one used to a life on the waves. But now, sat there, shoulders sagging, eyes focussed on the drink before him, shadowed with shame and defeat, that natural strength he had always possessed seemed sapped away from him. The mighty god of the sea had never looked so human. Even after the cataclysm Zeus had still saw him as an entity as strong as the oceans and tides themselves. Zeus was in disbelief that there was a person who had done this to Poseidon.

"I didn't think I'd see the day you looked so defeated." He said, his voiced laced with concern and judgement in equal measure.

Poseidon looked up at his brother, face set in an expression Zeus could not place. He had always been a man filled with rage and vengeance. Zeus had often been shocked by how far Poseidon was willing to go to defend his pride. But in this moment his response to an afront from his own brother was not rage but defiance.

"It will not happen again. I didn't expect him to be so capable. I've been beating men to bloody pulps for thousands of years. My arrogance must have got the better of me."

He maintained eye contact with Zeus as he let a small smile pull the corners of his mouth upward.

"Hades would have loved this."

He finished taking another drink from the long-necked bottle in front of him, having, as was his way, refused a glass. Zeus was surprised to hear the name, they hadn't mentioned their brother in a long time, but he had to acknowledge it was true. Hades had always had the best sense of humour amongst them. He revelled in the misery of others, never from maliciousness, but simply because he had always been able to find the humour in every situation. The three of them had rebuilt the divine order of the world together and Hades had made them laugh through every second of it.

"How odd of you to mention him." Zeus observed, his own mouth mirroring Poseidon's by rising into its own wry smile.

"I thought I was going to die" Poseidon's replied, soft and raspy; a withered and shameful confession spoken through cracked and bloodied lips. "I thought that last night that man would actually have been able to kill me, I thought my time had come and I would find myself opening eyes in the hall of Hades or even in Tartarus."

By the end, his voice was nothing but a tremble, each syllable falling gruffly from his mouth between pants and gasps. Tears were starting to leak from his eyes and roll down his torn cheeks.

Memories began to flood Zeus' mind as his brother spoke. Dirty tiled walls moving through his vision. His own screams rising high into the air to mingle with the other tormented sounds that snaked and curled around all those present. He recalled restraints pressing into his flesh, his desire to move and be free denied to him. He recalled dim gaslight, and beatings, and isolation, and falling asleep exhausted and devoid of life on a cold floor every night. He remembered being sure that he was dead, that this was how the fields of torment must look, a prison of tiles and cold glares. He shook himself out of the memory to look down at his weeping brother.

"You know as well as I do Poseidon that we can't die." He rested his hand on Poseidon's broad shoulder and squeezed affectionately. Gods were vengeful and powerful, but they were also loving siblings when the time was needed. "Whoever this man is, he is not strong enough to kill a god."

"Who are we kidding…" Poseidon began, raising his head before an interruption came.

Hera sauntered into the bar from the back room. She walked straight backed, cold eyes forward, focussing on her two brothers. The room stilled at her presence, even the air seeming to bow and pay tribute to her. The woman had spent thousands of years walking in the world of men and had never subdued herself to them. She walked with the purpose and poise of the queen of Olympus. Poseidon rose to his feet, straightening his back through the pain and exhaustion to greet Hera with a gentle embrace.

The goddess rested her hand on Poseidon's cheek and looked up into his eyes.

"You really do get yourself in some trouble don't you?" She admonished.

Poseidon didn't reply, he just sank against her, smiling softly, allowing that small spark of maternal nature within Hera to accept him.

Coldly she looked over the shoulder of her beaten and broken brother into the eyes of her husband.

"Your guests will be here in a few hours darling." She informed, her hand tenderly running over Poseidon's back. "It may be best if you go and get ready. Men who stink of cheap perfume rarely get respect."

Zeus left reluctantly, not wanting to leave Poseidon on his own after what he had been through. Poseidon did not take losing lightly and he feared that if he left hm to recover unattended his favourite bar would be in tatters again when he returned. Luckily, he was wrong. When he returned from an afternoon of sleep, bathing, and dressing in his finest suit the bar was at its best. He entered the small space, that before had been a sticky mess of bright lights and old furniture, to find it had transformed into a golden lit hall of music and joy. The band had ascended to the stage, each member swinging as they made their instruments sing. The deep thumps of the double bass danced effortlessly with the high-pitched blaring of the trumpet. The notes moved around the room causing leather clad toes to tap, and bead drenched shoulders to sway. The light of the lamps glinted off the finely polished glasses that were held in every hand. Men and women danced together, the upbeat rhythm moving through their bodies, sending long fringed dresses swaying wildly. Above it all rose the mingled scents of perfume, cologne, smoke, and liquor. The heady, intoxicating atmosphere of warmth and joy pulled Zeus in deeper. Nods of respect and gracious hellos greeted him as he moved through the bustling, booze-soaked crowd.

Zeus' guests were assembled in his office. The men sat around a small circular table away from Zeus' large oak desk. Wooden cabinets brimming with papers and files surrounded them, the crumpled pages threatening to close in on the guests at any moment. The room was a claustrophobic mess of glass lamps and chaos. None of the litter on the shelves was any real business documentation, but numbers and names peeped from, and creeped out of, the stacks in strategic places. Zeus had found long ago that misinformation was the key to running a successful empire.

As he walked in, he noticed one of the men peeking at a corner that had managed to come loose from an impressively swollen file on the shelf right at his eyeline. There was a maliciousness to his small smile as he thought he may have just gleamed useful information to use against his host. Zeus repressed his anger, nothing annoyed the god more than a poor house guest, other than a poor host. The man turned and noticed Zeus in the door, his large muscular frame dominating the space, looking as if it could almost cause the doorway itself to burst. The faint sound of joy and music drifted in behind him.

Quickly the man rose to his feet and simpered a greeting towards Zeus, his fear that he had been caught snooping clear on his face. Even in the dank orange light of the office, Zeus could make out the piggy features of Harry Winslow. The agent was shorter than most men and wider than most combined. He held his bowler hat in his hand, twirling it with shaking, sweaty fingers. Limp hair sat plastered to his head with sweat, the warmth of the room causing the rotund man to drip violently. He took a small handkerchief from his pocket and dabbed at the thick beads coating him. Zeus had often wondered how a man so clearly unhealthy had managed to end up as one of the most senior agents in the New York division of the bureau of prohibition. The other agents he worked with were lean and exuberant. In the early days many of them had chased down Zeus' cars, but not anymore. Harry's health didn't matter though. All that mattered was his influence and the fact that he could be brought with two things: little girls and large stacks. Luckily, Zeus had both in abundance.

"Gentleman," he began, sitting himself at the only free seat available. "Last night my bars were attacked, and my brother was beaten."

The men around the room shifted awkwardly in their seats. Each one of them had taken money from Zeus with the express understanding that they were to make sure his business ran smoothly. Each of them now drove the best car, lived in the finest apartment, slept with the most beautiful women, or in little Pete's case; men, because Zeus had been generous enough to put coins in their pockets rather than on their eyes. They now knew that they had failed him, and fear was beginning to twist its way round the room, pulling the men into hunched positions.

"Whoever this was Zeus, none of us knew about it. We were all surprised." Little Pete's voiced chirped up, a high pitch melody in the sombre room.

The diminutive man sat to Zeus' right and was dwarfed by the god's large frame. He was a spindly man with a face of smooth skin stretched over points and straight lines. His large nose cast shadows across the angles of his face as he moved in the lamplight, expressions wild and exaggerated. Zeus had always assumed that lawyers should be emotionless and guarded, never letting opponents even glimpse their thoughts or feelings, but Peter Lilly was a different type of man entirely and somehow, he had managed to rise to the most senior legal position in the city. The DA had been good to Zeus and an eager partner in his empire building; he had managed to maintain the air of legality and rule of law whilst never once allowing Zeus' profits to dip.

"I know Pete but that doesn't change the fact it happened, and I've lost cases of valuable liquor. I want to know how a man can operate in the streets of Manhattan without your people knowing about it."

He turned his attention to the man directly opposite him, sat in the corner, chair pulled back away from the table to avoid the damp and bloated body of Harry Winslow. The man met Zeus' steely gaze with one of his own, deep chestnut eyes almost burning in the room's orange light. Thomas' thick moustache covered his upper lip, the brown hairs sprinkled with greys barely hiding his poorly repressed snarl. As chief of police for the NYPD Thomas Shattney had the air of authority around him. He was large and imposing and wore his uniform crisp and perfect, the dark blue and gold emblems standing out from the drab black suits worn by his fellow guests. He was silent for some time, clearly trying to compose himself. He had been the hardest of the senior officials to crack; a stern man with a belief in justice he had tried to weed out corruption and bribery at the start of his career, but Zeus had found ways to make him cooperate. When he had refused bribes and proven too dreary to do anything that was worth blackmailing him for, Zeus had been forced to take extreme measures. Coming home to find Ares with a gun to his wife's head and his daughter tied up at his feet had made Shatterny much more cooperative. Little Shannon still worked as a barmaid in one of the downtown joints. Zeus would be reluctant to let his best bargaining chip out of his sight.

"We don't even know what this was Zeus," he began, his voice methodical and clear, each word spoken deliberately. "There's no evidence a new gang is trying to claim turf and to be honest with you this sounds more like a personal attack; a vendetta more than the start of gang war."

"Well, whoever it is had a gang because they hit more than one place at the same time."

"I shouldn't think it's hard for one man who hates you to find a few more Zeus."

"Now is not the time to test me Tommy." Zeus snarled at the police chief, anger starting to flare in him, as it always did when his authority was questioned.

"Gentleman let's not fight amongst ourselves." A soft feminine voice rose from the back of the room.

Hera had been sat quietly in the shadows sipping at a freshly made martini. The olive in her glass swirled in the thick, crystal liquid as the cocktail stick tinkled at the glass. Zeus had assumed she had left the room once the meeting had started, but clearly, she had taken a seat to watch the theatre of masculine incompetence. She walked over to the gathered men and rested her hand on the shoulder of her favourite judge. Justice Arthur Brewings was an old man with deeply wrinkled skin and stark white hair. He was a quiet man with thin lips that always seemed pressed together in flat pink line. He was smooth shaven, but his eyebrows were a wild array of grey and white hairs that jutted from his brow at every angle conceivable. He looked up and allowed himself a wry smile at the goddess. Bitterness had always been a key to Zeus and Hera's marriage, but so had respect and in this room of powerful men, she never once looked out of place.

"Whoever this attacker is he must know about our operation; he must have inside knowledge. That means he works for us," she said, walking over and gliding her hand along the back of Zeus' shoulders. "Or he works for one of you. We can handle our end, but you are powerful men with more staff than we can dream of."

Zeus couldn't help but smile as she spoke. If there was one thing that Hera did better than any other being that had ever existed, it was playing on the egos and arrogance of men. She continued to pace the floor as she spoke.

"We here think of you gentleman as partners and friends, we have shared our profits with you, our lifestyles. You have revelled in our highs as is right for friends, but we ask you now to support us in our lows. Or the consequences for all of us could be dire."

She pointed the thinly veiled threat at each of them. Her eyes meeting all of theirs in the silence that followed her words. She kept a hand on Zeus, and he gripped it back tenderly. If she kept on impressing him like this, he might actually spend the night in bed with her.

"None of us saw this coming" Tommy announced to the still air, "but Hera is right, you've pulled us all too deep into your cesspit of a world Zeus and I personally do not want to be drowned in shit with you."

For the next hour, the assembled men drank, their drinks and minds topped up by Hera. She was the most gracious of hostesses and played her role dutifully. They strategized, Zeus and Hera not letting slip their own plans or what had been set in motion earlier that morning, but helping the others devise how they would find out information. Informants, vagrants, spies, and rats would all be dragged before powerful masters to repeat the whispers and rumours that crept around the streets of Manhattan. Warrants could be issued where they weren't technically legal, arrests could be made, threats would be used. Zeus was ready to mobilise the army that he had been building since he arrived in the city. Once a strategy was in place the men rose from their seats and began filing out the back entrance, each one doing their duty as a guest and saying a pleasant goodbye to Hera and nodding respectfully towards Zeus.

"The problem is still going to be the Mayor" little Pete announced before he finally departed. "Word has it he's cutting out every agency and department, and starting his own task force to take you down Zeus."

"Don't worry about him, there's a plan in motion to make the Mayor's office much more pliable."

With those final words the door closed, leaving Zeus and Hera alone in the empty office. More drink was poured as they contemplated the plan they had just laid out. In time Poseidon joined them, his bottle accompanying their glasses on the table. He had not joined them in the meeting, deciding that as the face of a legitimate business within the empire he should not find himself in dubious and shady meetings. That, and the god of the sea hated pompous sycophants as much as drunk Irish fuckers. As Zeus and Hera informed him of the plan the conversation began to drift. They laughed at how Harry had been gleeful at finding false secrets, at how the judge had clearly had his fix that morning because his glazed over eyes had sparkled so much. They discussed how to manage the police chief if he finally decided to act as his own man again.

"I am worried about the mayor" Hera declared. "He has the resources and will to really hurt us Zeus, and our plan is slow."

"Don't worry Hera, we'll be fine. We just have to wait a few months and the mayor will be out. It will take longer than that for some fire happy attacker to take me down."

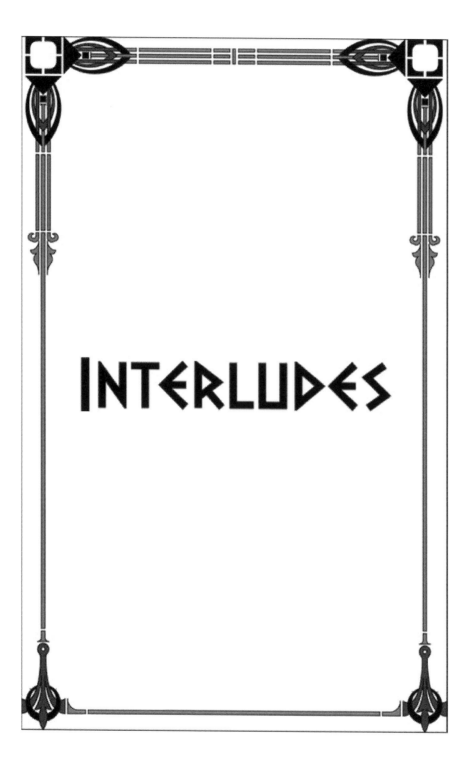

INTERLUDES

Interlude 1

Mount Olympus, Greece, 345 AD

The sun beat down a relentless thumping wave of heat over the dry grasses and dusty rocks of the Greek peninsula. The lapis blue of the Adriatic whispered with the faintest hint of a breeze that danced across its surface, breaking against the white sea foam that lapped the pristine sand of the coast.

High on Olympus, Zeus reclined on a stone bench, the white marbled with silver and gold. It glowed in the sunlight that surrounded them, coating the god in an otherworldly radiance. His ancient back fit perfectly to the contours of the slab, and as he moved the stone breathed and reshaped itself fitting to his every need and whim. He opened his eyes to see a small Nymph dance towards him, her pert breasts of sun kissed skin bouncing gently. She smiled as she made her way to the king, her plump limps inviting him in to kiss her. Zeus adored the Nymphs. The playful, sexually adventurous wonders of divine creation tantalised him.

She perched beside him and fed him grapes. Thick juice-filled fruits fell into his waiting mouth, sending bursts of sweetness across his waiting tongue. He ravished them, barely savouring the perfection of the delicacies that grew in his mountain kingdom. The Nymph looked at Zeus, her eyes changing colour, shifting through the spectrum as her pupils widened in anticipation. Zeus knew he shouldn't. The world below him, that existed underneath the thin veil of clouds, was slowly turning away from him. Cults and temples in his honour had been left to decay and fall into nothingness as a new religion spread across his land, imported from the wastelands to the east.

As he basked in his luxury the other Olympians moved amongst the people, exerting their influence where they could. Even the fallen gods, the titans, were trying to find a place in the ever-changing world. Zeus was not as worried as the other deities that surrounded him. He had seen new cults and new gods come and go. Being the king of Olympus had given him a view of the world other beings could only dream of. He had seen the empire expand into Egypt and import the cults of the gods that ruled over the people of the Nile. They did not last. He knew he would be safe from the Christian scourge. No matter how much they proselytised and banged on about their Messiah the people of his great land always came back to him and his family; the gods that walked amongst them, entered their homes, put on armour to fight in their wars.

He pulled the nymph close, his thick arm wrapping around her slender waste. He reached his other up and played gently with her nipple. She moaned softly into his ear. He stood up, pulling her up to wrap her legs around his waist. The two of the kissed deeply and passionately, and as their blood surged around them, heating their skin, their clothes simply melted away, turning to whisps that fell from them and sank across the peak of the mountain into the clouds that encircled them. Zeus could feel himself grow desperate, ready to be inside her, to feel that unparalleled pleasure.

Then the world shook.

The sky seemed to darken.

A scream, so loud, full of fear and pain, echoed around the rocky land and shook Zeus from his moments of pleasure.

Interlude 2

London, Great Britain, 1895

There was nothing more entertaining to Zeus that watching humans act important. He had walked amongst them, disguised as a mortal, for over 1600 years and they never failed to amuse him. The gentleman that surrounded him were the elite of British society, a collection of white skin and starched black fabric, straight backed against oxblood chesterfields. Their paleness stood out against the darkness of their clothing and the overly polished rosewood that coated every surface of the club. They held important conversations, with furrowed brows and twitching beards and moustaches. They spoke of politics, of economics, of social scandal, all things that mattered so little when one considered how little time they each had on this earth.

Zeus found himself smirking as his colleagues continued their conversation unaware of how little he cared about what they had to say. The brandy had been flowing well through the night and Zeus was finding it was having the desired effect. As he sipped, he found his head growing foggier. He found that he could barely contain the need to belch and hiccup like a common mortal. He tried to clear his thinking but instead he simply swayed in his seat. Though he had only been in London a short time he had managed to find his way into the upper echelons of this closed and slowly dying society. His colleagues were junior parliamentarians and landowners, industrial opportunists making money from the world that changed around him. They had embraced the god quickly, his sharp thinking and ruthless ambition helping to drive them to success.

Another brandy arrived, followed by even more. Zeus knew he had to leave. He had never felt himself so out of control before. Even when he had indulged in the greatest moments of hedonism in human history he had still felt in control of his faculties, but now he could feel them slipping away, slowly falling from his mind in great droplets of consciousness.

"Sit down old chap, there's more Brandy coming." One of the stuffed suits demanded of him.

Zeus could not tell who it was: one of the industrialists or maybe one of the lords. They all looked the same to him, fuzzy shapes with ridiculous accents. He waved the man off and stumbled away.

"I say man, show some decorum." Another voice commanded of him.

Zeus couldn't handle it. He turned in anger at the man and leaned over him, steadying himself against the chair.

"Listen here," He began, his voice a slurred growl of drunken anger. "I will do as I fucking want."

A hand touched his shoulder. He turned, swinging his fist wildly in the direction of the human who dared touch him. He felt his knuckles collide with the firm bone of a jaw and heard shocks and exclamations as a man fell to the ground. "I'm Zeus." He screamed. "King of Olympus, master of all Greece. You will not touch me."

"Someone call the constabulary." He heard above the din that followed his exclamation.

Men backed away from him as he began screaming. His rage felt boundless. How dare they touch him, how dare they talk to him like he was some worthless pion? He charged forward towards an amorphous figure, determined to show them all he was not to be trifled with. Men rushed to stop him, a hoard of starched and pressed suits descending on him in a pile.

"Don't touch me mortals or I'll throw you into Tartarus." He screamed.

Over and over, he bellowed at them, but they did not stop. The shrill whistles of the police sounded above the commotion and as Zeus wrestled with his oppressors. The men in all black dragged him away from the club.

PART II

Six

The Candidate

emember the conditions, stick to questions about the campaign and the candidate's plan for the city when he wins."

"Don't you mean if?"

"Oh no, I definitely mean when. Any personal questions and you'll never get an interview again." Anni smiled as she finished speaking, that charming smile that covered her face and let her teeth glisten and shine. The reporter she had been talking to smiled back, some hack from some local station looking to make a name for himself. Mediocre men with ambition were always the most pliable in Anni's experience. Not that she had much. Being anything but a secretary or a hooker was unheard of in the city. Anni always liked bucking trends. Tucking her hair behind her ear, she walked from the room towards her boss' office.

Private space was limited in any Manhattan building and the campaign headquarters was no different. Between the interview room and the office was an open space that teamed with people. Small meetings were being held in corners whilst secretaries sat at desks, their fingers quickly moving over typewriter keys; the clanging and tapping sending shocks of sound through the room. Bunting and posters hung from ever drab wall and ceiling beam. Placards were piled in every available space, each reading the same slogan in blue and red writing.

Anni weaved in between the throngs of campaign staff, she danced through their meetings and walks, she avoided spilling their coffee and treading on toes. No one moved for her, even junior aids and volunteers carried on their business ignorant of her presence. Anni had never been one for resentment but she couldn't help but think a man in her position would at least get a few averted glances.

She was the only woman she'd ever heard of who had been appointed as a campaign manager, and not for some hum drum, hick town school board, but for the next mayor of New York. She was giving it her everything and she was going to get the candidate elected. At his office door she gently tapped on the frosted glass waiting for a response. If there was one thing she had learned quickly in her job, it was the importance of waiting to be told to enter a room. When no response came, she rapped her knuckles on the door again. She moved her head closer to the glass and strained to hear any sounds. She thought she could hear a muffled voice but the cacophony in the main hall made it almost impossible to tell.

The door swung inward, and Hermes greeted her with a smile. She had seen him every day for months now, but he still took her breath away.

"Is it time for my interview then?" he enquired, his bright blue eyes twinkling as he spoke.

"Yes sir. Now it may be worth briefing you on the kind of questions you can expect."

Anni had to finish her sentence on the move as Hermes began his walk to the meeting room. As he walked the throngs of people parted before him. The campaign was in full swing, but everyone reacted the same way when Hermes entered the room. Looks of adoration and respect surrounded him. Every man wanted to shake his hand, every woman wanted to catch his eye. His walk was not direct, he weaved his way through the bullpen, stopping and talking to strategists, campaigners, and secretaries. Hermes liked getting to know people and after a few months he was proud that he knew the names of everyone working for him. He knew the small details of their lives that made them feel special. He knew Susan the typist was engaged, that Victor the strategist hated grapes, and that Larry from accounting was secretly in love with Susan the typist. Everyone he met got a handshake and a smile, usually a hand on the shoulder as well.

Hermes walked straight backed, his tailored suit fitting perfectly to his lean frame. His long legs took strides across the floor, tapping out a slow background rhythm to the noise of the office, as his leather sole met the hard ground. His blonde hair seemed to shine in the sunlight that streamed through the windows, each golden strand in perfect place, slicked back. His milk white skin was smooth and unmarked, even his hands were soft and supple. When one of his opponents had mocked him for his softness, he had simply replied that workers have rough hands, not leaders. Hermes looked young, not a day of his millennia on the earth showing in his face. He bristled with energy, his whole body alive with youthful exuberance. Eagerness was all over his face, obvious in his delicate features.

The interview didn't last long. Puff pieces never did. He talked about his plans for the city. He talked about fighting corruption and working in partnership with other agencies. He chastised the current mayor for being secretive and aloof. Even when he took a tone of judgement or disapproval he still smiled, and his voice still carried like a perfect melody in warm summer air. The interview was a live radio broadcast; a chance for him to speak directly to the people of New York. He made promises, repeated slogans, and quoted statistics. Hermes did what he had always done; fulfilled his purpose as an Olympian and delivered the message. Most people assumed that being a politician was about coming up with ideas and getting things done, but that was hardly true. The key to being a politician was to be a messenger; make sure people heard and believed what you told them.

When the journalist had gone Hermes returned to his office with Anni at his side. She did what she usually did: she rambled about budgets and markets, about ad time and campaign stops. She went through scheduling and speech writing, never thinking to take a breath. Hermes couldn't help but smile. Women like Anni always made him smile. He had spent his life around strong women who stood shoulder to shoulder with men, and he adored seeing it. Hermes loved the fight that was clear in Anni's eyes; that spark and drive to succeed. He needed it now more than ever. It had only been a day since Zeus had called him with news of the clubs, with the disturbing tale of what had happened to Poseidon. The family had faced enough tragedy since Olympus fell. He had to make sure nothing bad happened to them again, and that meant keeping the legitimate business fronts and mayoral campaign on track. Hermes was no warrior or spy; there were better gods for those jobs, but he was bright. He could stabilise the family and make them truly untouchable. When he won the race the family's criminal empire would be unbreakable.

"Does that work for you then sir?" Anni finished speaking looking at Hermes expectedly, her large notepad in her hands, fountain pen carving out scribbled notes across the white page.

Hermes had missed almost everything she had said, he couldn't even remember sitting down in his office, but there he was, straight backed in his chair, desk carved from rich oak before him. He hated when he ignored Anni, her hard work meant so much to him but sometimes she had to be drowned out. She needs a better messenger, he thought to himself.

"Whatever you decide will be perfect I'm sure." He replied, hoping she would sincerely believe he trusted her judgement and not that he was simply covering up his own ignorant behaviour.

"OK then sir, we'll cancel the meet and greets for today, and reschedule the strategy meeting for tomorrow."

"Yes… wait, why are we doing that again?"

"The fires sir. We couldn't cancel the radio interview, but it seems in poor taste to campaign the day they announced that twenty people died in fires in one night. A quiet, mournful, campaign works better for us now."

Hermes didn't reply, he just nodded his agreement and gestured that Anni could leave. She rose from her chair and smoothed out the pleats in her ankle length skirt, her silk top billowing slightly in the breeze that drifted through the office window. Shooting Hermes a smile, she left the office and busied herself around the bull pen: prompting, suggesting, and commanding as she went. Hermes sat back in his chair. Many times, he had wondered if he should start sleeping with women again; they really did impress him.

It didn't take Hermes long to decide what to do with his free afternoon. Campaigning was a hard and brutal slog; it required every ounce of energy that Hermes could pull out of his ancient body. He always smiled, always waved, always shook hands and signed pictures. He cheered his thanks and appreciation at every crowd that surrounded him. Any time that was spent alone was usually spent sleeping, so he decided he had earned the afternoon doing something truly outrageous. Hermes was going to have some fun.

His car made its way down the long streets of Manhattan until it crossed the Brooklyn bridge. The great colossus of stone and iron always impressed Hermes. He looked out of the window skyward, the criss-cross of cables stood stark against the cloudless summer sky. Sunlight danced off the rippled water of the east river, its surface moving in the gentle summer breeze.

The streets of Brooklyn always felt different than Manhattan. They seemed dirtier and more crowded, the air seemed more stagnant, and full of decay. Many of his friends and campaign staff had warned him that he was just being a snob, but he still never felt fully comfortable in this part of the city. Luckily, he was here for a person and not the surroundings. His car pulled up beside an old building; another inconspicuous shop that never seemed to have customers but always turned a tidy profit. Hermes stepped out of the car and, after reciting the correct password, was able to walk into the shop's backroom. The air was still and filled with the wisps of cigarette and cigar smoke from the smatter of patrons that were dotted throughout the joint. A gramophone sat on the bar and from its brass funnel the scattered notes of a jazz tune played. The hazy orange light of the room hid faces in shadows, and all seemed to agree not to look too long at the other patrons.

He moved over to the bar to find it empty. The bottles on the back shelf twinkled, their various contents distorting the light and casting a smudged array onto the mirror behind them. The bar top had been wiped clean, the dark wood showing no signs of the spills and watermarks that would have coated it the night before. A speakeasy was never an easy place to keep clean.

"Well, this is an unexpected surprise." Came a voice from behind him.

Hermes couldn't help but beam at the sound of it. Everyone saw Hermes smile, they all saw his perfect rows of immaculate teeth and the glint in his eye. That was part of the act; be happy to see everyone and they will be happy to see you. But this voice, the sultry English accent that swam through the warm booze-soaked air towards him, made him smile in a way that no other person had in a long time. He turned to gaze upon the man walking towards him. William towered over Hermes. His height and broad frame invited Hermes in; he wanted to skulk into the shadow that he cast across the bar and hide from the world in the tight embrace. William smiled back at him, thin pink lips moved up his face to expose his teeth, one or two out of place, crooked in ways Hermes had never seen before but that enticed him to keep looking at the ruggedly handsome man. A dark coating of stubble covered his chin, shadowing the angles of his square jaw.

"I had the afternoon free from the campaign so I thought I would come see my favourite barman."

Hermes winked as he spoke, spinning on his barstool to keep his eyes fixed on William who had walked to the shelf of booze. Like all the gods of Olympus Hermes adored alcohol, he loved the smell and the warm sensation it sent through him as he drank it down by the bottleful. He marvelled at how instantly it sent waves of comfort around the body and relaxed him. He enjoyed the confidence that surged through him after liquor filled his body. William had learned this about him quickly and now whenever they met there was a drink poured instantly. Hermes loved wine above all else and it was the rich crimson liquid that was presented to him. He gulped at it greedily, emptying the glass in a few mouthfuls. As soon as the empty vessel was on the bar William began pouring again. Hermes pulled out his wallet and passed a few notes over, enough money to make sure the wine flowed generously.

Hermes always felt a small pang of guilt at passing over his money to another family, but this was where William worked and so he had made the decision that his small sums for a few glasses of wine would hardly tip the balance in any crime war that could possibly emerge. Not that it was likely. The recent attacks had sent shocks through some of the other gods, but Hermes was less scared. Passion, anger, explosive personalities were all common amongst his family, but Hermes was different; he preferred a calm and measured response to most situations. He knew that even if some masked psychopath was going to launch a vendetta against his family, it would come to nothing. Even the other large gangs knew they had no chance against the Olympians. If it was on the island of Manhattan it was owned and controlled by Zeus. That was the new order, and a few dollars in a competitor's bar was hardly likely to change that.

"There's not many customers about. Shall we go enjoy a couple of drinks in the back room? I'm sure they can do without me for a little bit."

The back room was a quiet space tucked away behind the bar. It was part storeroom, part office, part slum bedroom. A small, dilapidated sofa was secreted in the corner, confined by crates and boxes all coated with a film of dust. Loose papers sat strewn atop every surface with pencils, pens and other assorted office ware keeping them in place. From some loose section of wall, a draft swirled warm air around them, gently rustling the papers and swirling small plumes of dust up into the air to dance in the flickering light of the bulb that hung limply from the ceiling. Every wall flaked dry paint, and every wooden floorboard was warped and creaked with the lightest step.

"Wow," Hermes said looking round the room. "You've come a long way since you were a message runner for Castle."

He turned and pushed himself up onto his toes so that he could plant a kiss on William's lips. As he did, he felt the man's strong arms wrap around him and pull him close. Hermes could feel the taught muscles pressed against him. The kiss dragged out, Hermes savouring every second that he could feel his lover's warmth seep through clothing to envelop him. When the kiss ended, he looked up into William's dark eyes, the deep brown almost indistinguishable from the black in the centre. He saw his own reflection in them, saw his beaming smile and blonde hair almost shining.

"From messenger to running Brooklyn's biggest speakeasy in less than a year. I wonder what else old Castle has in store for you."

William's smile faded and his tight grip on Hermes loosened allowing the god to fall slightly from his firm body.

"Frank has already told me he wants me to join his enforcement team. A few of the other Brooklyn gangs have been threatening territory and he needs all the help he can get."

He looked down, a sombre expression on his face. His eyes darted around the room, avoiding looking at his lover. Hermes read shame in his face; the way his eyes darkened, and his brows creased together. His posture fell, his shoulders slumping low as the heavy burden pushed down on him. He saw defeat in this strong man he was slowly falling in love with.

"It's just I don't like violence. I work for Frank because he pays well but I never want to hurt anyone. It's not who I am."

Hermes couldn't help but be a little shocked. He had always known William wasn't one of Castle's toughs, but he had always assumed it was because William was white. Castle was one of the most powerful black men in New York and he only trusted other black men to run his businesses with him. But now he realised that William wasn't just on the side-lines because of his skin, but because that was where he wanted to be. He felt sorry for his man. Hermes had lived a longer life than most and had seen the world change more than anyone could comprehend. One thing had never changed, though; there was no place for pacifists. He did not know what to say to William and so he simply rose on his toes again and kissed the man with all the passion and intensity he felt for him. The other truth he had learned was that all men were easily distracted by physical touch.

Their plan of hiding away in their small ruin of a refuge was cut short as a call came from the bar summoning William. Hermes walked with him, sure that his standing as a son of Zeus and next mayor of New York City would keep him and his reputation safe from whoever had called. He came to the bar to find Frank Castle standing there, but it wasn't the elderly black man that caught Hermes attention, it was the tall statuesque woman behind him; a woman who stood straight backed with a face of angles held in an earnest expression; the sister he loved and adored more than any. Athena.

Seven

Wisdom

A thena raised her eyebrows at the sight of her brother skulking in from the shadows of the seedy back room. The perfectly sculpted angles of her eyebrows rose, wrinkling her forehead, almost making contact with the few curls of jet-black hair that fell from her trilby. The wide brim cast a shadow over her face, obscuring the piercing blue eyes that stared at the little fool. Hermes looked how he always looked, charming with a dash of youthful rebellion. If he had noticed her disapproval, then he was not showing it. He simply smiled coyly and walked into the light of bar lamps, golden hair shimmering, soft skin glowing, and teeth glinting as he began greeting and shaking hands. Hermes really had been the ideal choice to be their man in the mayor's office. He had a natural sense of ease with everyone and oozed a calm and comfortable charisma that never once intimidated. He hugged Castle in a way that Hera had never seen Castle hug a man before and then moved to her.

Before he could make himself stand taller so as not to seem diminutive next to her, she spoke.

"A private word. Now."

Hermes' smile only intensified at her command. He was playful and calm in most situations and he found antagonising others to be more of a game than a problem that he faced. Athena excused herself from her guests and dragged Hermes by his forearm to a shadowed corner of the club. A mop stood next to them, propped up against the wall, its cloth tendrils writhed slowly in the bucket of brown water. A thick, pungent scent rose from the metal container, the smell of cleaning fluid and stagnant alcohol filling the air round the two huddled gods.

"What the fuck do you think you're playing at?" Athena asked in curt whispers, her glare trying to bore its way through Hermes skull to see what was going on in his idiotic little brain.

"I had the afternoon off from the campaign, so I came to spend some time with a lover. Is that such a heinous act?" Hermes' responded in a way that was neither curt or challenging, but casual and clearly unimpressed by Athena's reaction to his presence. Her eyes rolled as exasperation consumed her.

"Have you forgotten the last two thousand years?"

"Of course not."

"Really?" Athena worked hard to keep her tones hushed to hide her conversation from the gathered men at the other side of the club, but her anger was taking over. "Because you seem to think we're still living in a pleasure palace on top of a mountain." Athena kept speaking even as Hermes attempted to reply. "We are not gods in a world that worships us anymore, we are trying to thrive in a world of savage superstition and ridiculous ethics."

"I know that." Hermes managed to interject, giving the goddess time to catch her breath. "But I'm not holding orgies on the streets on Manhattan. I'm having a discrete tryst with an attractive young thing. Find me one politician who isn't."

His casual rejection of her worries didn't improve Athena's mood and she could feel the darkness of her fury starting to curdle within her. She knew her capabilities and she expected them to be respected and her instructions obeyed.

"Yes, but those politicians are spending their time with women. For whatever foolish reason, the people of this age detest two men fucking. If you are found out it's not just an apology and a kiss on the wife's cheek that will be required of you. Your political career will be over, and when that's gone our chance of controlling the mayor's office melts away."

Athena hated monologues, she hated having to spell everything out to everyone. If she understood the importance of something, then surely everyone else must. Hermes didn't respond, but she could see in his eyes that he was dismissing everything that she was saying to him.

"And furthermore, how can you call it discrete when you're getting bent over in Castle's back room?"

"William works here, it was simply a passing visit to see him, I wasn't getting bent over."

"Not yet." Athena retorted, letting some of the annoyance recede. Humour from Athena was a once in a decade occurrence, so she let Hermes enjoy it, let him scoff just a little bit. "But that's not the point, you're here, incriminating yourself, potentially making yourself vulnerable to our enemy, and when you're vulnerable the whole family is vulnerable."

"Castle isn't an enemy. He's too busy fighting for scraps of Brooklyn to bother us. You know as well as I do, that he needs to be on our good side more than we need to be on his."

"Anyone who isn't us is the enemy." Athena leaned into Hermes as she spoke, memories of rolling black clouds, of thunder, of the earth cracking, of blinding light and winds so vicious, they pulled columns from temples, burning in her mind. "You know why we only have each other. We can't trust Castle and therefore we must not make ourselves vulnerable to him. Do you understand?"

Silence was her answer. She gripped her brother's shoulder tight and peered into his eyes, glinting blue like the sea in the morning sun, no hint of despair or darkness in them.

"Hermes tell me that you understand."

"I understand Athena. It won't happen again." Hermes smiled up at his sister, allowing his respect and adoration for her to push back his pride and desire. "But if Castle is an enemy then why are you here?"

"There's been no hint of who attacked the clubs. Castle has one of the best networks of informants in the city. He may have information that can help us."

"You expect an enemy to help us."

"Not for free, no." Athena responded, raising her eyebrow again and casting a glance towards the assembled men, sat at a squat table sipping liquor and exchanging a hushed conversation of their own, having shooed the last straggling customers from the bar. "That is why Zeus sent me, I'll get the information if the price is right." She paused before her eyes locked back on to Hermes. "You're going to leave now and let me do my job. Your desire for your lover is not a priority right now. Correct?"

"Of course, correct as always."

Together the two of them left the oppressive shadow and corrosive scent of the corner and walked over to the table of men. The tall stranger that Hermes had come to visit was stood behind the bar cleaning glasses. He flashed a smile at Hermes as he walked through the door and up the stairs out of the club. Athena apologised to the men and sat down in the chair they had set out for her. It was a rickety old thing, some ancient wooden frame held together with rusted nails and aged joints. It sat lower than the other chairs and was furthest from the door. Athena couldn't help but be unimpressed. She had seen such simple and ineffective strategies used to intimidate people in negotiations for eons now. It was clear to her that the men she was meeting with were amateurs. Still, she sat straight-backed, raised to her fullest height.

Athena knew how to use her physical attributes to her advantage. The goddess was tall and lean. Her body was a towering pillar of sinew and strength. Even on her smaller chair she was still taller than the others. Some looked up at her, falling for their own trick and allowing themselves to be intimidated by her stature.

"So, Athena, you plannin' on telling me why we had to meet?" Frank asked. His southern drawl making each word drip with emphasis, a stark change to the snappy New York accent she had become used to.

She looked toward her host and smiled. Frank was an unassuming elderly man. In a line-up of average men Frank would have been the most average among them. He seemed to be designed to not stand out, and other than the few strands of grey that were poking their way through the thick black curls of his hair, there was no distinguishing feature that Athena could find on the man.

"As you probably know Frank, three of our clubs were burned down two nights ago."

"I fail to see what this has to do with me." Frank retorted, his gathered collection of sycophants nodding and murmuring at his words. Castle undid his jacket revealing the garish assemblage of colours that constituted its silk lining. In a seeming attempt to make up for his own blandness, Frank Castle enjoyed adorning himself with flamboyant accessories. His jacket was lined with sickeningly colourful silk, his belt was a colour of leather Athena had never seen, his tie was a jolt of simmering red fabric and the clip that held it in place was gold and coated with so many diamonds that the fine polished metal beneath it barely shone through the glittering.

"Let's face it Frank, you have the best network on informants in the city."

"In Brooklyn." Frank attempted to correct. "Your family practically banished me from my beloved Manhattan."

"Please, if you think I believe your informants are isolated to Brooklyn then you must think me a fool." Athena stared down Frank, whose southern charm seemed to flicker for a second as Athena called his bluff, but he continued to smile at her. "You hear every whisper that the streets have to offer so I want to know what's been reaching your ears."

Frank's smile didn't change but Athena could see the shift in his deep brown eyes. The genuine warmth and humour vanished. His face no longer looked courteous and polite. The way his eyes now glinted with self-satisfaction and smugness sent a small wave of annoyance through Athena.

"Are you telling me that the great Zeus has no idea how his precious clubs burned. How embarrassing." Each word seemed elongated as he let his accent move around them, savouring the sensation of getting to speak such things.

"You can gloat, or you can negotiate Frank. But you can't do both. We want information. What do you know and what will it cost?"

There was silence after Athena's words, the mob boss clearly taking his time to think through what he could get for what he had. He looked towards one of his associates, a tall and slim black man with small ratty eyes hidden behind silver spectacles. Athena knew a whisper gatherer when she saw one. The two men seemed to have a wordless conversation, sharing a sense of knowing between them.

"I want Ares." Frank declared after the elongated pause. "I've got a few territory issues and I can't handle them all with the enforcers I have. Ares and his friends are the best." He explained, clearly responding to Athena's confused look.

She must admit that she was surprised, she had expected Castle to want territory, control, or a partnership. Shit, she had even expected him to demand Harlem back, but asking for Ares to do what he enjoyed; mindlessly beating men to a bloodied lump on the ground, hardly seemed like much of a request at all. Usually when another of her family was involved, she consulted them, but she had extraordinarily little doubt that Ares would relish the chance to use his fists. Ever since the family had consolidated power, he had been a watchdog occasionally getting to dole out punishment to defaulters and loudmouth drunks. The chance of a real fight would thrill her fellow god of war.

"I'm sure that Ares can be persuaded to help you crack a few heads open Frank. So, tell me, what do you know?" She leaned forward to hear what he could tell her.

The man sat in silence, a long pause stretching between them as he thought how best to share his information.

"A few weeks ago, one of my associates was approached by a man who said he was recruiting for a job."

Athena sat silently letting the words fill the space between her and Frank.

"Apparently he was gathering together anyone who was down on their luck and with an axe to grind. Told them all that he would make them rich. Obviously, I tried to speak with the gentleman myself, but he has been elusive. Before your clubs were attacked there had been no word of territory disputes. Personally, I thought we were looking forward to a kidnapping or political assassination."

"Why did you think that?" Athena quizzed the aging gangster.

"Well, his name surely." Frank answered. "He's only been referring to himself as the Killer." He smiled at the look on Athena's face, the quizzical expression she had worn had instantly contorted itself into a look of annoyance and derision. "I know, my momma always said not to boast and a name like that is surely nothin' but boasting." He laughed gently as he spoke, clearly amused by the expression plastered onto Athena's stern features.

"What else can you tell me about this man?"

"Unfortunately, not much, every time I get a whisper of where he is, he's moved on. The man is good at keeping quiet. All I know is that if you find him you need a special word to get close to him. Clearly the skittish kind."

"What's the word?" Athena asked. Frank looked at her, the humour from his previous chuckles falling from the shallow wrinkles of his face. He was clearly debating internally whether any additional information was worth more than what he had already extracted from Athena. "Now is not the time to test me Castle. We had a deal; I expect it to be honoured."

"Of course, ma'am. I am a man of word, but you can't begrudge an old dog at least trying to think up a new trick." Frank raised his hands in mock surrender, fingers splayed beside his face. The men around him laughed, the humourless laugh of men desperate to write their name in a powerful man's good book. "It was a word I am unfamiliar with. Thanas, no, Thator, Thantos, oh my how did it go?"

"Thanatos?" Athena guessed, her eyes losing focus, the sounds around her seeming to fuzz and mute in the air before they reached her ears. The faces lost their clarity and became smudges of brown skin encircling her. She hadn't heard that name, that word in so long. Multiple possibilities and scenarios surged through her mind as she processed the information. It was unlikely to be the name as he had been banished from this world long ago, and she surely would have felt something, would have known if another god had returned to the world. That meant it had to be the word, but that answered even less questions. Athena slowly started descending into her own thoughts, into the web of information that she could almost visualise floating in the air before her. Through the haze she heard Castle's voice, but the words were indistinct, just hints of the southern drawl bouncing inside her head.

"Sorry can you say that again Frank?"

"You know this word then?" He asked, looking at Athena with a modest amount of concern.

"Yes, it's a Greek word, whoever did this knows about my family."

"You're Greek then?" Castle asked, as if the conversation were so easily turned to the topic of heritage and birthplaces. The old man would be asking for baby pictures next.

"Excuse me gentleman, but if that is all I do need to be leaving now." Athena rose as she spoke, prompting all those assembled round the table to rise with her. Manners and respect were an integral part of relationships, even between rivals and there was no way these men would let her storm out of their club without at least saying a proper goodbye and shaking her hands. She politely shook every hand and thanked them for their time. Once she had extracted herself from the group, she smoothed out her suit.

Athena always wore a suit, especially when negotiating. She had raised a few eyebrows dressing so masculine in a world that had become obsessed with segregating the sexes by how they dressed, spoke, and behaved, but she cared very little what these people thought of her. Athena had been born in a full suit of armour and she would not let societal convention put her in a beaded skirt and bonnet. In this city a tailored suit was armour, and she would wear it into battle.

When she reached the top of the stairs and had made her way to the street outside the shop she sucked in a deep breath. Cool air drifted over the road, coming off the river that lay behind a cluster of buildings over her shoulder. She needed to get back to Club Olympus urgently. Though the information wasn't extensive it was important. There was something to track now, a name and a pattern. This was what Athena thrived on, patterns were the key to war.

"Miss." A voice said from the alley behind her.

Athena turned at the sound. She recognised the tall, muscular frame and dark features peering out from the shadowed recess. Hermes' lover shifted his gaze nervously over the street before leaving his shelter and walking over to her.

"Frank didn't tell you everything, and I think you need to know."

"What would that be?" She asked, her tone dismissive, "and why would you tell me?"

"If it helps Hermes out, I'll tell you. I don't want him to get hurt." He went quiet again, hunching over to speak quieter, gaze still moving up and down the road. "We know who supplied the fuel for the fires."

Athena stared at the man as he spoke and gestured for him to get into her car that set waiting, engine rumbling, on the side of the road for her.

Eight

Irresistible

Richard Musgrave, Dickie to his friends, evil conniving monster to his enemies, useless shit to his wife, and target to Aphrodite was a man of influence, wealth, and luxury. His office sat high atop one of the skyscrapers that were beginning to dominate the Manhattan skyline.

From the vast panels of immaculate glass that filled the window frames of his office one could survey the bustling city below. Aphrodite looked down as people scurried and hurried, their lives effortlessly intermingling with the city that they found themselves in. She waited patiently for her host, keeping herself held tall and straight. Her dress hugged her figure, so different from the fashionable draped and pleated fabric of the secretary that had shown her in.

The city flowed; currents of people swirled around each other almost seamlessly.

"You know, when I moved here from my little town I was sure this many people in one place would mean my shoulders would be in a constant state of peril, but so far they had remained in perfect condition." The nasal Illinois accent squawked through the room as Dickie walked in.

In his youth Dickie had been a lanky imitation of a man. He had been tall and slender with ripples of rich brown hair and large hazel eyes.

He had been the kind of man who folded himself into seats and had to unfurl himself from them whenever he needed to stand. His clothes had hung off him like drapes hung on a line to dry, and every breath of wind had threatened to take him into the air. Middle age had claimed the body of the man now stood before Aphrodite. Where there had once been messy waves of brown hair, there was shiny pale skin with only wisps of brown and grey encircling it. His eyes, which had once twinkled, were now dull and bloodshot from sleepless nights and liquor. Years of sitting at his desk had turned small taut buttocks into sagging sacks of aged flesh. Aphrodite still let he lips turn into a wide smile, pearl white teeth glinting through red lips.

"Those really are perfect shoulders." Aphrodite purred as she slinked her way towards him.

"People know how to move in crowds, they understood how to herd themselves together. I respect the instinct: it can be extremely useful."

Dickie had only just emerged through the door when his eyes fully fell onto Aphrodite: the most wonderous and beautiful woman he had ever seen. She stood in the waning evening light surveying to office around her, her smooth alabaster skin not showing a hint of her thoughts, no crease or wrinkle appearing on her face. Her body was a sea of curves, each one drawing his gaze so that his eyes roamed across her. The dress she wore fit perfectly to every sensual curve, the fabric glittering. The dress stopped just above her perfectly round breasts, erect nipples clearly showing through the skin-tight fabric. Her shoulders were a sculpted, rolling cascade atop sleek collar bones that somehow glistened as she stood there.

Dickie started walking towards her, his steps feeling turgid and awkward in the presence of her grace. Her green eyes shone with life, tones of emerald catching the light, pulling Dickie into the black mysterious abyss of her pupils. As he got closer, he became entranced by her hair. Long strands of auburn, burned gold, strawberry blonde, and bright orange fell in effortless curls onto the soft skin of her neck and tumbled down her back. Aphrodite allowed herself to glow, and emphasised the scents of her perfume, drawing her target in.

"You're amazing," he cooed under his breath, his voice catching in his throat at the presence of Aphrodite's grace and beauty.

"So are you Dickie," she said moving forward, resting her hand on his chest. Her job was to draw him and his colleagues to her private club, but she could sense he wasn't ready yet.

The man needed his ego stroking, so she asked him about himself, allowing him to pour them both drinks as he began a long and rambling speech about his life.

He talked about how as a poor upstart some twenty years ago, he had a been one of the mass of cattle like residents. How he trudged and moaned as the city and its demands corralled him into offices and any other workplace. He had never resented it, apparently this was how the world worked. When you had nothing, you were nothing and when you had everything you were everything. Richard Musgrave had everything, and so Aphrodite would treat him as if he were her everything.

Dickie was a king of the stock market and outside the thick oak doors of his gilded office his subjects busied themselves in the noble pursuit of building his castle ever skyward, making him money Aphrodite wanted lavished on her girls. Dickie told Aphrodite that he loved his life. He had gambled, invested, and clawed his way to the top of the pile. He made money in quantities he had never dreamed of before. Reams of paper were dedicated to telling him how much he had made for himself and his clients. Everywhere around him was a testament to his brilliance. Some called him arrogant, which Aphrodite could not argue with, but according to him: when you start as a herd animal and end up as a king it is just realistic to assume your own brilliance.

The day was dwindling to a close, another day in which Dickie had increased the wealth of every shareholder he was responsible for. Aphrodite saw he felt empowered, strong, and virile. She could see it in the way his posture changed as he talked about his accomplishments. He drained the small remnants of whisky that was in the tumbler on his desk and together they contemplated how to spend his evening.

"I was thinking of gathering up the other senior staff and taking them to Olympus. The speakeasy is one of our favourite places in the city, it's so extravagant. Would you care to join me?" His invitation was accompanied by a pleasant smile and an extended hand. He was right: decadence oozed from every surface in Club Olympus, the alcohol was high quality and full of taste, the music was loud and full of joy, the women were exquisite and full of lust.

"I have a better idea," Aphrodite said, leaning forward, looking longingly into Dickie's eyes.

Now was the time to get him to start spending his dollars at the Cyprus Lounge. She had spied him at the club many times, often noticing that his attention moved from alcohol to women almost immediately. He was the perfect man to bring to the lounge. He was rich enough to pay for her girls but not rich enough that his money made ordinary women overlook his flaws. His belly hung in a paunch over the rim of his fine leather belt, the silk shirt and waistcoat struggling to keep it in place. No man would call him fat but there was a myriad of other words they would use to describe his less than elegant look.

"I know a place that can make all your desires come true."

Dickie made his decision immediately and left the office. Men in cheap suits bid him good evening, congratulating him on the day's trading. Men like him always liked sycophants. They enjoyed the company of people who were in awe of their brilliance and were not ashamed to demonstrate it in public, Aphrodite had found. Dickie placed a pile of letters he had been drafting onto his secretary's desk wordlessly and walked with his guest into the elevator. It descended uninterrupted to the ground floor and opened onto the bustling main atrium. Men marched across the entrance to the building, the leather soles of their shoes slapping against the crisp white marble, the whole space reverberating with the sound. No one chatted: business was done behind closed doors where secrets could be kept. Outside the car waited ready to whisk the pair off to Aphrodite's haven.

The Cyprus Lounge was the most elite gentleman's club in all of Manhattan. A fine establishment that catered exclusively to the desires of the influential and important men in the city. As Dickie entered, the scent of cigar smoke and perfume consumed his senses. All around him men lounged in leather wingback seats, the sage leather, looking soft and supple against the polished hard wood of the walls. The large sheets of newspapers obscured faces, cigars met lips to be replaced by great billows of smoke, and in every free hand was a glass of scotch or gin. Even though it was illegal, alcohol still seemed to be present in every aspect of life.

All around the patrons, moved the nubile young women that made the Cyprus the most enticing place on earth. The women moved through the men with grace and ease, each smiling and tucking loose strands of hair behind their ears as they made eye contact with Dickie. They wore nothing but lingerie, their skin barely covered by lace and silk of every imaginable colour. Large inviting breasts passed him, barely contained by soft pink silk and jet-black lace. Small breasts and pert buttocks came up to Aphrodite and Dickie and ran a hand over the man's shoulder, the pale skin contrasted with dark blue of her brassiere. She whispered something alluring and enticing into his ear and soon he found himself being taken by the hand towards the back of the club where the private bedrooms waited for them.

"Enjoy yourself, Dickie. My girls will make all your dreams come true."

"I want you." He declared, stopping in his tracks and moving back towards Aphrodite, his voice breathy, hushed, and laced with desire he couldn't comprehend.

"I'm afraid I'm not on offer," she replied with a smile, her voice husky and sultry. It seemed to float towards him, making the air dance as it did. "But Madeline here will make sure you are kept very happy."

"I have plenty of money. I want you and I will pay what it takes to get you." He reached out his clammy hand, fingers prickled with the dark strands of middle age hair, daring to touch her.

Aphrodite grabbed his wrist and pulled him close. She was used to the unwanted attention of males. She had been the greatest object of lust and desire in the world for centuries now. She had risen from sea foam as a perfectly formed vision of beauty, but she was still a god and she did not belong to men, no matter how often she laid with them. Dickie was clearly used to having exactly what he wanted at the point where he demanded it. Humans had always amused Aphrodite in this way, relying on power to get them what they wanted. He stood hunched, flabby, bald, with breath that smelt of decay. He was here because he could have what he wanted without needing to deserve it. At least her fellow gods, for all their rage and power and ego, were beautiful to behold.

"I told you, I am not for sale. You have your pick of any other woman who works here though." Aphrodite smiled at him and gently let go of his wrist, running the tip of her finger over his forearm. She preferred to allow men their fantasy of her, to use the desire that swelled and swarmed within them to her advantage. At first sight men wanted her, but eventually they all just wanted to please her, to follow her, to see the way she smiled as they fulfilled her every wish. This man would be no exception. "I do like to see my patrons happy, and it would make me so very happy if you were to follow the rules." She looked up at Dickie, the brilliance of her eyes meeting the dull lifelessness of his.

"If I'd have known I was going to be rejected here I would have just gone to Olympus. At least the drinks are cheap there. Would have been worth it, fire or no fire." His annoyance was clear, but he was obviously placated, moving away from Aphrodite towards the woman who had been leading him to the bedrooms.

Madeline smiled again at his approach and gently ran her hand up to her chest and teased her nipple, making it harden. The man moved quicker in reaction to her, getting close and running his hand into her blonde hair, the other tracing shapes on the exposed soft skin of her belly. It was only as they made it to the door that Aphrodite realised what he had said.

"The Olympus was on fire?" she asked, striding over to the man, the long steps moving her left leg through the slit in her dress, revealing soft, smooth skin, untarnished by hair or razor burn. The silk garter on her thigh drew the eye of every man in the room. Dickie was no exception, his thin lips hanging open as Aphrodite drew close to him. "You did say the Olympus was on fire?"

"Ermm, well, ermm." He couldn't get his words out, the long legs of satin white skin distracting him from any coherent thought that threatened to enter his mind.

Aphrodite leaned forward and drew his focus back to her eyes, she asked again in the softest sultriest voice she could manage, one hand resting on the man's shoulder, the other dancing small delicate patterns against his chest.

"No, my dear, the Olympus wasn't but apparently some others were. It's got us all a little worried about visiting them. Don't want to end up with flames up my ass now." He laughed a little at his own words as he finished speaking so Aphrodite did what all women must do to make men happy; she laughed with him.

"Fuckers." She murmured to herself as Dickie exited into the back rooms. She kept herself composed, tossing her hair behind her shoulder, and making her way across the lounge. She floated effortlessly, each step carrying her forward gracefully. Eyes followed her as she walked, some leering with lustful intent, some merely enjoying the sight of a goddess amongst them. The girls who milled around in their small lace costumes, carrying drinks to the customers, looked at her and smiled, some raising free hands to give her a small friendly wave.

Aphrodite considered herself a good madam. Her lounge was no back-alley brothel where any man could pay his due and have his way. There was no curtain covered cubicles where sailors could lower their stained and stinking pants and hump and grind until they fell in a rum soaked heap atop some poor, emaciated, homeless woman. She had seen those establishments more than she could count and she would not be found dead in one. She had decided she would run only the finest of brothels. She would have the best cliental and the most beautiful women. Gentlemen would spend their evening in sensual ecstasy, all their needs met, and her girls would be safe in the knowledge that they would not suffer at the hands of a drunk oaf.

Her head of security nodded at her as she passed the main door and slipped into a small hallway. The long, dimly lit passage ran down the back of the building. At regular intervals a small man or woman sat on a stool, their focus taken by walls that dripped plaster in a white shower over their shoulders. The wall was not what interested them. Where each person sat a small hole had been drilled into the drywall, and as they peered through them, they intermittently moved away and filled the holes with cameras instead of their own eye. Every private room had a place where Aphrodite could keep an eye on the men. Zeus knew nothing about it of course, but she couldn't take the chance that her girls would be left to anyone's mercy, so she had the pictures taken as insurance. Any man who found themselves on her darker side would soon fall into line when they realised their every dirty secret and hidden perversion was now committed to paper.

Once out of the passage, Aphrodite reached her office. The room was filled with soft light, hazy and muted beams cast soft colours into the air as the glow from lamps passed through silk scarfs that Aphrodite had draped over them. The walls were filled with paintings: art she had collected from across the centuries she had been wandering the earth. She had no specific era that she loved most so the wonderous history of artistic endeavour was displayed in full around her. She ignored it all and sat at her desk. She crossed her legs and reached for the phone. She dialled the number for Zeus and waited. She missed the sound of the operator's voice, the nasally overly formal tone of women forced to wear far too many clothes. When the receiver was picked up, she didn't give Zeus time to greet her.

"Were you planning on telling me that clubs had been burned down or was I just supposed to imitate Apollo and divine such information?"

"Who is this?" Came Zeus' confused murmurs, his deep voice rumbling through the telephone lines that connected them.

"It's Aphrodite. Answer my question, why on earth wasn't I told that clubs had been burned down?"

Zeus sighed. He had learned long ago that Aphrodite was far more than beautiful; she was as tenacious, furious, and awe inspiring as the rest of the pantheon.

"It was not information that you needed Aphrodite. It wasn't relevant to your role and…"

"Not relevant," she barked, not interested in what he had to say. "I'm assuming here that three clubs burning is no coincidence and these were attacks?" There was no response to her question, just the silence of a man who knew his words would be meaningless anyway. "I'll take that as a yes. So, if this person attacked clubs, it's very reasonable they would attack my lounge, or one of my other establishments. How am I meant to protect my girls if I don't even know they're in danger?"

"I don't give a fuck about your girls."

"Well, I do. That was the deal Zeus, I lure men in and in exchange I get complete control over the brothels. Don't mistake me for an obedient child or tired sibling."

"ENOUGH." Zeus' rage burned through the receiver that Aphrodite was holding, she swore she saw sparks dance over the casing, some long lost memory of Zeus' ability to create lightning stirring fear in the back of her mind.

She adjusted her tone. She may not be his child or sibling, but he was still the most powerful force that had ever ruled from Olympus. Their conversation carried on, the more subdued Aphrodite asking only that in future she be kept abreast of the situation. Zeus agreed and the topic turned to the clients of the week. Intrigue and gossip always caused revelry between gods.

Nine

The Farm

ionysus leaned back against the soft leather of the car seat. He allowed the supple brown fabric, with its abundance of padding, to surround him and cushion his neck. Some of the tension from the night before slowly fell away from his body, the memory of the lumpy motel mattress disappearing as he finally embraced the comfort of the seat. He had tried to keep himself alert all day as the car made its way through the fields of rural America, but the long straight roads surrounded by green and gold that stretched out to the horizon provided very little entertainment.

His books littered the seat next to him: scuffed pages of poetry folded, and dog eared, the paper turned yellow with age. They were the original publications he had collected over the centuries. Dionysus loved poetry, the way the words danced on the page, the imagery, the pain, sorrow, love and joy, all coming together for him, alone, to absorb and enjoy. But even poetry could only entertain him for so long. He closed his eyes and let his head loll backwards, giving into the exhaustion that he felt, letting the comfort take him ever deeper into the car seat.

Time slipped by as Dionysus allowed himself to drift in and out of sleep. The journey to Kentucky was long and tested his capacity to handle boredom. He was a man who loved to be around others. He had spent his years roaming the world enjoying the company of some of the greatest people in history. He had drunk wine with leaders of the French revolution, gulped vodka with the Tsars of Russia, and laid in euphoric bliss in the opium dens of china. Philosophers, poets, artists, and politicians had all filled his mind and time with wonder. He needed their entertainment, their voices to ring through his mind. That is what it had meant to be the god of revelry, not merely to drink and dine in abundance but to experience the ecstasy of good company. He already yearned for his bar, wishing he were there pouring the drinks and talking endlessly to the regulars. Instead, he was sat in a car on his way to a farm. Such torment should be reserved for Tartarus, he thought to himself.

When he fully roused himself, the sun was beginning to fall low into the sky. The bright blue that had been painted above him was slowly transforming, the colours of the setting sun bleeding across it, lighting the bellies of the clouds that drifted listless and sleepily in the sky. The driver turned a corner, taking the car off the main road and up a dirt track that ran through the fields. The sun's rays seemed to shine off the golden crops that surrounded him, that stood tall and swayed in the breeze, rippling as the gentle wind moved them. The track was less well kept than the main road, littered with potholes and loose rocks that caused the car to bounce as it made its way forward. Dionysus' bones rattled inside his slender body, his knees banging against the driver's seat in front of him. He could feel the car straining against the uneven surface, desperate to be free from the agony of carrying its load over such terrain. The driver had slowed the car, taking it easy, and whilst Dionysus was thankful of the caution, he felt he would be willing to suffer the indignity of his teeth smashing together and body trembling if it meant he got out of the car quicker.

Dionysus sighed with relief as the car's journey up the dirt road quickly ended. The car turned one last time as it came upon a squat farmhouse set in a baron patch of dirt amidst the fields. Dionysus took the place in as he always had and let his heart sink just a small amount. He gazed at the wooden walls where white paint flaked, and small patches blew away with the wind. He heard the creak of the shutters that hung limply from rusted hinges. Shingles sat precariously on the roof, each one threatening to fall and smash in the wind. A small porch ran around the entirety of the building, the steps leading up to it a wonky mass of aged timber that looked almost impossible to walk on without falling over.

As the door was opened for Dionysus he breathed in the warm sweet air, the smell of nature filling his nostrils. The smell was so familiar, the sweetness of plant life warmed in the sun, tinged with the heady aroma of flowers and animals. Bird song drifted into his ears, filling his head with the playful tones of the world around him. He thanked the driver when he stepped out and allowed himself to unfurl, his long limbs each stretching in their own direction in a bid to pull the aches and tension from his body.

"I thought you were meant to be here much earlier." A voice demanded of him.

He looked up at the dilapidated farmhouse to see the mesh covered door swinging gently backwards, as a plump, middle-aged woman walked through. He smiled at the sight of his new companion. As always her long brown hair, thick and rich with glossy colour, that rippled like the wheat fields around them, was tied into an intricate braid that wove its way around her head.

"Well, I slept in. What can I say? I do so enjoy the lice infested mattresses they have in Ohio." Dionysus replied, raising his eyebrow at Demeter's flat expression. "Oh, come on aunty, don't I at least get a smile?"

He began walking towards the house as she stepped down from the porch, the rickety stairs causing her no problem. She smiled gently at him as she walked, letting her good nature consume her. With each step the voluptuous curves of her body bounced, breasts and buttocks moving like time had slowed. The low-cut dress that Demeter wore left little to the imagination, the soft tanned skin of her chest gently glistening as the long rays of the evening sun met the small droplets of sweat that beaded upon her.

Once the distance between them was closed, the plump woman reached up and wrapped her arms around Dionysus. The simple dress she wore looked at odds with the elaborate suit of violent colour that clad Dionysus' slender frame. Demeter pulled him close and encourage his head to rest on her fleshy shoulder, the natural comfort of familiar contact helping to push away his weariness. He worried that the short hairs of his goatee would jab into Demeter but when she didn't react, so he allowed the embrace to continue uninterrupted.

Demeter had always been one of the more affectionate of Dionysus' family. She cared deeply for every single one of them and had sacrificed the life of revelry and joyous abandon they had in the city to keep the farm running smoothly. For a brief second Dionysus felt regret for coming here so reluctantly, she was one of the few people whose company he could tolerate without whisky coursing through his veins. Together they walked into the old farmhouse.

"So, what really kept you from getting here on time?" Demeter asked, gesturing for Dionysus to sit.

He shook his head in response, choosing to stand next to the old armchair. He rested one hand on the threadbare fabric, the last remnants of colour just visible if one squinted hard enough. Leaning was too much stillness for him after such a long drive. He began to pace, walking around the room, inspecting the assortment of figurines and trinkets that lined every flat surface. Pictures hung from the wall, pictures more valuable than any person would realise; faded, dull works of endless scenery that captured the monotony of the world. Dionysus had never been a fan, but the names signed in each corner meant that should the family ever need money they had something to sell. He much preferred Aphrodite's collection; she had a true appreciation of beauty.

"I had a small soiree in my motel room last night, nothing amazing but enough company to keep me somewhat entertained." He looked over at Demeter who gave him a small smile of exasperation. "But I was feeling a little bit rough this morning. Ended up sleeping in."

He poured himself a glass of water from a pitcher that sat on the table next to Demeter. The clear liquid seemed to rattle as it tumbled into the glass. The refreshing scent cutting through the mustiness of the farmhouse.

"You know you could just have one night without a party." Demeter retorted.

"And you could have a day without your breasts on show to the world."

"Always show off your assets I say." The goddess replied wryly. "Which is why I assume your trousers are made of such thick material."

Dionysus couldn't help but laugh. Despite his unhappiness at being away from the parties and social events of the city, it was nice to be away from the bulk of his family. Demeter always brought out the humour in him, something that was hard to find when Zeus and Hera screamed bloody murder at each other, when Hermes taunted Ares, when Aphrodite pouted in disdain or Athena glared down her nose at everyone who passed by. All of them had forgotten what it truly meant to have fun and to experience joy. Demeter remembered.

"The only thick material I see…"

"Is the material holding my dress together?" Demeter finished, looking up, her deep brown eyes, like pools of melted chocolate, glinting with cheek and amusement, looking straight into Dionysus' own. "You made fun of my weight last time you were here dear. You really should get some new material."

They laughed together as Dionysus poured and gulped down another glass of crystal-clear water.

The evening progressed with the usual chatter that the two Olympians had come to expect of each other. They teased one another and then moved on to poking fun at their fellow gods. They exchanged memories of times long past, memories that seemed to be a little fuzzier and more uncertain with each retelling. Dionysus had finally succumbed to his need to sit and taken refuge in the tatty armchair, his long slender fingers absent-mindedly pulling at the loose threads of the aged material. Demeter was curled up on the sofa, her legs almost completely tucked under her dress, pulled into the soft curvature of her body. The electric lights flickered as a servant turned them on, the two old friends unaware that the room had slowly started to be consumed by darkness as they had talked, and the sun had fallen behind the sweeping curve of the planets horizon.

"I guess we should discuss why Zeus has sent you back so quickly." Demeter finally said after the warmth and good humour had lulled Dionysus into a false sense of security.

He did not want to talk about this. Demeter didn't speak, allowing the silence to draw out Dionysus' words. He finally succumbed to the tactic, hating the moments of mindless silence that others could tolerate so well. He leaned forward and rested bony elbows on bonier knees. Either side of his open waistcoat fell aside revealing the crumpled white silk of a shirt he had been forced to travel in. He told Demeter everything that had happened, about the fires, about how they implied knowledge of the way the family operated, how Poseidon had been beaten to a pulp. It was the last fact that seemed to paint genuine concern and fear across Demeter's round face, that finally caused the soft pink of her cheeks to fade to an ashen white.

"So, Zeus sent me here. He thinks that if they know how we operate they could know about the farm, that they could try and do some damage here, cut of our supply line entirely."

"What does he want you to do whilst you're here?"

"Check for anything suspicious." Dionysus replied. "Make sure all locks are secured, that the staff know to be on the lookout for anything suspicious, make sure no one has already got in who shouldn't." Dionysus sighed and looked down at the floor, the faded pattern of the rug barely covering the warped and distorted floorboards that seemed to creak even when no one walked over them. "In all honesty I just think the old man is scared. He wants to feel like he's doing something so here I am. It will be good to check on the distillery staff though, make sure they keep everything locked down. That lot can be a bit slack."

"The newer ones aren't too bad though."

"Newer ones?" Dionysus asked, looking at his aunt quizzically. The last time he had visited there had been the same staff that there had always been.

"Yes, some of the boys in the distillery thought they would … erm … sample some of the product." Demeter smiled as she spoke, chuckling to herself. "I mean I'm not mad, boys will be boys, but they clearly sampled a batch that wasn't ready, went and made themselves very sick. A few of the girls knew guys looking for work so they're covering until the little toe rags are all better."

Dionysus couldn't help but smile as Demeter spoke, the way she laughed off theft and serious illness with such light-hearted abandon. Seriousness rarely seemed to be a feature of the woman. The rest of the conversation was dominated with plans, ways that they could make the distillery more secure. Locks, checks, even better wages all seemed to be reliable options. It wouldn't take long for Dionysus to be done here and then he could go back to the city, to the constant clatter and buzz of crowds where he belonged.

Their conversation was brought to an abrupt end as a servant entered to inform them that dinner was ready. The man stood before Dionysus was a vision. He towered over the room, his muscular physique casting a broad shadow across every surface. Enticing brown skin was pulled taught over large pecs that were just visible in the gaps between buttons of his casual work shirt. His furrowed brow shadowed his already dark eyes, drawing Dionysus in. As he spoke his lips parted to reveal two perfect rows of white teeth, and each word seemed to pull at the corners of his mouth making him smile at the two gods before him. As he turned to escort them to the dining room Dionysus' eyes roved over his back, taking in the perfect curve that led to his tight firm buttocks and thick legs. He drank in the sight of the man, allowing his senses to be overwhelmed by desire.

The meal was spent in a distracted haze. Demeter attempted to make conversation, but Dionysus could not remove his focus from the idol that moved around the table pouring drinks and plating food. He ate and drank, of course; food and liquor were just as important to the hedonist as sex. He was lucky that, unlike humans, he never put on weight. He tore at the meat he had been served and drank down glass after glass of liquor. Each time he did the man would come by his side and pour more for him to consume. The man's scent wafted over Dionysus, the thick musk of a man who worked in the heat, an aroma that intoxicated and delighted, that made his skin prickle and hair stand on end. It was at times like these Dionysus despised living in such a prudish society. He was not as dedicated to men as Hermes, but he enjoyed sampling every delight the world had to offer him, yet one suggestion to the wrong person and he would find himself beaten bloody. Damn Christianity! Still, he enjoyed the tantalising fantasies that the servant's scent conjured in his mind.

As the meal progressed and the night wore on Dionysus began to feel weary, and two days of travel and a night in a filthy motel made him yearn for the soft embrace of a real bed.

"Well, I think it's time that I went to bed. I suspect we have a long day tomorrow." He stated, rising from the table. The chair creaked under him as he shifted his weight, and the table, its wood free of shine or gloss, swayed as he placed his weight on it, its one weak leg threatening to break. Demeter bid him good night with another tight embrace, her cheeks now even rosier from the warm food and alcohol.

"I'll get Lilly to show you to your room." She declared, a slight hiccup accompanying her words as the food and alcohol threatened to follow them.

Dionysus was about to protest, having stayed at the farm multiple times over the past year, however the words failed him as a young woman entered. Lilly seemed to glow in the room, a cosmic presence amongst the tattered and worn-out furnishings of the farmhouse. He gazed at her soft skin, gently tanned from a life in the sun. He took in the petite figure, a body he could envelop with his own, that he could consume with passion and lust. Her dress was modest and revealed only small amounts of flesh. He envisioned tearing away at the fabric, allowing his hands and lips to explore every part of her that lay underneath. She smiled sweetly at him, blue eyes twinkling with joy. As he began to follow her a deep voice reverberated, behind him sending shivers down his spine.

"Allow me to escort you as well sir."

Dionysus turned to see the young servant smiling at him, a playful look painted across the dark features of his face. Dionysus allowed the two humans to lead him away from the dining room. Demeter sat still, her focus on pouring yet more liquor into the shimmering glass of her tumbler. The stairs groaned as all three ascended to the hallway. With each step the tension between them grew, sparking through the air, threatening to set the house ablaze. Dionysus reached out and locked his fingers in between the man's, then, reaching the other way, did the same with the woman. He felt uncontainable, like his clothes may fall from him from sheer willpower. They all exchanged glances: knowing, longing, heated with passion and consumed by lust. Then, as the door to the bedroom closed, they succumbed in totality to the desires that swarmed within them.

Ten

Men

T he whirring, buzzing, crunching, and growling of machines perforated the air, sending a wave of noise outwards to consume the workshop. The stench of oil and heated metal radiated through the air, filling the nostrils of anyone who came close. Sweat beaded on every forehead and trickled down every neck, running over leathered skin and squat muscular bodies as the heat enveloped the workers. No person was still, they moved with precision, a rhythm of workmanship oscillating and beating, pulsating between them all. Poseidon was always impressed when he came to the workshop. The men worked tirelessly, the heat, noise, and smell seeming to drive them on rather than deter them. He had found himself in an age where physical prowess, determination, and strength were no longer admired characteristics and he despised it. Yet, here in this little pocket of the world, strength and stamina, and raw personal power were still essential.

He moved through the workshop, wooden benches full of gouges and burns sat laden with metal contraptions. Piles of springs and warped metal panels filled overflowing barrels. Nuts, bolts, and rivets were everywhere. In one corner of the workshop cars sat, half assembled, raised up with men working their tools underneath. In another section men tinkered with guns of all shapes and sizes. Small pistols were polished and cleaned then laid down next to Tommy guns, their wide circular magazines virtually lifting them off the surface. Blows echoed through the air as one worker fired a pistol into a target, he frowned and then continued working on the gun, for some reason unhappy with how it had performed. Poseidon had never quite understood modern technology. He still preferred messengers to phones and would rather run than get into any kind of motorised vehicle. For so long the world had remained unchanged. Life had plodded along as normal, people content to walk and punch, but now, for some reason, they needed to drive and shoot. Humans never made sense to him.

He moved from the world of nonsense into a world of sheer absurdity. Hephaestus' office was a mess of papers. Plans and blueprints were taped and pinned and laid on every flat surface available. Hand drawn notes were across every single one, prompts in every language under the sun. Greek, German, English, Russian, and even a few of the dead languages sat side by side in squat messy writing. Some sentences were a mix of every language. The smell of smoke and oil was replaced by the overwhelming, bitter scent of coffee that rose from the pot on the table. Hephaestus sat at his desk, his body stooped over some drawing or diagram that made no sense to Poseidon. He didn't look up as his sanctuary was invaded, instead he continued to scribble manically on the page. Poseidon coughed in an attempt to get the man's attention. Nothing. He coughed again, a louder, more deliberate cough, but still no reaction came. Poseidon kicked the table, causing the wood to rattle and the legs to grate against the rough stone of the ground. Hephaestus finally looked up from his work.

Hephaestus smiled as he saw Poseidon. His dull brown eyes showed no sparkle of joy, their murky colour holding in all the light that they could. They looked huge to Poseidon, magnified by the thick glasses on Hephaestus' face. The contraption was startling, more than a metal frame with thick wedges of glass: they had multiple layers, handles and levers. One side looked somewhat normal, but the other was almost like a brass telescope that he had attached to his crooked face. The glasses sat wonky, an unfortunate feature of Hephaestus' face being entirely asymmetrical. His lumpy features seemed to have been thrown at his face by a blind man who had only heard vague rumours about what a human face looked like. His nose glistened with beads of sweat, each one seeming to magnify some lump, pore, or blemish that sat hideously upon his face. He rose from the seat and welcomed Poseidon, moving the contraption from his face. Poseidon couldn't help but laugh as the now unobscured face was revealed to have only one eyebrow, the space where the other had been only marked by the occasional singed hair. The god of forges did himself very few favours.

He reached out and shook Poseidon's hand, his brawny, knotted fingers, callused from lifetimes of hard labour, gripping tightly. It was rare that the god of the sea felt emasculated in the presence of another. Even Zeus and Ares had a whiff of femininity to them, they enjoyed luxurious perfumes as much as any woman or dandy that had graced the surface of the earth, whereas Hephaestus chose to walk around in a haze of his own musk. Poseidon had breathed salt air and battered the very rock of the earth itself, so with Hephaestus, a man of steel and sweat, of toil, and tirelessness, he was had found his equal, and a friend for eternity. Hephaestus mopped the sweat from his brow and pulled a bottle from under his desk. Pulling out the stopper with his teeth he spat it onto the ground and then gulped down the liquor, followed by a mouthful of thick black coffee, straight from the pot. He passed the bottle to Poseidon who did the same, except for the coffee: he had never acquired the taste for the bitter drink. Now that greetings had been done, they both sat, Poseidon doing his best to get comfortable on an upturned crate next to Hephaestus' desk.

"It's good to see you Poseidon" Hephaestus said, handing the bottle back. "Heard about that business with you and the arsonist. Bastard." The god's voice was gruff and hoarse, more of a rumble that seemed to catch in his throat and fall from his mouth than actual speech. His accent was unplaceable. Years of travelling, of gathering with every man in every tavern or warehouse he could find had turned his voice into that of a man with no home. Poseidon nodded his gratitude at Hephaestus. After feeling so vulnerable and exposed in front of Zeus and Hera he was looking forward to the company of a man who would ask for no such emotion from him.

"Fucker, more like." He replied taking another long gulp of whisky. "But it's not happening again. Next time I see him his guts will end up decorating my shack."

"Good, that shithole needs brightening up."

"Never took you for a decorator."

"Well maybe I'm expanding my horizons."

The two of them shared a chuckle, the kind of laugh that signified that everything said between them was good natured. Poseidon enjoyed Hephaestus' company more and more as the days progressed. Even though the god was obsessed with modern technology and revelled in improving upon every invention and contraption that came his way, he was the most consistent and timeless of the family. The rest of them fought, bickered, jostled for Zeus' approval, but Hephaestus simply worked with the single-minded dedication of a man who had nothing to prove.

"Well, I'm hoping you can stay in your horizons for me for a bit."

He handed back the bottle and took a deep breath. The god of the sea did not like asking for help, but with Hephaestus it was easy. The god did not judge, scoff, or mock like the others. He simply found joy in providing what help he could.

"Whoever this bastard is he's quick and he's tough. I want him dead, and I want it to hurt. I need weapons that can turn this fucker into paint." Poseidon declared as Hephaestus beamed his crooked smile at him.

The straggly beard hid his Hephaestus' lip, but Poseidon could see his face contort into a lumpy depiction of joy: a look that was like a hand puppet being made to look ecstatic. Hephaestus leaned back and ran his hands through the tangled mass of limp brown hair that sat atop his head.

"Are you saying you want to have a look in the toybox Poseidon?"

"No." He replied, rolling his eyes.

For years Hephaestus had been trying to get him to take an interest in guns, and rummage through the toybox; a collection of altered, tinkered with, and personally adapted guns that Hephaestus had been creating for years. Everyone had a toy from the toybox. Even Aphrodite had a small, bejewelled pistol that she kept tucked into some sort of lace she wore about her person. To date Poseidon was the only god who had refused one of Hephaestus' favourite little items.

"You know I don't use guns. But I want something that will catch the fucker off guard."

Hephaestus rose from his seat slamming his gnarled hands down on the table.

"Fine, let's see what else I have for you."

With that he walked out into the workroom. The wall of noise, odour, and heat collided with Poseidon as he re-entered. Men smiled and clasped hands with Hephaestus as he walked past. They called him boss, sir, and guv, one guy even called him champ. They showed him the kind of respect he deserved; the admiration men have for someone so unassumingly brilliant. They walked past the guns and into a small hidden corner of the warehouse. Here, men in leather vests hammered at thick shards of metal while others wearing complex glasses contraptions like Hephaestus' tinkered with elaborate mechanisms.

Hephaestus walked to a cabinet on the end wall: a broad structure made of metal bars and grates with a matte, worn surface that reflected none of the sparks that burst from the equipment around them. Flashes flew through the air and landed on Hephaestus' exposed arm, but the god didn't flinch. He simply pulled open the cabinet to reveal the array of weapons that had been harboured within.

Poseidon tried to take in the collection but there seemed to be little order to the assembled arsenal. Hephaestus rummaged for a short time before proudly bringing out a wide, brown, leather vest, studded with stout metal spikes.

"This," he declared proudly, "is especially useful for opponents that are quick. If you're going to struggle to fend off body blows then this vest will make the blows hurt them more."

"Isn't it a bit obvious? I might as well wear armour."

"It goes under your clothes, the spikes are dull enough that they won't pierce through loose cloth, they'll only stab through when pressure is exerted. It's got the element of surprise."

He threw the vest toward Poseidon who managed to catch it without piercing his own flesh. He ran his hand over the leather; it was lighter than he expected, and the studs were dull enough that he could touch them without drawing blood. The design seemed perfect for the intention.

"It's good to know that all these years working with machines you haven't forgotten how to make real weapons." Poseidon quipped.

Hephaestus just grunted and continued to rummage. He bent low making his worker slacks descend and reveal the sweaty crack that ran between sagging buttocks. He made no attempt to pull them up, still engrossed in his search.

"AHAH!" He boomed, drawing some attention from the rest of the room. "I knew I'd find them eventually."

He stood tall and presented Poseidon with two shafts of blunt metal attached to leather straps. Poseidon could do little other than send a bewildered look at Hephaestus. The other god just smiled and lightly clicked some part of the contraption that Poseidon had not noticed. A metallic ring echoed around them as, from within the contraption, a blade surged forward. The polished metal shimmered in the light of the warehouse, Hephaestus turning it so that Poseidon could see.

"These attach to your arms. When you're in a jam just put pressure on the switch and the blade will come out. Handy in close quarters."

Poseidon took the weapons and looked them over. He had never been a sneaky fighter, but the idea of hidden swords excited him.

Hephaestus continued to move through the collection with a purpose that Poseidon couldn't fathom. Some items prompted a shake of the head, others got a quizzical look and placed onto a pile, some were beamed at, but then discarded. Whatever was going on in the inventor's head was a mystery to Poseidon. He was provided with several other items: a watch with a hidden garrotte wire inside, shoes with secreted knives, even a belt with hidden compartments for small explosives. The array of tailored weapons made Poseidon's head spin, unsure of whether, or even how, he would use everything that he had been given. The final item that Hephaestus gave him seemed to bring the smith more joy than any of them. He beamed as he presented Poseidon with a small wooden box. Inside sat a metal lighter, the same tarnished tin device that could be bought at any stand or store in the city.

"This is a bomb." The god explained. "You simply act like you're lighting the lighter. This sets off a fuse, you have about ten seconds until it goes off. It will turn a man into a loose set of limbs in an instant."

Poseidon took the device from the box and twirled it in his fingers. He wanted to decline it at first; explosives felt too much like modern weaponry, but memories of burning and explosions in ancient wars, ones that him and his fellow gods had laughed over, reminded him that turning men into ash and assorted parts was a tradition. He put the lighter into his pocket and made an important mental note to never try and use it to light his roll ups.

"Fancy having a practice?"

Poseidon allowed himself to be helped into the array of gadgets that required straps, buckles, and laces to be affixed to various parts of his body. What surprised him most was how light weight it all turned out to be. He had expected himself to feel laden like an ox on the way to a market, but Hephaestus had managed to work magic into the wearable weapons. They somehow felt light on his person.

After he had re-dressed and secreted away all of the items, he moved around. Hephaestus had been clever with the vest ensuring that none of the sharp studs were too close to his sides. He could move his arms around freely without fear he would puncture himself. The arm blades were short enough that they didn't hinder any flexibility and the belt was made of a leather so soft and wearable that it felt like it must be made from the hide of some divine cow. He was looking forward to testing out what he had been given and was happy to see that his nephew had arranged a group of men to challenge him.

The workers were all built the same. Each one of them was broad and muscular with a body that was used to hard work and labour. They were strong and each wielded their weapons confidently. Poseidon reasoned that very few of them must know how to fight properly; any men that worked for the family and proved themselves handy with a weapon or their fists found themselves under Ares' wing, beating up debtors and protecting the bars and brothels. These were strong men, though, which meant they would probably rush him and use their power to overwhelm him. There were five of them. Each had taken their shirt off in order to improve their movement whilst fighting in the heat of the warehouse. The first one rushed him, raising a chain high and slamming it down. Poseidon moved out the way, easily dodging the sluggish attack. Behind him a crowbar swung.

Poseidon still ached from his beating, the bruises and cuts about his body only just beginning to fade. He pushed the pain aside, determined to give his all, even if it was just a sparring match. He hadn't expected the men to gather around him so quickly. Clearly these men had a little experience with confrontation. As the bar came towards his head, he raised his arm and allowed it to clash into the blunt metal casing of his blade. The impact sent tremors through his body, jangling his bones, but, luckily, he was strong enough that the blow didn't throw him off balance. Hephaestus hissed, taking a breath in through clenched teeth as the metal bar clashed against his invention.

"Fuck me, if you warp the metal the blade won't come out." He shouted at Poseidon who had now decided to be more offensive.

Poseidon flexed his arms in the way that he had been shown, which caused the blades to spring from their containment. He moved with startling speed towards the men. Each time they made to strike him he deflected the blows with his blades.

Poseidon's natural instinct to punch and grab and throw had to be curtailed. The only way to get the blade back was to push it in and he did not have time to do that in a fight. Instead, he used the blade to block weapon attacks and then used his legs to kick away or injure his attackers. The men were determined, though. They came at him as a group, each brandishing something metallic and heavy, forcing him to mix his speed with strength. After he had disarmed one of them, he allowed them to strike a body blow. The punch still forced the air from his lungs and sent a shock of pain through him, but it appeared to be worse for the other man, who let out a violent scream of agony as the vest stabbed into his hand. With the man now in pain Poseidon let his foot squarely meet his chest and sent him flying to a rest on the hard floor.

The rest of the fight progressed similarly: they came at him in a wave, and he fended them off, whilst managing to disarm and incapacitate one at a time. They grunted and groaned in pain, but Poseidon barely heard them over the continual cacophony of bangs and buzzing that surrounded them in the Warehouse. The last man standing was a squat man, short but rippling with sinew. He was glazed with sweat from heat and exertion, the fight leaving him panting and bruised. A small trickle of blood ran from his lip where it had been cut. Poseidon eyed him and then decided that the men gathered around them had seen enough of him beating workmen. He raised his hands in mock surrender, the blades from his arm mounted weapons rising above his head. The man smiled at his gesture and backed away with his own hands raised. The fight had not been genuine, but no man ever wanted to lose at a round of sparring.

Poseidon's chest heaved with deep breaths. His body felt tight, and he could feel some of his wounds from the fight with the killer aching again. He regretted letting the first man get a body blow. Above it all he felt ready. He had carried the shame of defeat on him like a stench that wouldn't leave for days now and he knew next time he saw the assailant he would replace shame with victory.

Eleven
Small, Petty Men

The ensemble of cars rattled and groaned as they made their way into the mess of dilapidated streets that was Harlem. Each car churned thick black smoke in their wake, the engines pouring out the toxins that churned within them. Zeus sat in the car that led the way. His perfectly polished, silver stallion almost seemed to sing with a guttural and primal voice, like a beast prowling and circling at the start of the fight. An aura of calm surrounded Zeus as he sat straight backed and motionless. With every bump in the road his body should have swayed or bounced, but in this moment, he was a statue: the world around him barely able to chip away at him. His face was not serene, his harsh features still carried the edge of derision and contempt that befitted a god amongst mortals, but it was no longer screwed into a mask of rage.

When Athena had first revealed to him who had supplied their enemy, he had allowed his anger to emerge from him in a wave of unadulterated destruction. His home, a sanctuary of soft furnishings and fine art, a haven of decadence and luxury that Hera had spent years crafting into a place where they could live privately and publicly, was turned into nothing more than tattered rags and broken wood in a sea of glass fragments and torn parchments. He had rammed his fist through an especially valuable piece from when they had lived in renaissance Italy and turned a priceless Chinese vase into powder.

There was nothing more Zeus hated than when he couldn't direct his fury towards the intended target, but Athena had been right: their enemy was more elusive and capable than any enemy they had faced in a long time and rushing in with his fists could result in him ending up battered and bruised like Poseidon. So far, the killer, as he called himself, had avoided all efforts to find him: federal agents, local police, and even slimy informants knew nothing. The man was almost a ghost, walking through the city unseen. Zeus had made more angry calls in the past few days than he could count.

Zeus knew his reputation was all that kept his family safe. His conquest of Manhattan had been swift and brutal. He had gathered men together and swarmed through the island like a plague. There was not a home or business he had not infected. Every official or person of means was in his pocket: every gangster, every hustler, every tiny little speak easy owner he came up against chose to work for him, leave Manhattan, or die. Warehouses, docks, and black alleys were permanently stained the deep burgundy of dried blood from where he had felled his enemies. Every board room gathered at his establishments and spoke his name in fearful whispers, and every public official treated wives and mistresses to gourmet delicacies thanks to the money he had slipped into their pinstriped pockets. He knew that if he were ever seen beaten and broken in a back alley his empire would fall. The gangs that fought for scraps of domain in Brooklyn would descend upon him and consume what he had. He knew he needed to be unstoppable and at times that meant listening to wisdom, luckily, he had a goddess for that.

Athena sat next to him, her posture somehow even more rigid than his. The goddess never slouched, never seemed to relax. Even when the alcohol was flowing and the world around them was nothing more than an orgy of sensual delights, there was still an alertness to her, a twitch that pulled her eyes to the corners and kept her alert and ready for action. The sun shone through the window casting her profile in shadow, highlighting the sharp angles of her face. Her nose jutted forth from her face, like blade had been thrust through the back of her head, her lips were thin, red like blood smeared in a line across her face, and her chin angled down. The scent of her cologne wafted through the car filling the small space. She reminded Zeus of the day she burst forth: strength and danger poured from her, seeping from her skin and consuming her. The only difference was instead of the golden helmet

JAMES MORLEY

that had once adorned her head she now wore a trilby, the navy-blue fabric stark against her white skin and hiding her long locks of black hair that she tucked up inside of it. It never surprised Zeus that the greatest civilization in history had taken their name from her. She had been by his side through everything, the one person he could truly rely on. He reached out and rested his hand on hers. She flinched slightly, always uncomfortable with signs of affection, but allowed the moment to exist before turning to Zeus.

"We're clear on the plan aren't we father?" She asked, her voice cutting through some of the apprehensive tension that filled the car. They weren't far from their destination and both of them were ready to spring into action.

"I think I know how to intimidate scum Athena. Don't worry about me." Zeus replied, his confidence never faltering.

They had had eyes on the shop for a couple of days and had seen no evidence that Poseidon's assailant had been anywhere near the store. If he was linked to this place, then the link was weak. The plan to find out was simple. The kind of plan that Zeus liked; he would enter with every strong and angry man he had, destroy the place, terrify the owner, and get all the information he wanted. If he didn't get what he wanted, then he would do what he was best at: he would destroy the man who stood in his way.

He felt the anticipation bristle and foam into excitement within him. He was a mix of emotions: a surging pit of anger, apprehension, and the ecstasy that came with his power. It seemed to spark under his skin, flowing through every part of his body, a storm brewing within him. He took a deep breath to calm himself, knowing he couldn't let himself get carried away, knowing that he couldn't let those feelings manifest, not like they used to, not now, not ever. He channelled the sensations into physical strength, tensing and flexing his muscles under his clothes, feeling the coarse fibres tighten against his flesh.

As they turned one last corner their target came into view. Drewery's Fine Collectibles was a beat down shit hole that sat on a dirty corner of Harlem's 125th street. The windows were covered with thick iron bars that, along with the grime caked onto the aging glass, hid the plethora of misused and abused items that sat in the window begging to be sold and free of their prison.

The collection of cars moved around the building forming a horseshoe to pen the building in place. The tires stirred up dust as they moved across the dry summer streets and filled the air with their mechanical rumblings. As Zeus stepped out from his car the rest cut their engines and silence swam around them. At Zeus' signal feet, clad in thick leather shoes, stomped out of every car door and a swarm of stone-faced men moved towards the peeling paint and chipped wood of the shop door.

The door burst open, the thud of the kick that sent it swinging almost loud enough to drown out the whining squeak of the hinges. The inside of the shop was dim, only cheap dirty lamps scattered around the interior provided any light and the bright sun of the day struggled to get through the murky glass of the windows. The warm air of the street seemed to pour into the chilled space as Zeus' men filed in. The smell of must and damp greeted them, the air stagnant and still. Men in three-piece suits, straight backed and weighted with muscle, made their way through the rows of shelves, taking positions throughout the shop. The owner wasn't present and there was no one sat behind the dust laden counter at the furthest side of the shop away from the door. Zeus and Athena followed their men in, each of them allowing their faces to twist and to contort into a sneer as they look around the dirty and pathetic assemblage of useless and broken trinkets that occupied the shelves of the shop.

There was no order to the place; chipped and aged figurines sat next to string-less guitars, old and tattered books were heaped on top of weapons, and clothing sat in dirty bundles surrounded by withered, colourless paintings. The shop looked like someone was attempting to sell a junk yard without hiding the fact that everything was junk. Zeus understood why, but it didn't annoy him any less. The shop may just be a front for illegal activity, but it should at least look like a place where people might buy things rather than a place where a person might find themselves waking up after a heavy night.

The thick dust in the air and the chill from lack of heat or sunlight made the place distinctly unpleasant. The air felt oppressive, like it was trying to hold Zeus in place. He began to pace the shelves, letting his thick hands, clad in leather gloves glide over the assortment of filth and garbage. Every man he passed stepped silently and unprompted from their space, even those with backs to him managed to crane their necks and look from the corners of their eyes to make sure not to get in his way.

A commotion sounded behind the counter. The mumbled cries of protest and surprise barely made their way through the door that hid the dank office of the shop's owner. The muffled sounds began to grow, the sounds of desperate pleas becoming almost distinct and the soft thuds of a fist meeting a belly audible to all those in the shop. The sound erupted into the room as the door swung open. Ares appeared, stepping from the darkness of the back office into the gloomy light of the shop. He seemed to cast a shadow in all directions, his heaving, gargantuan frame consuming the doorway. Muscles rippled under his clothing, pulling everything that adorned him tight. His neat crop of brown hair seemed to be lost above him, unnoticeable from the angle that most people had to look up at him from. His face was set in a stern expression, his blunt features, and flat nose marred by pot marks and scars. His mouth twitched slightly with joy as, behind him, he pulled a squirming mass of Irish fear.

Ares threw his quarry on the counter and, for the first time, Patrick Drewery realised that he was not alone with the mammoth that had attacked him. Blood was already trickling from Patrick's lip and one eye was closed. A fresh red bruise was beginning to blossom around the scrunched-up socket, the shimmering green iris slowly becoming lost to swollen flesh. Zeus stalked forward as the little man stared, fear radiating from every part him. His mouth hung open, bottom lip quivering, his hands barely able to keep him propped up. He moved his mouth, looking like he might try and speak, might try and offer some of his Irish charm and patter to soothe the tension that was circling throughout the room, but the words would not come, lost in his dry and terrified throat. Zeus smiled.

"We had a deal Paddy." He stated, impressed by how calm he managed to sound.

At his words, men began to trash the shop. Every item that could break would break. China, glass, and pottery all fell to the hard floor and an assemblage of crashes rang in the ears of everyone present. Paddy tried to move forward, in some feeble attempt to protect his assortment of tat. Ares grabbed his shoulder and slammed him down, driving the air from his lungs. Paddy could do nothing but lay atop his counter and gasp for breath as Zeus walked closer.

"I let you keep living and working and in exchange you don't sell to any of my competitors. You supply for small time jobs by pathetic men."

The assault on the collection within the shop continued. Shelves were pushed over, the wood kicked and battered until it formed nothing more than chunks. Paddy looked on in horror. The hoarder hated to see his lifetime of work trampled so easily into dust.

"Please." He finally managed to gasp. "I've never broke our deal Zeus. By God you know I wouldn't." His lyrical Irish twang seemed to dance over the sharp and harsh noises of the destruction that was happening all around him. "I've turned every crime boss away. I sell old guns to drunk men who hate their wives, or to dirty little muggers who want to make the back-alley game easier." He looked up at Zeus, his eyes imploring him to be merciful.

Zeus had no time for mercy. With a nod of his head, he commanded Ares to continue his onslaught. The brute raised the man up by his neck. Patrick's small and frail body tried to fight against it, his loose-fitting shirt and baggy trousers twisting around his body as he flailed desperate to be free. His mop of deep, muddy red hair seemed to dance as he twisted and contorted. Finally, Ares slammed the small man onto the counter and in one swift movement, bent his arm and snapped his bone. The crunch and the scream that followed rang high above the noise of destruction. Zeus moved close and loomed over him.

"Don't lie to me." This time he did nothing to contain the anger in his voice. He allowed his words to shake the air, to rattle the earth. He felt his fury swell within him, felt like it was pushing against the inside of his skin making him grow and glow. "We know you sold flammables to an enemy, flammables that were used to destroy three of my clubs. Tell me everything you know, and I might let you keep one of your limbs."

With Zeus' final word, Ares raised his fist, like a boulder, and slammed it down onto Patrick's knee. Another sickening crack and desperate scream sounded through the shop.

"I don't know anything. It was just some guy looking for a way to start a fire. I didn't know he was after you Zeus. I swear on the virgin Mary."

"Swear on something that isn't bullshit and I might believe you." Zeus thundered into the face of the desperate man, spit flying from his mouth and landing on his opponent.

Paddy's eyes were red, and tears were streaming across his cheeks, falling in great droplets on the counter.

"Please. I'll tell you everything." Silence immediately followed his words as the assembled men stopped their destruction. By now nothing remained in-tact except the lamps that illuminated the scene. Every shelf had been torn down and reduced to kindling, every ornament lay in a heap of broken china, clothing had been torn to shreds that now lay strewn across the assembled chaos. Dust rose into the air where it had been stirred by the violence. The smell of Paddy's fear; the piss, sweat, and blood mingled with the stale odours of dust and damp around them. Zeus looked down at his captive expectantly.

"I got a note through the door. Three times the asking price if I agreed to drop off a large shipment of flammables and small explosives and ask no questions." Paddy panted the words through his pain and distress, each one ending with a small gasp. "I needed the money, so I agreed. I never knew it was to hurt you Zeus, or I'd have said no."

Zeus let the silence hang for a moment after letting Paddy speak. Just as he was about to command Ares to break another bone when a voice rose from the shop floor.

"If all you got was a note then how did you communicate your agreement with the buyer?" Athena asked, her voice stern yet calm. She plucked her way through the assembled mounds of broken items, deftly avoiding everything with a grace and agility that seemed at odds with her rigid and powerful stature.

Together, she, Ares, and Zeus made an imposing force. Each of them was tall and broad, with bodies sculpted and defined by strength and musculature. She looked down at Paddy with visible disdain as he began his rambling answer. Whoever their enemy was he had thought through things well. Messages were delivered by a popular courier service to public locations, meaning there was no known address or location to track him to. Money never directly changed hands but was always delivered by courier, and large deliveries were made to abandoned warehouses across the city. Paddy provided little of use other than that every note was signed with a K, but given that that had appeared on the coins and the man was known as Killer it was hardly a surprise, or new information.

"Burn them both." Zeus ordered as he turned from the soaked wretch before him and made his way out of the door.

He barely heard the cries of panic and protest as he left. Barely smelt the gasoline as it was poured, liberally, in great gushes over the destroyed store and screaming man. As Zeus got into his car and the engine rumbled back to life he barely looked back as a match was lit and the shop rose in a flurry of bright orange flame. He sat quietly and contemplatively, Athena back at his side. Her stern expression was deeply embedded in her features as was his one of concern and misery. The trip had been a waste, giving him nothing but another burned out shop and dead Irishman.

"Father." Athena began, her solemn tone barely carrying her voice through the silence of the car's interior. "We will find the assailant, but we must be prepared for revelations that seem impossible."

Zeus turned to look at her quizzically, the apparent truth that was so clear to her, not yet obvious to him. She had always been smarter than the rest of the gods. It was why she had never lost his love or trust.

"Whoever this person is he knows that we are Greek, which is concerning since we haven't spoken about our origin to anyone in hundreds of years."

The seriousness of the situation began to dawn on Zeus.

"We have to consider that our enemy is just as immortal or just as godly as we are. Which means they could be virtually unstoppable. We know there are other Pantheons out there and luckily we have avoided them, but this could be a war, some Norse or Egyptian trying to take what we have."

The air seemed to thicken around the words and both great Olympians sat in a silence as the car headed south through the streets of Manhattan.

Twelve

Fear

emeter fell slowly into the soft mottled fabric of her favourite armchair. The threadbare surface lightly scratched against her exposed skin and sent her small hairs standing on end. She took a deep breath and smelled the aroma of nature that had clung to her clothes. The sweet smell of summer lingered around her; the tang of tree sap, the earthiness of wheat stalks, and the freshness of flowers and fallen blossoms. She took it all in and allowed the orchestra of scents to settle her weary mind. In the corner of the room one of her maids awkwardly fumbled with the radio, sending small thuds and crackles of static into the room. Eventually the slow melody of smooth jazz music wafted towards Demeter, letting her fully relax. She reached awkwardly at her skirt, unclasping the tight fastening. She let out a deep breath as her body took up the extra room it had now been given.

It had been the longest day she had had to endure for a while. Ever since Hermes had left the full scale of keeping the farm protected had fallen to her. He had devised and installed ways of keeping the farm safe in his brief visit but now that he had gone back to the city Demeter was left alone with a laundry list of startling length. There were locks, alarms, security staff, and dogs. The dogs were what Demeter hated the most. She had never once found a slobbering, whining, burden that hadn't instantly turned her stomach. Being a goddess of nature, everyone assumed that she must love animals. She knew that somewhere in some damn museum or gallery there was a picture of her frolicking with small animals and birds. Demeter, however, had no time for animals. She was a farmer at her core, she was devoted to the land, to growth and agriculture. She marvelled every day that she saw a crop spring fourth from the dry dirt of high summer. Animals got in the way of that.

She had spent the day on her feet, circling the fam, checking the health of the crops. She had walked the new fenced areas and made sure that every metal link was safe and secure. She had spoken with the new security staff, if they could be called that. The Bury brothers were an assemblage of thugs from a small farming town just down the road. They had made a name for themselves as merciless brutes and Hermes had decided that was just the kind of people the family needed guarding their most precious location. Demeter sighed thinking back to the days when the people who guarded sacred places were noble men who stood tall and proud in gleaming armour with spears and short swords. Now they were relying on hicks with tatty clothes and floppy hats wielding guns and clubs. Zeus' attempt for the family to maintain their glory seemed to be slipping further and further away. Granted, they were richer than they had been in centuries, but the grandeur and splendour that had defined them was gone. Not that it mattered much to Demeter. She enjoyed the mess, and she hated the pretence that they were rulers again: they were sordid criminals. It was better than the wretches they had eventually become in London, but not by much.

The worst part of Demeter's day had been inspecting the distillery. Outdoors was where Demeter thrived. She only felt at home in air that moved and swirled around her. She only felt comfortable when she could feel the rough earth beneath her feet and smell nature bursting into life around her. The distillery on the other hand was a brick and metal shrine to death. Inside the air was a pungent aroma of slowly dying vegetation. She had walked the halls and the large rooms; she had seen the machines that had just been installed, that moved the decaying plant carcasses in giant liquid vats. She was no opponent to alcohol, like all her siblings she had earned the right to indulge in the finer intoxications that eternal life had to offer, but machines made her nervous. She did not know if she could trust alcohol that had not been made by real hands. What scared her most though was that it confused her. Hephaestus had limped around and made slurred exclamations of joy when he had finished modernising the distillery a year ago. He had ranted for hours at the farmhouse table about his accomplishment using words like efficiency, technology, and electricity. Demeter had understood none of them, instead filling her mouth with wine and her mind with thoughts of the serving boy she had hired that day.

Despite her misgivings she had done her job dutifully. All locks, alarms, dogs, and security staff were just as they should be. It would take a lot more than one mask-wearing creep to do any damage here. She should try and talk Zeus into sending Hermes out permanently; this was too much work for a goddess whose work history was purely seasonal. Just as she managed to let her mind rest, a shrill sound pierced through the soft, still air of the house. Shocked, and screaming profanity, Demeter rose and walked to phone in its small, dark corner, hidden under stacks of letters and other assorted papers.

"What?" she answered, her tone sharp. She made no effort to hide her displeasure and annoyance at being roused from her brief moment of peace.

"This is how you react to the slightest amount of work in your day?" Hera asked through the line.

Demeter had recognised her voice instantly. The calm aura in every word, the crisp diction, the slight hint of humour that ran through every judgemental thing that her sister uttered. Demeter smiled ever so slightly.

"Well, you know me, work just isn't one of my skills." She replied, chuckling softly. Hera was one of the few beings that existed that Demeter felt fully at ease with. They had had trouble in the past, the kind of squabbles that sisters would have. Zeus, for a long time, had been the focus, but over time they had come to realise that all they really had was each other.

"I was calling to see how the new security measures were doing but it sounds like you'd rather talk about anything else."

"They're fine." Demeter hesitated a little, Hera was rarely this evasive. If the queen of Olympus wanted to talk about something, then she would have happily nailed a hapless victim to a chair so they could do nothing but listen. "What would you like to talk about Hera?"

"I think he's done it again." She replied, a stiffness in her voice that Demeter knew existed, only, to hold back a wave of pain and sorrow.

Demeter didn't need to ask what her sister was talking about. Whenever the woman who had stood so tall sounded this small it was because of Zeus.

"I am used to his infidelity and wandering eye. I have accepted he will never change, but he could at least not keep impregnating them. I have to keep this family safe, and he makes that impossible by spawning little bastards all over the world. I don't want to kill another." Hera's last words had been spoken softly, the regret for centuries of clearing up after Zeus' indiscretions were starting to take their toll on her.

Demeter let out another deep sigh, prepared to console her sister. Before, and after, their fall Hera had done all she could to keep the family safe. Zeus may take credit for every success, but Demeter knew that for every deal Zeus struck, every man his power influenced, Hera had been behind him, holding him up.

Just as Demeter felt ready to speak an alarm sounded in the distance. The wailing seemed to surround the house and shake the crumbling timber walls. The sound of barking came next, the rumbling, growling, guttural noise of animals ready to fight. It warred with the siren for dominance. A battle of noises was being fought all around her, consuming her. The door burst open and one of the Bury brothers fell through the doorway. His round face, dotted with sporadic clusters of beard, was bright red, and he held his chest as he panted, desperately gulping at the din filled air.

"Hera, I have to go."

She placed the phone back down and waited for her security to catch his breath.

"Ma'am. There's someone in the distillery. We think we got him trapped but he's armed." The deep southern accent felt like an assault on her ears, yet another amongst the wailing and howling.

She nodded and followed him out of the door. She was sure the mortals could handle one intruder, and she was by no means a fighter, but she would be there when the man who was hurting her family was shot dead. She was not going to miss that.

Demeter didn't run to the distillery, instead they took a small truck that she had parked up around the back of the house. The machine was a dilapidated blue wreck that juddered and shuddered as its wooden wheels bounced and creaked over the stone strewn road that led from the house to the distillery. Flakes of orange-brown rust flew into the dark night air as they made their way to their quarry. The road was a mystery to the driver, the small light at the front flickering on and off with every bump they encountered in the road. The chill night air raced passed Demeter's face and managed to pull loose the occasional strand of hair form her immaculate braid. The distillery came into view, a grey monolith that sat as a shadow against the deep black and silver stars of the night sky. The truck stopped with an ominous spurt and screech, belching black smoke from the tail pipe. A problem for another day.

The boys had shut off the alarm, so the blaring had ceased and the wild howling of the dogs had settled to disgruntled, rage filled, rumbling and deep growls. The men explained what had happened, that one man in black had broken the lock and ran into the distillery. They said they had seen him enter but that all exits were now covered. They had gone in and were pretty sure he was in the mixing room, but it was large and filled with innumerable hiding places. They were ready to go in, but he had shot at them. She understood their hesitation. The hider always had the advantage. They would be able to choose a spot that gave them good a good view of the enemy whilst keeping them hidden. Demeter stood and pondered for a short while. There were enough of them that they could surround any position, and even if some of the mortals were shot and killed, there was only one assailant and they could be caught. She gave the order for them to enter.

The inside of the distillery was a dark space filled with shadows and ominous sounds. Every step taken echoed against the bare walls and metal machinery that ran through the building. Every softly spoken word seemed to smother itself against the walls and creep into the ears of each person present. Breathing felt impossible, even in the open space. The mixing room was a vast arena of mechanical equipment. Even though stillness consumed them, soft clangs and thumps seemed to sound from every possible corner. The dogs had even gone quiet as the tension within the group had swelled. Demeter was surrounded by burly men, each one with a revolver and some crude tool that was designed to smash open a skull. Her wall of human guards towered over her and the scent of their sweat provided a reassuring barrier of strength.

"Ah Demeter." A strange voice uttered from within the darkness.

The group started and all turned to try and pinpoint the location of the voice that was laced with elegance and threat in equal measure.

"I am sorry I have to kill you first, but I need to cut off Zeus' supply."

Demeter let herself smile a little as he spoke. Clearly, he did not know who he was up against. It didn't matter how many guns he had stashed on him, he would not kill her.

"Come out and fight me properly" one of the brothers shouted into the dead, dark air of the mixing room. Only silence greeted him. He shouted his threat again, spitting the words out into the night.

"I have no quarrel with any of you men. Leave the woman to me and you get to live." The reply wasn't shouted, screamed, or demanded.

The cool tone sent shivers down Demeter's spine. This man truly believed he was going to kill her, and for just the briefest second Demeter started to believe him. Her circle of protectors remained fixed and steady. Not one of them flinched or made to move. She caught glimpses of their stern faces, dark eyes darting around the room, still trying to find the source of the threats. She didn't assume that they were loyal to her, but they were clearly proud of their own physical strength and ability. Not one of them was going to back down.

"Fine."

The air exploded with noise, like thunder had been contained within the building. The cacophony was followed by the sounds of screaming as a hailstorm of bullets ripped through the men gathered in the distillery. From all around the room innumerable bursts of light filled Demeter's vision. There was clearly more than one of them. Each gun sparked as it fired mercilessly into the room. The men tried to lift their pistols, but bullets ran through them sending sprays of blood into the air. Thick droplets mixed with fine mist as men screamed and fell in agony. Demeter ran. She didn't know where she was going but she knew she had to hide. Behind her, men yelled, shot, and died. The dogs barked in fury and fear, then wailed in anguish as bullets hit them as well. The noise consumed Demeter, even her own mind was drowned out. She couldn't think. She couldn't reason. She just ran. There was clearly more than one intruder, this was an ambush.

As Demeter ran, a bullet sliced her shoulder; her flesh and bone seemed to be no obstacle for the piercing metal as it went straight though her. The pain blossomed around the blood seeping wound, but she managed to bite her lip and keep running. Another bullet ran through her calf and she fell to the ground, blood smearing against the grey concrete. Fear filled her. She knew she couldn't die but had no inclination to feel pain. She crawled and pulled herself behind some contraption and wedged herself between it and the wall. She felt her wounds and winced. She couldn't stop panting, her body consuming air at a rate she couldn't maintain. Fear raced through her, every part of her was tense and shaking. She didn't know what to do. Her mind swam with noise, and pain, and fear. Tears started to well in her eyes. Run, was all she could think. A doorway sat a few feet from her, and so she obeyed the command.

She managed to slip through the doorway without getting shot again and closed it with a metallic clunk. The hallway she found herself in was pitch black. She felt against the wall, her hands staining it with blood, in a desperate attempt to find some sort of light. The coarse skin of her squat fingers found the switch, and, after a few flickering seconds, the hallway was filled with light. Demeter looked down at herself. The dull fabric of her clothing was consumed with the crimson red of pooling blood. Her shaking hands were coated red too, and she could feel her hair, loose of its braid, starting to absorb the viscous liquid from her shoulder. She put her hand to her mouth and held back tears and sobs, desperate to keep herself silent and hidden. She didn't know the distillery, didn't know which way would see her to safety, so she chose randomly and limped as silently as she could.

She had only travelled for a short time, following an array of corners and twists in the corridor before she heard a sound behind her. She turned and saw a man, tall and lean, clad in black, his face covered in a mask. She gulped and tried to push the fear within her down. This was him. The killer that had fought Poseidon and had burned down her family's assets. She could feel herself losing blood, the wooziness and light-headedness starting to send her vision into a tunnel. She couldn't outrun him, and she definitely couldn't fight him. Luckily, she had the advantage because he couldn't kill her. He could shoot her and beat her, even bury her, but overtime she would heal and keep on living. She ignored the pain that surged through her and pulled herself up to full height. She might as well get the agony over with.

Her assailant walked forward, taking long, confident strides. His shadow stretched and contorted beside him as he made his way under each bulb. His face was hidden. Demeter couldn't tell what he was thinking, what he was feeling. His approach was silent, confident.

Demeter trembled as she sensed the pain she was about to feel. She bit her lip and stared defiantly at the man, brown eyes dewy with tears. The attacker moved his arm and pulled something from behind his back. Demeter only saw it for the briefest moment, something curved, and sharp, and black. The attacker's motions were fluid and with one swoop of his weapon he had severed Demeter's head from her body. Both fell with sickening thuds and he stood over the goddess, now in a world of darkness, as dead as any mortal.

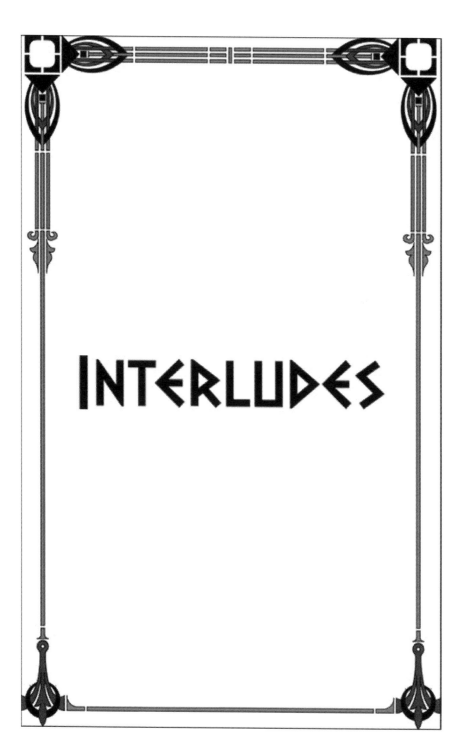

INTERLUDES

Interlude 3

Greece, 346 AD

This is getting out of hand. Zeus there has to be something you can do!"

"What would you have me do Hera? I don't even know what's causing this."

The two of them were stood over the body of an oceanid. The poor creature writhed on the beach in agony, its wails echoing off the jagged rocks and outcroppings that surrounded them. Its naked body of slick blue skin and patterns of iridescent scales was beyond recognition: mutilated and burned, its limbs broken into an array of sharp angles and protruding bones, eyes gouged out and tongue torn from its mouth. Poseidon had found the poor thing desperate for help under the thunderous waves. It was one of many that seemed to have suffered the same terrible fate. They were scattered along the pebble covered beach, convulsing, and coating the area around them in their black blood.

Zeus almost wept at the sight of the death around him. The oceanids were mighty beings. They dominated the waves, rivers, and lakes of his land. They protected the waters from the destructive nature of man, keeping nature in balance, and now they lay in unimaginable pain in front of him. They could not die. They were immortal beings like the rest of the pantheon, but he knew that their fate was sealed. The first being to be found like this was a Leimakid: a year ago her mutilated form was found in her meadow, the grass around her burned and scorched. No matter how she was cared for, or how long the gods around her waited and gave their strength, she would not heal, and her anguish continued. There was only one way to help the victims of this new plight.

Zeus closed his eyes and drew on the power within him. He felt the world below, the writhing mass of souls that made the underworld: the empty darkness of Hades, the burning pain of Tartarus, and the gentle release of Elysium. He communed with Hades, the master of the afterlife, and with his blessing the ground below each poor Oceanid opened. The stones fell underneath them, into vortexes of grinding earth and rock. They each descended, their pain easing as they entered into the unknown world of afterlife, their pain ending forever as they spent immortal life trapped in a paradise prison.

"Hera go gather the rest of the family. We need to discuss this" Zeus commanded of his wife. She did not question his order, instead vanishing on the wind to gather the Olympians. Zeus stood in his solitude, breathing in the salt air of the sea, the smell of blood coating every other scent. He set his jaw firm, determined to stay strong.

"Hello Zeus." A voice sounded behind him; gentle yet cold. He turned to see a man he had never seen before. He was tall, with pale skin that seemed to glow with a silver light, and hair so blonde it was like a crown made of curled gold.

"Who are you?" Zeus asked, suspicious of a being who could see him without his consent.

"My name is Jophiel, I'm a representative of God."

"Which one?"

"Huh," he let out a small laugh, "the only one, or at least the only one that matters now. We're moving away from the concept of one of many."

"I don't care. Leave me alone."

"I'm here to make you an offer."

"Do I look like I'm in a business mood, child." Zeus snapped at the young man, his anger over the interruption radiating from him.

"I'll be brief." He replied, smiling slightly. "My lord has visions of being the only god worshipped, and we'd like to offer you the opportunity to go away. If you and the rest of your … friends agree to never seek worship or use your powers, we will leave you be." He announced, hands wide opened. Zeus didn't know whether to laugh or throw lightening at the upstart.

"Fuck off." Was what he settled on, growling, as he stalked forward. The man in white made no effort to move.

"It's a shame you are so reluctant." He replied, his eyes glowing with an intensity Zeus had never seen, even on Olympus. Above him the swirling grey of the clouds broke open and jets of light fell to the ocean, the water stirring in great, frothing torrents.

Zeus watched in horror as, around him, the seas turned dark with blood, and the bodies of even more Oceanids rose to the surface.

"Every day you resist our efforts more of your fellows will suffer and our offer will become less generous." With his final words the assailant vanished, no evidence of his presence left.

Interlude 4

London, Great Britain, 1896

The stone at Zeus' back was cold, like blocks of ice pressed against him. He still wore the same shirt that had been on his back when he was thrown into the sanitorium. The fabric had almost ceased to exist, the thick weave of cotton now nothing more than scant threads and holes held together by the grime that coated him. The smell that came off him was rancid: the aroma of filth and human waste. He had surrendered to his world of shame, a world of cold surfaces and iron bars, a world with no warmth and comfort. The walls echoed and sounded with the cries of other patients, each one of them desperate for the voices in their head to cease their relentless onslaught. The voices had invaded Zeus' own mind, whispering venom into him as the days in confinement continued.

"Visitor." A gruff voice announced through the bars of his cell, the man indistinguishable from all his other tormentors in the dim light of the gas lamps that lined the wall of the corridor.

"Zeus? Is that you?" Hera asked, pressing her round face between the bars.

Zeus wept at the sight of his wife. He had not seen friend of family in over year. The mahogany of her eyes looked so warm and inviting. He crawled over to her and clasped her hands in a desperate attempt to feel human touch.

"What have they done to you?"

"I think I'm in Tartarus." Zeus replied, his dull blue eyes darting wildly around his prison.

"Don't worry Zeus I'm going to do something to help you. Aphrodite is with the owner of this place right now. Working her charms."

Hera clasped his hand, reaching one of her own up to gently caress his cheek, catching the scraggly grey hairs that surrounded the bush of his beard. The stayed like that for some time. Zeus relishing the human contact. The feel of skin against him.

Aphrodite descended the stairs to the cellar of iron bars with the warden in toe, the little man looking up at her with wide eyes, drooling slightly at the sight of her. She cast her eyes around, a look of horror and disgust contorting her perfect features.

"The warden has very kindly offered to move Zeus to one of the nicer parts of the hospital."

"Move him?" Hera snapped. "He's been locked down here for a year. I want him released."

"I'm afraid I can't." The warden replied. His eyes still dreamily focussed on Aphrodite, one hand held slightly aloft as if toying with the idea of touching the goddess. "I answer to many powerful men and they want your husband here."

"Why?"

"He embarrassed them. People won't deal with his associates so I'm to ensure no one can possibly be associated."

Hera stared coldly at the man, her dark eyes like portals to the underworld in the dimness of the basement prison. She could feel her lips pulling into a long thin line, twitching with anger. Ever since Zeus' arrest the family had become outcasts. They could barely make ends meet. In order to recoup losses, thugs had been sent to collect on debts. All their great collections had been shipped away. Hera knew it was time to leave London, but she couldn't go without Zeus.

"This isn't over." She sneered at the warden, managing to pull her hand away from the whimpering, shaking, malnourished mess of her husband.

After his wife had left Zeus felt the cold grip of despair on him again. The sensation didn't ease when two burly men arrived, thick beards shadowing their faces, and took him up the stairs to the hospital. Long corridors of white tiles snaked around rooms filled with muttering and howling. Zeus' eyes darted to every small, barred window, nervous of which place he would find himself. Eventually he was thrown into a solitary room, one with a bed and bed pan: luxury Zeus never thought he would encounter again.

Around him the walls still ached with the oppressive misery of those contained within the hospital. Only the sounds of pain met his ears. He began quivering, until, through the cacophony of sadness, he heard the first sounds of joy.

"Hello, my name's Mary."

PART III

Thirteen

The Twins

Apollo woke with a start, chilled beads of sweat coating his golden skin, tracing thin ribbons of moisture across him as they slowly dipped onto the soft white linen of the bedsheets. His soft curls of wheaten hair were drenched, and the sweat soaked into the pillow beneath his head. Goose bumps began to raise on him as he fixed his blue eyes to the ceiling, mock renaissance art looking back at him. Fear and pain seemed to move within his mind like serpents biting at his consciousness, poisoning his thoughts. Nausea sat in the pit of his stomach and every time he contemplated falling back to sleep or awaking fully his entire body would reel.

Apollo had found Zeus' ban on the use of magic harder than the other gods. His mind was connected to everything; the whole of reality buzzed at the edge of his consciousness. He knew he should control himself and not use his power, but he found it difficult and had found his psychic tendencies useful over his long life.

He contemplated what could have happened that would have aroused his sense so fully to have left his body panic stricken, the temptation to use his powers fully harder to resist with every second. He did his best, simply remaining atop his bed staring up at the ceiling. He breathed deeply, hoping that the air would force the fear from his body. Minutes stretched around him as he fought for the strength to push his anxiety aside and wake up. It was clearly morning. The large curtains that hung from a brass poll were smeared with the light of day. The intricate pattern woven into the fabric looked bold and full of wonderous colour compared to the dimness of the room where light had yet to fully penetrate. He knew he should rise and open the curtains, knew he should embrace the day, but the malevolence that his senses were aware of held him to the bed.

Just as Apollo had resigned himself to his fate as a fearful, bed-ridden invalid, the door to his room burst open and strength stepped into the threshold. Artemis' entrance had exposed the room to more light, as the hotel's hall bulbs shone their beams straight through the open doorway. The goddess looked around the room and shook her head. Light now swarmed around masses of bodies that covered the floor and the other half of Apollo's bed. It shadowed where it met the peaks and troughs of muscles, breasts, and groins. Light glinted where it met sweat slickened skin, of every possible colour, and where it invaded newly awakening eyes.

"It smells like Hephaestus' bathwater in here." Artemis remarked with her typical air of annoyance. She wasn't wrong. The smell of sweat, the must of human bodies, and the lack of fresh air made the atmosphere in the room heavy.

Ever since they were children Artemis had been annoyed by Apollo. Sibling rivalry was to be expected, though Apollo had never been bothered by it. He loved to do things that would bring the characteristic sneer of annoyance onto Artemis' face. He had even made it a game at times; he liked to challenge himself to see how far he could push her annoyance before she tried setting her dogs on him. She secretly liked the game.

With the presence of his twin sister Apollo felt the fear that had been consuming him push away, his senses returning from the mystical to the real.

"You should probably stop smelling his bathwater then, pervert." He responded, sending a smirk towards Artemis.

Apollo pushed himself up to sitting position only to realise now that the buxom woman next to him had her arm, soft white skin aglow, strewn across the firm muscles of his chest. He brushed her aside causing her to stir and roll over, the mix of alcohol and exhaustion from the previous night keeping her locked in a deep sleep.

Artemis didn't respond to her brother's jab, instead she picked her way across the room, her feet, clad in thick, worn boots deftly avoiding the entangled and heaped masses of naked bodies that covered the plush fabric of the carpet. Some nasal announcer spoke on the radio, ushering in a tinkling of jazz as Artemis made her way to the window. With one graceful motion she cast the curtains fully open and allowed the room to be consumed by the sun. The assembled hedonists woke with a start, wincing, moaning, expressing shock an annoyance. Only Apollo remained unphased. The sun had been his for a long time and even in his post orgy, hungover haze he embraced the harsh light it had to offer.

"Everybody" Artemis announced to the room, "you need to leave now, gather your clothes and return to your families. Quickly!" With her final word she left the room, careful to avoid contact with the people that were now beginning to move and writhe in a desperate bid to find their clothing.

The men seemed to move the quickest, Apollo noted. Each one of them was desperate to leave the room where they had succumbed to the temptation to embrace another man, or several men. Their eyes were cast down as they hurriedly pulled on pant legs and thrust their arms into shirts, careful not to make eye contact with each other. Apollo found it sad to live in a world where people felt guilty after an orgy rather than free or elated. Humans had moved so far backward since his family ruled the heavens. This Christianity they all seemed so attached to really had spoiled everything.

Artemis marched down the hallway, annoyance prickling inside her skin. She wasn't angry, having realised that being angry at Apollo was a waste of time. For centuries she had raged at him and his immature hedonistic ways. He would only ever smile and call her prudish or virginial. She was sure he enjoyed seeing her get angry.

She returned to her room and slammed the door behind her. They had been away from the rest of the family and stuck in the cesspool that was Chicago for days now. They had a job to do, and it would not be done by spending the night writhing around with every human that could be dragged from speakeasies and brothels, or spending the day sleeping off the hangover and making love with the stragglers. She paced the room muttering to herself all the things that she wanted to yell into

Apollo's face. She said them to herself now, knowing that if she said them to him, he would take no notice, but also knowing that if she didn't say them out loud, she might well explode from rage. She had to admit that he was not the only source of her anger. She had pleaded with Zeus to let her hunt the arsonist who struck the clubs, but he had decided keeping the Chicago gangs out of New York was more important.

Her feet carved out a path around her room, taking her past the broad window of pristine glass that looked out across the brick buildings of the city, past her four-poster bed of deep carved oak and smooth sheets that had never been touched since she had started her stay. Finally, she passed the bundle of furs in the corner where she had decided to sleep.

Artemis never felt comfortable indoors, in a bed. She was the goddess of the hunt and she found comfort in the howling wilds of the woods. She wouldn't be so irritable if she had had a decent night sleep, but Apollo had stopped her from sleeping in the park. She missed the smell: the damp dirt that hid under fresh grass, the smell of fur and discarded feathers. She craved it.

"Sleeping in a park isn't normal Artemis. You would have drawn attention." Apollo stated as he pushed open the door to her room, now dressed in a casual shirt and slacks that seemed to hang loose from his frame, yet accentuate his strength and toned physique at the same time.

He looked so effortlessly attractive Artemis thought, whilst she, with her sheer build of straight lines and taught, tense muscles, and with her desire to cover herself in thick, coarse fabrics looked like a statue someone had decided to use as a clothes hanger. She didn't care much as she had no interest in being attractive, she just found it odd how different her twin brother could be.

"Stay out of my mind Apollo. If Zeus found out he'd beat that pretty face straight off of you."

"I don't have to use my psychic abilities to know what you're thinking Artemis, you have a very expressive face." He smiled and gestured for her to lead the way out of the hotel. "Shall we?"

As they walked Artemis noticed the last few stragglers of Apollo's night of decadence lurking around the hallways, moving through the shadows, trying to extricate themselves with as little notice as possible. Many of them wore fine silk suits, now wrinkled, dishevelled, and stained with various liquids. Men and women of power and status surrounded them trying to hide their shame.

Artemis couldn't help but roll her eyes at what she saw. It wasn't that she was prudish like her brother accused her of, or that she was disgusted by sex, she just saw no purpose to it. She had lived thousands of years without the intrusive need to be entered and found her life perfectly fulfilling. The only thing she craved was the hunt, the wind whipping her wild brown hair into a frenzy as she tore through the trees, the smell of nature and fear in the air, the snarl of dogs and the whimper of prey surrounding her. She got lost in her contemplations and it was only when she felt Apollo's elbow in her ribs that she realised they were now outside the hotel.

The streets of Chicago were alive with activity. The morning rush had filled them with people, each one scurrying frantically around, deftly moving to avoid colliding with the other commuters and the cars that seemed to be ever increasing their presence on the roads. Apollo was like Zeus, he stared lustfully at the curves and colours of the vehicles that spluttered and roared their way past them. Artemis paid no attention, the noise and fumes just acting as more annoyances in the world. The twins made their way through the streets, each one of them keeping their senses alert. They were unknown in Chicago, and so far, had not been recognised as part of the New York family, but these were dangerous times, and they had no interest in being found out before they were ready. Artemis looked up at her brother as they turned into an alley and made their way silently in the filth and shadows.

"You look distracted." She finally said as the mouth of the alley came close, bathed in sunlight. "Was last night so fun that you can't think straight today? Not that you ever do."

"I know fun's not your thing Artemis, but can you try and say the word without the hint of disapproval." He replied, smiling and winking at her, but soon his face returned to a look of concentration. His perfectly soft skin was furrowed, and small lines began to creep across the strong jaw and around his dazzling eyes. "I woke up with a feeling of fear and panic this morning. A sensation I've never felt.

Something is happening and it was terrifying." Apollo confessed to his sister.

He was glad to have said it, but now he wanted to move on, and Artemis had no idea how to respond, fear not being her area of expertise, so, they stood in silence. All the gods had the ability to connect psychically with the world around them, but some, like Hera and Apollo, had stronger senses than the rest of them. Artemis had rarely used or honed hers, she was not concerned with the ethereal or the possibilities of the future. Her and Apollo talked on everything, but on this she had little to say. His senses were rarely wrong, which meant something was coming or was already here.

Their quarry came into view and allowed both of them a new focus. They had been sent to Chicago to hunt down and kill Jimmy Short Stack. He had been a low-level gangster in New York before the family had taken over Manhattan. He had agreed to work for them and had been made an enforcer and given control of a few speakeasies. The family had treated him well. Apollo had been there when he had taken the deal. He had even tracked and killed a few of his enemies to help keep him safe when he worked for the family. Artemis had spent more time with his dogs. It hadn't taken long for the rat to betray them, he had skulked away with suitcases of the family's cash and enough information to do them harm. Now he was in Chicago sucking up to every Italian and Irish who had visions of taking on New York.

Apollo clenched his fists. He had no time for traitors. The family were gods and had been worshipped. Now tiny little men betrayed them for fistfuls of money. Artemis was hunched next to him, face set into a sneer, shoulders raised and skin quivering, ready to pounce.

Jimmy had been hard to track. He'd gone underground as soon as he'd got to the city, but it hadn't taken the twins long to figure out his pattern and routine. Each one of them had senses that surpassed any mortal or god. Apollo felt the presence of anyone, and Artemis could sniff out a guilty man better than a bloodhound. Short Stack would eat here and then he would go back to his safe house to make calls and send letters, trying to get some support. So far, he hadn't been successful, but something was stirring up the city mobsters and he was starting to get attention. Now was the time to act.

"Right when do you think we should get him?"

"Not now, we don't want to cause a scene in the diner. Zeus wanted this to be a quick kill. The last thing we want is the mobs of Chicago coming to New York"

"Well, we can't get him at the safe house, that place is full of security and alarms, one wrong move and he'll be out of there."

"What about the bathroom?"

"The bathroom?"

"He always uses the bathroom before he leaves. If we could get in there and wait for him, we could kill him quickly without being seen."

"I can work with that."

With the plan set the two of them moved back into the shadow of the alleyway. They knew they couldn't approach head on. Short Stack knew their faces and the diner was all window, they would be spotted and evaded quickly. They had skulked around the diner over the past few days, and both knew the layout pretty well. They moved into the street and then into a different alley making their way up past the garbage and through the small puddles of discarded dish water, until they found themselves at the back of the building. The windows to the bathrooms were small and set high into the wall. Luckily, no one had thought to fit bars, so Apollo was able to boost Artemis up the wall so she could squeeze her narrow shoulders through the opening. Artemis was halfway through, her hands running down the inside wall, keeping her well balanced, as she began to try and turn to pull her leg through. It was only then that the door to the toilets swung open and two women walked in. The chatter between them and the harsh, shrill notes of their girlish giggles bounced around the walls and pierced Artemis' ears. They only silenced when they noticed the torso of a goddess protruding in through the window. They stared at her in disbelief. Artemis rolled her eyes and slinked backwards allowing herself to fall into the alley next to her brother. With a fluid motion she slapped the back of his head, making him wince.

"Again?" He asked, getting nothing but an annoyed nod in response. "In my defence what are the chances it would happen three times?"

Artemis had lost count of how many times she had been pushed through the wrong window, but she knew it was more than three.

No man entered the bathroom as Artemis slipped gracefully through the window. Apollo jumped up and managed to pull himself so his face poked through, but he couldn't get any further, his broad shoulders making it impossible to squeeze through the small opening. Before the twin could decide what to do footsteps sounded outside the door. Apollo fell and Artemis silently moved into a cubical and bolted it shut. She was happy to finish the mission alone. She waited silently listening to the footsteps and breathing outside the cubicle. She breathed deeply, ignoring the smell of bleach and urine that filed the air and stabbed at the back of her throat. Instead, she forced her sense to focus on the cologne that coated the skin of the man in the room with her. It wasn't Short Stack, she would know and recognise his scent anywhere.

Time passed and Artemis waited. She began to doubt that her prey needed to use the bathroom, but sure enough the door opened, and Artemis' ears pricked up. She recognised the way his feet patted out a rhythm on the floor, she recognised the way he breathed and the scent that lingered on his skin. She moved out of the cubicle and tuned to see the back of his head. The little man stood at the urinal, trousers slack around his waist where he had unbuttoned them, cock in hand. Mindlessly he went about his business. Artemis pulled the knife from inside her trousers and walked softly towards him. She knew how to get close to prey silently. Her footsteps and breathing went silent, her heart beat softer somehow. Within seconds she was behind him.

Her hand clasped over his mouth.

"Never fuck with Zeus" she whispered.

She raised the knife, but Jimmy managed to wriggle free, falling into the splashes of his own piss.

"Please." He begged, wiggling away from her, his trousers pulling down to his ankles. "I didn't mean to screw you over, I just didn't know what else to do."

"What else to do? You had everything because of us." She snarled.

"I know, I know." He whimpered, lip wobbling from fear. "Someone's coming for you guys, a war is brewing in New York. I had to leave. I can't fight another turf war."

"Who's coming?" Artemis demanded.

"I don't know, but he went to everyone. He's coming and he's ready to fight."

"Unlike you!"

She moved deftly and plunged her blade straight into his neck. Blood spurted against the cubicle door next to him and then began to pool on the floor as his body slipped down the dirty tiles. Artemis looked down at the man, soaked and full of fear. Her face, tanned and coarse from years in the wilds and sun, was splattered with blood and was pulled into the widest smile. She loved the kill as much as the hunt. With her quarry now dead, she signalled to Apollo and, using the sink, climbed back out the window. Both were glad that they could return home, but the news of a coming turf war soured the mood.

Fourteen

The Queen

awn slowly crept across New York city, the black sky of night, devoid of stars, shifted away as the light of the sun started to paint the eastern horizon a deep shade of burnt orange. The colour seeped into the sky like dye and the darkness retreated, blanching the heavens of their mysterious radiance, and replacing it with the shining pale blue of day. Hera stood at the tall window of her bedroom, one hand pushing aside the thick curtains so she could see out into the city that was breathing back to life beneath her. The other cradled a crystal tumbler that had been filled with a generous helping of rich amber whisky, an essential if she was going to deal with the day that lay ahead of her.

She continued to stare out at the city that slowly allowed itself to be bathed with the light of the sun, and drank. The sip she had planned to take became a gulp, which soon became several, and with one motion she had consumed every last drop. The call she had made to Demeter the night before still weighed heavily on her mind; something had happened at the farm, and regardless of how much she called there was no answer from Demeter's telephone. Something twisted in her gut. A feeling that something wasn't right was burrowing deep inside her.

She had tried to send word to Zeus but, as she had expected, he had been hard to track down. After millennia of marriage Hera was no longer foolish enough to expect her husband to return to his marital bed at night. He was a king and kings had concubines. She accepted it begrudgingly, but, still, the knowledge that no matter how hard she tried she would never be good enough ate away at her a little bit each time she saw their bed. Her side was a mess of twisted blankets and misshapen pillows, his was still untouched and unused, as always.

She felt like she needed him in this moment. Demeter was their sister and the closest thing to a friend Hera could claim to have. Zeus had grown as tired of Demeter as he had of Hera. She took comfort in being around a woman who posed no threat to her marriage and who had experienced the harshness of Zeus' rejection too.

As she stood in her window, bathed in sunlight and sorrow a call was being made in the other room. She heard the clang and thud of the receiver and knew that, yet again, they had been unable to get through. The housekeeper conformed it. Hera nodded a curt reply and continued to stand, deep in thought. Self-pity was only allowed the briefest of moments with the queen of New York's underworld. Sucking in a deep breath she began to ready herself for the day. Calls would be made to the farm and attempts would be made to speak with Zeus, but she had other duties to attend to and an entire family to protect.

With her back straight and eyes clear she dressed for the day. Hera missed the days of draped robes, the elegance of materials cascading over her body, like waterfalls of white silk embellished with gold and fine gems. However, she was growing to love the modern fashion. She had despised the corseted, rigid clothing of the past century. Victorian London had been nothing but a prison of heavy fabrics and whalebone, but now she was able to pull on a loose dress, adorn herself with long strings of pearls and finally, her favourite part of the process, she shrugged her shoulders into a mink coat of irresistible and decadent softness. The rich tones of soft browns and hidden greys that marbled across her, matched perfectly with the deep brown of her hair and shrewd darkness of her eyes.

She looked at herself in the mirror and smiled. She had never been a beauty to rival Aphrodite, but she did not care. She ran her hands over her hips, and smiled as she felt them, still suitable for childbearing. Her body was firm yet curvaceous and, even clad in fur, her breasts were noticeable. Her face gave only the smallest hints of age, lines around her eyes and mouth were beginning to form but they were not deep set and, as she inspected herself, she found no sign of a wrinkle.

Hera's first task was one of the grim realities of her life. Her mood, that she had managed to lift as she dressed, descended into gloom again when she had entered her car. Now, she sat in one of the run-down, dilapidated corners of the city. Rows upon rows of worn-down apartments and tenement buildings surrounded her, rising like rotted sentinels to guard the poor and wretched that swarmed the streets here. The smell of subway steam and uncleaned streets managed to penetrate the protective shell of her car as the shouts of still-drunk men reverberated through the street. Drunks stumbled, workers in dirty clothing trudged, street walkers strutted. Every person seemed broken down, defeated by life, shorter and smaller than humans should be. Hera had never been a goddess of the common people and had little time for the impoverished masses. She had ruled over the greatest kings of the world and had been the source of their awe and wonder. She much preferred a banquet hall than anywhere else in the world. Even in the family's lowest moment when Zeus had been taken and their resources were low, she had still considered herself a lady of good standing.

Luckily for Hera she did not have to wait long in the filth before the young woman she had come to meet had left her building. She recognised the girl almost instantly. Her hair was an effortless gathering of shimmering blonde ringlets that cascaded around her pearl white face. Her eyes glinted, like beacons in the grim greyness of the squalor around her and her lips were a pale pink, and plump, like ripe fruit that one could not help but bite. She walked with grace and poise, the loose cotton dress she wore clinging to her body and accentuating her curves as a gentle breeze meandered through the street. Hera noticed that she was not the only person looking at the girl: eyes followed her as she moved. Both men and women admired her. Betty had been a singer at the club, a fancy of her husband's and now she was pregnant. A problem Hera had to deal with.

As instructed, Hera's driver pulled up beside the girl and drove slowly, the car matching her walking speed. Betty noticed and glanced uncomfortably at the vehicle. Hera rolled down the window and looked up at her. Their eyes met and recognition blossomed on the young things face. Hera regretted opening the window and allowing more of the stinking air into her car.

"Please join me." Hera commanded with a tone that implied she was usually obeyed.

The car stopped. Betty stopped. She looked nervous, unsure what to do. Her eyes scanned the street, clearly deciding whether she could get away if she ran.

"I don't like to give instructions twice," Hera continued, staring into the young girl's face.

It did not take long for the door to open and the small young thing to slide in. Her pale face was now flushed, and her effortless beauty shrouded with fear. Hera enjoyed the fact that her mere presence could cause such a reaction.

"Miss Hera I am so sorry, it was a moment of weakness, I never meant…" the girl stammered, every apology or excuse she could think of erupting from her in a desperate last attempt to stay safe.

Hera had silenced it all by raising her hand. The goddess stared out of the window as the car picked up speed and made its way through the city. The noise of New York was almost deafening if one didn't learn to keep it out of the mind, but at times Hera enjoyed the cacophony. It helped distract her and let her compose herself. The girl's apologies were insincere and selfish, but she had no need of rage today.

"Pretty little thing. I haven't come to hurt you." She said as she turned and faced the girl. "My husband has fucked and raped his way across the world. He has bedded queens, whores, and maids. I have sat back and wasted nights alone as he has had his way with the appealing things that distract him. I do not have time to punish you all."

"Then why are you here?"

"You're pregnant." It was not a question. Hera knew already.

The girl's eyes widened in shock and as a reflex she placed her hand on her belly. Her mouth parted, but Hera continued.

"I have spies everywhere my dear. If you know something, assume that I also know it." Hera kept her eyes fixed on the young girl as she spoke.

No word was said, but the expression plastered over the young girl's face was enough.

"Where are you taking me?" Betty asked, fear still obvious in her voice.

"My husband forgets himself when he is around beautiful women. He forgets that every time he sires a child, he is creating a rival for himself and my children. He forgets that he deposed his father, who had already deposed his own father. I have no interest in the cycle continuing. My family, and all we have worked to achieve, are too important to me, even the bastards he has brought into the fold." The response was not clear, but Hera felt she had done enough to put her point across.

The girl still looked at her perplexed.

"I can't have you giving birth child. I'm taking you to a doctor and we are going to have the thing inside you destroyed."

"It's not a thing." The girl retorted, looking up at Hera with fear and disgust. Her bottom lip quivered, and her eyes swam with tears that had yet to break free. "I don't want to kill my child. Please, I'll leave the city. I won't tell Zeus. I'll do anything." The tears had begun to break free and were cascading down her face. She started to blubber, repeating the word please over and over, begging the goddess not to kill her unborn child. The car continued on its path.

"I take no joy in this you know, but it's what I must do for my family. You will have this procedure, or I will have you killed. There is no other option I'm afraid." Hera offered no comfort to the girl, instead she just sat in silence as the car made its journey and Betty continued to try and contain herself.

The doctor that Hera used for these eventualities was situated in one of the nicer buildings in the city. The cream stone was exquisitely carved, and the windows gleamed, reflecting the light of the day back into the street. Low black railings guarded the front of the building from the street and a small tree, coated with bright green leaves, stood outside, gently waving its thin branches in the breeze. The putrid smell of poverty was replaced by the fresh scent of perfumed women and freshly planted window boxes. The sound of cars began to drown out any human sounds as the rich buzzed through the streets in their favourite toys. The sidewalk was empty, but for a few people in fine dress meandering their way through the tranquillity. It stood in stark contrast to the scene inside Hera's car. The woman still cried and blubbered, still begged to be allowed to keep her child and leave. Hera remembered how it had felt to hold life inside of her and she almost started to pity the poor girl, but this young thing was not the first to beg and Hera doubted she would be the last.

She prompted the girl up the steps to the door. The wood was painted a deep black that seemed to absorb the heat of the day and project it back onto the two women waiting to be seen. The brass plaque that announced the doctors name was freshly polished and glowed against the darkness of the door.

Hera rang the bell, and it wasn't long before a plump, yet stern faced, nurse, dressed head to toe in white, answered the ring. She recognised Hera instantly and, acting as usual, gently pulled the tear coated girl inside. As they walked in the girl was led off to the operation suite. She cast one last mournful glance at Hera, her eyes begging to be released from the nightmare she had found herself in. Hera simply watched her go, feeling only the smallest amount of remorse for this latest victim of her husband's excess.

"Ah zere is ze most beautiful fraulein that haz ever graced ze vorld." The thick German accent punctured the air as Hera walked further into the office. Dr Roland Meyer was a man who appeared stretched beyond all reasonable proportions. He rose from his chair and moved over to Hera, firmly grasping her hand in both his and raising it high to his lips so that he could gently place a kiss upon it.

Hera looked up at the man, his thin flat chest and long slender arms seemed to move like liquid as he breathed and gestured. His face was nothing but an assemblage of angles and points with his eyes deep set behind square cheeks and brow. He wore small round spectacles that had glass so paper-thin Hera was sure that they were just for show. He smelt, as always, of disinfectant. The cleaning fluid that coated every surface of his offices leaving its pungent aroma on his skin and clothes.

"You have brought me anozer patient I hear. Zat huzband of yours is a buzy man." He chuckled softly, somehow managing to find some lightness and humour in the situation.

Meyer was a doctor of high renowned, but also a gambling addict of little talent. He commanded the highest fees for his work, but it had never been enough to satiate his appetite for card games. Hera had been there for him. She paid dizzying sums to have Zeus' problems dealt with knowing it would all find its way back to her through the family clubs and gambling dens. They made idle chat for a while as the nurses in the other room made the girl ready for the procedure.

There had been times that the doctor had tried to discuss what he would do with Hera, but she had no interest in the intricate details. As long as there was no child after the procedure, she considered the work done.

When a nurse came to inform them that girl was sedated and ready for Roland, she took it as her cue to leave. She was not the girl's mother or friend. She would not sit in the waiting room or pace back and forth in worry. She had done her job and now she would leave. In the office she left two envelopes, one was filled with money to pay the doctor the other, a much smaller and lighter envelope, was to be given to Betty when she was done: enough money to settle her rent and get out of the city. Few of the girls felt like returning to singing and dancing after what had been done to them and Hera had no inclination to keep them around.

Outside, her car waited patiently for her, the driver sat mindlessly thumbing his way through one of the daily newspapers. She had often considered bedding the young man. He was attractive and had a glint in his eye whenever he saw Hera, but she knew she would be doing it purely to irritate Zeus and it would fail. There was no way that he would ever know or care who she was with. Their marriage had become a job to him, a promise that he was keeping and nothing more. They each had roles to play and as long as they each did the bear minimum, they could sleep easy, no matter how tiring the loveless crevasse between them was becoming.

Hera considered where to go next. The worry of the early morning was starting to creep back into her mind. She knew she should go to the temperance meeting. Ever since prohibition had been enacted the movement had slowly been dying off. The men and women who had forced sobriety on the land felt their work had been done. Hera needed to keep the movement alive and fired up. Illegal alcohol had given the family the path to their fortune and to their new empire. If it was ever made legal again then they would find themselves struggling and she was not about to let that happen. Some lawmakers were already talking about ending prohibition and she could not have that. Her worries for Demeter were still very real, though, and she felt the urge to return home to see if there had been any contact with the farm or with Zeus.

She sat back in her car seat and let the decision move through her mind. She was a woman of decisive action, she knew her duty was to keep the family safe and productive. She knew there was nothing she could do for Demeter now. Whatever was happening at the farm was a security issue and that was not a task to which Zeus had set her. She resolved to protect the family the way she could. She had removed a potential threat by forcing the woman to the doctor and now she would keep their business alive by keeping the temperance movement ignited. She informed the driver of where to go and the car spluttered to life at her command. She saved a passing glance for the doctor's office and then fixed her stare firmly ahead. Goddesses did not look back and Hera knew deep within her soul that she need not regret the things she did to protect the family she had worked so hard to keep together.

Fifteen

Revelation

T here was no lightening and yet thunder sounded through the dark night as if the wind rolling through the clouds had set the entirety of the air aquiver. Rain pelted against the glass, stone, and brick of the city, turning walls and pathways dark, and soaking the unlucky dwellers that found themselves outside. The great grey clouds that clustered above the land swirled and churned with fury, the light of the moon unable to penetrate their ominous façade. Hermes' car made its way to the family. He sat alone staring out at the wind strewn city, watching as wet leaves and sodden litter were pulled from the ground and thrown about in the air around him. When he had left his office only a short time ago the night had been clear and the air full of warmth, with the scents of summer mingling in the city. The rain and wind had pounced on them. Hermes would be suspicious that Zeus was behind the storm but when the king of the gods was enraged there was always lightening and, so far, the sky had remained dark.

Zeus had been brief when calling the meeting, stating that it had something to do with Demeter and the farm. He was unsure how his presence would be of any help to the family. He had never been to the farm and he could hardly say he had missed Demeter whilst she had been away looking after the family investment. He had no problem with his aunt, but she was a simple woman who enjoyed a life of quiet luxury, whereas he had grown to love the complicated intricacies and never-ending wonder of the city. He had no interest in nature or in wild things;

people and their creations were the most fascinating things in the world to him. He adorned his wrist with the latest, and most stylish, watches, he attended fashion shows, and bought his suits from the finest designers. He was not drawn to simple. When they had come to New York he had vowed never to leave the city again. It had enthralled and enraptured him. He knew that even if Zeus commanded him to go the farm he wouldn't.

He did not expect Zeus to issue such a command though. Hermes was a key feather in the family's hat. Once he was mayor Zeus would be unstoppable. There was no way that his father would risk the final stage of his plan because Demeter was in trouble. He had used her up for everything she was good for long ago, like every other woman that crossed the mighty king's line of vision.

Hermes couldn't help being somewhat anxious though. His role in the family was to present a legitimate face, which only worked when he couldn't be tied to any of the illegal activities. He was to keep his distance, maintain his reputation, and build legitimate connections in politics, the papers, and wall street. It was a simple plan that would see the family rise to new heights. Something serious must be afoot if they were willing to risk his deniability by summoning him to a family meeting. He rubbed his eyes and exhaled. If only Zeus had just told him over the phone, then he would be able to avoid all the anxiety and worry that was plaguing him.

The apartment building that Zeus called home was an old stone block building in one of the finer corners of Manhattan that overlooked central park. The front door to the building was a blend of brass and polished glass filled red with the coats of doormen, eager and ready to help and escort the wealthy cliental that called the building home. They kept their pockets large and empty in anticipation of the tips that flowed from lonely widows and tipsy bankers. As soon as Hermes' car stopped one raced forward with an umbrella in hand. The young man, black skin glistening with droplets of rain, and wearing a broad smile, escorted Hermes to the door, doing his best to make sure the rain was kept far away from the pristine blonde hair, the grey pinstripe suit, or the shining black leather of his spats. Hermes pulled a collection of notes from his pocket and slipped it to the young man with a thank you and smile. He always tipped well. He knew when you're in the public eye it pays to be generous. Stories of miserly behaviour were not good for an election campaign.

Hermes almost forgot to breath the entire elevator ride from the ground floor to Zeus and Hera's penthouse. He had been here before and usually the elevator attendant was an old man named Jack, a sweet man that mumbled incoherently in a way that should have been entirely annoying but somehow seemed charming. This evening, however, Jack was nowhere to be seen, instead the elevator operator was a nameless beauty, a man who seemed to brush the top of the elevator with thick black hair that had been effortlessly styled. A man whose height fit perfectly with the broad musculature of his chest and shoulders that a shirt and waistcoat failed to hide. Even pressing the button had caused his arms to tense and his shirt to tighten against sun-kissed skin. Hermes didn't dare open his mouth, fearful of the pleas that he would utter.

Hermes had always been addicted to handsome men. He had always found them intoxicating and almost enslaving, but he had never been intimidated. He had been able to speak, to shine like the god he was even when their bodies caused his jaw to drop. That had changed when he met William. The young bar man had been gorgeous beyond words, he had seemed to shine like one of the gods themselves. Hermes had been so awed and so obsessed with this man he had found that he had agreed to be with him, and only him, as long as their relationship lasted. Hermes, like the rest of his family, had found the concept of monogamy strange and unsettling at first. Sex and love were not the same thing in their world. Sex had always been the activity that gave life its greatest pleasure. It was a release of need, desire, and passion. For it to be contained between two people alone was unthinkable. For William, though, Hermes had agreed. He felt no regret for his decision, but the unintended consequence was that he now found himself tongue tied around other gorgeous men, the guilt he felt at desiring them holding his tongue in his mouth and making him stare like an idiot.

Luckily, the elevator ride didn't last long and after tipping the young man more than generously he went into the apartment. The entrance hall was a lavish display of wealth. Hera had taken on the decorating responsibility and had turned the penthouse into a temple of decadence. Hermes could feel the softness of the rugs through the sole of his shoe. The brief spaces of wooden flooring that could be seen had been polished to a perfect sheen, the dark wood reflected the light from the crystal chandelier that hung above his head. Hera had built into the apartment upstairs to create one great space that had ceilings twice as high as they needed to be. Around the chandelier, artists had worked day and night to paint rolling and swirling patterns of colour that cascaded down the walls and moved around the vast collection of art. The family had the greatest collection in the world. Every one of them had taken the pieces they loved and kept them close throughout their long lives. Hera loved epic scenes, battle pictures, portraits of military leaders, cityscapes that showed the roaring and hurtling of life. Vivid colours almost oozed out of the canvases towards Hermes, filling the air with a brightness that fought for dominance over his senses with the sour scent of lemon cleaner that had been applied to every surface.

In the lounge only one other god was present. Ares sat on one of the long sofas that was facing the fireplace. The purple velvet strained not to rip under the weight of the giant.

"Hera must have had the sofa reinforced if you're able to sit on it." He said as he walked towards his brother.

Ares turned at the voice but did not respond to the jab. Instead, the god of war simply contorted his face into a look of disgust and annoyance and turned his gaze away from Hermes.

"Wow, I think that might be the most intelligent thing I've ever heard you say."

"I didn't say anything." He growled, still not turning to look at Hermes.

"Exactly." Hermes kept his eye on Ares as he spoke, making his way to the liquor cabinet. He could see his brother's body tense, even shake a little, but he managed to hold himself back and not rise to the bait. Only two jabs and he was already enraged, Hermes couldn't help but smile, his favourite sport might be a little easier tonight. "I don't suppose you know why Zeus has called this little family get together do you?"

"No"

"To be fair my question could have ended after the word 'know' and your answer would still have been the same."

He sat down on the opposite sofa, drink now in hand, the tumbler filled halfway with some clear spirit Hermes was hoping was vodka. He glanced at Ares who threw cold and angry looks towards him. The air between them seemed to grow dark and rumble with disdain. Hermes' smile only broadened. He allowed the silence to linger between them, sipping at his vodka, which he was now thinking was gin, and waited for the right time to strike. In the hallway he heard the ping of the elevator and the thud of the front door.

"I wonder who that is about to join us, perhaps your lost brain, I know you've been without it for a while."

Ares rose from his feet with speed that anyone looking at the large collection of oversized muscles would have found impossible. He deftly moved towards Hermes and within seconds he had his thick callous hand around the small god's throat. Hermes dropped his drink and sent the clear liquid spilling across the rug and polished floor. The sofa creaked as both Ares and Hermes' weight were focused on one spot. Ares squeezed hard. His hand pressing down on the windpipe, his fingers pushing deep into the side of his neck, cutting off the flow of blood to Hermes' brain. Hermes' vision began to swim. He knew Ares couldn't kill him, but he had no desire to start off the family meeting unconscious and being tossed around like a dog's chew toy. He clawed at Ares hand and looked up into his brother's murky brown eyes. The colour was almost lost, his pupil large and full of joy. Hermes tried to speak but couldn't. Ares always reacted to his jokes. He always shouted and threatened, then every so often he would kick Hermes to the ground, but he had never reacted with such rage before. Tensions were clearly running high.

"Ares get off him." The voice was filled with command but little urgency.

Ares hesitated for a moment and then loosened his grip and moved away from his victim. Hermes took in deep raspy breaths, filling his lungs as best he could. In the very short scuffle, his fine suit had wrinkled, and several hairs had fallen out of place. He stood and started to straighten himself out. Presentation was key and he was determined to always look good, even when he was with family. Ares, on the other hand, made no attempt to neaten his clothes. His trousers were already dirty from whatever activities had occupied his day. He had untucked his shirt, which was covered with wrinkles and creases, the top two buttons undone to reveal a plume of thick brown chest hair, and his suspenders hung limp at the side of his legs. There wasn't a waistcoat or jacket to be seen, but definitely some dried blood, Hermes realised.

When he was finished making himself look presentable, he turned to see his saviour. Athena stood in the doorway, her strong build and straight back making her look like a giant striding in a world of lesser beings. She rolled her eyes as Hermes smiled at her.

"Next time he chokes you I won't make him stop until after you're unconscious." She said as she walked to join Ares at the bar. "Have a drink and cool off. I don't know why you let him get to you like this."

Athena poured a glass for Ares and patted him on the back as he made his way to his original seat, the padding and velvet still dented and creased from his first period of relaxation. Hermes was tempted to say something but thought better of it. It wasn't so much that he feared another attack from Ares, but he did not want to have to deal with Athena. She was not the oldest of the children by far, but she was the most highly respected. She commanded the room effortlessly and it always felt right and natural to obey her, just as it did with Zeus. Of all his children she had inherited his ability to lead and command. When the old man finally stepped down and relaxed, they all knew it would be Athena who would lead the family in their endeavours. Hera had tried to keep the family together when Zeus was locked away some years ago. It had been a dark time for the family, and it was only when Athena had come to London that they had united and come up with the plan that secured Zeus' freedom. The ordeal had guaranteed that she would be the queen when the king fell.

The three of them sat in silence, each of them nursing their drinks, swilling the glasses so the liquid approached dangerously close to the rim. Normally Hermes would continue his light teasing, targeting Athena. The goddess was far more intelligent than their hulking monstrosity of a brother and she could play along with his games. Tension sat in the air today, though, and after Ares' outburst Hermes decided he would be better served sitting in silence than anything else.

As the night drew on the rest of the family that were still in the city began to assemble. Hera was first back, clad in her waves of deep brown fur that seemed to move across her body. They dripped and glinted with the occasional droplet of rainwater that had managed to hit her. Hermes could tell she had just come from her temperance meeting: her face was screwed into a look of repressed annoyance. Her lips were pursed, as if to keep in the words of condemnation she knew she could not bellow at the repressed and uptight women held within her. She moved to sit next to Ares, affectionately stroking his hand and pulling herself close to him. It was a poorly hidden fact that Ares was the only offspring she cared for.

Aphrodite was next, her sensual figure and relaxed features the absolute contrast to Hera. She smiled broadly at the assemble gods and winked as she saw every one of them admire her. Aphrodite transcended sexuality, she was lust incarnate. Even her smell was nothing more than desire made reality, her naturally perfumed skin smelling like a meadow of summer blossoms.

Hephaestus and Dionysus arrived after, two men who were somehow related despite their looks. Dionysus was a lean and elegant soul who seemed to skim across the floor to the drinks cart, whereas Hephaestus merely clomped his way through the gathering. Both were a let-down after Aphrodite, the smell of stale cigars and whisky on Dionysus and the dank scent of oil and sweat that lingered around Hephaestus, drowning out her pleasant aroma.

The room was a mix of mutters and tense chattering which only silenced once Zeus entered the room. He stood tall among them, greeting them with friendly familiarity as he poured himself a drink. Hermes could see, though, that his eyes were shadowed. He began to speak, his voice, usually steady and strong, shaking. Hermes couldn't tell if the king of gods was full of rage or fear but there was something inside him that was unsettling. Zeus made no attempt to ease his family into his announcement.

"The farm has been destroyed." He announced.

The family shared looks and glances of concern, every one of them steadying themselves with a drink.

"I received words from some friends: the farm, the distillery, even the house has been burned. Everything is destroyed."

The importance of what was being said started to dawn on the assembled gods. The farm was their largest source of drink: if that were destroyed, they would lose more money than they could count. Without money they couldn't pay bribes or enforcers, and their empire would start to crumble. The family sat in shocked silence, each of them digesting the news, a few trying to create plans that could help the situation.

"What of Demeter?" Hera asked, her soft voice pouring gently through the silence.

"I don't know." Zeus confessed.

The next harsh reality dawned on them. Demeter was immortal but she could still be captured, hurt, tortured for information. Hera and Dionysus stared blankly at the floor. Zeus pushed the conversation forward along with Athena. They asked for ideas on how to keep the family businesses afloat, how to keep paying men and bribes. They reminded everyone of their immortality and the family's ability to survive trials and tribulations. As they spoke the storm outside raged. The thick droplets of rain fell heavier, the wind whipped up faster. The glass of the windows around them sounded out a cacophony as the water threatened to smash it to shards. The storm felt ominous, as if something worse approached them.

The elevator sounded, the door creaked open and thudded shut, heavy footsteps sounded on carpet and polished floor. The lounge door opened and within stood the figure of Poseidon. The god was wearing a thick trench coat that dripped pools of rainwater onto the floor. His long dark hair, streaked with grey, and thick, ragged beard were drenched, plastered to his face. Despite all the rainwater that coated him the other members of the family could see his eyes filled with rage-fuelled tears. His body shook and, in his hands, he held a box, the bottom corner of it stained deep maroon and brown. He trudged forward silently and passed the box to Zeus. As soon as Zeus' eyes met the contents his face twisted into a shape Hermes had never seen before. Every horrid emotion a man could feel seemed plastered into one expression. Suddenly the storm that that been free of lightening crackled and burst to life. Every person in Manhattan hunched in fear as the rage of Zeus tore apart the sky.

Sixteen

Aftermath

Ω

Zeus had to leave the city, there was too much that his wrath could destroy in that place, and he had no intention of turning his new empire into heap of smouldering rubble. The storm followed him as his car sped its way along the roads that gave him passage from the dense collection of buildings. Dark grey clouds rolled and surged above him, thunder rumbled through the air and lightening tore apart the sky. Every great fork of intense light illuminated Zeus' face, twisted in pain and rage. His blue eyes seemed to glow and crackle, and his hair seemed to whip in a wind that was not present inside the protection of the car. His destination was still miles from him and so he focussed on driving, trying to keep himself sane enough to not decimate all those around him.

It was hard, all he could see every time he blinked, every time that he allowed his vision to darken, was her head in that small box. Her eyes closed and covered with coins, her skin, once a beautiful olive from so long spent in the sun, turned white and ashen with death. Her hair, usually worn in an intricate braid that turned her simple brown hair into a woven work of art, nothing more than a matted clump of blood pasted to her. Tears fell from his eyes as the storm above him worsened, he needed to find his secluded spot. The state of New York was littered with mines and quarries and he just needed to find one empty enough that he could unleash his power. He knew he shouldn't, knew his deal forbade it, but he didn't care. All he could focus on was destruction. All his rage commanded was ash and rubble. The human race had enraged him before, and he had wiped them out. He was rusty, but confident he still had the power to destroy rocks and dirt.

As Zeus drove, Hera sat in her Manhattan penthouse and wept. There had been little discussion after the revelation of her sister's head in a box. Some had refused to believe it. It was impossible, they had shouted, for a god to be killed, they were immortal after all. Some had said it was some vile trick or prank. Hera knew otherwise. She could feel it deep within herself that her sister had been taken from her. Ever since their phone call had ended, she had felt something in the pit of her stomach, she had felt the sense of impending loss and mourning. Even when she tried to supress her sense of premonition it still found ways to tell her that pain was coming.

The queen, who had spent her whole day poised and clad in the finest symbols of her wealth and status: furs, diamonds, designer clothing and immaculate make up, now sat in nothing but a night gown on the edge of her bed, weeping. Tears fell in great streams from her deep brown eyes, now bloodshot red. She had taken down her hair, letting the brunette strands fall where they may. For centuries she had had her sister by her side and now she was gone. Hera had prevailed through everything that the world had thrown at her. Even in the darkest of times: when she was adrift without her husband, her family was in ruins, and Zeus rocked back and forth in a cell, she had continued, strong.

Grief consumed the goddess, it held her down, making her sink deeper and deeper into the soft furnishings of the bed. She made no effort to lay back, no effort to sleep. She simply gave into the command to stay still, to give up, to surrender herself to the pain, fatigue, and sense of pointlessness. She looked down at the ground, at the spot where her tears fell and darkened the polished wood of the floor. She dared not look up or close her eyes knowing that both risked her seeing the face of her sister.

Athena had been the last to leave the penthouse. She had stayed back so she could study the head they had been sent. She wasn't the first to argue it wasn't real, that there must have been some sort of mistake or it was some horrific hoax, but she was the last to argue it. She had remained to study the head, examining, poking, prodding, and doing everything she could think of to prove that Demeter was not dead. After all her efforts there was no denying it. The head was definitely real, it was definitely Demeter's and she was definitely dead. She was not the first of the family to be decapitated. They had spent some time in revolutionary France when decapitating people was the fashion. Usually, the head just turned to smoke and a new one appeared as soon as the neck was free. She had seen it, even experienced it. There should be no head. Gods could not die. Even the cataclysm hadn't killed the non-Olympian gods, they had simply been banished to one of the underworlds.

She now found herself hunched over an assemblage of books in her private library. Over their long lives the gods had cultivated every kind of collection one could think of. Art was popular among most of her family. For Athena it was books. She had a library that could rival Alexandria or Oxford University. She had rare and unpublished scrolls, manuscripts, and even doodles. She had read each and every one of them and remember their contents in depth and detail. She could not mourn whilst the death was unsolved, she could not cry while there was an answer she needed but could not have. She poured over the information, desperately seeking some sort of answer. Tomes had been written about her family tree, but humans had little in the way of real information, just whispers told over campfires and speeches given by arrogant blowhards. There was much truth in the myth, but they rarely had truths she had not already known. Still, she searched, desperately clawing at withered yellowing pages for some scrap of information that would allow her to mourn.

Ares didn't need to think, he didn't need to solve the problem. He had no grief to deal with, no mourning to attend to. Ares did not have to figure out a riddle to feel his emotions. His emotions were always there, just below his skin, pushing against his physical form, desperate to be on display, desperate to be released onto the world. He did not feel sorrow or sadness in this moment, he did not feel tears falling from his dark eyes. Instead, he felt only rage, the likes of which he had not felt in a long time. The anger within him was white hot, he could feel its glow, its heat, searing his inside. It felt like his own anger would liquify his organs. It commanded him to let it free, to be released onto anyone or anything within his sight.

For the past two nights he had been upholding his end of Athena's deal with Casper and making use of his size and strength to intimidate local agitators who were causing the gangster trouble. He had taken to it half-heartedly at first, scaring petty dealers and thugs. He had landed a few blows but nothing that would lead to anything more than a few days recovering in bed. Tonight, was different though. He had dealt with worthless trash before, but now every person who crossed his path seemed to be the lowest form of life he could imagine. Each one of them deserved the beating that he was going to deliver them.

The man who currently faced his wrath was some young thing, skinny with only the smallest dappling of hair upon his round face. He had been caught spying on Casper and a price needed to be paid. Ares hadn't brought his team with him tonight, he didn't need them. They slowed him down. He wasn't weak like Demeter, even on his own there was no risk to his life. He could kill anyone, no one would stand against him. He let his rage move his fist. His knuckles connected with every part of the man he could find. Blood spouted from the poor man's nose and mouth, and bones shattered beneath Ares' unrelenting onslaught. He would beat the weakness from everyone who crossed his path until his nose was full of the metallic smell of blood.

Hephaestus pounded his hammer against the strip of metal in front of him. Sweat dripped from his brow as he went about his work, the exertion slowly starting to soak his messy clumps of dirt brown hair and his loose, rough clothing. Finally, after all his exertion, the metal began to yield to him, slowly taking the shape that he willed. Hephaestus kept working. When one strip was complete, he would grab another and begin the process again. He wasn't sure how many he would need or how many strips he had to work on, but he simply kept hammering. It was all he could do. He didn't know anything else.

The death of Demeter was weighing heavily on the whole family, but it sat so much heavier on his shoulders. It pushed them down, threatening to force Hephaestus into the dirt where he belonged. He was a monster that limped and clomped his way through a life filled with perfect beings. He was not fit to walk amongst them: they all knew it, with their faces that seemed to glow with iridescent beauty. Hephaestus had found his place with the family by being useful. When they needed something, they turned to him. He had developed their cars with hidden compartments to transport alcohol, their weapons and, most recently, their security systems.

Guilt stung at Hephaestus more bitterly than any pain he had ever felt, more than the white-hot sparks that spattered against his fingers. He would always remember being a babe falling from the height of Olympus. He could remember the agony and deformity it had caused. Since that day he had proven himself worthy of his place, but now a god was dead. The impossible had happened because he had failed to protect her. So, he worked. He hammered through his sweat, through his pain. He hammered through the dark of night desperate to create something, in the acrid smoke of the workshop, that could redeem him before he was thrown down again.

Hermes felt himself collide with the wall. His hand ran over the textured pattern that had been embroidered onto the wallpaper. William held his wrist tight and pushed him firmly into place. Hermes smiled to himself as he felt William get closer, as he felt his breath on the back of his neck and the warmth of his body close to him. He arched his back, pushing his lower half towards his lover. Hermes craved the passion that he found in William. He desired it more than anything. The physical sensations that coursed through his body were the same ones he had felt for millennia and they seemed so incomparable to the joy he felt at being held against the wall by the man he had come to love more than he knew possible.

He revelled in the moments when they were together, when they were so close and so intimate that their breathing even started to sound the same. He craved the moments where William didn't want to talk and didn't need to, when they could enjoy each other's company in a heat filled, sweat drenched silence, with nothing but heavy breaths and soft moans between them. Hermes felt safe with him. Ever since they had met, he had found sanctuary in the thick muscles of this man, the sensation of security that was to be found simply resting his head on William's shoulder as they slept.

When their passion had finally reached its end, Hermes turned and looked up into the sapphire eyes, the rich tones seeming to swim in a sea of light that lightly lapped as the deep recess of his pupil. Their warmth seemed so inviting that Hermes found it almost impossible to stop. He embraced the smell of the man next to him, the sweat that fell from them both, steaming into the air and dampening the sheets. He had never been close with Demeter, but her death was a shockwave, something that sent fear surging through his body. Hermes found himself talking about what had happened. He kept much of the truth to himself, knowing what happened to gods who revealed themselves to mortals, but he expressed everything that was within him, every fear, and anxiety that his aunt's death had moved in him. In this space he knew it was safe to ease the burden.

Aphrodite told no one, she was old and wise enough that her circle of trust included only herself. She didn't even trust the family. She knew that each and every one of them, as well as the mortals that surrounded them, were only hoping to look after themselves. She had found herself in conflict with the other gods more than she'd found herself working with them. Even her role in the family business was separate. She looked after the girls and paid no mind to the booze, drugs, gambling, racketeering, or violence. They were not hers to invade just as her parlours were no concern of theirs. As long as the money continued to roll in, she could be guaranteed a life of solitude from the rest of the clambering, squawking gods. That was how she liked it. She enjoyed her solitude.

She had grown up alone, had been married off to a man with a hideous face and a personality duller than a soup spoon, and had never been more than an object of lust to every other person who saw her. She had learned long ago that her solitude was her greatest strength; the less people who could see her the less they would want her. It was a system she was quite happy with, moving within the walls and shadows of her establishments, keeping her girls safe and protected, sharing what she knew. Tonight however, her confidence in her strategy was wavering. She was shaky, drinking slowly from a glass that tremored in her hand. Demeter had lived a life of solitude and now her head was in a box. Aphrodite could not die, she knew what it would mean for her girls.

She sat, dwelling on the horror of the evening, on the realisation that immortality might not exist for her anymore, the only certainty she had had. She sat and thought, surrounded by lavish art and stunning beauty, the sound of music coming from the radio, swing tunes blaring around her. She thought on what she could do to keep the girls safe should she die. Mortality was a new and daunting concept.

"Mor .... Mor ...... mortalality?" Dionysus slurred, desperate to get the word out without letting any vomit join it in its escape from within him.

"Yeah, that's what a family death makes you think about." Replied the blurred figure that seemed to split into multiple people every few seconds.

Dionysus knew who he was talking to, he knew everyone, but the name seemed to escape him at the moment. He decided the blur was no longer worth his time and turned away to survey the scene around him. The fuzzy shapes of humans filled his apartment. Every surface was covered in them, and every corner and alcove were filled with them. When Dionysus threw a party the whole of Manhattan attended. Every one of them was as intoxicated as he was. They talked, they drank, and they fucked.

There were no rules when you drank with Dionysus: the bedroom could host a political debate whilst the lounge saw orgies and grape eating, and it was best not to discuss the kitchen. No eyebrows were raised at the lavish excesses that occurred and everyone agreed that to be in the presence of the master of ceremonies was to end the normal code of conduct. Dionysus felt another pang of grief, that unannounced desire to cry, to blubber like an infant separated from its mother. As soon as it emerged, he grabbed the bottle next to him and drank, hoping that each drop would supress the emotion that was moving through him. He sought nothing but freedom from the pain.

"More revelry!" he demanded of the room and with a cheer more revelry surrounded him.

The roar of the sea and the wind whipping against Poseidon drowned out the screaming rage that filled his mind. Nothing could remove the image that was seared inside him and burst into view in any darkness. The sea air did its best to mask the smell that was stuck in his nostrils, the salt trying to blast away the putrid smell of decaying flesh and dried blood, but it was no use. The moment he had opened the box storm clouds had swelled above him. He remembered everything in such detail it was like it had been painted on the inside of his eyelids. His beautiful sister had been reduced to a pale and bloated head clad in its own blood. The killer had even gone through the effort of placing coins over the eyes, a way of signalling he knew who they were and what he could do.

It was in times like these he wished he could act as Zeus did and summon lightening. He wouldn't be so gentle or diplomatic about its use. Their enemy was in the city, reduce the place to ash and their enemy would be ash also. Zeus had more patience. He was more deliberative, even when enraged. Poseidon knew he could not be trusted in the city, so he had taken his boat and come to the sea. He had always felt a connection with the ocean, even before it had been allotted to him. He felt it surge beneath him, felt the waves crash against the hull and the spray coat his face. He embraced the darkness and mystery and as his connection grew the wind, and thunder, and rolling clouds grew in size and ferocity. There was no purpose, no end goal, but the sea was his domain and as long as he lived, he knew could use his power upon it.

Seventeen

Scandal

ermes woke to the shrill ringing of his telephone. The piercing sound seemed to surround him, jabbing at him like sharp, bony fingers, urging him to wake from his peaceful slumber. He didn't mind waking early, it was usual for him. Whilst most of the other gods would be sleeping, he would be beginning his mornings. He hated being woken, though. He once rose to the sounds of a gently flowing water or the wind moving softly through an olive grove. Now he was beckoned to wake by the screams of a machine he was enslaved to. If it wasn't his phone summoning him to a social interaction he had no energy for, it was his alarm clock screaming at him that he had to begin his day. All around him was noise. He tried to ignore it. He kept his eyes firmly shut, scrunched tight against the wailing racket that was battering against him. He curled himself up tight in his blankets and imagined sleep, imagined the warm embrace of the peaceful darkness where his dreams would play.

The noise didn't stop, and his dreams stayed distant from him. Finally, giving in, Hermes rose. He threw the sheets off himself in a dramatic show of annoyance. There was no one there to witness it but he had always maintained that a little drama, even when alone, was good for the soul. Sunlight was just beginning to seep into his apartment turning the floor from a dark and dull brown to a glowing amber. Hermes rubbed his eyes, hoping that the brief moments they didn't have to deal with light could help ease him back into sleep. He hadn't bothered to put on his robe, confident that this would only be a temporary intrusion into his rest.

Hermes always slept naked. Pyjamas and all other sleep wear were far too restrictive, and sleep was for freedom and escape. In his sleep his aunt hadn't been killed and he was enjoying the pleasures of life without stress or worry. He was not having clothing ruining it for him. Like all the gods, Hermes was comfortable with his nudity and had no shame for his body. He may not have been muscular or dominating like some of the others, but he didn't' much care. His skin was soft and unmarked by blemishes or imperfection. Every part of him was slender and lean. He moved with grace and precision, every step showing off another piece of perfection. He was sure hulking gods like Ares saw him as small and weak, but he felt strength in his movements. There was nothing to obscure his natural muscles, and it took little effort for him to show off his impressive abs and taught buttocks. His small stature and slender figure had come to define him over the years, and he had embraced it.

Finally, he reached the parlour where the phone was sat. Sunlight failed to penetrate the room. Thick curtains of royal blue hung over the windows blocking out all light. The room was bathed in shadows, a den of darkness and high-pitched wailing. Hermes clicked on a lamp and pierced the gloom. It was a simple room: a pair of wood framed chairs clad in luxury sat facing a fireplace with a small oak table between them. Every surface had been waxed and polished making it look like the wood gave off a lustre of its own, warming the room. One wall was covered with books: collections of literature and poetry he had gathered over his years. The room smelled of paper, the crisp dry aroma of tomes that were well cared for surrounding him.

Hermes adored poetry and music, anything that conveyed real and genuine emotions, anything that could move him. Records sat in long rows on shelves that reached the ceiling. He had every possible artist and genre. He had the music of Beethoven played by the London Philharmonic and jazz records straight out of New Orleans. Stacked with the gramophone discs was sheet music, that was starting to yellow and go crisp on the edges and poked out between the carboard sleeves. Sometimes Hermes could read the sheets and hear the music in his mind as if he were sat in a concert hall.

The god let himself fall into the chair next to the phone and exhaled a final huff of exasperation before answering. The sudden silence that enveloped him was a brief moment of bliss, a tranquil second between the high-pitched blaring of the phone and the gruff voice that now spoke to him.

"Get here now." The voice demanded and then nothing but the hum of the phone line.

No look of confusion came across Hermes face, no sense of wonder or worry crossed his mind. He had spoken to Zeus enough times in his life to recognise the demanding voice. Most people would have made the demand sound more like a request and would have at least furnished the recipient with some details, but not Zeus. He expected to be obeyed and for everyone to know and understand his will perfectly. Lesser beings explained themselves and Zeus was by no means a lesser being.

Hermes rose from his chair, sighing with annoyance and muttering to himself. All he wanted to do was sleep and now he had to go through the drudgery of getting ready and being lectured.

"Do I need to prepare some of the men to leave?"

"Fuck!" Hermes responded, jumping with fright. He turned to the shadowed corner of the room to see one of his security team stood there. "Maybe make your presence known a little more subtly in future Frank."

He had forgotten about the increased grunts. Ever since Demeter had been killed the rest of the family were on high alert and some had been given men to watch over them. Zeus had been determined that he would not lose another relative and so Hermes was constantly trailed by an ensemble of burly men in jet black suits. Each one had their hair shorn and small beady eyes that looked out from chiselled faces of worn skin. They were former soldiers according to Zeus. The one advantage of them was that they seemed perfectly comfortable with Hermes' nudity. Most people seemed to feel a sense of bashfulness around naked bodies but not these men. Hermes supposed that a life of showering and shitting in the open with every man you worked with increased the threshold for embarrassment.

Hermes got ready quickly, making himself look as presentable as possible with the short amount of time that he had. Luckily, he had an extensive closet and so finding himself a suit was an easy task. He chose a well fitted suit in a duck egg fabric. His electric blue eyes and golden hair shone in comparison to the matte texture of the cloth. He wasn't as flashy as Dionysus, but Hermes always liked to look good: he was, after all, the face of the family. Every time a person saw him he had to make a good impression, even if he was only seen by a labourer on their way to work in the small hours of the morning. With a trail of security, he left his apartment and made his way to Club Olympus. Zeus hadn't specified that this was where they were to meet, but he never did business at any of the other clubs, drug dens or brothels. At this hour he wouldn't have a meeting at his home. That would mean going in to find Hera checking if he smelled of whisky and cheap perfume, which he undoubtedly did.

The club was still being cleaned from the night before. A teaming mass of young men and women were running brooms and mops over the floor and wiping down tables with rags that went from white to murky brown before his eyes. The air was filled with every unpleasant aroma Hermes could think of. Stale cigar smoke hovered above him, and the sticky scent of walked-on alcohol and cleaning fluid rose towards him from the ground. The faintest scents of cologne and perfume were tangible, but he dared not sniff too hard to try and enjoy them. The band had gone but the stools and music stands were still all set up and some poor young person was slowly disassembling and moving them, whilst someone else was sorting the microphone. Hermes had always thought the thing was redundant. The bar couldn't get too noisy, so the volume was always down low. The singers could have just sung a little louder and it would have had the same effect, but image was everything to the family.

Hermes found Zeus in the club's back office. The old man sat in a chair at a large round table, his eyes staring off into the distance. Hermes couldn't tell if it was the dimness of the room or his father's current mood, but his eyes were dull and full of darkness, the usual bright and piercing sapphire now looked to Hermes like a dark and murky pool. Zeus noticed Hermes and nodded for him to take a seat.

"We were so close" Zeus stated, his voice gravelly and weighed down with sadness. "So close to reclaiming our former glory, to ruling over an empire again."

Hermes wanted to ask what had happened now. He knew the death of Demeter had hit them all hard and the fire at the farm was affecting business, but they weren't out yet. They still controlled every person in town and had a decent stock of alcohol. They just needed time. Hermes was about to speak, but before the words could leave his mouth Zeus slid a paper over to him.

"You've ruined our ambition son."

Hermes stared down at the page before him and his smooth face, usually free of wrinkles, filled with boyish charm and delight, shifted into a mask of shock. The page was nearly filled with a picture of him. It was black and white, and all the edges seemed fuzzed, but there was no mistaking it was him. He was stood on his apartment terrace. His top was off, and his pale skin was bathed in the light of the sun. His eyes were closed, and joy was spread across his face. Next to him was William, the tall and muscular man towering over him. He too had a face filled with pleasure, as the pair of them shared a kiss, their hands roaming over each other's bodies. The picture, that contained within it a memory so full of joy, now struck horror into Hermes. The headline did not help.

HOMOSEXUAL SINNER IN BID FOR HIGH OFFICE.

All Hermes could do was stare at the page in disbelief.

"We needed you to secure the mayor's office. Without it there will always be infractions on our turf, always be people we can't control. Now it's over, because you can't control your lust, boy" Zeus wasn't screaming, he barely raised his voice. His anger was not the seething storm of rage it had been when he had seen Demeter's severed head. It was a quiet, cold rage that was mixed with disappointment and contempt. "You had one role in this family, and you ruined it."

The hush between them held them both in place. It was a cloying stillness that couldn't be broken; Zeus staring at Hermes, Hermes staring at the paper, neither one of them knowing how to break it.

"There must be something we can do?" Hermes breathed between barely parted lips.

"Like what?"

"I could deny it. Say it's faked, with a lookalike or some form of trickery." Hermes started to feel some tiny semblance of hope as he spoke. "We have powerful friends, if they come out and say that they don't believe it then that will lend credence. If we keep denying, then this looks more like a smear campaign than real news."

Zeus' expression didn't change as Hermes spoke, he kept his cold stare on his son.

"Our powerful friends won't even take my calls. They've clearly been told about this, told about our precarious situation and they've decided they can ignore me. It's going to take more than lies to fix this. I still struggle to believe that you would do this, that you would put your own family at risk for sex."

"It's not just sex."

"Of course, it is, you're like all of us; a creature of lust and decadence. It's how we were born. At least the rest of us have the decency to keep our fucking in the shadows, away from prying eyes.

"I love him."

"Gods don't love mortals son, not anymore. They always leave, they always die, and we're left without them." Zeus responded mournfully, his face shadowed as he spoke, old memories hiding in the depths of his eyes. "Anyway, your desires and urges aren't the point here. The consequences are. You know this society. This backward country on the edge of the earth has strong feelings about men being with men. We all yearn for the days when sex was uninhibited, but this ensemble of prudes has made it otherwise. There is no way your campaign can continue. The money will dry up, no one will host you, everyone will disavow you. You're finished and so are our aspirations."

Zeus leaned back in his chair, the gloom seeming to pull at him. He looked up at the ceiling and let out a heavy sigh. He did not dismiss Hermes, but he didn't need to. The conversation was over. When Zeus made a declaration that was it, there was not continuing the argument, no more discussion or debate. The matter was settled.

Hermes had been reluctant, at first, to present the legitimate face of the family, but as he had worked and campaigned, he had grown to love it. He had a role that he was excelling in and the family would grow stronger than it had been in centuries because of him. He had embraced his role, his place, his mission, and had devoted himself to it fully. Now he had nothing. His shame consumed him. It numbed every part of his body and held his mind in a haze. He wanted to weep but he couldn't, his body was frozen, his mind nothing but a blank void of sorrow. He needed to think of a way to make this right. Instead, he simply sat in silence, wallowing in his own failure, the shock of the early morning news keeping him in his seat.

"We all make mistakes Hermes. We all fall short. You just did it at the worst time. Our supply is running low, the family is haemorrhaging money on security and constant transport. Our reputation is failing. There have been four raids the past three nights. I am disappointed in you, but I don't have the time to deal with you. Go home, I have an empire to try and save." With those final words Zeus rose from his seat and left the office.

Hermes stayed where he was, not wanting to leave whilst his father was still so close. He would wait until some business took Zeus' attention and then slip out.

Hermes couldn't believe what was happening. The family had been doing so well, they were unchallenged as mobsters of the most important city in the world. Yet in just over a week one man had brought that crashing down. Whoever it was knew the family and its operations well enough to exploit the weak points. Unfortunately for Hermes it turned out he was one of the weak points. He realised suddenly that he had nowhere to go. His days so far had been planned out meticulously. He campaigned relentlessly and to a schedule that was so precise it would have made Kant jealous. He almost smiled thinking of the old philosopher. Hermes had spent a whole summer changing his clocks just to mess with him, but even that memory couldn't push aside the sinking feeling in his gut. There was no schedule, no campaign, no role for him to play.

As the early morning hours crept onwards Hermes skulked out of the bar, hoping to be hidden by the small ensemble of workers that were making their way home. He had initially decided to return to his apartment to drink and wallow in his misery and defeat, but as he entered the light of the street, he decided against it. Even though he had no campaigning to do, he had a campaign office and a campaign team that had been the centre of his life for months now. He had staff who believed in him and who had worked hard to help him. If they were all about to find themselves out of a job and with no purpose, then the least he could do was face them. Hermes was many things that he was not proud of, but he was not a coward. He would face his problems and the consequences of his actions, even if that filled him with even more regret.

Eighteen

Interception

New York was never dark and never empty. As Hephaestus' convoy slowly made its way through the streets, flagged by apartment blocks and newly constructed office buildings of metal and brick, light and eyes fell upon it. Cars and trucks had become a regular sight in the city over the past decade. Horses had fallen out of use except for the occasional buggy and now everything was motorised. But to some the sight of a small convoy of trucks was still something to gawk at. The streetlights filled the road with a soft orange glow that shimmered against the coating of water on the ground: the remnants of the day's brief rainfall that had given way to the clear and warm night. Hephaestus sat back in the passenger seat of his truck and allowed the breeze to wash over him, taking a short puff on his roll up cigarette.

The man next to him was one of Ares' grunts. Hephaestus had wanted to bring along some of his mechanics, but that was extra weight and Zeus wanted him accompanied by fighters. The driver was a young man, skin free of wrinkles but marked with scars, some still new and some faded to only thin white lines. His eyes looked at the road ahead when necessary, but the rest of the time they darted in all directions looking for danger. Hephaestus was sure that his paranoia was unwarranted; the family had been going through a tough time, but one man could only do so much to them, and they had the resources to rebuild. Hephaestus was also sure that his handiwork was undetectable and unstoppable.

Zeus' demands had been a lot. He had insisted on a constantly mobile warehouse that was undetectable and defensible. Hephaestus had always been able to design and construct wonders, he was the one who had been able to harness Zeus' lightening as a weapon and not just angry flashes in the sky. If he could harness the raw power of nature, then he could certainly make a few sneaky trucks. They were able to move around the city and surrounding areas with ease, people only looking because of the noise, but never caring what was in them. They were bigger than anything that had been made before and Hephaestus had been proud of the fact he had managed to adapt an engine so it could handle the size and weight of his machines.

The concept was simple. Never stop for more than a few minutes, never look the same for more than a few hours, and never take the same route more than once. The outer shell of the vehicle was interchangeable by pulling a lever inside. There were five options that rotated around the van, everything from a bakery shell to a medical supplier. The back half could be removed and fitted to a different front so when they needed to refuel, they simply moved it across to a front already gassed up and then drove off. No sitting around waiting. The booze was hidden behind façade boxes and wrapped and sealed so as not to be smelled. The most important aspect for Hephaestus was that there were guns everywhere. Each van had a stash of shooters that would make the army jealous, and it didn't matter where you were, you could get to a gun.

He had come out with the convoy on its first few runs to make sure everything worked properly. He had no doubt it did. In the thousands of years he had walked the earth, he had never made anything that broke. He may not be as attractive, or sexual, or awe inspiring as the rest of the gods, but he was the most useful. He liked to think that without him they would fall apart and so was content to work quietly in the background. Demeter's death had shocked him into action as well, making him follow any order so he never failed the family again. He also knew that he needed to be here in case anything went wrong. The other mechanics would never understand what he had made. They alone couldn't fix it if it broke. The demands on him had been huge and so he had broken the family rule; he had used magic.

Hephaestus didn't feel bad. He knew that Apollo still used his psychic powers and that Aphrodite still used here powers to control people, even if she didn't realise she was doing it. Magic was in all of them, and it had to be released. They were gods after all. He also comforted himself with the rationalisation that he hadn't used much power. He had infused some of the mechanisms and materials with magic to make them stronger. He had also cast spells to disorientated anyone who got on the truck without permission. Any cop who tried to see what they were hiding could look straight at a bottle of whisky and think that they were looking at a crate of sponges. It had been the most magic Hephaestus had used in a long time and it had been exhilarating to finally make something that pushed him outside the bounds of reality.

As Hephaestus dwelled on his creation, the collection of vehicles sputtered their way through the city, the wooden wheels causing the metal bodies to shake and rattle as they ran over uneven paving slabs. They had just finished dropping off the alcohol for the night and were ready to leave the island and move around the less populated areas for the day. They always took a convoluted route through Manhattan, never heading straight for the bridges. That had been Athena's idea. Hephaestus had thought it was overkill, but he wasn't going to argue with her. Athena had a way of coming out on top in every discussion. She always got what she wanted, even without people realising they had lost. Now he simply settled into her lectures and did as he was instructed.

The convoy turned into a quiet street. The buildings sat low and squat, and darkness swamped the convoy. The lamps here were few and far between, and the oppressive blackness of night almost consumed them. Hephaestus came out of his contemplations to look around him. The driver kept his eyes combing the area. His hands gripped the wheel tighter and every now and then he glanced down at his gun as if to make sure it hadn't left his side. There warm summer breeze continued to waft through the window but instead of smelling the scents of the city it was tinged with something else that assaulted Hephaestus bulbous and misshapen nose, something acrid that stuck to the back of his throat. He breathed deeply pulling the air into himself to better determine what it was. The driver had also smelled it and they looked at each other, both with quizzical and puzzled looks on their faces. Then in a flash Hephaestus realised.

"STOP!" He bellowed to the diver, his rough gravelly voice chewing at the air as it rose above the grumbling engines.

Tires and brakes squealed as the van came to a halt. Behind them the others stopped. Hephaestus' timing had been impeccable. A few feet in front of the truck the street burst into flame. A wall of fire spread from building to building consuming the street in a bright blaze of ferocious oranges, reds, and yellows. As the wall of flame rose higher the heat beat against Hephaestus, the warm summer breeze he had been enjoying now became a scorching incandescence that made his skin tingle. The heat and flame didn't bother him, nor the heavy scent of smoke. He had been master of the forge and was used to it, but he knew instantly they were in a trap.

"Reverse these trucks now." He commanded to the driver.

The man turned to Hephaestus and nodded. The sound of gears grinding marked the transition and the van began to back up. It almost hit the one behind until it also managed to get into reverse and move backwards. The convoy now slowly reversed, every man holding their guns ready, eyes searching the street, ready to shoot any shadow that moved or person that emerged. Before the vans could back up more than a few feet another blaze erupted behind them, penning them in. The driver next to Hephaestus looked panicked. The vehicles stopped and nothing could be heard but the soft rumbling of their useless engines and the roar of the fires that contained them.

There was no movement, nothing seemed to happen. Hephaestus should have smelled the gasoline earlier and realised what was happening. He couldn't let the alcohol be taken or destroyed. He gripped his gun tight. He loved guns, loved how they worked, loved how they had been invented, but he was no expert at firing them and with only one good eye his aim was shockingly bad. He wanted to avoid this fight more than anything but knew that was impossible. These trucks needed defending, and someone was attacking. He gulped and nodded to the driver, signalling that they should get out of the vehicle.

The driver slowly opened the door, gun in hand, and stepped down into the street. He was the only person out there, illuminated in the flickering light. For too long the street was silent. He walked slowly and deliberately, every step was accompanied by glances in all directions, his gun raised, pointing at every shadow, at every indefinable shape that seemed to move and slide across the floor with the waves of light and heat that pulsed in their new enclosure.

A bang sounded in the street. The loud crack of gunfire rang in Hephaestus ears, above the engines and the flames. His driver fell, the back of his head flying across the street. A spray of blood and brains smeared the dark ground and his body fell lifeless, surround by a pool of crimson liquid within seconds. His eyes remained open, no longer alert and piercing but lifeless and staring up into the dark abyss of the night sky.

A storm of commotion erupted around Hephaestus. Bullets pummelled the side of the trucks. The noise was beyond anything he had heard before; a cacophony of pure chaos entombed him, echoing through the street. It was an explosion of noise the likes of which Hephaestus could hardly stand. Gunfire screamed above the sharp clangs of bullets meeting metal. Glass smashed and shattered as men screamed and yelled instructions at each other.

Some hunkered down in their seats and fired blindly out the windows hoping to hit whoever was shooting at the convoy. Others escaped their vehicles and ran for cover hoping to get a lay of the land, using the large vehicles as cover from the bullets. Hephaestus knew that he couldn't just stay in the truck, so he jumped out. It seemed like the bullets were coming from one side of the street. A group of his thugs were huddled behind the vans, each one looking desperate. They needed a leader, and, reluctantly, Hephaestus knew it had to be him.

He had never lead men before. He had teams and employees, apprentices and admirers of his work, but he had never led. He knew his machines though. He started shouting instructions to the men. His voice shook a little as he did, his gravelly tones giving way to the occasional stutter and pause that ran too long, but he kept going. He raised his voice above the din of war and told the men what to do. He showed them where the secret stashes were, where they could find shotguns and tommy guns. He told them where they could find secret explosives and other weapons. The men listened to him. They gathered what weapons they could without entering into a firing zone and each of them leaned against the side of the trucks taking in deep breathes. They panted, sweat dripping from them, each of them consumed by fear, but filled with savagery.

Men darted out and began firing. Hephaestus couldn't tell which guns were making noise, but only a couple of his men fell at first. The rest kept shooting and moving forward. The thick black tommy guns erupted with sparks of light as they fired on the enemy, the circular magazines holding enough rounds to turn a sheet of metal into nothing but flimsy mesh. Some of his men shot up at the roofs of buildings, whilst the others shot into the dark recesses of the alleyways that peppered the walls they were walking towards. Screams could be heard from the enemy in the shadows, as lucky bullets found their marks and pierced flesh. Hephaestus signalled to the other men waiting and, with a small click of a switch, a small ladder appeared in the side of each van. The men climbed to the top, careful to keep low, and with another subtle movement they managed to pull up a gun on each roof that had been hidden from sight.

These were Hephaestus' masterpiece. He had taken the automatic firing of the tommy and attached it to a gun that was thicker than a shotgun. Using all his knowledge and a small amount of magic he had been able to create something remarkable. The gun could fire rounds that were as large, powerful, and destructive as a several shotgun blast in one. The thing was enormous and had to be fixed to something secure and heavy. Hephaestus took a moment to marvel at his own creation. The sleek metal shone in the light of the fire that surrounded them and seemed to burn before his eyes like it was in the forge itself. When they fired, his heart skipped a beat. The noise was incredible, they roared and bellowed like a charging elephant. Each shot shook the vehicle it was attached to and echoed in the space of the street, their broad barrels erupting with sparks. The men firing winced at the sound and shudders, but they kept their finger on the trigger, firing monumental rounds of destruction into the street.

The whole space was consumed by smoke. The fire had caught onto some of the nearby buildings and was starting to spread, sending thick columns into the air. The guns were contributing too, each shot producing a small puff that was starting to get lost in the gathering grey cloud consuming and choking them. War really was like the forge, Hephaestus thought to himself. Stone and brick dust mingled with the smoke as Hephaestus' powerful weapons shredded the building in front of them. The atmosphere was acrid and choking, the smell of metal, smoke, and blood dominating. Still bullets rained down on Hephaestus and his men. His weapons and inventions were doing well but they were sat in the open and their enemy was hidden in shadows.

He didn't know how long his men could last out. Despite their earlier success the ones in the open were starting to fall and some had even run back behind the vans. Ammunition was low and the enemy was unrelenting. Hephaestus was just hoping that his big guns would last long enough to scare the enemy off.

His hope was short lived. From the roof above, a collection of small flames descended through the thick, grey air. Time seemed to slow as Hephaestus recognised what they were. The improvised explosive bottles crashed onto the tops of the vans, the glass giving way, and the flammable liquid coating the roofs in a sea of fire. The men who had been shooting stopped and started screaming, their bodies consumed. They tried to stand and move, but the heat disorientated them. They writhed in agony and fell to the ground, rolling and flailing, doing all they could to try and extinguish the flames that were eating at their body.

The remaining men scattered. The realisation that they could not win dawned on them and without consultation or discussion they fled in every direction. Some were gunned down immediately, falling in the smoke, their bodies covered in their own blood. Others made it into the shadows or alleyways, no longer feeling shame at abandoning the supply. Hephaestus knew that he had to do the same. As quick as he could, he made his way to an alley. His limp made him slower than most, but he still moved with drive. He was not inclined to get killed today. He had lived for thousands of years and he would live for thousands more. The attacker probably only wanted the booze anyway, there was no benefit to them in chasing him down.

Hephaestus made it to the mouth of the alley but as he entered the shadows, he saw that the ground was littered with bodies. His men, every one that had escaped, lay dead on the ground, great pools surrounded them, colour lost in the darkness. It was like a swamp of death, nothing but immobile human shapes contained by thick liquid. He hadn't noticed the new shots from behind him amid the noise and chaos of the street. He started walking backwards slowly but within the dark space a figure moved forward. It was just how Poseidon had described him: tall, clad in black, and his face covered with a dark mask. Hephaestus was frozen in fear. Whoever this person was they could kill gods and he was walking towards Hephaestus. The god of forges raised his gun and pointed it at the attacker. Poseidon had only had fists when he confronted this man, Hephaestus had more than that.

Before he could pull the trigger, a bullet sliced through his shoulder. He screamed in agony as more bullets hit him in the back, sending bursts of blood from his body. His arm fell, weak from his wounds, before he finally collapsed to his knees. He knew he could heal from bullet wounds, but it took time. They kept firing. None of them killed him, but pain coursed through his body, infecting all of him. His gun lay useless next to his immobile arm. His fingers twitched trying to grab the weapon, but it was no use. As the bullets stopped, he managed to glance up and see the towering figure in black looming over him, a misshapen, golden coin glinting with firelight in his leather clad hand. Hephaestus closed his eyes and within seconds he was dead, his life taken with a single thrust.

Nineteen
Alliances

T he days that followed Hephaestus' death had been nothing but a sea of indefinable misery for the family. Grief walked amongst them like an eternal spectre turning everything that they loved to ash. Food became tasteless, sex lost its pleasure, and music and art seemed dull and lifeless. Above it all was the knowledge that they had lost something more important than another member of their family. They had lost the very last of their supply, the thing that kept them funded. They all knew that without alcohol they couldn't survive. Without it they had no money and without money they had no power. Zeus yearned for the days when he had power because of his name, when the whole of civilization shook at the mere mention of his wrath. Now, unless he had money to pay thugs and grease palms, he had nothing.

The family had not had the time to grieve properly. There was too much to be done. Every contact that they had was harassed and every favour that they could call in was called in. They had reached out and tested every lifeline that they possessed and managed to get together enough liquor to keep the clubs open. Three more had been set on fire and they were rapidly running out of places their patrons could drink. Spies had found that small time gangsters were setting up their own bars in the city, making money where the family could not. Zeus didn't even have Ares to knock them about, his work for Casper still not finished yet. He felt trapped, like a lion backed into a corner by a band of savage hyenas.

The hardest part had been the return of Artemis and Apollo. The twins were his shining beacons, both of them incomparable in their beauty and ability. Together they could even rival Athena in his affections and admiration. Seeing the look on their faces when he had told them he was failing, that gods were dying and that their criminal empire was turning to rubble had almost hurt more than the loss of his sister and his son. Artemis had stayed calm as always, but he saw it in her eyes - the way her honey irises were consumed by black pupils and the way her thin, pale lips were pursed tight to stop them quivering. She had been silent, motionless; a vision of primal strength never letting her weakness show through. Apollo had been more obvious in his despair, falling to the ground wailing and screaming for vengeance, piercing blue eyes shimmering with tears, golden hair waving wildly as he used his head to gesture every emotion, his hands too busy ripping his own shirt off in a display of anguish.

For anyone who didn't know Apollo they would have found it a dramatic over reaction, but to Zeus it was heart wrenching. Apollo was the sincerest of the family, feeling no need to hide his emotions and his soul. His pain, rage, and anguish were all true and all-consuming. Artemis had managed to console the poor boy and take him back home. He was glad to have them back, even if the pain they were in was hard for him to watch. They had always been his trackers and assassins, they could find and kill anyone. They would end the killer lurking in their city. He knew they would never stop, never give in until his head was served up on a platter to Zeus.

Time was of the essence to him now. Until the enemy was subdued, he had to keep his business going and that was why he found himself in a small speakeasy that smelt of nothing but stale sweat and cigarettes, in the shit hole that was Brooklyn. Ever since he had created his empire Zeus had refused to leave Manhattan, having no interest in anything that happened in the slums that surrounded it. Times were desperate though and he had killed everyone in Manhattan that had been strong enough to oppose him, unfortunately that was also everyone strong enough to help him in his time of need.

He sat at a small table, the chair beneath him creaking and wobbling every time he moved, threatening to crack under his weight. The furniture clearly hadn't been updated in a long time; the wooden surface of the table faded and coated in water rings from every drunk who had passed through the place. The air was heavy, and the lights dim. Smoke was swirling around him as Aphrodite exhaled from the last drag on her cigarette. She sat to his left, her eyes looking firmly off into the distance as if in thought. She looked as impeccable as ever. Her red hair was worn down in beautiful curls that seemed to swirl like the smoke she was exhaling. Every strand glistened and shone, none dull or tangled. She wore a tight-fitting dress made of black, shimmering fabric with a long slit up the bottom showing off the smooth skin of her leg. Her back was straight, yet she looked relaxed and comfortable.

Aphrodite hadn't been entirely happy with her role in Zeus' plan. There was a time when she would have had sex with anyone for any reason. Lust was her role in the pantheon after all. It was what she did better than any being, what she exuded from every part of her body. Over the years, though, she had grown tired of men and women lusting after her, of giving them all the pleasure they could ever desire, and so she had simply decided to exploit that lust. It was why Zeus put her in charge of the brothels; no creature in existence could convince a man to spend more on hookers than Aphrodite. It had been a long time since she had been with a man, she hadn't explicitly deemed worthy and, so, to offer her up like a piece of meat to a hungry animal had been repugnant to her, but Zeus had no time to consider her feelings. The family needed her to step up.

"Can I interest any of you in a drink?" a voice drawled from the doorway in front of them. Zeus hadn't noticed Casper walking in, his entourage behind him, fanning out as they all made their way to sit down. "From what I hear it's been a while since any of y'all had one." He let out a small laugh as he finished speaking, his eyes meeting Zeus' as he sat down, testing and bating the opponent to see what reaction he could get.

Zeus never let a man like this get under his skin. He had lived amongst the most arrogant men civilization had ever spewed forth: he could handle some jumped-up, small-time gangster.

"No thank you Casper. I've already had plenty of water today, your whisky isn't needed." He replied, his voice kept serious and professional.

Casper's smile disappeared at the jab and Zeus saw Athena, sat to his other side, shoot him a look. She may be wise, but she didn't know men like Casper. Even when you needed them you had to show them that you weren't desperate or intimidated, or they'd walk all over you.

"What can I do for you fine folks then? It's rare we get a visit in little old Brooklyn." As he spoke, he leaned back in his chair gesticulating, his hands open wide as if to invite them to make any request.

Zeus saw the way his hands were calloused, years of hard labour evident on the man's dry and worn skin. Casper had clearly had a different life before he found his way into the underworld. Zeus had no time for men who had crawled their way up. Power was something one was born with, it was a part of who you were. In this moment the urge to leave became almost too much to control, but he managed to contain himself. He would not enjoy treating Casper as an equal, but if it was what he needed then he would do it,

"Frank, you're probably aware we've been under attack lately." He said, keeping his tone as calm as possible.

No reply came, Casper just looked at Zeus, his eyes barely visible in the patchy lamp light of the bar, his expression unreadable except for the small amount of wry amusement that he seemed to be getting from Zeus' pain.

"We need liquor, and we need it fast. I know you keep a healthy supply and I'm willing to buy it off you and offer you a little something extra." He gestured towards Aphrodite who switched effortlessly from disinterest to sultry seduction.

Zeus had always admired Aphrodite's ability to convey her sexuality. She was never obvious or vulgar: she simply moved her body, made her eyes sparkle, even made her breathing just a little deeper and more obvious. Every part of her signalled that she wanted Casper, that he could have her now in front of everyone. Zeus could see Casper's eyes widen, see the way his lower lip fell just a little, the way his awe was written across his face as he stared across the small table at a woman who seemed to be glowing in the gloom of the small bar.

For a moment Zeus felt something, like his senses became just slightly more alert, a tingling or humming that touched on the edge of his awareness. He glanced at Aphrodite and realised what was happening. Every colour she wore seemed more vivid; the red of her lips glowed and the soft tan of her skin shimmered. Even her scents seemed more obvious and intense, not just her perfume but the smell of her hair and the powder she used on her skin. She seemed so obvious, so present, like everything else around her was merely background. It wasn't until then that Zeus realised Aphrodite was using magic, and not like he had, in some rage fuelled moment of chaos. She was intentionally using her powers. He had to stop her. Fear shoved him forward.

"So, Frank" Zeus began, loud enough to shock the room out of their staring. "Do we have a deal. I buy your booze off you and you get a night with Aphrodite. Not a bad deal is it? I think …"

"I want Harlem back." Casper interrupted, catching Zeus off guard.

He stared towards Casper unable to think properly. He had offered up a goddess and still this man felt he could negotiate. Casper could see Zeus' shock and he seemed to enjoy it. He leaned forward and placed his hands on the table.

"You kicked me out of Harlem, and I want it back, as well as the money and the wonderful woman next to you."

"What makes you think we would give up our territory?" Athena asked as she leaned forward and met Casper's gaze. She was staring at him with an intensity that Zeus had rarely seen in her eyes.

If Aphrodite's sensuality was irresistible then Athena's determination was unstoppable. Frank continued to look into Athena's eyes, but he eventually looked away, unable to match the severity of her stare. His dark eyes wavered, and he looked at Zeus, knowing that no matter what Athena said, no matter how hard she stared, the decision would finally be down to him.

"You have no alcohol and little money, your clubs are near to closing and customers are fickle. You can keep going with my moonshine and lose Harlem or you can leave here dry and empty handed, and I will watch the vultures pick at your territory and take Harlem for myself. It's up to you Zeus."

"Fine. Harlem is yours." Zeus replied.

He didn't delay, he didn't even bother to act like he needed to think about it. He could feel Athena's eyes burning into him as he spoke. She would want to discuss, to think, to plan, but Zeus knew there was no time for it. There was no time to waste. He had to agree and when they had the time and resources, he would crush him again, and that time he wouldn't push the rat into Brooklyn he would drain the life from him.

"Well, a deal like this definitely deserves a drink" Casper said falling back against the back of his chair, beckoning to the bar man across the room.

As drinks were poured, Zeus managed to make polite conversation with Casper. He kept his anger and frustration under the surface, acting as if he didn't want to throw the table aside and throttle the man. He knew that he and Athena could beat every man in this room to a bloody mess with their bare hands, but over the years he had found that people worked better for him when all their bones were in one piece. As his thoughts turned violent, he found the conversation naturally moved to Ares. Casper's time with Zeus' son was coming to a close and the man from Brooklyn had nothing but praise to laud on him. Zeus had tried to find out what Casper was using Ares for, but the man was not forthcoming. Even Ares didn't know why he was beating men to a pulp for Casper. Soon Zeus would have his guard dog back on the chain where he belonged.

Eventually the conversation turned to the details of the deal. Liquor flowed as the two men bartered and negotiated over every detail. Casper didn't just want bars in Harlem, he wanted everything: the brothels, the gambling dens, the protection rackets. Casper was relentless, he refused to look away from Zeus, even when supping on his drink, even when Athena or Aphrodite spoke. Aphrodite had almost walked out the room when Zeus agreed to let Casper run the brothels. Over the years in the city, she had become so protective of her girls, but Zeus knew the longer the negotiations went on the longer he would be without product. He agreed to more than he had ever agreed to before. He felt so restricted and oppressed. His mind flashed back to a cage, to a cell not fit for an animal, to being so restricted he felt he couldn't breathe.

Zeus pushed the memories aside, desperate to keep going forward, but he could feel the sweat on his brow, feel his hands shaking in balled fists under the table. He kept his composure but everything he agreed to give away was like a knife in his chest, a pain that stopped him breathing, that stopped him focussing, that took him back to that squalor in London when he was barely a man, let alone a god. He felt the repression and constraint in his mind. He loosened his tie and rolled up the arms of his shirt, desperate to do anything that would bring a sensation of liberation.

Finally, the meeting came to an end. Everything had been agreed and several bottles of whisky had been consumed. The air around them was thick with the scent of cigarettes, alcohol, and testosterone. The men surrounding Casper seemed shrouded in darkness as they rose and went about their business. Zeus left as quickly as he could, eager to let out his frustration away from the prying eyes of opponents and rivals. He needed to bellow like a storm, or he would be consumed. Athena accompanied a host of Frank's men to one of his warehouses to collect the product. She looked like a giant amongst them. The tall and burly men who usually looked so threatening seemed small compared to the statuesque figure of Athena, her posture and poise never slouching or slacking.

Aphrodite left with Casper, trailing slightly behind him as if being led, her hand in his, walking so demurely, like she was merely floating along the ground. Every time Casper looked at her, she smiled at him, her teeth perfectly white, sparking in a light that did not exist. She had no idea where she was being taken. She rarely got involved in the politics and spying of Zeus' empire building and so she knew little about Casper. He was charming though. He had a confidence and ease about him that made him enjoyable to be around. Even when he had been pressuring Zeus, he had never raised his voice or shown an emotion. He had simply taken the process in his stride. Aphrodite couldn't help but admire that about him. Men were emotional beings who rarely had the social skills to impress her. Casper seemed to be the rare exception. She still wasn't happy at being treated like a bargaining chip, but at least, she told herself, if he was pleasant company, she would be merely annoyed rather than enraged.

She also knew she needed time with Casper. The negotiations had been quicker than expected and too much had been decided in too short a time. She was about to lose control of a lot of girls, and she needed to know that they would be well looked after. She couldn't see another young woman abused just for making money with her body. She would take this night to daze Casper, to give him an experience that he would remember until his dying day, and then she would find a way to make sure he looked after her girls. In a moment she had slunk around Casper, standing in front of him. The man wasn't especially tall and so she bent her legs slightly so he would tower over her. She looked up at him, her green eyes wide and shimmering. She placed one hand on his chest, her immaculate nails gripping at him slightly, as if in unrestrained desire, and then she tilted her head up and moved to kiss him. Their lips met, beginning a night of unrestrained and unrelenting passion.

Twenty

Lust and Power

Aphrodite awoke in a haze. Her mind felt empty, as if the only thing she could hear were a breeze blowing through it. She tried to open her eyes, but they would not move, the lids feeling as heavy as lead. Something felt wrong, her body did not feel the way it had when she had fallen asleep in Casper's arms. She had drifted off with soft cotton sheets caressing her skin and her head rested on Casper's surprisingly strong, yet comfortable shoulder. She could no longer feel the softness of the cotton or the presence of a man next to her. Soon she started to realise that she wasn't laying down anymore. Her head was lolling, her chin resting against the very top of her chest. She tried lifting it, but it felt as weighed down as her eyes. Her whole body had the sensation of being held in place, as if her muscles had vanished and her bones had been turned into stone.

As time started to pass, her grogginess and confusion lifted. An array of scents began to enter her awareness. Smoke and liquor danced on the edge of her senses, as well as the smell of freshly laundered sheets, the crisp soap smell managing to penetrate through the stale odours of decadence. Above it all, though was the smell of perfume. The sickly-sweet smells of every conceivable brand surrounded Aphrodite. They swirled, dominating her newly awakening mind. Then something else emerged, something repugnant that entered her nose as she tried to breathe in more of the perfume's heady aroma. She sniffed more, trying to determine what she was smelling. It was only when she opened her eyes that she knew what it was.

Death surrounded her. Corpses littered the floor of the dimly lit room she found herself in. Each one was female. Each one was naked or wearing only the silks, satins, and laces of lingerie. Aphrodite's vision was still blurred but she knew instantly who she was looking at. The girls of The Cyprus Lounge had been strewn around her carelessly. Some lay alone, some were next to each other, still holding hands. They were still hunched, a pile of bones and flesh coated in blood, heaped in the corner of the room. It was difficult to tell which corpse had once been which girl. There was little light in the room and every body was covered in blood, their hair discoloured and matted, their eyes gummed shut with the drying, viscous liquid.

Aphrodite couldn't help but stare at the scene she had found herself in. Her whole body was shaking, her breathing deep and laboured. Shock and fear filled her, a pain like no other. Tears began to stream from her eyes, cutting a damp path down the alabaster skin of her cheeks and falling from her chin onto the naked flesh of her body. She tried to move but couldn't. She no longer felt heavy and immobile, and it was only then she realised she was sat on a small chair with ropes holding her in place. The thick bindings were tight against her. Her wrists were lashed to the arms of the chair, her ankles secured to the legs, and yards of rope had been circled around her waist to keep her firmly pressed against the meagrely cushioned chair back.

She began to squirm and writhe, desperately trying to pull herself free of her restraints. Nothing seemed to work. The ropes had been tied well, and tight. The more she moved the more the ropes seemed to tighten against her, cutting into her flesh. She knew she should stop struggling but it wasn't in her nature to give up. She was already consumed by anguish and remorse for the fate of her girls. She would not add a feeling of hopelessness into the mix. Whoever did this could have killed her, but they wanted her alive for some reason. She resolved that they would never get to use her. She pulled at her restraints and still they tightened as if they possessed a will of their own.

"That's pointless and a waste of your energy." A voice behind her informed. Whoever it was they spoke calmly, their accent unplaceable, the kind of voice that reeks of pretention and arrogance.

Footsteps sounded as the new entrant walked towards her. Aphrodite craned her neck to try and see who it was, but she saw nothing but shadows.

"Who are you? Why have you brought me here?" She asked desperately.

"The same reason I've visited two other members of your family so far." The captor answered, emerging into the soft glow of the lamp that was sat in the corner of the room, offering what light it could. The tall figure clad in black, face covered by a mask, picked his way through the corpses, careful to avoid standing on any of the girls, making the occasional footprint in the pools of blood that were beginning to dry and congeal on the floor. "You're going to die."

Aphrodite stared up at the masked face in horror. She wished she could make out some sort of expression, but the mask didn't even have eye holes, just shimmering sockets of darkened glass, covering the assailant's real eyes. She wanted to see how serious he was, how determined. All she could make out was the sound of his breathing: deep breaths pushing against the inside of his facade. She didn't know how to respond. Part of her wanted to beg for her life, to offer him anything just so she could continue to live, but the stronger part of her, the part that had risen from sea foam, that had been worshiped, and depicted in art, the part of her that was bestowed with the power and dignity of the titans would never let herself sink so low. She held her quivering red lip as still as she could and continued to stare up to the obscured face.

"If you were going to kill me, I would already be dead."

"You have one purpose first."

With that, he signalled to the doorway and a young man entered. The assistant carried a phone with him. The black cord trailed behind, smearing a thin line of blood across the tiles that weren't already soaked. He looked scared, his eyes darting around the massacre, his pupils dilated as he took in everything his boss had done. The short little man quickly handed the phone to the killer and scurried from the room, the cuffs of his oversized suit soaking up blood as he stepped in yet another pool. The smell around Aphrodite was becoming unbearable, the metallic tang of blood infused with the terror induced shit and piss of the dead was a heinous assault on her senses. She wanted nothing more than to leave this room.

"You heard all that I hope." The killer said down the line, speaking to whoever was on the other end of the phone. "If your still not convinced I can make her speak more."

There was a pause as the killer listened to someone reply. The silence was unbearable. Aphrodite wanted to know who he was talking to and what was being said.

"Fine" the killer finally replied. He held the phone up to Aphrodite, but before she could make a sound, he pulled a small knife from within his long black coat and rammed it into her belly.

The goddess let out and ear-piercing scream, the type that could curdle blood. The pain came as a shock, a searing bolt of agony that slammed into her and spread through her entire body. The killer didn't remove the knife, leaving the metal inside of her, blood pooling around it and spilling out of her torso. She stared up at the mask in unhidden pain and horror. Silently the killer ended the call.

Aphrodite breathed through gritted teeth, hoping that the air would carry the pain away. It still remained within her, consuming her. Every now and then a whimper escaped. She hated herself for them but there was no way she could hold them in.

"Why are you doing this?" She managed between ragged breathes, the words quivering as she spoke. "Why did you kill my girls? Who were you talking to?"

Her questions were met with nothing but silent stares.

"Tell me!" She demanded, screaming the words, their ferocity powered by her pain and anger.

She wished she could work her magic on this man, wished she could charm him, but she couldn't focus. She had clearly been drugged to keep her asleep and the effects of that had been replaced by terror and then by agony. Her mind couldn't focus on conjuring charm and allure.

Aphrodite's vision began to swim again, the blood loss and over exertion seemed to cloud her mind. The edges of her vision blurred, becoming nothing but a muted haze of skin tones and deep red. As her vision condensed into a pin prick, and the sound of the world around her was replaced with nothing but the sound of her blood thumping through her body, she saw the shadowed figure walk towards her. In that moment, as her head pounded with the sound of her own heartbeat, she knew she would die. A curved blade emerged before her, the metal jet black as if it had been made of the night sky. The killer raised the weapon and pieced it through the goddess' chest into her heart. The pounding stopped and Aphrodite died in fearful silence.

Ares had not witnessed such wanton death and destruction in so long. He walked through the brothel, his stomach turning as each room seemed to contain more and more slaughter. The bodies of prostitutes and clients were scattered everywhere. No person had escaped the rampage of death that had moved through the place. Everywhere he turned he saw naked flesh and fine suits soaked red, empty lifeless eyes staring in every direction, faces contorted in pain and fear. The smell of decay was everywhere, penetrating the air with ribbons of odour. He could almost taste the blood and bodily fluids that caked every victim.

Eventually he came to the washroom that Aphrodite had been held in. She was still tied to the chair, her lifeless body pale and limp, soaked in blood. Ares had always marvelled at the beauty of the goddess, like everyone, but seeing her like this she looked so ordinary. The curves of her body meant nothing when she was not present to move them or wink about them. Her once bright lips were a faded pink and her hair sat flat against her, the ends a deeper colour as they met the wound on her chest. Her head was tilted backwards, and coins were rested on her eyes, the way they had been on every other body in the building.

Ares felt his revulsion and anger merge within him into something new and potent. He had witnessed death before. He had caused more of it then he could ever remember, but it had always been in a battle. Ares adored the scent of blood and sweat on a battlefield. He loved the cries and the cheers of war. He could stride through a battlefield happier than any being that had ever existed. He had seen combat in all its forms, and he had showered in the blood of his enemies. He despised death for its own sake. Battle was a truly divine experience, but murder was the act of cowardice, especially the murder of women. Ares shook with unrestrained fury as he continued his search through the brothel.

The hulking behemoth made no effort to step around the blood and other substances that had gathered on the floor. He walked deliberately, storming into each new room hoping to find his prey, knowing he wouldn't stop until the person responsible for killing off his family was found. Ares had never cared much for the family members he had lost so far. None of them impressed him, not like Zeus or Poseidon. None of them had been strong or leaders, but it was his job to protect the family and he had failed. He was the winner of battles, the decider of wars, he did not fail. The death around him felt like shadowed claws pulling at him, demanding he remember his failures. The thought of Aphrodite tied to the chair, her immortality taken from her was enough to send his blood boiling.

He came to one final room and with a swift kick he sent the door flying from its hinges. The wood groaned as the sole of his massive leather shoes collided with it, causing it to fall to the floor with a loud clatter that echoed in the space. The room was well lit and free of corpses. It was clearly some kind of storeroom. Crates and boxes were scattered around, and some were pressed up against the wall. The place stank of perfume and alcohol, clearly the two things patrons wanted to smell when they came to a brothel. None of this caught Ares' eye because, across the room, sat on a box, was a man dressed in black, no face to be seen.

Ares snarled, his mouth curling up into a wicked smile. He had found his prey. He felt his body tense, the thick muscles that coated him coiling up, ready to strike, filling themselves with power. The man remained silent, the black eyes of the mask fixed intently on him. Ares wished he could see the look of fear that must be plastered on the real face. The mask was annoying him, it had been made to look realistic but only in general strokes, there was little definition and the expression it had been shaped into was one of disinterest. When he was done killing the man, he would crush the mask beneath his boot.

Ares didn't speak. This man knew he would be killed on sight and so no explanation was needed. He stalked forward, closing the space between them. With each step his anger grew a little more. His fantasies of destroying this man were close to becoming a reality. With one final snarl he lunged forward.

Metal crashed around him and Ares felt his body collide with solid rods as his attack was cut short. A cage had fallen around him. The latticed metal cube enclosed him, keeping him in place. Ares looked up to see a hole had been cut in the ceiling to hide the contraption. The killer must have been prepared for this moment. Ares didn't care. He was a god, it would take more than a few iron bars to hold him back. With all his might he threw his fist at the cage. The sound echoed through the room, and metal grated on tile, but it barely moved, and the bars remained unbent. He tried again and again but still nothing happened. Ares used his magic, throwing the rules away to fight his enemy, but still the bars remained in place.

"You won't smash your way out of that cage I'm afraid."

"I will, and then I will smash my way through your skull." Ares teemed with rage. His body bristled with it, his hairs standing on end as it begged to be released from within him. He continued hammering the bars. "Fight me you fucking coward." Ares bellowed, his eyes staring, trying to burn his way through the mask. He conjured more power within himself, the kind that drove men to conflict and war and focussed it all on his opponent, urging the killer to fight him, but the man seemed unaffected. He continued sitting on the box, looking at the caged god like some sort of wild beast.

"I don't want to fight you Ares, I want to help you."

"I don't need help from you. You've been killing my family."

"I've been thinning the herd." He replied, no hesitation, no thought.

Ares stilled himself as the man continued to speak.

"Zeus is weak and has let his family grow weak too. New York needs a real leader. I want your help to take him down, and in exchange you will lead. You will have a greater empire than he could dream of." The man leaned forward as he continued to speak.

Ares couldn't help but smile at the audacity of the man in front of him, at his foolishness and stupidity.

"You think I would betray my father for you?" He sneered.

"Look at what I can do. Look at how I have trapped you. I know a cage can't hold you Ares and yet I made it work." He cast his arms out as if to usher Ares forward. "I have tracked you and caught you. I have done the impossible, the unthinkable. I am more than your father and together we can be even more than that; more than him or Casper or any other low life criminal." The man continued.

Ares took a moment to think on his words. There was a voice within him urging him to talk, to learn more about the man who could trap and kill gods, but Ares' anger drowned out his rational inner voice. Smashing his fists against the cage even harder than before, he roared at his captor.

"You are nothing to me but an object to be crushed. You think you've broken us?" He was panting, pushing the cage to emphasise his words. Dust stirred where metal pushed against the tile. "I will watch your head explode little man."

Silence followed as Ares continued to stare at the man, desperate to bait him into a fight, to hurt him and break him.

"Your loyalty is admirable…"

"Save your admiration for someone who gives a fuck" Ares retorted.

"Fine. If you change your mind, if you come to realise your place is on the top, then contact me. I'm always watching your little gang. If you want to be my partner, then let me know."

The killer opened the door and walked out into the street.

"The only place I belong is standing over your corpse." Ares managed to yell in reply before the latch finally closed.

The god of war stood alone, caged and useless. He wanted nothing more than to be free and to continue his hunt, but he couldn't. His anger was beyond words, he raged at his enemy, at himself, at Zeus for failing to win this war. He seethed and shook, the whites of his eyes almost red as they cast about the room looking for a way out.

He paced the cage, searching his enclosure. His eyes darted everywhere, looking for any way he could escape. Beneath the matte metal that ran along the bottom of his enclosure he saw the cracked tiles, the parts of the floor that had given way to the weight of the falling object. Arcs fell to his knees, pulling at the chips and cracks. He clawed at the broken floor until there was a gap that he could push his fingers through. He grasped the cold metal tightly and lifted. His body tensed and filled with strength, his muscles forced him up, taking the cage with him. He raised it as high as he could before slipping through and letting it fall again behind him. He turned to the door, tempted to run after his attacker, but he knew he would be long gone by now.

Twenty-one

Earth Shattering

The back door to the club slammed shut, quivering as it thudded against the frame. The sound shattered the air in the dark alley, causing the small pools of water that were gathered on the uneven ground to ripple. The air was cool and dry, the clear warmth of day had given way to a crisp evening. Poseidon stormed down the alley, the thick leather of his boots beating a marshal rhythm on the ground. His trench coat billowed behind him, the scent of salt air wafting off of him, from years of living by the sea. His grey eyes stared forward, intensely scrutinising everything in front of him. The tangle of grey and black hair that made up his beard hid the thin line of his lips and clenched jaw, the matt of hair that hung from his head obscuring the throbbing vein in his temple that signalled his rage.

Poseidon was finding his place in the family intolerable. He had been the one forced to witness Demeter's head, coated in blood and placed in a box. Seeing his sister like that had been a trauma the likes of which he had never experienced before. Even the cataclysm hadn't hurt as much as seeing a sibling dead. He had been the one who had fought the killer, who had experienced his strength and skill. He had been the one hunting him, checking every abandoned spot, talking to every underground contact. He had not needed Zeus' instruction or approval. The fact he had managed to uncover little, other than how well paid the killer's crew was, was a constant source of even more frustration. Yet, despite all this, whilst the rest of the family made deals and sold alcohol like common shop keepers, he sought true revenge and retribution. For this, they cast him aside.

They had been presented with an opportunity. The killer wanted to meet Ares, he wanted to talk, to make a deal. That was a way to find him. It would bring their enemy to them and, finally, Poseidon would be able to get his hands around his neck and squeeze until the whites of his eyes turned blood red. He craved his revenge, it had been all he had thought about since he had fought the killer. Every other task was delegated, every woman was passed up and ignored, every second of sleep was missed. Yet Zeus had said no, had refused to put anyone at risk. The fool didn't realise that as long as they sat like caged rats in their dens and clubs they were already in danger.

Even Hera had not been able to soothe his wild outburst. Usually, his sister could calm the rage within him and there had been many occasions when his hot temper had been mellowed by her reasoned approach to revenge. He found her cunning and wickedness like a salve that eased away the red-hot pain of his own anger. Tonight, however, her clever words and call for caution had fallen on deaf ears. Poseidon was done working in line with the rest of the family. Time on earth had made them weak, almost mortal. Poseidon could try and determine why and how the family had come to this, but he didn't have the time or inclination. After turning his bottle into nothing more than a smear of alcohol and shards of glass he had left the club, determined to find the enemy.

Poseidon made his way from the club to the docks. The city was teaming with life, even at night. People moved in the darkness and shadows, eyes scanning for pearls, jewels, and wallets. The wall street wealthy and Brownsville beggars swirled around each other, careful to never get to close. Drunks stumbled into alleyways, each one carrying the looks of joy and regret intertwined on their faces. Poseidon moved like a ghost through it all. The god walked tall but kept his eyes downcast. His dirty grey clothing, that hung from his thick and carved body, stood out from the well fitted suits and elegant draped dresses of those around him. He towered above most, like a statue was being pushed through the street. People stepped aside as he approached, not wanting to get too close to the brooding monolith.

The docks were even busier than the rest of the city. Ships were beholden to the tide, not the clock, and so sailors would disembark at any time of the night. From the looks of it several ships had just arrived. The area teemed with drunken men staggering around each other. They clustered into groups, some singing old songs, some talking between deep gulps of rum, or whatever drink they could lay their hands on. Some cut through the crowds like wolves on a hunt, their noses high in the air and eyes focussed as they searched for their first woman in weeks. Poseidon wanted to smile at the scene; at the wrinkled dark jackets of officers that had been unbuttoned and hung off one shoulder and at the small round hats that had been picked off the floor and placed back on heads so many times the dirt was more obvious than the original colour. He wanted to smile at the noise of laughter and cheers, at the smell of salt air, damp wood, liquor, and cheap cologne. At the sight of his people in a glorious cacophony of joyousness.

Poseidon couldn't smile. His mood was too dark for even this sight to bring him joy. Part of him wanted to leave, to curse them all for not feeling the pain he felt, for not being filled with a rage that destroyed any happiness that they came into contact with. He knew he couldn't though. He needed these people if he was going to catch a killer. Whoever was hurting his family had spies and knew everything about them. Poseidon knew that this man wanted an ally in the family to help bring down Zeus, so all he had to do was tell everyone he came into contact with that he was willing to play that role and eventually one of the spies would report back to the killer. He wondered how many of the people he'd let close to him were spies, how many had gloated about how he had screamed at the sight of Demeter's severed head.

As he walked into the crowd he was instantly recognised. Men cheered for him, some clasped his hand, others placed a firm palm on his shoulder. He was swamped by respect and adoration. Every man who knew him offered him a warm welcome and those who didn't act with deference, clearly aware they were in the presence of someone who deserved it. Poseidon managed to plaster a smile across his face, pulling the corners of his lips high. His eyes remained dark and focussed throughout, as every face he saw, every person who treated him like a king, was a potential enemy. The constant raucous conversations and shows of respect slowed Poseidon's journey to a crawl, but finally he reached his shack.

He placed his hand on the rough wood of the door, feeling the dampness and rawness of it. He breathed deeply smelling the ocean trapped in the coarse material. The wood was aged, the constant battering of briny air had changed the colour from a dark brown to a murky grey, with patches of green swirled across it like camouflage. Despite its appearance it was sturdy: men leant and sat against it, they even tripped and stumbled into her sides. Over the years dozens had pissed against her walls. She stood strong, unshaken by man or the elements. Poseidon placed the key in the lock and with a great flourish he pushed the twin doors open and revealed the ragged splendour within. Tables and chairs sat in clumps around the space. The mismatched furniture was as aged as the cabin but a lot less sturdy. Chairs with splayed legs were pressed up against the walls and tables that leaned, like the drunks who put their drinks on them, were scattered about haphazardly. Empty bottles and cigarette butts littered every surface, sending the smells of tobacco and alcohol into the already damp air.

Poseidon had rejected the idea of electricity in his shack and so as he walked around, he lit the paraffin lamps that were fixed to the walls. The soft flickering light barely managed to pass through the murky glass that surrounded each flame, but together they gave the shack an ambient glow. Poseidon pulled what supplies he had left from behind the bar and placed each bottle atop it. He had more than he remembered and eventually the untreated wood of the bar was filled with bottles, the contents hidden by the dark brown glass. With the place illuminated and the alcohol available Poseidon walked to the door and, above the din of the men drinking around him, managed to bellow the invitation for all to come back to the shack and drink for free.

His invitation was met with a thunderous cheers and roars of approval from the crowd on the docks. Now, hours later, the bar was still crammed with every sailor that New York had to offer. Officers sat with their subordinates, merchant sailors brushed shoulders with navy men, honourable seamen laughed with smugglers and crooks. The shack felt like it had before; the life of the ocean beating through it. Poseidon spoke to everyone that entered. He mingled through the crowd, striking up conversations everywhere he could. With each conversation he managed to bring the topic back to his family, he managed to tell everyone how unhappy he was.

Poseidon refused to mince his words or be unclear. He told how he had argued with Zeus. He told them how Zeus was destroying the family through weakness. He screamed that he could do a better job as leader and raged that he was now willing to do anything to see Zeus killed and the family put back on track, even if that meant working with an enemy. As the night drew to a close the shack began to empty. Men stumbled away, swaying as they tried to walk, their eyes unable to focus on the steps ahead of them. Many had a whore on their arm, some playful young thing who twirled her hair and laughed at the incomprehensible idiocy that fell from their mouths.

Poseidon sat in the corner surrounded by a few sailors he had no recollection of meeting before. Each one of them had arrived only a short time ago and so he had taken the opportunity to speak to them. Poseidon swayed in his seat, each word he spoke, followed by a hiccup. He held his breath to try and regain control. Small droplets of spit flew from his mouth, his words slurred but understandable. He gesticulated wildly. The booze in his almost drained bottle swilling around, rising dangerously close to the lip. The shack stank of spilled booze, cigarette smoke, and vomit: all assaulting the back of his throat. The alcohol had flowed more freely tonight than ever before, and every sailor had taken advantage.

The men Poseidon was addressing looked at each other as he spoke and then one leaned towards him. The man was clearly not a sailor, he wore the uniform too well; a real sailor had turned his starched and pressed clothes into a wrinkled mess by the early hours. His black hair was slicked back across his head, the elegant style of a city boy, not the short cut of a military man, or the wild tuffs of a man from the sea. He got close to Poseidon, the warmth of his breath stroking the side of the god's face.

"Our boss is in the next building. The cargo holds to your left. He is willing to meet with you." He said, then leaned back and looked at Poseidon.

He had not expected a reaction to come from the killer so quickly. He didn't reply but stood up, swaying as he rose. Then, slowly, he staggered away from the men, out of his shack and towards the warehouse. He made a mental note to never forget their faces and to kill them in the most brutal fashion possible when he had the chance.

"I was hoping for Ares." The voice greeted him as Poseidon entered the Warehouse. The sound seemed directionless, oozing out of the shadows that consumed the space.

The warehouse was full of crates, arranged in rows around him, like a Labyrinth of darkness. The smell of age and must was everywhere, coating every surface like a veneer.

"I needed his men, but I suppose Zeus' own brother betraying him has a certain pain to it that I like."

Poseidon wanted to roar that he would never betray his family, but he needed to see his opponent first.

"Come out." He slurred. "No games, just talk." Poseidon's words fell from his mouth, like heavy objects he needed to be free of.

There was silence between the two of them, Poseidon hoped that his drunkenness hadn't made the killer reconsider. Then in front of him, from within the darkness a man in black emerged. It was just how Poseidon had remembered him: the posture, the clothes, the mask. Everything was the same in this moment as it had been in the last. Poseidon's fear, anger, and pain consumed him, he felt his body shaking, desperate to act.

"I don't usually do deals with drunks but…"

"You're not doing a deal with me fucker." Poseidon stated, his voice strong and calm despite the tempest within him. He was going to kill this man. He knew it. He could feel his victory looming over him. He stepped forward, straightening himself up, his steps deliberate. "I'm not drunk, and this time I'm ready for you."

"So am I." The killer said.

As he spoke, he reached into his coat and pulled out a blade. Something about it pricked at Poseidon's memories. It wasn't a sword, not even a curved one. In the dimness of the warehouse, it was hard to see the jet-black blade clearly. Poseidon could have sworn it was a scythe. His turbulent emotions allowed him only a second of curiosity before they screamed within him to charge. Poseidon heeded the call and ran towards his opponent. Part of him expected the man to retreat back into the shadows but he ran forward too.

The killer raised the scythe and swung it down at Poseidon. Poseidon raised his arm and a loud clang reverberated through the warehouse. The blade was sharp, it had cut through the material of Poseidon's coat and shirt, but had made contact with the hidden, retractable blade Poseidon now wore at all times. He silently thanked Hephaestus, repeating his vow to avenge his fallen friend. He allowed his instinct to guide him. As the killer focussed on pushing his scythe down the god slammed a fist into his gut. The killer stumbled back, and Poseidon pounced. He lunged at his opponent and grabbed his wrist, careful not to let him gain momentum over the scythe. With the other hand he grabbed the killer's neck and lifted him into the air. He took in a deep breath, fuelling himself with every ounce of air he could, then threw the killer to the ground.

He heard the man grunt as his back collided with the hard floor. The scythe clattered on the stone, bouncing out of the killer's grip. There was a second of shock before the killer made to try and grab his weapon. Poseidon raised his foot and slammed it down to crush the leather clad hand of his opponent. The killer reacted quickly though, pulling his hand away and rolling to the side. Poseidon pursued him, kicking and stomping, forcing his opponent back towards a wall and far away from his weapon. The killer was quick. He managed to evade Poseidon and gain enough distance to get back on his feet.

"I beat the shit out of you with just my fists before and I can do it again." He taunted, pulling his fists up in front of his face.

Poseidon charged again. He knew he couldn't get the first punch in, knew his opponent was too quick and so he left his midriff open. As expected, the killer slammed his fist as hard as he could into Poseidon. The air rushed from his lungs and a web of pain blossomed in his body, but it was worse for his opponent. The spikes on Poseidon's vest had rammed through his shirt, through the killer's gloves, and into knuckles. The spikes severed flesh, tore at tendons, and scraped bone. Poseidon heard the crunch, even as the killer screamed from the agony that ran through him. Poseidon seized his opportunity and sent a fist into the side of his enemy's skull.

The black clad figure fell to the ground, dazed and disorientated. Poseidon smiled down at him, a great grin of triumph. He had hit the man right in the temple, full force. He was lucky to be alive, let alone conscious. Poseidon walked over to his opponent and bent over him, resting a knee on his neck. He applied as much pressure as he could without choking the man to unconsciousness. He placed his other knee on the man's arm, keeping him immobile. The figure beneath him flailed, his black clothing rustling against the rough stone. His hands clawed at Poseidon's knees, one oozing blood over Poseidon's tattered old trench coat.

From under the mask, he heard the man trying to speak. Ragged breaths tinged with meaning sought freedom. Poseidon pulled off the mask and looked down into the face of the man who had destroyed his family. He felt nothing. The man was nothing, he reminded Poseidon of no one and stirred no memories. Poseidon had expected some great moment of revelation but instead all he was looking at was a dying man, some empty shell of a human who had tried to take down his family and destroy an empire. Poseidon sneered at him and placed his palm on the man's forehead. He breathed deeply, almost panting, as he prepared himself to finally end every trouble his family had experienced. With the smallest of gestures, the blade secreted up his sleeve burst forth, the metal sending a spray of blood out as it pushed through the man's eye and into his skull. The cause of all Poseidon's misery died silently. It was only then when he looked up from the corpse he had created, that he realised the scythe was gone.

"You did well." The tailored voice of the killer announced behind him.

Poseidon had no time to react, no time to move. The thick black blade fell with a force Poseidon could not have anticipated and sliced through the side of Poseidon's neck. As the killer pulled the blade free streams of god shot through the air and smattered on the ground. Poseidon felt the life drain from him. He knew he was about to die. In his last moment he sought his revenge, his weak fingers finding the explosive lighter in his pocket. He tried to make it spark, but he couldn't. Desperation filled his dying moments as the killer grabbed his arm and pulled his hand from the pocket, the lighter rattling to the ground. The limp, lifeless body of the great god Poseidon fell on top of his last victim and the shadowed figure of his killer walked away with his blood-soaked blade.

Twenty-two
On The Hunt

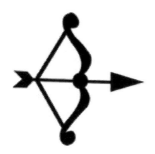

Artemis prowled the halls of the squat, little building. The house had been beautiful from the outside. It stood out like a white, wooden beacon amongst the brick that surrounded, and towered above, it. Everything about the place oozed luxury. The fine fabrics that coated the furniture and hung as light drapes in the darkened window shimmered in the lamplight. The oak panelling that ran along the base of the wall accompanied the bar top so exquisitely that Artemis could have sworn they were taken from the same tree. The carpets were plush, and her boots sank into them as she walked, the vibrant colours changing as fibres were cast into shadow.

The blood that was splattered and smeared on every surface was the only part of the place that didn't scream luxury. Even the bedrooms, where every imaginable debauchery occurred, were decadently decorated with a taste level that Artemis had to appreciate. She examined every room closely, looking for any clue about the killer. She loomed over a king size, four poster bed, the sheets once a swirl of colours now brown, coated in dried blood that had soaked into every last strand of material. The frayed edges stood rigid, the hardened blood holding them in place. Three young women, each with lustrous black skin, scarcely hidden by lace and silk, were strewn across its surface, surrounding a man who seemed bloated beyond what death would do to him. His belly rose above the girls around him, like a rotund mountain casting a shadow over a city. His mottled pink skin was covered in the fuzz of grey hair, now soaked. Each one of them had eyes wide open, lifelessly staring at the canopy above them.

This was the fourth room she had found like this. It was a slaughterhouse now, not a brothel. She moved the bodies looking for clues. Nothing appeared to her. There were hairs, smeared fingerprints, and bodily fluids coating the bed, but they could all be expected at a massacre. There was nothing distinctive about this room, the same as there had not been about any of the other rooms. Artemis sniffed at the air, then pulled her face close to the corpses. She had tied her hair up into a bun to avoid it dipping into blood. The thick curly strands were held loosely atop her head, the occasional hair falling loose from the improvised style. Her deep sniffs confirmed her suspicion. There had been a different group of men in this room to all the others.

Every man smelled different: their sweat, their choice of cologne, their breath. Everyone was traceable. So far, she had recognised several of the scents that filled the whorehouse, turned tomb. The men who did this were mainly men who worked for Casper, goons she had sniffed out years ago when the gang wars had started for Manhattan. They still lingered in her memories. Artemis couldn't help but be frustrated when she smelled the familiar scents of Ares' thugs. Men who worked for the family had helped their enemies. She was sure neither Zeus nor Ares would tolerate betrayal.

She had hoped that a place like this would yield some clues as to the Killer's identity, but she could not smell anything but mediocrity and death. The scent of the Killer she had smelled in the laundry room was something new, something she had never smelled before. That was nothing useful. Artemis left the bedroom and continued down the stairs to the main reception area. More bodies lay scattered around. The walls were riddled with bullet holes, fine white plaster oozing over the lavish patterned wallpaper. The smell of slowly decaying bodies polluted the air around Artemis, her acute senses almost commanding her to gag on the stench.

She found Apollo in a small back room, he had cleared it of bodies except for one. Aphrodite hadn't been moved. She was still sat naked, hands and ankles tied to the chair. The once beautiful goddess looked so small, so pathetic and mortal. Artemis had never been amazed by her in life the way others had. She had never craved her the way every other being seemed to, even if she had appreciated and understood her beauty. It was gone now, hidden behind a death mask of pale skin and bloated features. The scene around her was something unique. Apollo had cleared the room and lit incense to mask the smell of decay, filling the air with the sweet scent of herbs and dried flowers. He had dimmed all the lamps and the room was cast in a hazy golden light that seemed to be seeping out of the very air itself. He had manoeuvred a chair into the room and now sat opposite Aphrodite with his hands on her temples.

Her brother was weeping. Tears fell from his eyes, rolling down the golden skin of his cheeks and falling onto his lap. Small dark pools appeared on the fine silk of his suit. His blonde hair moved in a breeze that did not exist as power radiated out of him. It had been a long time since Artemis had seen Apollo use his powers properly. His psychic links could be powerful, air splitting events. She couldn't help but be impressed. He opened his eyes and they blazed. The bright blue of his irises shone like lanterns and his skin let out a final breath of power before the room returned to the eerie dimness. The god sat in silence, tears still falling, his typically happy face set into a mask of horror and pain.

"Are you OK Apollo?" She asked, the concern making her voice waver. Apollo did not speak, but simply nodded, grasping the hand Artemis had rested on his shoulder, and tilting his head against her weather-worn skin. She could feel his tears running over her. "What did you see?" she asked, keeping her voice soft.

She may have been using her powers too, but her sharp senses didn't give the emotional insight and pain that Apollo's gave him. He would have felt every second of Aphrodite's death as she had, would have felt the fear and even the sensation of the kill.

"This is personal." He replied, taking a deep breath before continuing. "I sensed something from him in Aphrodite's memories. He's not just doing this for money or power. He wants to hurt us." He took a long pause allowing the silence to stretch between the two of them. "He wants revenge."

"Revenge for what?"

"I don't know. Senses through visions and memories are difficult, but this man seriously hates us."

He rose from his seat and turned towards his sister, wiping his tears away and brushing the pained expression from his face. He smiled toward Artemis, his brilliant white teeth on full display. Artemis had to smile back at him. Even in these moments he refused to let his pain become hers. He had always been the same.

"What did you uncover?"

"This was a huge attack. Dozens of goons came in and slaughtered everyone quickly. Most didn't have time to run or hide. I recognised the smells of Casper's men, and even some of Ares' thugs. Clearly, they've decided to do a little moonlighting. This killer has a large gang which means he's rich enough to line a lot of pockets."

Artemis couldn't keep the smile on her face as she spoke, she had hoped to be able to provide more, but even using their magic the two gods failed to find their quarry.

"There wasn't a uniting scent either, they aren't all based in one place."

"Do you think he knows what we can do?" Apollo asked, his smile also faded from his face.

It was clear that this killer knew the family were gods, but the way they were hiding their tracks, the way that they were able to kill them, the cage that had imprisoned Ares, all suggested he knew the details and intricacies of their power. This man knew them in a more intimate way they had thought possible. Athena had floated ideas that they were other Gods, from the other edges of the world, but Artemis had smelled old Gods before, and she wasn't convinced. Something struck Artemis in that moment.

"What killed Aphrodite?" She asked. The question seemed to trigger something in Apollo. He looked up at her, shocked he had not thought to focus on that more.

"Some sort of curved blade."

"Athena said Demeter was killed by a blade, probably curved or hooked, Hephaestus was killed by a blade, and now Aphrodite. Everyone else was gunned down but they had to use a blade on the family. He's found a specific weapon that can kill us."

"Is that even possible?" Apollo asked, his brow creased with worry.

"Clearly it is. I'm going to call Athena from the payphone down the street." She said heading for the door.

Apollo followed, making sure to describe the blade as best he could. With Artemis gone Apollo could only stand in the entryway to the brothel and take in the scene around him. Triggering his magic had been liberating. He had felt the raw power of his godliness flowing through him for the first time since the cataclysm. Now, though, it was becoming too much to bear. Even without focussing, his mind was connecting with the past of the corpses around him. He could hear their cries of anguish and pain. He felt bullets ripping through his skin, the way they had. He felt their fear, the warmth spreading round his crotch as they had wet themselves in terror. He tried to shake his head clear, but death circled him, every emotion and sensation pouring into his mind.

Apollo rushed through the front door, slamming it closed. He took in deep breaths of the cool evening air. The sun was just beginning to set, its golden light had turned a deep orange, and the sky was coated in the last lingering rays of light, darkness beginning to melt across it in the east. Apollo looked to the sky and continued breathing, the small distance from the slaughter inside allowing his mind to clear. He pulled his cigarette case form the silk lining of his suit and lit it quickly, the spluttering flame finally allowing him to suck in a lungful of stress relief. He leaned against the wall, and began sucking in longer drags, taking out his quarter and flipping it into the air. The repetitive task focussed his mind away from the death rattles that sounded behind him.

Within minutes of his freedom a car pulled up beside him, the lights on its roof were off but Apollo could tell what he was looking at. The doors opened and a pair of cops emerged. They walked over to Apollo, their uniforms perfectly pressed and well fitted. Long dark coats with glinting silver buttons covered everything but the bottom of the trousers and the shiny leather of their shoes. They each wore hats, but as they approached, they removed them, tucking them under their arms. Apollo couldn't help but admire them. They didn't cast the same strong figure as him but both of them looked lithe and well groomed, the way a man should look in uniform.

"Good evening officers." Apollo greeted them. He knew that Zeus was losing influence, but the police should know better than to ask any questions that would get them on his bad side. He reached into his pockets and pulled out his wallet, a few notes would be enough to keep these men out of his way.

"Good evening sir. We had reports of an incident here, came to check it out."

"Nothing here to interest you fine gentleman, but here's a thank you for your hard work." He stepped forward, pushing the collection of green bills into their pockets, receiving a smile and a wink from one in return. "My contact information is in there as well if you ever want some company." He mumbled as he moved away. He knew now wasn't the time, but he couldn't help himself: attractive people weren't always on offer or available, not as much as they used to be.

"What have you found out?" One of the cops asked, his eyes focussed on Apollo, his hand not making any effort to reach for the money he had just been handed. Something was off.

"Like I said, it's nothing that concerns you." He replied.

"I still think we should know, sharing information helps us all."

The cop stepped forward as he spoke, his intensity growing. Apollo squinted his eyes at the man, confusion replaced by suspicion. There was a rule that anything that happened at a family business was of no interest to the cops as long as money exchanged hands. Either this cop didn't know the rules, or he wasn't a cop at all. As the reality of the situation dawned on Apollo, Artemis flew into his vision, launching herself at one of the men.

The fight that broke out was over quickly. There were few beings that had ever existed that were as quick and ferocious as Artemis. The men went for her, but she managed to dodge every blow they threw her way. She leaped at them, throwing her fists and feet into every tender part she could get near. They tried to draw their guns, but they had no time. Artemis moved between them, keeping them distracted and busy. Apollo heard bones breaking as the huntress made the two men her prey. Within minutes one was unconscious on the ground and the other was laid on his front, an arm twisted behind his back, Artemis bearing down on him.

"These two smell exactly like men that were in the brothel." She said through gritted teeth as she pulled the man's arm higher, making him squeal in pain. She pushed his face into the filthy ground. "They must work for the killer."

The exchange that followed was brief. The man realised quickly that Artemis would not stop until she knew everything that he knew. Unfortunately, he didn't know much. The killer's identity was a secret even to him and most of the other men who worked for him. They still worked for Casper and everything was done through his businesses. He didn't know what he was planning, other than taking over Manhattan, and had no idea what was happening next. Whoever the killer was he only told the men what they needed to know at the time they needed to know it. The rest of the time they just worked Casper's jobs. The killer left little trace. The only useful information he had was his hideout, an old apartment block on the north of the island.

The apartment building that the two went to was nothing special. It didn't look run down, but Artemis and Apollo could tell it hadn't been looked after in a while. The building was dirty, the grime of city life coated on the outside wall. Every window was closed, the occasional glass pain cracked and not replaced. Even from their vantage point across the street, atop the roof of another building, the two couldn't see inside. The windows were covered with a layer of dirt and thick, heavy curtains. The place was locked down, every possible way in or out secured with hefty metal locks. Apollo extended his senses. There were only a few people inside and three that were stood smoking on the roof. If they could get inside there could be information they needed, or at least clues to other safehouses. The two of them knew they had to get in as soon as possible before the killer found out his fake cops had been compromised.

Taking out the three men on the roof was easy. Apollo and Artemis had spent the early years of their lives as hunters. They were master archers and both of them could shoot the wings off of a fly. On the roof opposite the apartments, they unloaded their masterpieces. The rifles that Hephaestus had made for them were exquisite with long barrels like streaks of ebony in the evening light. The gods pieced them together, clicking and latching everything into place. Their aim was flawless. The first two men died as soon as they heard the bang of the guns, bullets flying through their skulls and sending their bodies lifeless, falling in piles on the ground. The third man tried to run, the sound of guns cracking the air alerting him to the attack. He wasn't fast enough. He fell as he ran, Artemis' second bullet cutting open his neck and killing him in an instant.

The two of them worked together to get onto the roof and slip into the doorway. The men that confronted them died as quickly as those on the roof. Apollo and Artemis worked seamlessly. They moved around each other in an elegant dance of battle, each one of them using their heightened senses to keep them ahead of the enemy. Apollo knew when an attack was coming, and Artemis had the reflexes to plan a way to deal with it. Gun shots sounded through the building, the sharp crack of rifles, the deep booms of pistols, and the cacophonous rattle of tommy gun fire. The gods were unphased, their abilities guiding them from room to room in an effortless motion, no bullet even coming close to meeting their flesh.

It didn't take long for them to clear the building of their enemies. The massacre was useless though, every room either used for sleeping or eating. There were the occasional scrunched up pieces of paper containing instructions, but they were for old jobs that had already gone down. It was clear the killer was well funded: there were no instructions to rob or gain money in anyway. They had started this with enough cash to keep them going. Either Casper had been doing better in Brooklyn than they thought, or the killer was rich in his own right. Unfortunately, that wasn't much of a clue as to his identity. The city was filled with people who were rich beyond imagination. The stock market and massive industries had produced a plethora of men whose wallets would never be big enough, and any of them could have a motive for wanting to take down the family.

"Artemis get over here." Apollo yelled.

Artemis made her way towards him to find her brother stood at a door, turning the knob and pushing against it as hard as he could. The door didn't move. Artemis raised her eyebrow. Every other door that they had come to had been open. Together they pushed against the wood. When that failed, they took running starts, slamming their shoulders against it with all the force they could manage. Eventually the frame gave way and they fell through the opening. Wood flew out in splinters as the metal lock ripped through it. The two gods crashed to the ground together. Darkness consumed them, and as they collided with the floor something sounded around them. The sound was deafening, the thud of something heavy colliding with the hard floor, the sound of metal ringing and reverberating as it made contact.

As their eyes began to adjust to the darkness the twins noticed that around them something had fallen. An intricate lattice of metal encircled them. They were in a cage, trapped in darkness.

Twenty-three
Bargaining

The New York Police Department headquarters loomed over Zeus as he sat next to Athena in the car. The impressive stone façade and rising dome gave the building the feel of some impregnable, yet holy, site, as if it the work going on there was somehow sacred and separate from the rest of the city. Zeus knew otherwise. He had personally greased the palms of half the men in that building and knew that inside the perfectly cleaned exterior was a cesspit of corruption he could exploit. That was how he had kept a tight grip on the city. Now he was worried that grip would be lost forever. He had had to resort to only bribing the most senior officers. The rest of the beat cops were walking around without his money and that had been causing him trouble. Information wasn't flowing to him as freely as it had been before, and he needed it now more than ever. It was time to squeeze Shatterny for all he knew.

He stepped out of the car, his grey pinstripe suit pulling tight against him as he moved, the buttoned jacket holding tight to his broad shoulders and thick arms. He had made an effort to look his best, deciding that he would be every bit the businessman he claimed to be. He knew he couldn't rely on just intimidation with Shatterny. The old walrus of a man had taken steps to protect himself and his family ever since Zeus started losing control of the city. His daughter was no longer under Zeus' watch and he couldn't afford to bribe the cops who kept Shatterny safe. The chief had even started arresting cops who were still taking bribes. These were all things Zeus would have to rectify when he started to reclaim his territory.

Casper's booze had been distributed to all of Zeus' clubs. He now knew the man had a role in killing his family, after Artemis' call to Athena, and had used it to leverage getting Harlem back, but it didn't matter. The money generated by Casper's act of arrogance would be used to pay for his funeral. For now, he needed to remain focussed on the task at hand.

"Are you ready?" Athena asked coming beside him, her brown suit and trilby looking drab and lifeless next to the silver of his.

Zeus looked like a rolling thunder cloud, illuminated by the power of nature, whereas Athena looked like the earth itself: strong and immovable, but not flashy or impressive.

"I'm always ready Athena." He replied, walking forward and climbing the stone steps in a few strides.

He pushed the glass doors open and marched across the marble floor. Desk officers looked up from their stacks of paperwork and buzzing phones to see Zeus striding before them. None of them attempted to intercept the gangster. They simply sat, mouths agape, staring at the man who so openly defied their laws. Zeus kept his eyes forward, burning like gas lamps in his skull. His jaw was firm, everything about him screaming strength and determination. He pushed through another door and made his way through the winding corridors and staircases that lead up to the chief's office.

Shatterny was stood outside an oak door, his moustache bristling with unconcealed fury, the thick strands of brown hair standing on end. His skin was beet red, all blood diverted to his flesh to show the world the extent of his rage. Zeus was not impressed. Shatterny would have seemed like a mildly perturbed child compared to the rage filled monsters the Hellenic pantheon could become when provoked. Zeus kept walking with purpose, Athena to his side keeping pace with long, elegant strides. The two of them made an imposing force, a wall that most men would not be able to penetrate.

"Shatterny, you've been ignoring my calls. I thought I'd pay you a visit."

"Leave my building now, or I will have you arrested." Shatterny seethed, his teeth grinding as he spoke.

"No, you won't. Let's sit down and see if we can't come to some arrangement." Zeus replied, stepping forward and reaching out a hand. He may have been capable of great bouts of rage, but he was equally capable of cunning. He knew Shatterny would just meet anger with anger: the man's pride and slavish devotion to law and order would see to that. He just needed some tenderness. Shatterny didn't respond, he simply opened his door and gestured for the gods to follow him.

The office was sparse, as if it had been decorated by a spartan bureaucrat with a fetish for dark wood. There was nothing but four walls of oak panelling and mahogany desk with chairs. The lights illuminated the naked space, casting scant shadows across the crimson carpet. Shatterny still didn't speak as he moved to his chair and sat down. Zeus and Athena lowered themselves to sit opposite him and let the silence linger. Zeus was in no rush to make Shatterny talk, he wanted to make the old man feel uncomfortable, and nothing made him feel that way more than dealing with criminals.

"So, what do you want from me, Zeus. What more can you take from me?"

"You've been causing me trouble recently Shatterny. My informants have found themselves in cells, my friends in the NYPD are gone or silent. I feel like you've been taking liberties with my business."

"I've arrested criminals and removed corrupt cops. It's my job."

"We had a deal Shatterny, remember we made it in your kitchen when that lovely daughter of yours was getting a midnight snack." Zeus leaned forward as he spoke, letting his face twitch with anger as he reminded Shatterny of how far he could be pushed.

"I know, but you can't hold up your side of the deal anymore, and there's only so much I can do."

"Do about what?" Athena asked. She was always the one to ask more, to find out everything. It was why Zeus brought her with him when he met tricky customers like Shatterny or the other power players in New York. "There's not another rival is there?"

"Casper's got to some men, they're taking his cash to arrest your guys and squeal on corrupt cops." Shatterny leaned back in his chair. "I would put a stop to it, but every cop I cross is another one who will happily shoot me."

"I'll happily shoot you." Zeus snarled.

"At this point I might welcome it." He sighed and closed his eyes, rubbing the bridge of his bulbous nose with his forefinger and thumb. "You two have torn up my city in this war. Fire bombs in Harlem, shoot outs everywhere. Fires raging in every building. I've dealt with gang war before, but this is too much. I'm staying out of it and when I have dirt on anyone, I'm personally making the arrest and walking the paperwork to the mayor and DA. I'm done being a pawn in your games."

"Like fuck you are Shatterny. I want the name of every cop on Casper's payroll." Zeus demanded, thumping his hand against the desk.

"You think I know that?" Shatterny huffed in response. "The chance is every cop who takes cash from you takes cash from Casper too, and any other alley rat with an eye on your clubs." Shatterny looked broken as he spoke, a life dedicated to law and order falling apart like wet tissue paper before him, the gangs of New York turning his vision of a safe and decent city to nothingness.

"If that's true then you have to help me."

"I'm not getting involved until I have what I need to see you rot in jail."

"Will you agree to just stay out of my way? No more arrests and no more raids? If I lose any more guys this turf war will get even worse. The guy we're both dealing with won't stop with me and my family. He'll kill everyone who helped us and right now that includes you."

The two men stared at each other. The determination both of them had to win was palpable between them. Zeus admired the man to a degree. He liked strong people who stood up when needed, but Shatterny and his entire police force were proving to be an obstacle. The urge to summon a storm and render the building to charcoal was more than he could bear. The smouldering ash would smell better than the constant odour of wood polish he was forced to endure in this office.

"Fine, you guys have left plenty of death around my city to keep us busy anyway. End this war soon Zeus, I won't have this city destroyed because of your greed." Shatterny conceded, his voice heavy. Zeus didn't respond, gesturing to Athena that they could leave.

"I need to know one thing before we leave." Athena said, disrupting the men from their staring competition. "How much has Casper got to the others? Are we up against the DA and feds as well?" There was no response at first, Shatterny simple thought in silence, his face giving nothing away.

"They're hedging their bets. No one knows how this will end up. You beat Casper once, but this guy he's working with is unknown. They're not going to help either of you. They're going to watch you tear each other apart and then whoever is left in the blood pool will be the new paymaster." He replied, every word thoughtful and commanding. A statement of facts made without bias. "I wouldn't bother trying to talk to them either if that's the plan. Whomever is after your turf is paying well and scaring the shit out of them. If I were you, I'd leave quickly. Get out of the liquor game Zeus. It's bad for your health."

Shatterny clearly didn't care who won this war and he wasn't going to step in to help out the family. Zeus did his best not to show his anger. He had lined the pockets of everyone in this city in order to buy their loyalty, but all he had was pathetic men who would tun on him for a dime more. Without a word he rose from his chair and stormed from the office and then out of the building.

"I told you this was a waste of time." He bellowed at Athena as she joined him in the street. His rage could not hide within him anymore. It was a caged animal that needed to be released.

"It wasn't" Athena replied calmly, careful not to let Zeus' anger infect her.

"What do you mean? We gained nothing."

"We've got impartiality. We needed them when we didn't know who we were dealing with but now we know it's Casper that's not important. We know where he's based, how many enforcers he's got, and that we can kick his ass. The best thing the authorities can do is get out of our way and let us win." She walked toward Zeus smiling and placed a hand on his shoulder. Sometimes he forgot she was a warrior, born to fight and survive, and win. He let her hope infect him, her determination and eagerness for battle. In that moment Zeus felt the tide of this petty street brawl turn.

"We gave him Harlem, gave him cash, gave him access to Aphrodite. Let's make that old fucker pay!"

The glass doors to the precinct burst open and streams of men in dark uniforms poured down the steps. The sound of ringing phones and commotion followed them, flowing into the silent darkness of the street. Every man ran towards their cars. Engines revved and sirens blared as they made ready to leave. Tires squealed as they pulled away, the cops inside chattering loudly and signalling the directions to their partners. None of them even looked at Zeus, each one too caught up in the mania of whatever had happened inside.

Shatterny emerged bellowing instructions towards his men.

"The ambulances are on their way. They take priority. Your job is to keep them safe, let them help."

"Shatterny, what's ging on?" Zeus asked, raising his voice above the commotion that enclosed him.

"This is your fault you bastard." He shouted in response. "If anyone dies it's on your head!"

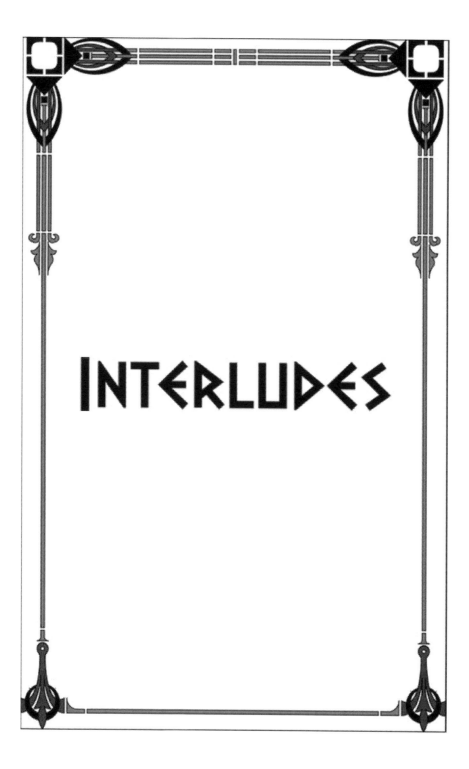

INTERLUDES

Interlude 5

Mount Olympus, Greece, 347 AD

T he sky had never looked so dark to Zeus. The nights, usually a great painting of silver stars on the black canvas of the sky, had vanished behind a thunderous rolling of heavy clouds. No light penetrated through the thick layer, and on his mountain, Zeus looked down at a world slowly dying.

For the past year the number of gods falling prey to his new enemy had only increased. It had started with the nymphs and beasts being struck down, but now the children of Olympians and Titans fell foul to the wrath of the god who sought to control the world. Zeus had refused to tell anyone about Jophiel, his pride making a mockery of his common sense. He was the king of Olympus, he had fought more than one god in his time, and he had always been the victor. He would not need the rest of his family to deal with this upstart.

That had been how he had thought before, his arrogance pushing him forward, slowly witling away at the pantheon that strode the lands of Greece. He stood alone, his hand running through the long black locks of his hair. Sweat dripped from his forehead, the exhaustion of another failed day pressing against him. His shoulders sank and his face fell into an expression of unrestrained despair. He felt his failure taunting him, swirling around him like a dark mist, daring him to do worse, daring him to be weaker. Finally, he called out the name he had hoped never to say again.

"You called?" Jophiel asked from behind Zeus. His voice carrying like a plucked lyre on the air. The silver illumination of his skin cast long beams of light against Zeus, elongating his shadow against the stone ground of the mountain top. Zeus turned and looked at the angel, trying as hard as he could not to give away his desperation.

"I'm ready to accept your deal." Zeus declared, his voice booming, echoing off the clouds around him. "Leave my pantheon alone and we will disappear."

Jophiel didn't reply immediately, the smooth skin of his face making no expression. "That was the old deal Zeus. It's not going to work for us."

"You came to me with that deal." Zeus snarled in response to the angel's arrogance.

"And I told you every day you ignore it, it gets less generous."

"I should turn you to ash."

"If I'm ash then there's no deal at all, and your petty little gods get mutilated for all time."

"What do you want?" Zeus asked, his defeat and rage pulling him in half. He held himself firm, determined to do all he could to protect the beings of Greece."

"Here's the deal Zeus: you and I will open the doorways to the underworld, every one in your pantheon will be sucked into the pitiful pit you call an afterlife, trapped for eternity, then you will leave Greece and never give me cause to talk to you again." Jophiel walked forward as he spoke, each word punctuated with a step, or a sneer. Zeus could almost reach out and grab the fucker. He could feel his limbs twitching with the desire to grab the curls of gold hair and rip the angel's head off.

"You would have me banish everyone I've ever known, loved, and fought, to the underworld, then walk the earth alone for eternity?" Zeus asked, his body trembling.

"No of course not, I will let you keep Olympus safe, and the little inbred troupe that live up here with you, but the rest go to Tartarus, as a thanks for my generosity."

"No"

"Then no deal, and there won't be another. You reject this and I will make you watch as I flay each of your children alive and turn their organs into hummus." Jophiel spat, his eyes sparkling with a sickening glee Zeus had barely seen in his immortal life. In that moment he knew he could not win. He had known the angels allied against him were powerful, that the god seeking to take his lands was determined, but he had never imagined how much they enjoyed the work they were doing.

"Fine." Zeus replied, his defeat finally on display for all to see.

That night as the Zeus called the Olympians to his throne, he enjoined his power to Jophiel, and over the rocks, mountains, beaches, coves, grasslands, forests, and fields of Greece a fire burned. No mortal eye would ever catch a glimpse of the torrent of heat and pain that scorched the divine. No mortal ear heard the wailing, as desperate cries from beings of great power and history, radiated up the steep slopes of Olympus. From on high the twelve members of the Olympian family watched in horror as Tartarus consumed the Hellenistic world and a cataclysm of wind, flame, and rolling earth changed them forever.

Interlude 6

London, United Kingdom, 1897

Mary giggled as Zeus pulled her quietly into the small hospital chapel. The silence of the room soothed the both of them, allowing them to embrace, allowing them to feel the joy of each other. For a year they had managed to meet in secret, their rare moments together filling Zeus' heart with a sense of joy and wonder he had not felt in years.

Mary was a vision to him, her crooked teeth and uneven eyes gave him palpitations. The way she snorted when she laughed or twitched when the quiet became too much for her gave his soul reason to exist again. He kissed her passionately, running his hands down the curvature of her back. They had never had sex, their secret moments consumed by conversation, by kisses that lasted for eternities, and by tears of joy at having found another lost and broken soul to share their time with.

Zeus had told the young woman everything. She had been his catharsis. She had heard every word and believed him, singing his praises and worshipping him as the god he was. Every word he spoke to her she absorbed. She listened and cared about every detail of his life; the life he had before his deal with Jophiel. She did not judge him, or hate him for the choices he had made, instead she only loved him more, fawning with glee over his imperfections.

Today something felt different; there was an urgency to her kisses, a desperation in the way she held him close. Where she had once gently caressed him, she clawed at him. Their clothes were ripped away, and on the floor of the chapel he entered her. She moaned into his ear, her thighs rising and stroking at his sides. He felt an ecstasy like nothing he had felt before; a sensation that swam through every part of him, making his skin tingle. As their love making ended, he kissed her and rolled beside her, panting. His long streaks of grey and black hair stuck to his sweat coated skin. He turned to look at his love, smiling at the sight of her beaming, wet face. Before he could speak or touch her again a voice sounded from outside the door.

"Zeus, where are you? Get here now." The voice commanded. One of the men charged to keep the hospital safe must have noticed he'd slipped away from the dining hall.

"Wait here dearest." He whispered to Mary, pulling his clothes back on and planting a soft kiss on her forehead.

"Must you leave?" She begged in hushed tones.

"Don't worry my dear. I'll never leave for long. You are mine forever." With his final words he slipped out of the chapel to face the guard.

"What were you doing int there without the chaplain?"

"Just prayer." Zeus lied, averting his gaze. Years of subservience to these men had given him the habits of a dog, desperate to avoid the punishment that came in a syringe.

"You have a visitor." The guard informed, leading Zeus away to the main foyer of the building. Light spilled through the hospital windows, illuminating the broad staircase that ran from the entrance to the upper floors. Dark wood absorbed every ray it could, creating streaks of blackness against the cold white tiles. Hera and Athena stood waiting for him, starched dresses hugging tight to the corsets that crushed their waist.

"What are you doing here?" Zeus asked, his hands reflectively moving to cover his unfaithful cock. "It's been so long since I've seen you."

"I know," Hera replied stepping forward, her hand reaching up to his cheek, "but, they've agreed to let you go. As long as we leave London, but I was going to do that anyway."

"I can't go." Zeus snapped in response. "I'm sick. I need help." All he could think of was Mary, the small ray of light illuminating the path ahead.

"Don't be silly Zeus, you need to come with me. We need you." She looked up at him, eyes wide and imploring. "Athena has done what she can, but you're the one who has kept us together. Please, your family can't survive without you."

Conflict raced within the god. His eyes twitching as the uncertainty took over. Finally, he made his decision, and taking Hera's hand he walked out to the fresh air and sunlight, leaving behind the promises he had made.

PART IV

Twenty-four

Poison

The night was in full swing. Club Olympus had never been so full. People filled every lamp lit and shadowed space, their faces and fine clothes softly illuminated by lights that sat on the tables and hung from the walls. The air was full of smoke and music, both swirling around the patrons, blending with the alcohol in their veins, making them lightheaded and giddy. The low rumble of chatter, the constant murmur of excited conversations, buzzed between them all. The words mingled with the rhythmic jazz music to create a bubble of sound that enclosed and encased everyone.

Dionysus lent behind the bar, his slender frame standing in stark contrast to the curvaceousness that surrounded him. For the first night in weeks the family had enough alcohol to sell without restraint or worry. Casper had really come through for them. The women behind the bar were some of the most gorgeous that Dionysus had ever employed. Each one of them had large eyes that glistened and twinkled with mischief. They had each mastered a wry smile that emphasised their plump lips and knew how to lean forward just enough to show off the soft, supple skin of their breasts without flashing. They did their jobs well, enticing men to the bar. Dionysus couldn't hear what the patrons were saying but he heard the soft giggles of response, noticed the way their hands, with long, elegant fingers caressed the upper arms of the men trying to gain their attention. Their fashionable clothes well in a waterfall of shimmering beads over them, their curled hair held up tight.

No glass was left empty: liquids, both crystal clear and rich amber, flowed as if pouring from some eternal spring. Bottles emerged miraculously from storerooms and behind the bar to replenish every patron who had drained their drink. The glasses clinked together as small groups gave cheers to their companions. The moonshine sloshed out in great, thick droplets onto the table as men cast their arms around one another to praise their friends. Women were less boisterous, their martini glasses held high to thin faces, smiling coyly as they drank, their hands running over the pearls that decorated their necks and chests. They let out small laughs at comments from their friends, casting seductive glances to the men around them.

Dionysus couldn't help but admire the clothing that covered every man and woman in the bar. The family owned every speakeasy in the city and so every person who lived in Manhattan had to drink with them. Club Olympus was unique. It had never been some drinking hole hidden behind a false wall. Olympus was for the elite; it was a member only club of refinement and decadence. There was not a poor person in its walls. The men and women that sat in this club were the wealthy and privileged of the city; the financiers, businessmen, and politicians who kept the city running. Every one of them wore clothes from the finest designers and tailors. Every man was impeccably dressed in tailored suits. Even with their ties loosened and jackets thrown carelessly over chair backs they looked stylish. The women all wore loose fitting dresses - silk, velvet, and cotton cascading over their bodies. Their hair was perfectly styled into waves, like seas of blonde, brunette, and auburn in the room. Some wore small bonnets, but most embraced the fashion for diamond head bands with a flurry of feathers. Every woman looked like she was ready to stand and perform.

Dionysus stood enamoured: fashion was the purest expression of indulgence that humans had developed since they first made alcohol. Over the centuries he had watched humans go from clothing themselves in sheets and furs to designing elaborate costumes and outfits that were more impressive than any sculpture or artwork. He had worn powdered wigs in France, ruffs in England, and silk robes in China. New York had a different flare than anywhere he had been before. Looking wealthy meant fine fabrics and jewels. Size wasn't important, it was the name on the label and the fit on the body. Dionysus had his suits hand tailored, each one bold and almost skin-tight. He looked down at his emerald waistcoat and trousers on top of his aubergine shirt. A matching jacket hung in the back room. Every button was hand sewn and was made of precious metal with a jewel set into it. Dionysus stood out.

He moved around the bar, sauntering from table to table. Everyone wanted to talk to the barman. Compliments about his alcohol poured from every mouth. They marvelled at the decadent tastes, the sweet scents, the smoothness. Every drop that was drank in Olympus was like a moment of unparalleled bliss, a second in heaven. Every gulp sent heads racing and hearts beating. One patron delighted that he could hear the angels singing to him as he drank. Dionysus smiled at every compliment he had received, happy to let the appreciation wash over him. It had been too long since he had served his own special blend.

Everything about alcohol was perfect in Dionysus' mind, not just the effect it had on people but its taste and texture. He had spent his immortal life working to improve it, and with every bottle he worked on he had managed to get a little better. Tonight, Club Olympus had played home to his very own blends and recipes. Casper's supply had been fine but tonight was the family's turning point, their moment to emerge from the shadows. It demanded the best. He had spent a day toying with every bottle they had received. It was only an hour ago he had been bent over a large tin tub, his sleeves rolled up to his elbows, his finger dancing on the surface of the alcohol, infusing it with light and energy, with sensation and emotion.

Magic was forbidden, but ever since his family had begun dying the rules had seemed meaningless, especially after Demeter's death. He still struggled to think of his aunt without the image of her head intruding into his mind. He refused to focus on that tonight, though. He had a goal to achieve and the skills to achieve it. He wasn't going to let Zeus' rules stop him, he knew the others weren't. He had strengthened the alcohol whilst reducing the bitterness, pulling out the sweet flavours which had been hidden within it. In those moments he had been the master he had once been on Olympus.

As the night progressed the merriment continued. There was no hostility in Club Olympus; no turf wars or battles to fight. The band stayed on the small stage through the night. The double bass was plucked, the trombones blown, the drums gently rasped, beating out the jazz rhythm that made leather clad feet tap themselves against the polished wood floor. Political and social enemies spoke like old friends, their differences and animosities reserved for the world above. In Olympus there were no newspapers to spread venom, no public forums to argue, no intrigue or deception. Olympus was home to fine women, fine music, and fine alcohol. The bar ran like clockwork, the alcohol flowing like an unstoppable force, with no delay and no intrusion. Extra security was at the entrance, on lookout and even scattered around the room. Men pulled women close as they danced, their beaded dresses swirling in a frenzy of colour as they circled their dance partners. Smiles were plastered on every face, genuine joy filling them. The music urged everyone into a manic expression of happiness that no other bar could create.

Dionysus had been warned by Ares and Athena that there may be some form of attack, but nothing seemed to be coming for them. The room rose in applause as the young woman who had been singing took her final bow and left the stage. Her voice had been perfection. An effortless stream of notes had come from her, filling the room with the sounds of a happy soul. Once she had left and the music continued with no voice, the chatter soon rose again. As the voices blended together, the shrill sound of the phone blared from the back room.

"Hello." Dionysus answered as he picked up the receiver, eager to end the shrill noise cutting through the electric atmosphere of his club.

"Dionysus, you need to come here quick, something's not right" The voice shouted. Dionysus recognised it immediately. Phillip was one of his barmen, his voice, usually weak, rang like a high-pitched wail down the phone line, the panic obvious. He had been the barman of the Pantheon, a small speakeasy a few blocks away, for a year now. The man was capable and wouldn't have called unless he had to.

"What's happening?"

"It's the drinkers, they're sick, every one of them. I don't know what it is but they're not well."

Dionysus didn't ask any more questions. He knew he could get there quickly and find out what was happening. Morning was drawing close, and Olympus had reached the point where the crowd would slowly begin to melt into the concrete jungle around the club. He slammed the receiver down and pulled on his jacket with a flourish, the velvet moving around his body in a great wave. The phone rang again.

"I'm on my way Phillip."

"It's Jeremy, you need to get here now, everyone's really sick."

Dionysus' eyes widened in shock. He couldn't believe it. How could two different places be having the same problem. He hurriedly explained the call he'd just had and then hung up. He ran his hands over his slicked back hair, his fingers digging into the base of his skull. He breathed deeply, focussing himself. He needed to decide what to do, and he was not the best god to take control of a crisis. The Pantheon was closest. It made sense to go there first. The air was pierced once more by the phone.

Dionysius began to lose count of the number of calls he received from his clubs. The story was the same from every one of them. Patrons were ill, even dying. Every club that the family owned was full of people throwing their guts up all over the floors.

Dionysus didn't know what to do but he had to see for himself. He tried to contact Zeus and Athena, but there had been no answer on the phones. He needed guidance but there was no one to give it to him. The bars had been left in his hands, the more responsible members of the family attending to other business. He rushed out into the cool air of the early morning. The sun hid under the horizon, the soft rays of light it threw into the darkened sky hinting at its approach. The car ride to the nearest club was quick. The driver sped through the streets as fast as he could, the tires squealing against the road as he turned onto the small street the club was on. The street was full. Police cars and ambulances crowded the main doorways. Stretchers carrying limp and pale bodies flowed out of the door, men with grim looks over their faces carrying each end.

There was no obstacle to the god entering the building. Every person present knew he was one of the owners and stepped aside as he walked forward. He wasn't a towering behemoth like Ares, but he was a member of the most powerful and dangerous family in the city, for now. The scene inside the club was ghastlier than outside. Bodies littered the floor, each one with a head resting in a thick, sticky pool of blood-streaked vomit. Hollow, gaunt faces looked out in every direction, lips, dried and chapped, unmoving. The air was rancid, the stench of stomach acid and bile putrefying. Dionysus almost gagged, holding his hand to his mouth as the stench caused him to wretch violently. He pulled his coat over his nose and tried to control his breathing. His lungs and stomach ached, but he forced himself to stand his ground.

He found the bar staff in the back room, guarded by the police. The family could get out of any scrape, but a mass death scene would not be easily explained, and the police had to do something. He felt bad for the small group, each one of them wore a look of shock and horror on their face, the trauma of what they witnessed plain to see. He pulled a chair from the corner and sat with them.

"I need to know what happened here." He asked, speaking as softly and calmly as he could manage, looking at each of them to give him some answer or explanation. It took some time for any of them to gather themselves together enough to speak.

"It seemed like a normal night. Lots of drinking and smoking. A couple of fights broke out but nothing big."

Philip was an old guy, a veteran of the New York bars before prohibition. He wore a white shirt and suspenders, his hair slicked back revealing a face of age lines and wrinkles. His eyes were dull, focussed on the floor as he spoke, as if he were afraid to look up.

"Then about an hour ago people started getting sick, they couldn't control themselves. Then it was everyone. It all happened so fast." The man's voice quivered as he spoke. Dionysus placed a hand on his and nodded his appreciation.

He spent the next hour travelling the city. Every bar and club he arrived at had the same scene unfolding and the same story to tell. Dionysus felt lost. He hadn't heard from the rest of the family and he had no idea what could have happened. The answer seemed obvious to him though. There was only one thing new at all the clubs together, only one thing every person had had: the alcohol that the clubs had been serving. The booze must have been poisoned. Dionysus chastised himself for not sensing it when he had played with Olympus' stock. His senses were dulled from years of inactivity.

The final club that he needed to visit was at the top of Manhattan, a small bar close to the edge of Harlem. It was the one furthest from any other, a club frequented only by the poorest and most desperate, a back room of a rundown shop that let men drink for cheap as long as they could put up with silence and filth. Most desperate men could. The outside of the bar was empty. No ambulances or police surrounded the place. Dionysus wasn't surprised. The bar was never that full and the people who did drink here wouldn't matter to the police or be able to pay for medicine. That was the curse of black neighbourhoods in this city. The inside of the bar was as grim as the outside. A small amount of light barely penetrated the gloom, and the silent air was filled with dust and smoke. The scent of vomit was absent though, only stale alcohol intruding on Dionysus' senses.

He walked through the empty bar, the only sound around him the slap of his soles on the floor. He was sure the barman here had called to say there was a problem, but the place seemed more abandoned than sickly. Something sounded behind him. The thud of the door and the click of a lock reverberated through the small, drab space. Dionysus turned and saw the shadowed figure stood before him. There was no face, but a black mask staring straight towards him. Dionysus froze, fear gripping him, sending his heart racing: the sound of it pounded in his ears. He didn't know what to do. This man had killed Poseidon, a great warrior, had killed Hephaestus, with all his strength, and outsmarted Athena by hiding from her sight. He knew he didn't stand a chance, but as the imposing figure moved towards him, he did not accept death.

Dionysus ran to the end of the room and launched himself over the bar. The wood creaked as he vaulted it, but it held strong. He hunkered down, thinking, the sound of the killer's footsteps drawing closer. There was nothing around him but alcohol, not even a gun or baseball bat hidden by the bartender. Then it dawned on him: he was surrounded by the thing he knew best, the substance he had control over. He grabbed a bottle of liquor and pulled the top off. Closing his eyes, he placed his hand over the lip. It took all his willpower to focus on the process rather than the sound of his impending doom, but he knew it was his only chance of survival. Dionysus' power flowed from him into the alcohol, rearranging the structure of the chemicals within it.

He rose from the bar and, only a few feet from his attacker, launched the brown glass container towards him. The killer raised his arm, hoping to render the glass and alcohol useless. As the bottle erupted into shards, the liquid immediately soaked through the killer's sleeve making the fabric hiss and smoke, melting it away to reveal flesh which started to scald and burn instantaneously. The killer let out a blood curdling screech beneath his mask and stared at his arm. With a gloved hand he tried to wipe away the burning liquid that coated him. In ancient times rearranging the structure of a substance was called alchemy, but to Dionysus it was a fundamental aspect of himself, a power he cherished and had perfected millennia ago. Even though it was hard and draining he knew he could do this. He quickly grabbed another bottle and used his magic again. He threw it towards the killer but this time the black clad figure slid out of the way and rushed behind a table, taking shelter.

Dionysus smiled at himself. As long as he had bottles of alcohol, he could fend off the killer and possibly even escape. He just had to keep him pinned down long enough to reach the door and unlock it, or burn the bastard so badly he couldn't even try and attack him. Dionysus repeated the process over and over, despite how tired it was beginning to make him: pulling bottles from under the bar, changing the composition of the liquid and then launching the chemical weapons at the killer's position. There appeared to be no movement from the small table the man had taken shelter behind.

"I hate that you've made me do this." The killer sneered from his hiding place.

Bullets filled the air. Metal flew in an unending maelstrom from the killer's position towards the bar and Dionysus. Glass smashed all around him sending out a spray of liquor. Bullets ripped through the bar, wood chips flying with abandon as everything behind it turned to ribbons. Dionysus' own flesh wasn't safe, his skin splitting and pouring blood. The killer rose, a tommy gun held towards the bar. Dionysus couldn't think, his body was full of agony and exhaustion. Every glass shard, wooden splinter, and metal bullet felt like it had struck him. He fell to the ground, the savage storm of debris flying above his head, the floor soaked with blood and alcohol. Suddenly the killer had rounded the bar, his gun no longer firing, a thin streak of smoke rising from the tip of the barrel. He stalked forward, dropping the weapon, and pulling out a curved blade from within his long black coat. Dionysus closed his eyes, not wanting to see the moment of his own death.

Twenty-five
The Rules

The warm air of the summer night caressed Zeus' skin. The soft breeze that gently drifted through the city stroked against him, sending small tingles through his body. The grey hair that coated his bare torso quivered like reeds in a stream. His skin was taut and tanned, stretched across his chest and broad shoulders. He was starting to show signs of his age though, his skin not as flawless as it had one been, the occasional sag and liver spot beginning to emerge. The king of the gods was still an impressive specimen. He leaned on the edge of his balcony, the rough stone pressing against his arms, and sucked in a long breath, devouring the scents of the city. He allowed the moment to consume him, letting the smell and the sounds wash over him, clearing away his thoughts. He heard the rumble of cars, the sound of people, the soft melody of music dancing through it all.

A tear fell from his eye, a solitary droplet of pain cascading down and dropping from his skin, leaving nothing but a dark patch of stone in its wake. The effort of trying to keep his family together, and the knowledge that he was failing, was becoming too much of the ancient king to bare. In one night, he had lost so much: his bars had been ruined, his son had been killed, and the twins were missing. He had been to more funerals than he could bare, each one taking a piece of him and burying it in the ground with his family.

The strain pressed against him, his anguish at his own failure choking him. He tried to push it from his mind, but the guilt was all consuming. He looked down at the collection of coins he had amassed over the past weeks. Each one left at a raided or burned bar, at a decimated brothel, or on the eyes of a dead god. The killer had been leaving his mark everywhere, taunting Zeus with his presence. The man wanted Zeus to recognise his handiwork and to be scared. The king felt trapped, constantly backing away, and hiding from this new enemy. Nothing he did was enough, nothing was keeping his family safe.

He clenched his jaw tight, determined not to give into his sorrow anymore. He had survived so much more than this. He had stood above the cataclysm as his world and culture had died, he had survived the horror of a London Asylum, and he would survive this petty turf war. He was the king of the gods and if he fell apart now his family would be left with nothing. He pushed himself upright on the stone, hoping that the sheer act of doing so would force his sense of hopelessness to just fall away from him. His hands gripped the railing of the balcony. He kept focussed on survival, his hands clenching ever tighter. He cast his eyes forward, the deep blue blazing with intense fire in the light of the city. As he steeled himself, the stone cracked, and his hands clenched into fists, sending chips and dust around them.

Zeus looked down at the accidental destruction, the soft yellow of dust coating his hands. He let out an exasperated sigh, annoyed with himself for losing control yet again. Ever since the cataclysm he had managed to follow his own rules, never giving into his powers, and keeping his family safe. Now he was no good at either. He wiped his hand against the dark fabric of his trousers, the stone debris smearing on them, and then downed the last of his gin. Turning to go back into his apartment he stopped still at the sight of a man in the doorway.

The man smiled, his pale skin dimpling as his lips rose. His eyes were like emeralds shining in the night, bursts of green in the darkness around him. He wore a tailored suit in white, every inch of it pristine, no mark or scuff to be seen. His blonde hair was effortlessly styled, falling in platinum curls around his angular face. Zeus stood motionless, staring at the man before him, enraptured by his presence and frozen in a terror he had not felt in millennia.

"Nice to see you again Zeus." The man said walking forward, extending his hand. Zeus gulped down his fear and walked as calmly as he could manage towards him. Their hands touched and Zeus could feel the man's power buzzing on the edge of his senses, feel it radiating from his skin.

"It is not nice to see you again Jophiel. I hoped it would never happen."

Zeus snapped his hand back from the angel's grasp, his eyes boring into his, refusing to show his fear, refusing to break his stare.

"Why are you here?"

Jophiel smiled again, breaking Zeus' gaze. Zeus had no illusion that he had managed to intimidate the angel, but it felt good to not be the first to walk away. Jophiel sauntered across the balcony, making his way to a set of chairs that Zeus used for entertaining. He lowered himself into one, careful to pull his trousers just right to stop the fabric wrinkling. He held out his hand and in an instant a glass of wine appeared in his grip. The crisp liquid smeared itself along the inside of the glass as the angel moved it in his hand, before finally bringing it to his lips. He sipped, eyes closing briefly as he savoured the flavour.

"We had a deal Zeus."

"I've kept to that deal." Zeus barked at the angel, turning to face him, as if daring him to provoke him further.

"A sudden, unexplained lightning storm a short time ago would beg to differ." Jophiel didn't raise his voice as he spoke, keeping himself calm and stern as if talking to a toddler on the edge of a tantrum. Zeus held back his anger, walking towards Jophiel and sitting opposite him, his body looking bulky compared to the trim, lithe figure of the angel.

"Demeter died." Zeus managed to say, breaking the silence that had grown between the two of them. He looked down, careful to hide his pain from the enemy. "I was angry someone had managed to kill her. My power slipped out, but that's it."

"It's not." The angel retorted, staring at Zeus, his eyes flashing with a brief hint of anger. "Do you think I'd be wasting my time here if the only problem was you losing your temper."

Zeus looked up at him as he spoke, unable to hide the look of confusion on his face.

"Practically every other member of your family has been using ancient magic lately, for everything. I'm surprised they haven't summoned storms just to blow the paper closer to the doorstep."

"I don't believe you." Zeus fell back into his seat, his thick fingers pressing against his temples, the stress of the night pounding in his brain. "My family know the rules and have followed them for centuries. They wouldn't start breaking them now."

"I didn't come here to have a discussion Zeus. I came with a warning." The once sparkling emerald of his eyes began to fade, the brilliance replaced by a darkness that seemed to swallow the light around him. "I'm here to warn you, if the choir senses any more magic from any of you, we will destroy you."

"I don't respond to threats." Zeus snarled.

"Yes, you do. It's why you're still here and every other part of your little freak show was wiped off the face of the earth."

"Don't talk to me like that."

"Or what?" The angel demanded, his voice rising like a wave above the city. "You were too weak and cowardly to fight us centuries ago and now you're a fraction of the god you once were."

As Jophiel chastised him, Zeus seethed, but felt unable to move.

"Our deal was simple, you help me rid the mortal plain of magical forces and I let your Olympian family live an eternal magic-less existence. You could have fought Zeus, you could have rallied them all together against the army of Christ, but you knew you'd lose, and we are stronger than ever now." With his final word he rose from the chair. "If I have to return it will be for war."

Zeus didn't know what to do. He had felt too weak for too long now. Inside him every emotion span, screaming and demanding his attention. He could feel every drop of blood within him coursing through his veins, boiling hot like molten lead pouring around his body. He was losing everything: his empire, his family, his dignity. Even his sanity felt like it was falling away from him, dripping out of his head. He could not lose again, could not allow an angel, some pawn of another god, to speak to him like that. He rose from his seat and stared at the back of the figure walking away from him.

"We're not done." He bellowed at Jophiel.

"Yes we …"

The angel began to turn as he spoke, a smug smile painted across his face. The words faded and the smile vanished as Zeus surged forward, ramming his shoulder into the angel's chest. Jophiel's feet lifted from the ground as his body flew through the balcony doors. Glass smashed into shards, and the angel landed in a winded heap on the living room carpet. Zeus marched towards his adversary and picked him up by the scruff of his neck. Jophiel growled, ready to unleash the vengeful power of heaven upon Zeus, but the old Olympian was quick. He smashed the angel against the wall and pressed his back into the light switch.

"Hephaestus may not be here anymore to turn lightening into a weapon, but the humans have done a pretty good job of that themselves."

As he spoke, he felt the flow of electricity behind the wall, the power circulating through the entire building. He pulled it towards him, willing it thorough the switch and into Jophiel. The angel began to convulse and smoke, screaming in agony and the volts pulsed through his body. When Zeus was done, he released him and let him fall back to the floor.

The white form of the angel smouldered, a small trail of smoke rising from him. Zeus stood, eyes cast down at his quarry. Jophiel rolled over and groaned. His suit was no longer pristine, now covered in tears and burned patches. His eyes stayed closed, but he was clearly conscious. The great god moved to the sideboard and grabbed a lamp, pulling it to his foe, careful not to snap the cable. He smashed the bulb and stabbed the broken glass into angel's face sending electrical power into his flesh. Jophiel screamed, his green eyes opening in shock, as pain poured into his body. He looked at Zeus, fear spreading through him.

"I should have fought you all those years ago." He whispered into Jophiel's ear, still forcing lightening into the angel. "I have a new deal for you to take back to your god and his army. Once I've dealt with the fucker killing my family, I will go back to not using magic, but for now I have bigger priorities than keeping you lot happy." With that he removed the lamp from Jophiel's head. The angel remained on the floor, his breaths ragged and weak. He coughed and spluttered as he tried to move. As Zeus looked down at him, the body began to fade, the edges turning to mist as he closed his eyes, the white vapour trailing into nothingness as it rose from the spot where he laid. Zeus looked on in shock.

"You have one week." The angel announced.

Zeus turned and looked behind him. Jophiel stood in the smashed doorway, his body the same as it had been when he had first arrived, his white suit once again immaculate, untouched by dirt or damage.

"I have consulted with the choir and we agree that at this time we don't want to waste our energy on your family, we have bigger plans in motion. So, you have one week to wrap up this issue and then crawl back into darkness."

The angel disappeared, the space where he once stood now empty. Zeus could only stare at the spot, his mouth agape. He was a god of Olympus. He had seen great wonders and had tapped into magics beyond mortal comprehension, but even he had to marvel at what these angels could achieve. He had filled the being with raw power, the electricity never stopping, and within seconds the angel had been able to form a new body. In that moment he knew he had made the right choice all those centuries ago. Even if he had amassed an army it would not have stood a chance against the angelic hoard. He despised the Judeo-Christian god, but he had to admire how he put together a militia, and how he spread his word. Even at his height Zeus had never had as many worshippers as this god.

Zeus made his way through his apartment, his mind consumed by what he must do. The killer was still out there, still had capabilities that Zeus didn't even understand. His family, his whole organisation, had failed to find him and now he had to track him and kill him in a week, or he would have an army from heaven to contend with as well. For the first time he felt like abandoning what he had built. He was losing his family over a turf war he could walk away from. He could gather the last members still alive and leave the city, let the vultures fight over the carcass and tear themselves apart. He could go build a new life, away from the killer who was pursuing them, away from the war which was breaking his spirit, away from the need and temptation to use magic that was bringing down the wrath of an even greater enemy.

Zeus knew he couldn't run, though. It was not in his nature. He had never backed down, never hidden in fear. He had faced up to his own father when he was young, he had conquered enemies and created the greatest pantheon of beings to ever exist. It was not in his character to flee or to let fear conquer him. He needed to find a way to win. He was out of alcohol, out of friends, and almost out of family. Yet, he knew the only thing he could do was fight to the bitter end and when he came face to face with the killer, the enemy of his family would feel a pain that they could not even imagine.

Zeus fell onto his bed. He stared up at the ceiling, allowing his vison to blur, allowing himself to lose focus. He pulled his glass to his lips and supped at the liquor, savouring the taste. He had spent tonight in a state of emotional agony he had not known was possible. The news of Dionysus' death had just been the start.

Hera had been the one to tell him. She had been so calm, so ready to handle his inevitable anguish. Yet, she had shown no pain of her own. She didn't care about his bastards. He hated her for that, wanted to blame her indifference for their death, but he knew it was his weakness, knew she was right when she had told him that only he could save what was left of the family. She had seen him weak before, seen him dragged into an asylum's cell, and she knew as well as him that when he was weak the family suffered. He laid still on the bed waiting for either an idea or sleep to claim him. Neither did, and as the night dragged by, darkness began to consume Zeus' mind.

Twenty-six
Ray of Hope

Hermes clung to William, his small, slender hands, clasping at the warm flesh and firm muscle of his lover's arm. Sleep still held him tight, pulling him into the darkness of dreams. His small body quivered as the nightmares of failure and defeat he had every night since the newspaper article surged through his mind. The look on Zeus' face; the absolute disappointment of a father he had loved and adored was seared into his subconscious. Hermes couldn't close his eyes without seeing his father's face coated in a scowl, his azure eyes downcast and full of shame. The ghost of his failure moved through his mind, the blurred black and white images of his own lust and lack of self-control could not be escaped. They surrounded him, a wall harder than stone trapping him in the darkness. Even clinging to his rock who anchored him was not enough to keep his dreams at bay.

He awoke with a start, his eyes snapping open as cold beads of sweat ran over his forehead, soaking his golden hair to his pale skin. He looked up at the darkened ceiling, the early morning light failing to penetrate through the thick curtains that hung over the windows. Hermes didn't move. Instead, he lay still, breathing slowly and deeply, allowing the breaths to calm his shaking body. He kept his eyes open, scared that if he blinked the nightmarish visions that had plagued him for days would return. His grip on William tightened, his hands desperately trying to pull strength from the man.

Zeus had tried to ban Hermes from seeing William. The phone had rattled with the sound of his voice as he commanded Hermes never again to see the man who now gave his life meaning. Zeus was convinced that William was behind the leak on behalf of Casper, especially after Artemis had confirmed to Athena that Casper was part of the plot against the gang. Zeus told him that the relationship was a lie, and that Hermes was a gullible fool who had been taken in by a good-looking man. Hermes didn't care what Zeus, or even Athena, thought. Both had tried to talk him out of seeing William, but he had lost too much already. The god had no role, no purpose, no place in the family, his reputation was in tatters. He couldn't even go to social clubs anymore, the prudish men of the city scared that he might taint them with his homosexuality. He refused to spend the time alone, crying by himself in the dark.

William had always been more than a gorgeous man to lust after. The love he felt for him was as real as any he had ever experienced. His heart thundered in his chest whenever he thought about him, whenever he looked up into his eyes or smelled the sweet musk on his pale skin. He knew this man could not hurt him, could not betray him. William loved him in return. As well, Casper would never trust a man who poured drinks with an important job, like bringing down a member of the family. William wasn't some trusted lieutenant; he was a barman.

Hermes couldn't help himself but smile when William shifted in his sleep, moaning softly as he turned and gently pulled him into a tight embrace. The god moved with him, allowing himself to be held. He knew he wouldn't sleep anymore. He didn't dare encounter his dreams again, so he laid still and peaceful in his lover's arms.

His mind raced though, unable to fully enjoy the peace and serenity he should feel in this moment. Ever since the news story had broken, he had been trying to think of ways he could get back in the race and earn the respect of his family. Anni had been devastated when she saw, but she was still employed by the campaign so she came over every day to help him think of ways they could make a comeback. Each day she looked a little more dishevelled, a little more defeated.

Everything about his campaign manager had been graceful and poised: she wore her dresses pressed, her hair in neat curls, and her makeup was flawless. In every meeting, though, something slipped: a creased dress, hair tied in a messy bun, no makeup or jewellery. She had always believed in him and watching her give up on his campaign was growing steadily harder.

He knew he had to come up with a plan, fast. The family was falling apart and if he could reignite his campaign, he could give them some hope. If they could hold out until he won, then he would hopefully be able to use his influence to end the attacks that were plaguing them. He had tried reaching out to the family connections and that hadn't worked. He had tried denial, aiming to set up interviews, but no paper would talk to him. He had even suggested they ignore it and carry on campaigning with the aim of the scandal just fading away, but no venues would host him, no donors would pay, and no one would attend. Hermes felt so alone, so lost.

As the morning dragged on Hermes reluctantly freed himself from the shelter of warmth and affection that was William's embrace. He pulled himself away from the tanned skin and soft silk and entered into the darkness of the room around him. He had been determined, through all this, to rise at a sensible hour, clean, dress, and do something. He refused to sit or sleep in hopeless squalor simply because he had failed. His regret and despair were always on him, like vipers coiled around his throat, ready and threatening to bite, and he was determined to keep them at bay for as long as possible. He went about his morning routine, trying his best to move in darkness and silence so as not to wake William. The man had been there for him in ways that no other person had, and he would let him sleep and rest as much as he needed.

Hermes was shocked that William ever managed to find the time for him. As Casper's empire now extended into Harlem, he had kept his staff busier than Hermes could fathom. Casper demanded William at every possible time of the day or night. He was draining the life from him, making him work on fixing up joints as well as serving drinks. He had come home with bruises and a serious burn on his arm from some sort of tool he'd been forced to use. The man was exhausted, barely able to make it to the bed without falling to the floor in a heap. Still, he took the time to kiss Hermes and hold him before he fell into slumber.

Fully washed and dressed, Hermes went to the kitchen. The cold chequerboard tiles of the floor stung at his bare feet, and the white fittings that surrounded him, bathed in the light of morning sun, shone, almost blinding him, as his eyes failed to adjust from the dimness of the bedroom. He poured himself a coffee, the thick black liquid rattling as it hit the sides of the mug, the bitter scent rising with the curling ribbons of steam from the dark surface. He sucked at the beverage, allowing his brain to spark and ignite from the caffeine's influence.

Still, no idea came to him, no ingenious thoughts occurred on how to solve his problem, but he sat and sipped, flicking through yesterday's paper, reading stories of mass sickness, poisoning, even more street murders. The city was in chaos, the family no longer the only people suffering from the killer's actions. He needed to end this man's terror, and since he wasn't a warrior, he would need to get back into the campaign and use the full might of the city.

A knock sounded at the door, an urgent rapping that echoed through the apartment, the furious sound bouncing off every surface, filling the place with noise. Hermes jumped as his silent contemplation came to an abrupt end. The banging continued, growing louder and more demanding. Hermes rushed from the kitchen to the source of the sound, eager to make it stop. Yanking the door open he saw Anni before him, her knuckles raised in the air, her eagerness to make more noise distracting her from the fact that there was now no door in front of her. She looked up at Hermes and for the first time in days she beamed, a wide toothy grin spreading across her pink, flushed face.

"Something good has finally happened." She managed to say between pants. She walked into the apartment, pacing up and down the hall desperately trying to catch her breath. "Sorry, I couldn't get a cab, so I ran here. I think I'm going to throw up."

She stopped pacing and pushed her hand against the wall, her fingers clutching at the wallpaper, her eyes bulging as she tried to control her breathing. Hermes held her under the arms and escorted her to the kitchen, sitting her at the small breakfast table and pushing a glass of water under her face. The young woman drank quickly, thin streams of water running down her chin as she gulped.

"So, are you going to tell me this great news?" Hermes asked as she finished her drink, panting like a dog as she swallowed down the last drop.

"I got a call today. Someone wants to help us."

The excitement in her eyes was obvious, they glowed like golden orbs in the sun's rays as she looked at Hermes.

"Who is it? I've not had much luck with allies lately."

"I don't know." She confessed, her voice still rippling with hope and excitement. Hermes looked at her confused. Anni had always been pragmatic and efficient, it was unlike her to get carried away, especially when she didn't know who she was dealing with.

"Sorry if I ruin your elation Anni, but a mystery supporter hardly seems like cause for celebration."

He looked at her, wondering if at any point some realism would enter her expression, but, still, the wide-eyed excitement continued to move across her features.

"He said he owns one of the big papers and he wants to run a story for us, denouncing the original tale as a hoax, he even has experts lined up to prove the pictures were faked."

She leaned forward and clasped Hermes' hand, shaking with unconcealed joy.

"He also said he will donate a huge sum to the campaign so we can get going again. This could be it Hermes, this could be the chance we need."

She tightened her grip on his hand and looked up at him. Hermes had to admit to himself that the offer sounded good. Whoever had contacted Anni was offering them everything that he needed to get back in the game and help his family.

"It's not as if I have anything to lose." He replied, smiling gently at Anni's look of unrestrained joy. "What do we have to do to get all this support?"

"There will be favours down the road I'm sure. There always is for any amount of support, but he hasn't said what they are right now."

"I look forward to receiving his calls regularly" Hermes responded, leaning back in his chair. He took a sip of his coffee, peering over the rim at Anni, her face had mellowed. "So, what does he want right now?"

"He wants a meeting with you."

"Well, that's easy enough …"

"And with William."

She looked down as she spoke, the guilt obvious on her face. She must have already agreed to the terms in her excitement, but now, sitting in front of Hermes, she had to know he would refuse. Hermes had never once allowed William into his work life. What he did was for the family, and it was separate to the man he loved. William was a decent man who had already been pulled enough into a dark and scandalous underworld that he was too good for. Hermes shook his head, ready to speak, then footsteps sounded in the doorway, followed by a soft cough that brought his and Anni's attention to the muscular, half-dressed man.

"Give me a few minutes to get dressed and I'll come with you." William said softly through a half smile. Hermes wanted to protest but William left the room as quickly as he arrived.

Hermes tried to talk William out of it, tried to keep the boundaries firm and strong, but looking up into the pools of his eyes he couldn't help but give in. William held him close, running the broad palm of his hand slowly up and down his back, every now and then moving his fingers to trace some unknown shape across him. Hermes finally relented and allowed William to come with him.

It was clear he felt some guilt over what had happened: the damage that had been done to Hermes and his relationship with his family. Hermes never wanted the man to carry that guilt with him, so he would let him help, but they agreed that if William was asked any personal questions or if anything was to be written about him, then they would simply leave.

The office building they went to was one of the finest Hermes had ever seen. Manhattan had boomed over the past few years and all around them the city swirled with style and elegance. Glass doors greeted them as they entered, everything styled to perfection. The marble of the lobby gleamed in the sunlight as bright beams cut like razors through the high windows. A crystal chandelier fell from the ceiling, every last cut of glass sparkling. Light seemed to envelope them as they walked, ushering them forward.

They had no problem getting past reception and into the elevator: a cocoon of dark wood and polished brass. The attendant smiled, the old black man tilting his head toward Anni, before pulling the cranks and sending the box flying into the heights of the building. They had only risen a few floors before the elevator jittered to a creaking stop, finishing its ascent slowly but surely.

Hermes was surprised to find the newsroom they had entered was completely empty. The wide-open space surrounded by windows had desks and cabinets in place but no people. He had expected to see the hustle and bustle of an active newsroom: expected to see men in fine suits dashing around, and to hear the constant tapping and shrill ringing of typewriters, as secretaries and writers hurried to meet deadlines. The room still smelled of dust, the soft scent of an empty and unused space washing over the three of them.

Hermes walked forward.

"Hello." He called out to the empty space but was met with nothing. He continued walking forward scanning the room for any clue of where they had gone. There was no emblem, no prints, no photographs, no business cards. The place looked like it had been set up but had yet to be used. "Anni, did you get any more…" Hermes stopped, his voice ending in horror as he turned to see Anni, her eyes wide in fear, mouth covered by a brawny hand he recognised so well.

William stood behind Anni, towering over her, staring forward, the inviting eyes Hermes so loved, now dark orbs leering at him. Hermes, couldn't move, he stood frozen in place, his legs like rock, his heart thundering within him, echoing in his skull. His mouth was dry and beads of sweat started to form on his face. Silently, William let Anni go. She spluttered and coughed as she fell to the floor, her body landing with a thump, a small pocketknife jutting from her back. Hermes wanted to speak, wanted to yell out and run to her, but he couldn't.

"Why?" he managed to ask, the word coming out as a rasping breath of desperation.

William walked forward. His face set into a scowl of determination, the sunlight that filled the room showing every line and shadow of his face.

"Please, why?"

William reached Hermes, still silent, and grabbed him by the neck. Hermes reached up, finally managing to react. He clawed at Williams hand, trying to pry it free from his neck, but the man was too strong. He walked forward, dragging the god in his wake. Hermes started squirming to try and free himself. He screamed for help, hoping that someone, anyone would hear his desperate pleas and come to his aid. William dragged him to a large oak desk that sat in the corner of the room. He threw Hermes on top of it. The impact drove the air from the small god's lungs, and he struggled to catch his breath. Still holding him in place, William reached down and pulled a blade from under the desk.

Hermes looked up at the man he loved in fear and confusion. Tears began to stream down his face. He begged, softly gripping William's arm, trying to pull him closer, to kiss him, to talk to him, to convince him not to hurt him.

"I thought you loved me." He managed to blubber through his tears, the words sounding so weak and pathetic in his mouth.

William froze, hie eyes burning into Hermes', tears slowly starting to form around the bloodshot whites.

"You do love me, don't you?"

"Of course, not" William growled in response, his smooth skin wrinkling with anger. "How could I love a monster like you?"

He didn't raise his weapon anymore as he spoke, breathing heavily, panting through his rage.

"Then why have you shared my bed for so long?"

"Because you talk when you're happy. You gave me so much information, and I got to bring down one of Zeus' plans. I stayed with you because you were the weakest link in his armour."

"But, you stayed, even after my campaign was destroyed. You made love to me when I was useless to you."

Hermes ran his hand up William's arm, his fearful grip replaced by a tender, desperate touch.

"There must be something real here. You must want me."

"I want revenge more. I want Zeus to see his family die. I want him to fall to his knees and despair like I have, that everyone has been killed by something unknown. I want him to watch his life burn as he tries to find the man killing his family." William babbled at Hermes, his eyes wide with manic energy. "That's why I brought you here. Your corpse in bed is suspicious, but here, in some abandoned office; it's one less connection to me."

William was almost incoherent, speaking frantically, his grip on Hermes' neck tightening and relaxing as he spoke, almost to himself. The strong, warm façade that had lured Hermes in slowly began to melt away, revealing the tremoring madness underneath.

"Please William, don't kill me. I don't want to die." Hermes blubbered, tears rolling over his face as the fear consumed him. The madness of his lover was too much for him to bare.

"I have to do this Hermes. Love is for other people. I'm not sorry, but I hope you understand your heartbreak and your death are necessary."

The blade was raised, the thick, black metal looking like a jagged shadow in the light of the room. Hermes didn't know what to do, he didn't know how to escape, so he made one last decision, he sent a message. For the first time in centuries, he tapped into the magic that was part of him and sent out his last moments as a vision to the rest of the Olympians in the city. He showed them the face of their attacker, showed them the weapon that was being used to kill them, and as his last act: he apologised, his heart breaking as he admitted he had failed.

Twenty-seven

Prepare for Battle

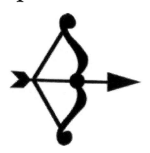

"How many more times are you going to keep trying this before you realise, you're wasting your time?" Artemis asked, leaning back, lightly banging her head against the golden latticework that made up the corner of her cage, thick strands of dark brown hair catching on the metal joints.

Days had passed with her and Apollo trapped in the abandoned basement and there had been no sign that they would ever be free. Another morning had arrived, bringing with it thin shafts of light through the high windows that hunched themselves against the room's ceiling.

"I'm going to keep trying until I get some sort of reading." Her brother replied, the glow fading from his skin, brilliant light rising off of his body like wisps of silver mist.

He opened his eyes, the last vestige of electric light giving way to the normal tone of his eyes. He had been glowing for hours, using every last bit of his magical strength to try and make a connection with the world outside the cage.

All he had been able to see so far was darkness, as if the whole world around them had vanished, turned to ash. Artemis was having the same problem, her senses, no matter how much she honed them, no matter how much she connected with the wild beast within her, could not smell or hear anything outside. There could have been a parade an inch from her and she would not have known.

Luckily light had been able to pass through the bars and so the two of them had not had to endure total darkness. Unluckily though, they had had to resort to undertaking bodily functions in the cage, the call of nature too much for them to ignore. There was a time when they would have had complete control over their physical forms, but as the millennia had drifted by, and they had grown used to letting their powers fade from their consciousness, they had lost that control, and the trivial matters that had once been the burden of mortal creatures had soon become theirs. They had been wise enough to designate a corner for the purpose, but the smell was starting to become more than either of them could handle. The thick and clinging odours of piss and shit constantly filled their nostrils.

"You know that whatever magic made this cage blocks ours. So, you'll never get any kind of reading."

"Then it seems that I will just keep trying forever then." Apollo retorted, shooting a long glance at Artemis.

The two of them had always quarrelled, always goaded each other, and tested each other's patience, but they loved each other dearly. The cage was starting to test their bond, the two of them desperate for freedom, miserable, cold, and uncomfortable. Artemis despised being caged. When she wasn't sitting, bashing her head against the bars, she was pacing the floor, desperate to find herself out in the wilderness, running free through hidden woodlands and along sequestered riverbanks. Apollo simply persisted in trying to break the magic of their confinement.

"Whoever did this has the powers of a god, it could even be one of the family."

"None of the family would do this, and the killer didn't have the same sensation as any of us when I read him in Aphrodite's memories."

He closed his eyes and sidled over to his sister, gripping her hand tight, his golden skin enveloping the sun-kissed bronze of hers.

"Whoever this is, isn't an Olympian, but they do have godly powers."

"Every being like that is gone though: the titans, the demigods, the Oceanids, the primordials. We were there, we saw them cast to Tartarus. They couldn't escape and they couldn't do this." She gestured at the golden frame that surrounded them, the metal shaped into intricate patterns and symbols within the grid framework.

Artemis couldn't help but admire where they were, even Hephaestus himself would have to marvel at the blend of magic and craftsmanship that had created this prison. Athena was almost certain it wasn't one of the other pantheons attacking them, but the power that was being used against them was beyond any mortal.

"Then he must be something new, something created after the cataclysm."

"A new god?"

"Or a new demigod."

The two of them sat in silence contemplating Apollo's words. If he was right, then they had no idea of their enemy's limits and no way to truly understand him. There hadn't been a new deity in in millennia. The twelve of them were the only survivors and they had all been careful not to reproduce, always checking on their conquests, always cleaning up their messes where they occurred.

"Who I am is of no concern to you." A voice uttered from in front of them, soft but confident.

The two of them looked up to see the killer before them, the black clothing and mask just as they had imagined. He loomed over them, a shadow cast into flesh that stood tall. The twins stood up and walked to the edge of the cage, their faces only inches away from the mask. The urge to leap forward and tear off his disguise coursed through both of them. They could feel it in each other: a thought and desire they both shared.

"Why don't you stop hiding and come in here and fight us properly?" Apollo challenged him, his face pressed up against the cage, the soft skin of his cheeks poking through the gaps in the metal, his eyes boring into the dark mask of their oppressor.

Artemis moved forward, her arm pressed up against Apollo. She snarled at the killer, challenging him to open the cage and let them be free.

"I have no need to fight you." The killer replied, moving forward.

He brought himself close to the pair of gods. Artemis could see the fine cracks of the mask's wood and smell the sweat and cologne that radiated from the enemy. Her senses buzzed with urgency, her bloodlust commanding her to rip the man to shreds.

"I am going to kill you and I don't need to fight you to do it. I don't care how you die or how noble my battle with you is, as long as you lie in blood at my feet. I'm happy." The killer declared, backing away from the cage, making space to allow a small man to step into his place.

The man lifted something in front of his face: a black box with rubber protrusions. A mix of metal and glass moved towards the two of them and, on the top, a small bulb flashed with a brilliant white light. Artemis hadn't seen many cameras but recognised it instantly.

"I know I'm gorgeous, but did you really need a picture of me when you have me in a cage."

"Oh Apollo," the killer replied "you're nothing but bait and now I have the picture to lure my target I have no need of you. Though, I still haven't decided whether to kill you now or later. Try and convince me to keep you alive a little longer."

"Let Artemis go." Apollo demanded, his eyes still boring deep into his captor.

"What?" The killer asked. The shock visible in the way his body went rigid.

"You heard me, let her go and then keep me as bait. Artemis can run off to the woods and you'll never see her again."

He reached back and grabbed his sister's hand squeezing it affectionately. For all his taunts he loved her more than the world itself.

"You're the second one of your kind to act like you can feel love today." The killer sneered. "Don't mask your ambition as affection Apollo, the lies that cover you stink."

As the killer began his taunting, the small man with the camera ran from the building, the few hairs that were scattered across his pale scalp moved in the gentle morning breeze. His dirty, green, chequered sweater pasted to his belly as he made his way to the photo lab. His master had instructed him to develop the picture immediately and deliver it to the enemy. The lab work was quick and by midday he was stood at the entrance to club Olympus, the enveloped photo clutched in his sweaty palm, his stubby fingers threatening to crinkle the prize within.

Athena had been working furiously for days. When she was not out with Zeus trying to forge new deals and partnerships or strategizing with Ares about how to best use the limited manpower they still had, she was in her study combing through books she had not pulled out in centuries. For too long she felt like she was going insane, unable to reason how she would solve their problem, unable to figure out what was killing her family. Her hair, which was normally hidden under a hat, tied tight to keep it from her face, had transformed into a tangle of brown that fell over her head like a weeping willow after a storm. She no longer wore her suits pressed, with every button done up tight. Instead, a pair of slacks and a white shirt were thrown on each morning, to keep some semblance of modesty as she worked.

Things had changed over the past days. Even as the tragedy of more and more of her family dying had hit her in waves of agonising grief, she had managed to find the small glimmers of hope and promise that had been laid out for her. Artemis' call and Hermes' psychic message had given her enough information to form a hypothesis. She felt her confidence surge back within her, felt the thrill of battle teasing at her mind rather than the sting and pain of defeat.

She sat in the dimly lit bar of the Olympus club, the only place that had not been taken over by the police or federal agents: the last refuge of their empire, the last place they could gather together and plan. The remnants of her family surrounded her. Zeus was a shadow of his former self. He was a rumbling storm cloud, darkening the horizon of her vision. He had barely spoken for days, each blow to the family a knife plunged into his heart. He had never looked older to her, his proud bearing now a hunched frame, his skin pale and sagging.

Realising Casper had definitely been behind everything, using the killer as a tool, had been a blow to him. He had been outsmarted by an enemy, and a mortal one at that. Ares and Hera sat at the other side of the table, Hera as poised as ever, a cocktail in her hand, Ares standing strong by her side, his face cast in an eternal scowl.

"I know how he's killing us." She announced.

The three gods looked at her, their expressions unreadable, each of them waiting to see what she revealed.

"Based on what I saw in Hermes mind during his last moments I think the killer is using the scythe of Cronos."

"Not possible." Zeus declared, barely looking up from his brooding contemplations.

"Why is that?" Athena asked, incredulous that she had been dismissed so quickly.

"I would know it anywhere: its blade was perfect. The one used on Hermes was black and twisted, marked and chipped." His voice still boomed, even in his disheartened and dishevelled state. "You're wrong Athena."

He waved his hand dismissively, as if to throw her words away from him, to repel her ideas.

"Besides, the scythe can't kill us, just hurt us." Hera added, sipping at her cocktail, the heavy furs of her coat slung over her shoulders.

"I believe he's roasted the scythe in a fire made from the entrails of the Ophiotaurus. A fire with that power, imbued into the scythe, and used on gods that have only grown weaker over time is the perfect killing weapon." She finished, trying to hold back her excitement, wise enough to know that now was not a time to revel in her own intelligence.

The family looked at her, each one of them waiting for her to finish.

"Knowing this gives us an advantage we never had before. We now know that as long as we stay out of arms reach, he can't hurt us. There's nothing special about his guns or bullets, he doesn't have power over us. If we always keep him at bay, if we always have eyes on him and fire power to pin him down then he can't kill us."

She grabbed Zeus' shoulder as she spoke, trying to pass over her hope and optimism through touch. The great god looked up at her and smiled. The first smile he had shown in a long time.

"Now we know that the killer works for Casper as well, this is turning into nothing but a turf war, and I can win one of those." Zeus said reaching out and clasping Athena's shoulder in return. "Casper made a big mistake setting back up in Harlem. I know every way to slip in and out of those clubs. That fucker will be dead by nightfall."

He looked up to Ares as he spoke, watching as a grin appeared of the war god's wide face.

"The only thing I haven't managed to deduce is who this William is. He's got to be more than one of Casper's pawns and we have no way of determining how he knows we're gods. We know there are other deities out there, but it doesn't make sense it would be them. Plus, everything so far has been Greek: the passcode, cage, and scythe." Athena puzzled.

The rest of them sat in silence. The mystery had been pushed to the side as they had tried to rebuild their empire and keep themselves from crumbling. Athena was determined to find out, she was determined to solve this last piece of the puzzle, to make it fit into place.

She downed the last of her water, and as she did, she looked ahead to see a small pale hand emerge from the shadow of the stairwell and place a brown envelope onto the floor.

The contents of the envelope were shocking. The family circled the table looking down at the black and white rendition of Artemis and Apollo's faces. The two of them cast dark looks towards a figure that could not be seen, pressed against intricate metal work that Athena assumed was some form of cage. The killer had them and judging by his note, he was prepared to use them to get the rest of the family.

"Fuck this man!" Zeus thundered. "I will find them and bring them back. I will not let any more of my family die."

"He wants me again." Ares stated. "I should be the one to go, he's lured me before. I won't get trapped again. I'll let him think he's broke me, that he can get close and then I'll rip his head off."

"No Ares, you're not going up against him. I've lost too much already." Hera said as she drank, looking up at her son, sadness and desperation radiating from her.

"I'm going to go." Athena announced.

Protests began to ring out from the other two gods. Ares was desperate for conflict, he seethed with anger that made his muscles and veins bulge under his skin. His strength rippled within him, waves of divine fury pulsing through him.

"I've let this go on long enough." Zeus declared. "I have sent too many of my family, too many of my children, into danger and I won't do it again. I'm going to go and face him. I'm going to kill that son of a bitch and I'm going to make him suffer for what he's done to us."

"He won't expect me to go." Athena began, the other two started to speak again, but she raised her voice above them. "According to this note we have enough time for me to plan a way to pin him down. When I've done that, the two of you can be the ones to fight him."

Athena knew they would hesitate, but she needed them to agree. Her plan required distance, that no one to be close to his weapon, and she couldn't trust Zeus, or Ares especially, not to rise to his taunting and baiting. The family had suffered because they had grown used to sheer strength winning them the day, but now was the time to be cunning and deceptive, and no being on earth did that better than Athena. She smiled to herself as she convinced the two gods to hang back. Tying her hair up and smoothing down her suit, she made her way out of the club to begin preparations.

The golden hands of Athena's pocket watch clicked as they moved to mark three pm. Athena's car rounded the corner of the warehouse district, rows and rows of brick buildings coated in dirt with windows scuffed, broken, and boarded lined the streets, ushering the vehicle to its destination. Athena breathed deeply, steadying her nerves as she came to a halt. The smell of wet air greeted her, the dampness of a humid summer day lingering around the ocean-soaked brick of the abandoned factories and warehouses. The scent of rusting metal was everywhere.

Her plan rested on staying far away from the killer, but she didn't know how fast he was or where he would be located. She hated when there were elements she had to leave to chance, but she had learned long ago that there were things in this world outside of a goddess' control. Her spats clapped against the sidewalk as she walked into the warehouse that was to be her meeting point. The doors were wide open, so Athena made her way into the darkness of the cavernous space.

"Welcome Athena." The voice of the killer floated through the room as the lights above her flickered on.

She cast her eyes around the space looking for any attack, but it was only when she looked up that she saw anyone. The killer stood on an observation railing looking down at her through the dark eyes of his mask. He must not have known that Hermes sent out his last moments to the family if he was still hiding his identity. As Athena's eyes roved around him, she noticed the two forms of Artemis and Apollo, dead, heaped by his feet, their sublime faces coated in blood, eyes staring into the nothingness. She did nothing to hide her hatred or disdain for this man.

"I was expecting Ares. Where is my old friend?"

"I'm afraid he's busy," Athena said, pushing her hand into the pocket of her suit jacket, allowing her fingers to run through the contents within. "But I'm here now and I'm sure I'm just as capable of killing you."

"You don't know what you're dealing with" the killer spat at her, his hands gripping the railing.

As he spoke doors at the other end of the warehouse slid open, the wheels that moved them creaking and groaning, echoing in the abandoned space, reverberating off the old equipment that lay huddled in dirty corners, the smell of oil and grease everywhere. Men walked forward, clad in black suits, aiming tommy guns at her. Athena gulped at the sight, careful not to let any fear show on her face.

"You were a fool to come her alone."

"You're the fool if you think I'm alone."

Twenty-eight
Battle

Athena stared up at the man who had been terrorising her family, her eyes cold; the usual piercing blue turned grey in the light of the warehouse. She didn't move, keeping her focus on her adversary. The dark mask looked down on her imperiously, a face of disdain and unrestrained superiority. She couldn't help but smirk at him wearing it, couldn't help but enjoy the fact he clearly didn't know that she had seen Hermes' last moments and knew exactly who was stood in front of her.

She didn't want to reveal that knowledge, but she could feel the men across the room starting to twitch, their bent fingers desperate to contract just a little more and pull triggers. They wanted to fill her with holes and watch her bleed to death. No matter who this man was and what he wanted from the family, for these men it was simple gang warfare. She needed to buy herself some time, her plan not ready to be realised.

"I have spies all over this building and this street. If you had come with people, I would have known about it." The killer announced, raising his hand, a clear start to the signal that shooting should commence.

"Really William?" Athena shouted up to the rafters, causing his hand to stop mid-air.

The shadowed figure of black cloth and leather stood motionless, staring down at Athena, who, with feigned confidence, reached up and tucked a stray curl of brunette hair back behind her ear.

"You think I would be foolish enough to come alone. You know who I am and you know what I can do. Ask yourself if a line of men with Tommy guns is going to be enough."

She continued to meet the glazed black eyes of the mask, hoping her gambit had worked, hoping he would take the bait and talk just a little longer.

"It's a shame to have to kill someone so smart."

William removed his mask as he spoke, the black leather façade peeling from his golden skin. He pushed his black hood back, and ran his gloved hand through his messy hair, sweat coating the long, wavy strands.

"I would ask how you figured out who I was, but I don't think I care. You're just another obstacle in my way."

He raised his hand again. This time Athena knew that nothing she said would stop him. She had spent so many years surrounded by gods, visiting with kings and queens, walking the earth with wise men, scientists and poets. All of them loved to hear the sound of their own voice, indulged themselves in hearing their thoughts said aloud, even if no one around them cared to listen. Now she was stood before someone who didn't care to speak, who didn't have words to say, but actions to undertake, and a goal to complete. The thrill of real competition electrified her body.

Athena felt a pulse at the edge of her senses as her hands felt a spark of energy: a surge of life force that rippled up her arms.

She had been shocked when Zeus had told her she could finally use magic again, even if it was just for this task. She had had so many questions, being the only other god who knew why it was banned, but she had not had the time to ask.

All of a sudden, her plans had changed. All of a sudden there was more potential than she could imagine. She had almost forgotten what it had been like to use magic, to feel that thing that made her special, that made her so much more than human.

She had run from the club in a frenzy of ideas, her mind swirling with possibilities. She did not have to put herself at the mercy of this madman, and stumble into his trap with the hope she had the wits and intelligence to escape. She could plan and prepare, making herself unstoppable. No matter what the killer threw at her he would be ready to fight back, and magic would be the key.

Hephaestus must have known this too because his workshop was full of creations that she could use. She had found herself there first, the smell of metal and oil filling the, now cold, workspace. Every forge, fire, and piece of equipment had become a relic, a ruin in the cold, dark garage. Each one was a monument to Olympian greatness. Hephaestus had helped make the family strong, as they all had, and Athena knew she would find help in his last workplace.

The gadgets she extracted were amazing, designs so intricate and detailed she could not believe he had managed to think of them. There were devices so small she was sure they could be nothing but trinkets, yet they had power beyond belief. Everything she found changed her plan, everything she touched made her smile with glee as her brain comprehended new strategies and devised new means to destroy the enemy. Wisdom and adaptability were the same thing to Athena. Rigidity in the face of new challenges and opportunities was as unwise as anything.

She had sat, crossed leg, the endless expanse of the workshop around her, the darkness nestling against her, wading through diagrams, sketches, blueprints, and instructions. She pulled leather and metal towards her, her fingers dancing across the cool surfaces as she decided how she would use the cornucopia of weaponry she had discovered. The plan had been formed and she had never felt so ready and eager to face off against an enemy who underestimated her.

As Athena smiled to herself, the killer's arm almost rose to the full. The men at the back of the room looked towards her with unrestrained glee, their eyes glinting with the bloodlust that coursed through them. Before they could give into their desires and pull the triggers Athena reached round her back and pulled a short golden spear from the quiver she was wearing. She was glad no one had entered from behind and seen the unsightly bulge in her suit. She wanted every moment of this to be a surprise. As bullets began to boom from the barrel of the guns, the tip of the spear rammed into the ground, Athena using all of her strength as a goddess. With one last smile of self-satisfaction, she let out a pulse of magic.

The room erupted with light, a golden glow that bathed everyone present, turning the dim space into a majestic hall of illumination. The spear shone with the radiance beyond worlds, and where the light began to fade, golden wings had appeared. The wall of gold stood between Athena and the shooting men, bullets ricocheting from its surface, the sound of heavy lead meeting the wings ringing above the cacophony that came from the enemy guns.

Silence followed the first round of bullets. A stunned silence as men, who had never encountered gods before, stared in wonder at the protective barrier around Athena. The wings stretched across the room, the metal glinting in the light left from the transformation, every feather carved with detail. Each one looked so thin and fragile that it could float away on the breeze, but woven together they were strong enough to stop bullets.

Smoke rose from the tips of the guns, the men behind them peering through the haze, unable to believe what they witnessed. The smell of gunfire and the smoke rising from barrels was everywhere, covering the smell of must and age.

Athena didn't look at the enemy and tried not to focus on the marvel that had protected her. She reached back into her pockets and pulled the contents free. She ran down the length of the wings placing the small figurines at strategic points. She barely heard the enemy scream for the men to keep firing, before the protective wall rattled with the sound of bullets. Athena kept at her task, taking the small figurines from her pocket, and placing them on the ground. The bullets continued to fire at her as she worked, but she was confident that Hephaestus' shield would hold. She could feel the power radiating from the protective barrier. Every time a bullet hit, the magic she had imbued into the spear would flow to the area and repair the metal. No bullet would be strong enough to penetrate it.

"Is that all the great Athena can come up with? A wall?" William yelled as the second wave of bullets ceased to rain down on her position.

She placed the final figurine in place and moved back to the centre of the wall.

"How are you going to stop me when all you can do is quiver in fear."

"Again William, you are surprisingly stupid."

As she spoke, Athena closed her eyes and concentrated, reaching out her senses to the figurines that she had laid across the barrier. She had not lied to the killer when she said he was a fool to think she had come alone, and she knew that a spear was no real companion. She pressed her hands against the cold ground feeling a connection with the world. She sniffed at the air, the smell of gun smoke and sweat beginning to fill the cavernous space. Then she felt them, the minds of the people she had transformed. She could feel their confusion, their fear and loneliness. She could sense them trapped in their new forms, consumed by a silent word of darkness.

Athena had been a master of transformation magic. She had made Medusa and countless other beings of extraordinary shapes from simple humans. Her powers to change the world and the people around her made her truly great, and so turning an array of men into miniature figurines had been a task well suited to the goddess, even if she was a bit rusty.

She sent her power out to the men, felt their bodies in her mind, the way they had been before she had transformed them. She felt the beating of their hearts, the growth of their fingernails, the sweat dripping from their brow. She felt all the things that made them human and gave that back to them, releasing them from the darkness and silence of their stone existence. The figurines around her grew, the stone falling away from them in cascades of grey dust. Flesh and clothing appeared before her and the men all began searching the room for signs of what had happened to them.

Athena knew she didn't have time to explain, and that even if she did the men would not believe her. She didn't need scared and confused men, she needed the tough, gang-ready thugs Ares had given her. She ran down the line and spoke with each of them, commanding them to do as they were instructed.

Every one of them was a loyal man. They had been with the family from the start, each one of them trained and paid by Ares. She had no doubt that they would fight to the bitter end for them, and by her count she had more men than William. She screamed above the raging torrent of gunfire for them to pick up their weapons and be prepared to fight.

The men did as they were instructed, raising their weapons ready, eager to show what they were made of. They shook their heads, desperately trying to get rid of the fuzziness that came with being transformed. They rubbed their eyes and clenched their jaws in determination and then with a roar they turned and raised their weapons above the golden barrier and let loose on the enemy.

A cry of shock rang out alongside the gunfire. The killer looked on in horror as a wall of death surged towards his goons. The weapons held by Athena's men were more than mere tommy guns, each one specially designed and crafted by Hephaestus.

To her right a young man with ice white hair and stern green eyes fired his gun towards the killer's men. His eyes flashed as he pulled the trigger, his mind connecting with the bullets that flew from the barrel, each one bonding with him. His eyes opened wide, sweat pouring from his brow, the experience unique and unexpected. He willed his bullets to meet their target, their course altered through the air to sink into the flesh of one of the enemies. The enemy screamed as the bullets tore at him, falling to the ground clutching his stomach. Thick red blood poured from him, running in a stream to bathe the cold, grey ground.

Next to him another man fired a gun loaded with large explosives. The room erupted in a sea of smoke, the ground tearing apart in the wake of the onslaught, chips being flung into the air, the shrapnel bouncing off Athena's wall, but cutting at the enemy ranks.

Weapons of every imagination assaulted the enemy. Light flashed as bullets that summoned illusions flew through the air sending images of animals towards the men opposite them, terrifying them and sending their line into disarray.

Every weapon Hephaestus had made, and been forbidden from using, was now in Athena's possession, laying waste to those who would bring her family harm. The enemy's ordinary guns were no match for what she was attacking them with. They screamed, their death cries sounding out amidst the hailstorm of bullets and explosives that drummed in her ears.

She glanced up towards the walkway and saw William look down on the scene, horror strewn across his face, the mask now totally abandoned.

Athena wanted nothing more than to run to the walkway and fight him herself, to see the look of defeat in his eyes. She knew she couldn't though. As long as William had the scythe of Cronos, he was a danger, and she knew she needed to keep her distance.

She shouted to the men, ordering them to raise their fire to the walkway. If she was lucky, she would be able to kill William now without having to move from her fortified position. The men raised their guns and fired towards the walkway, a thunderous maelstrom of death surged upward. Smoke, and fire, and bullets rose into the air in a storm that dazzled even Athena.

It took time for the smoke to clear, but when Athena looked upwards there was no sign of William, dead or alive. She banged her fist against the ground in frustration and then commanded men to follow her. She ran away from the protective wall and out into the light of the street.

The intense brightness of midday had passed, giving way to the gentle glow of the afternoon. The street seemed so peaceful compared to the warzone she had just emerged from.

She stood silent, thinking of where she could go. If there was an observation platform there was likely a fire escape on the side of the building for those on it. She gestured to the men and they ran beside her, keeping pace as she slid round the corner of the building. Her hat flew away from her as she ran, air rushing past her head, blowing her hair out of its perfect shape and into a wild mess of brown curls. The goddess didn't let it slow her down. She wanted to catch the bastard who had killed her family, so she ran, calling for the men to keep up.

As she made her way down the thin alley, she saw the fire escape before her, the back and forth of metal pressed tightly to the edge of the building, holding on to the brick. She saw him, his black coat billowing behind him as he fell from the final rung of the ladder and onto the ground below. He began to run but Athena was quick.

"William. Stop!" She bellowed towards him.

The call worked and the killer stopped in his tracks, turning towards her. He panted, his face set firm, anger spreading across his features, his eyes boring into hers. Athena slowed as he turned, making sure to not get too close, to stay back and keep her distance.

"This is the end for you." She said between deep breaths, the exertion of using so much magic and running so quickly starting to catch up with her.

"I underestimated you Athena." William admitted through gritted teeth. "You still haven't killed me though, and I don't think you can. Especially not before I kill you."

"We both know you need to get that scythe close to me to kill me, whereas I just have to shoot you."

William's eyes widened in disbelief as Athena spoke, his expression changing from one of disdain to one of fear. Athena basked in the expression, glorying in having outsmarted him. She wanted to talk, to explain to him how she knew everything, how she had planned for everything. She wanted to watch his horror turn to defeat and watch him fall to the ground and beg for death. Instead, though, she had only one question left unanswered, and he was the only one who could give her what she craved.

"Who are you really William? Why have you attacked my family?"

"I'm not telling you anything. Just kill me if that's what you want to do." He spat at her, eyes bulging with hatred. "But you can't can you? The great Athena has to know."

Athena stood deadly still. She couldn't think properly. The only tactical decision was to fill the man with holes and paint the alley with his blood, but then she would never know. She would be left to wonder at the mystery for the rest of eternity. She didn't know if she could live that life.

"Just tell me!" She ordered.

"No!" He shouted in response, a smile curving across his face.

Bullets rained down the alley towards Athena. She jumped back falling behind her men and ordering them to return the fire. The alley way filled with metal and brick dust as the two sides fired towards each other. Athena reached into her coat to grab her revolver, but by the time she had stood and drawn, William and his allies had escaped the confines of the alley. Two men lay dead, their bodies filled with bullets, and in the distance, Athena heard the screech of tires as William's car drove away from the ambush.

Twenty-nine
Failure

T yres screeched as William's car pulled away from the warehouse district, turning a sharp corner onto the main street that led up town. Sunlight streamed in through the windows, bathing the interior of the car in gold, shimmering on the polished leather of the seats. Noise consumed the inside as men argued over the battle they had just left, the small band of survivors in uproar over their failure. Shadows flickered in William's vision as the car gained speed and made its way through the bustling metropolis. People jumped out of the way, and other cars came to screaming halts, as their driver made a desperate attempt to free themselves of their enemy.

"Are they following us?"

"Do you think they have more men?"

"Do they know where we're going?"

"Did you see that light?"

"Where did those men come from?"

"What the fuck was all that? Did one of you drug me?"

The panic rang inside the small metal shell, each man desperately looking around them, clambering to see what was going on, whether there was another car behind them, it's tyres pulling at the ground, advancing on them, a woman with hair streaming behind her like a cloak, riding for them, sword drawn like a warrior. William was surprised she hadn't. She had had the edge from the moment that she had stepped into the warehouse. She had had every moment planned and thought out. She knew he would have armed men and had prepared for it. She knew he would not meet unless she came alone and so she had prepared for that, concealing her men so well. He couldn't help but be impressed, Athena had proven to be the master tactician the legends said she was. He should have killed her earlier. He had decided to dance at the edge of Zeus' empire, slowly destroying him, bringing him down a bit at a time. He should have gone for the kill straight away, cutting his jugular. Now his plans had been halted.

His was still in shock at the sight of such blatant magic use. He had been told they couldn't use it, and ever since he attacked their operations, he had encountered no magical resistance. His plans had depended on them not being able to act like they had on Olympus. He didn't know how he would handle Olympians wielding magical tools and objects. He had planned a gang war and street fights in New York, not some ancient, mythical battle.

William sat silently amid the chaos. He gripped at his arm, applying all the pressure he could to keep his blood at bay. Shootouts always meant a lot of stray bullets and one had managed to find its way to his arm. He could feel the tender flesh beneath his fingers, the stinging that pulsed, as thin streaks of crimson seeped through his fingers. He needed to regroup with Frank and find a new way to attack the family. Now that Zeus knew who he was it wouldn't take them long to find out that Frank had been supporting his destructive efforts, if they didn't already know.

The car sailed into Harlem and the men let out a sigh of relief. The panic that had consumed them fading away as they found themselves in home territory. William did not allow himself to relax. Zeus had taken over the underworld of Manhattan by storming into other territory and claiming it for himself. He may be weaker now, but he was not too weak to wage war on Harlem. William knew the man too well, knew he would do and say whatever it took to get what he wanted. The man was a monster, a scourge on the world. He needed lancing, removing, burning to ash and William was going to be the one to do it.

As the car stopped the men piled out, guns drawn despite the street full of people. They shouted for the pedestrians to run, to get off the street, careful to keep their eyes focussed on anyone who seemed too at ease with the weapons or too hesitant to run when a gun was waved in their faces. William had taught them how to identify spies and enemies near them. With a groan, William managed to pull himself from the car and lean against the metal shell, breathing deeply, his vision focused on the sidewalk. The edges of his sight began to blur, blood loss and exhaustion taking its toll on him. He had to stay focussed, could not allow himself to succumb to his wounds. He breathed deeply, trying his best to calm himself and take stock. A hand came under his shoulder and, resting against one of his men, he made his way slowly into the building.

The gloomy, smoke-filled interior was a deep contrast to the bright sun that was painting the streets of Harlem outside. The room was a work in progress, nothing but a stage and half constructed bar surrounded by assorted tables and chairs. Frank's flagship club was going to be the jewel in his Harlem crown, but right now it was nothing more than a dark and dilapidated space. In the centre Frank sat with his favoured goons. The huddled men surrounded a small table, each one of them sending plumes of cigar smoke into the dank air whilst drinking greedily from their glasses. They barely looked up as the door opened and William limped in, continuing to stare diligently at the cards and chips, letting their game unfold. Casper spoke and the rest laughed their hollow sycophantic laughs. As chips clattered to the table, Casper looked up and saw the bleeding wretch that had just entered his bar.

"I hope the other guy looks worse than you Billy boy." He crooned from across the room, waving his hand for some silent attendant to rush to William's aid, not bothering to rise from his seat. He ran his hand over his cropped black hair and winked at his friends, the dark skin around his eyes creasing, showing off his approach to old age. "I know Ares is tough, but I was hoping that you would kick his ass."

"It wasn't Ares," he replied through gritted teeth, his wound stinging as the assistant began to tend to it, the pungent smell of the antiseptic invading his nostrils.

Frank was always sure to have someone with basic medical knowledge in the room at all times. There was no way this man was going to make himself one of the most feared and respected men in all of New York only to have an illness bring him to his knees.

"It was Athena. She came prepared with weapons and men, and magic." He thought he had said the last two words quietly enough to not be heard, whispering them to himself, but from the look on Casper's face he must have said them clearly.

"Did you just say magic? How bad is that wound boy? It's got you imagining things." Casper chuckled, causing another wave of falsified laughs to ripple around the circle of men.

William didn't respond, now fully contemplating the magnitude of the challenge before him. He realised he wouldn't only have to face Athena using magic, but inevitably he would have to deal with the power of Zeus. His mother had been so certain that the gods did not use magic, it had been how he knew he could defeat them. If they were using magic now, if William had to face off against godly powers, then he would need more than the ragtag assemblage of shooters and thugs that he had.

"Frank you need to get every man you have into Harlem now."

"Boy, you know that's not possible. I have enemies all over Brooklyn. If I bring every man here in one go, I'll have nothing left there."

"They know who I am, they know I'm working for you. They will come and they will kill us."

Frank rose from his game, dropping his cards onto the table as he walked over to William. The killer didn't flinch. He had never found Casper intimidating. The squat man looked so ordinary, so human, to him. His stout frame looked so breakable. The mob boss clasped his hand on William's shoulder and smiled at him.

"They don't have enough men, they could barely keep them paid before their clubs vanished." He said, tightening his grip on William's shoulder. "If they come, we will have enough men to blow them away. Let them come, it's time we finished them off."

"Athena had more men than me today." William admitted, his deep blue eyes staring into the back of Casper's head. "We haven't had any thugs trying to join us. They've managed to keep their enforcers. If they come, we will be outmatched. Frank, we need ..."

"That's enough." Frank snapped, turning back, small flecks of spittle flying from his mouth. "I supported you because you told me it would take minimal men and I would be kept at a distance. Now you want me to risk my territory and host a full out turf war in Harlem. If that is the case, then you have failed, and our business is concluded."

"It's the final push Frank. Risks have to be made."

"It's easy for you to speak of risk when you have nothing to lose, just some street thug with an axe to grind. I have territory, businesses, a reputation. You have nothing more than a bad attitude and daddy issues."

William surged forward, his soul consumed by anger and hatred. His body acted through instinct, severed from his consciousness. His muscles were taut and primed, years of training making him ready to fight. His eyes burned, seeming to glow in the dim light of the room. His thick hand grabbed at Casper's neck, clutching tight to the soft, dark flesh they found. He pressed the man against the half-constructed bar and squeezed. He barely noticed the men at Casper's gaming table rise and draw their guns, barely heard the sound of the hammers clicking back as they prepared to fire, their fingers twitching on the triggers. Across the room William's men pulled their own guns free, pointing the long black barrels towards Frank's sniggering toadies. Silence filled the room, nothing but the sound of Frank's desperate attempts at breath rattling the air.

William allowed the haze to fall from his mind and looked into Frank's face. The man's eyes pleaded for release, bulging in their sockets as his small pudgy hands clawed at William's, trying to pry them away from him. Eventually William released him, letting the man slide down the bar and suck in deep ragged breaths. Frank waved at his men to lower their weapons, William did the same to his and reached out to pull Casper back to his feet.

"Well, that was my fault William, I should know better than to make a business decision personal."

"I'm telling you Casper if we don't have a decent number of men here, soon, then Zeus and the rest of his family will destroy us. We're so close to achieving our goals."

"I won't lose Brooklyn." Casper declared, and before William could interject, raised his hand and kept speaking. "But I know a way we can out man and out manoeuvre Zeus without pulling in any of my Brooklyn guys."

The next half an hour passed in a blur. Phone calls were made, and messengers were sent. Men passed in and out of the room in a flurry of activity. William sat with Casper discussing everything that could go wrong, everything that needed to be sorted. By the time things were arranged the room was transformed. Bright lamps had been set up around the club and serving women moved through the assembled men carrying drinks and cigars as soft jazz played from the record player standing on the bar. The atmosphere of tense apprehension and fear was still there, clinging to everyone present, holding them in place, but the drink and music allowed them to partially ignore the impending battle that was looming over them, breathing down their necks, setting William's skin on edge.

The men that Casper had managed to gather were the elite of New York, the men who pulled every legitimate and legal string that the city had to offer. For years they had been the allies of Zeus and pulled those strings to help him build and maintain his criminal empire. Now, with Zeus' bribes falling short, they were open for business, looking to line their pockets with others' ill-gotten gains. They were prepared to do what it took to keep themselves gorged on women and alcohol, and had no scruples about crushing a former ally beneath their boot.

William disdained men like this. He valued loyalty and honour above all else, having seen the devastation that could be wrought by lies and treachery. He had no desire to work with these men, to watch them lie and cheat and manipulate their way into his victory, but he had no choice. His plan to work his way through the family and the empire until he had his foot on Zeus' throat was now in ruins. He had no way of breaking them apart and chipping away as he needed to. He knew the only way to win was an all-out assault; a war against gods with every willing soldier he could find stood at his side. He sat in the darkest corner of the room glaring out at the men as they talked and strategized.

Shatterny had been the first to arrive. The chief of police for the NYPD had always been a reluctant partner to Zeus and was willing to do whatever it would take to end the life of the man who pointed a gun at his daughter's temple. He was followed by a legion of police, each one standing straight backed in their dark, starched uniforms, surrounding Thomas in an impenetrable shield. The man looked like he needed no protection, his large and imposing body reminded William of an Ox, a terrifying monstrous man who looked like he could flatten anyone who stood before him. His thick moustache had bristled with delight, unable to cover the smile that stretched wide across his face, as he was told of the plan to finally dethrone Zeus. He had been helping where he could in the shadows up until now, keeping men and supplies in police stations so that Zeus couldn't track them, using the police network to keep William up to date on Zeus' activities. William was impressed with how well he had hidden it all from Zeus, lying to the god's face on so many occasions. It was because of him that William had been able to track down Hephaestus' moving storerooms. He promised Casper every man he could find without delay.

Harry Winslow had done the same, managing to utter out promise after promise between mouthfuls of food. He threw plates of sauce covered meat down his gullet, cawing like a seagull feasting on scraps. He told Frank he could have every federal agent that was in New York here in the next hour, ready and willing to take down Zeus. The man was nothing but slime and sweat crammed into a fatty carcass, a disgusting traitor that William wanted to rip to pieces. He had been feeling the pinch since Zeus' income had dried up and William had attacked the brothels. The pig had an addiction to young things he could crush beneath his mass and he was clearly desperate to instate another king of the underworld so that he could indulge his perversions. If William could do it without him then he would, but the man had some of the best trained men in the city and if he were going to bring Zeus to his knees, he needed talent as well as numbers.

Little Pete, the DA, had been the biggest surprise of the afternoon. William had spoken to him before and the timid little man had always appeared useless, a quivering mass of nerves scared to settle on any decision, wrapped with fear. Now he sat amongst these men and proposed the most daring part of the plan that William had heard. He had stammered his way through the proposal, but had been ready, clearly shrewd enough to see that Zeus was about to fall from his ivory tower.

The plan came together slowly, each one of them leaving to make calls and set things in motion. William could sense the impending battle, the electricity that hummed through the air. He could taste it on the back of his throat. He was ready, prepared to fight Zeus and bring the man to his knees. Finally, he would have the revenge he had been craving his whole life.

Thirty
What Happens in Darkness

Athena collapsed into her seat, the old wood creaking and swaying beneath her weight. She was still breathing deeply, even after the car ride from the warehouse, the exhaustion she felt not beginning to fade. She unbuttoned her jacket and let it hang loose from her shoulders, cascades of thick black fabric brushing against the soft white shirt she wore underneath. She couldn't remember the last time she had felt so tired, or when she had used so much power and pushed herself to this point. She closed her eyes and let her head fall back, hair that had come loose during the confrontation falling back to sway in the stagnant air of the bar. She wished she could have stayed up on the street, breathing in the warm, fresh air that coursed through the wide city streets, but she had to report what had happened to Zeus and he was not prepared to sit vulnerable in the open.

When she had arrived the three other Olympians had been sat in a dark silence, each one of them sipping from a glass and shooting anxious glances at the door. Hera had yet to remove her coat, still nestling herself in the decadence that swaddled her. She barely looked up from the floor, her cold, dark eyes unfocussed, roaming the wood as if searching the pits of Hades for her lost family. Athena couldn't help but feel for her. She had kept a family together that wasn't entirely her own, and now her sister and brother and child had found themselves ripped from the world by a monster she had no hand in creating. Fate had played a cruel trick on the queen of Olympus over the past few weeks, and she bore the pain with grace. Athena's pity for the woman was also filled with admiration, even as she saw her hand clutched to Ares' arm, her manicured nails digging deep into his shirt and the muscle that lay beneath.

Ares had been the first to stand up when Athena had staggered through the door, holding herself against the frame, barely able to speak, vision blurred and mouth as dry as the Egyptian sands. Now she was sat, slowly allowing her strength to flow back into her body, and he was at the bar pouring the last few drops of scotch they had into a tumbler for her. He made no attempt to hide his frustration that Athena had gone to face the killer instead of him, but he was a soldier, and he would not leave a comrade stranded and beaten without a drink. The hulking man made his way over to her and handed her the crystal clad amber which she supped at, sending silent thanks for the refreshment. Athena had never been as fond of alcohol as the other gods, preferring a level head and clear vision over the futile and intangible ecstasy of intoxication. In times like these though, a large glass of scotch pouring down the back of her throat, sending warm sensations through every part of her body, was more than she could ask for.

In the dim room Zeus sat furthest away, barely visible as an indistinct shadow on the stage, his form almost blending in with the instruments that littered the place. When Athena had arrived alone, he had known she had been unable to save the twins. Her elation that she had survived the confrontation didn't last long. She wanted to explain to him that they had been dead when she arrived, the killer having no intention of letting them live, but she was too tired and weak to make excuses for herself. She embraced his pain and watched in pity as the mighty king of Olympus, the god who had ruled over humanity's greatest and most defining moments, was reduced to a silent shell of a man, huddled in his own shame and failure. She had never seen him like this, so consumed that he had surrendered to the misery and loss, but then he had never borne the pain of death, only bestowed it upon others.

Athena drained the last of her scotch and let out a satisfied moan, a soft thanks for her nourishment. Pulling herself up, she readjusted her waistcoat, moving it into position to compensate for her loose and sloppy jacket. Her voice was hoarse, the words pulling at the flesh of her throat as if to bring it with them.

"I didn't kill him," she managed to confess to the family members around her. "He got away, but I was able to put a dent in his gang. Most of the guys he brought died."

Her information was met with silence, the kind that lives by choking the words in the mouth of everyone present, that revels in the dank and squalid air of terrible times and small spaces.

"If you killed enough of his goons, is he weak enough to attack?" Ares asked, his gruff voice bludgeoning the silence, reverberating through the atmosphere that encased them all.

"I would say so, we still have plenty of our own guys and we know he's likely gone to Harlem. Right now, he's weak and doesn't have the support he needs for an all-out brawl." She managed between panting breaths, the exertion of speaking almost too much for her. She gripped the base of the chair to steady herself, keeping her eyes focussed on Ares even as her vision began to swim.

"You should stay here" Ares suggested, looking in concern at the sister before him, swaying, panting, and sweating in her seat.

"No." Athena snapped in response. "I just need to recover, I am not sitting out this battle. I'm going to watch him die."

She kept her eyes fixed on Ares, staring into the darkness of his glare. She resented him trying to keep her away from the brawl. He was not the only warrior in the room, not the only one who craved battle and felt the bloodlust and thrill of it in their body. She would not sit out the most important fight of her life. She would not miss the chance to avenge her fallen family, not today, not ever.

"Fine, then let me be the one to get everything sorted. We have plenty of men who you didn't take. I need to call them in and prepare them."

"Make sure they're well-armed, his goons had more ammo than I thought possible. Give them every weapon you can find, there are more special ones in Hephaestus' workshop, give them out too."

"I didn't realise you were the head of the family now Athena." Ares retorted, his petulant temper searing through him.

"Just do it Ares" came a command from the shadowed stage.

Zeus barely moved, his voice filled with sorrow, handing the command to Ares with a little of the strength Athena was used to. She couldn't help but be slightly happy that he had not given up completely. Ares only sneered in response and then stomped from the room, the sheer bulk of him sending ripples of anger and aggression through the floor, shaking Athena where she sat. She glanced over to the bar, desperate to take another drink, but not trusting herself to stand and walk across the room. She could still feel pain and weariness radiating through every part of her body.

The room, once again, became silent, none of the gods knowing what to say. The plan was in motion and now it was a matter of time, waiting for the call to arms. Athena had originally planned for Zeus to come with her and Ares to the fight, his power having once been unmatched by anyone, but looking at the shrunken man she was unsure if he would be of much use in a fight.

"What I don't understand is who this person is" Hera announced into the baron air. "Did he give you any clues about that or how he knows about us. Why is he doing this?"

"He didn't say anything." Athena replied, the anger she felt at her own ignorance building within her again. "But there are some clues."

"Such as?" Hera asked, rising and moving to the bar with her glass in hand, the long stem and conical top shimmering along with the last few droplets of her drink.

"Whoever they are they know more about us than just who and what we are."

Athena allowed her mind to work, plucking through clues she hadn't given herself time to notice, allowing memories of the battle to run through her mind. Clear and distinct visions presented her with information she had not bothered to pay attention to in the moment, too consumed by the combat to focus on minor details.

"He was surprised that I was using magic against him, genuinely shocked when it happened. If he knows we're gods, though, then he must have expected that. He's not just deduced who we are then, he actively knows. He knows we're gods and that we have been forbidden from using magic, or that we are unable to." Athena was rambling now, but she didn't care, the deductions and conclusions were consuming her mind, filling her every piece of consciousness. "If he knows that then it's someone who has been close enough to one of us to be told secrets. Which definitely rules out the other Pantheons."

"He was close to Hermes, maybe he told him." Hera suggested, her voice slashing at Athena's concentration like a hatchet.

"No, he had this all planned before he met any of us, seducing Hermes was part of it. He knew what we were before anything happened to us."

Athena knew she was right, but she couldn't make it make sense.

"The only problem is none of us recognised him. We all saw William at one point or another and none of us recognised him. That would be impossible if he was a former associate. So maybe he's not the person one of us got close too, maybe he was close to someone else who knew our secrets and is using that knowledge to hurt us."

"That still doesn't explain his motives."

"Unless we hurt that person. We've all got close to mortals over these past millennia and then hurt them in some way. What if one of those told this man, this William, our secrets and now he's getting revenge for them."

Athena wasn't certain if she was right, but the conclusion made sense. She needed to keep thinking, to keep explaining. Her voice was still hoarse but talking was making the pieces fit together. She had to go on. She pushed herself up from the chair, muscles straining as she moved, slowly limping towards the bar.

"There was something else about him too, something that seemed so odd, when I was using my magic. I could feel something from him, a presence, a dormant power or strength, something almost godlike. Though, that doesn't make sense if he's not part of another polytheism."

"That would explain how he was able to beat Poseidon in their fight." Hera responded, almost prompting Athena to go on, urging the answers out of her.

She finished making her martini, pouring the liquid from the cobbler to the glass, the whole time keeping her gaze fixed on Athena as she struggled towards the bar.

"But how could they possess magic? The knowledge of that was lost to humans long ago." Hera asked, almost as inquisitive and desperate for the truth as Athena.

"This is true, but he found the scythe of Cronos, maybe he found other means to wield and use ancient power."

Athena managed to circle the bar, holding herself up against the polished wood, her fingers smearing the smooth surface as she dragged herself around towards the scant bottles that littered the underside of the bar, eager to pour herself another. The smell of alcohol surrounding it all, drawing her forward.

"The only alternative is that William is a demigod."

"That's impossible." Hera snapped at Athena.

"I know it is Hera, we've all been careful to clear up loose ends where they occur, and we've all watched out for each other. The only way William is a demigod is if he was conceived at a time when we couldn't keep an eye on one of our own."

Athena spoke as she poured her drink, but the words were enough. She didn't need to think anymore, she didn't need to try and work it out or draw conclusions, it was there in her mind, the undeniable truth that she had come to see so clearly. She was unable to focus on anything but the revelation, her body was motionless, the scotch pouring into a glass that was now full, spilling and pooling on the sleek surface of the bar.

"Athena, what are you doing? What's happened to you?" Hera demanded, staring at the sight of alcohol flowing away, now dripping to the floor. Athena barely heard the words, instead staring into the shadowed stage where the crystal eyes of her father stared back, menacingly out of the darkness.

"It's you." She said, the words stumbling from her.

"That's enough Athena." Zeus commanded rising from his huddled heap, standing tall. An imposing figure of darkness.

Athena wanted to stop, wanted to keep the secret as commanded, and obey her father. It should have been easy. She had kept his secrets her whole life. She had protected him. She had been the only member of the family to know about his deal with the angels and his role in the destruction of every other member of the Greek Pantheon. She had figured it out early, but she had kept it quiet, knowing she would have done the same, knowing the odds of living were only increased by giving in. She had accepted it, allowed him to live without the hatred of the rest of the family. She should stay silent, she knew she should, but she had deduced everything. Weeks of searching and asking the same questions over and over in her mind had almost broken her and now she was free, unburdened of her ignorance. Zeus began walking forward, the stage creaking as he moved towards her and Hera.

"William is your son, you conceived him when you were in the asylum in London."

She stared at Zeus, looking for confirmation in his face, and she found it in the anger that contorted his features, in the betrayal and shame that filled his eyes. He stood still, meeting her gaze, neither of them noticing the horror that now coated Hera's face.

"You were alone for a year, locked away and mistreated, you must have found someone, a woman to help ease the pain."

"So, what if I did?" Zeus replied through gritted teeth, his skin rippling with fury as he stared at Athena. "I was trapped, me the king of Olympus, by ignorant and bigoted fools. Cast into squalor and humiliation for telling the truth. If I could find solace in that despair, then do not begrudge me that."

"I will begrudge you that." Hera replied. Her voice did not wobble as she spoke, but Athena could see the pain writhing within the woman, the lies and deceit stabbing her. She held herself firm, smooth jaw trembling, eyes watering as she spoke. "I have spent my life cleaning up your messes, holding your family together. I have kept us safe, kept us from facing annihilation by another generation of gods just as we destroyed the titans. Now I find out it was for nothing. Whilst I was working furiously to free you, you were in bed with some insane hussy, getting your rocks off to some mad little harlot." She screamed up towards Zeus' face, having strode forward, anger pulling her in.

"Enough Hera!"

"No, it's not Zeus. You did all this, you killed our family because you couldn't control yourself, you couldn't keep your urges in check, even in a sanatorium. You know what I wish, what I truly and deeply wish? I wish that I was surprised." Hera's voice began to crack, tears now streaming from her eyes, the fury within her forcing them out. "I wish I was shocked by your selfishness and recklessness, but I'm not."

"Hera." Athena limped towards the goddess as she spoke, eventually reaching her and planting a hand on her shoulder, squeezing tightly. "I know this is hard, but this doesn't help solve the problem, please let us get back to focussing on what to do now.

"What to do now is I leave. I have nothing to do with this boy or his grudge against you. He's killed to get to you." She snarled, stabbing a long, elegant finger towards Zeus. "The further away from you I am he safer I'll be."

She raised herself onto her toes to stand as tall as she could against the towering figure looming down at her from the stage.

"I have sacrificed so much for you Zeus and given you my all. I can't do it anymore, not now."

With that Hera turned and walked across the bar. She downed her drink and, as she moved to the stairwell, let the glass fall with a thud against the floor. Her fur lined shadow disappeared into the darkness and she left nothing but gentle sobs in her wake.

Athena looked up at Zeus, his face set firm and jaw clenched as he stared into the doorway, as if the sheer force of his will could bring her back. Nothing happened. He and Athena stood in the gloom of the club, the two of them letting the realisations wash across them. Athena couldn't focus on anything but the truth she had deduced. She could not believe that another demigod had been born, that another child of Zeus walked the earth. It had been centuries since one had existed and now there was one the other side of the city, waiting for them, burning with rage at them. There was one last thing she needed to know, one last question that was clawing within her.

"Why didn't you tell us that you had had sex in that place? Why did you keep it a secret? Hera's known for your whole marriage that you take lovers. Why didn't you clean up after yourself or let one of us do it? You must have known it was a risk?"

"I loved her." Zeus said, his focus lost, eyes staring into the distance. "She was my world when I was trapped in that place. I couldn't let her get hurt."

"Yet you abandoned her, left her there alone."

"We must always abandon mortals, they do not belong with us in this family."

Zeus' focus snapped back, and he looked down at Athena from his stage, the rage he had shown her earlier gone, a grim determination now setting his eyes ablaze.

"Come Athena, we have a battle to prepare for."

Thirty-one
Decision Time

Hera slammed the door as she entered her apartment, the thick wood swinging back against the wall with a thud that sent the ornate picture frames lining the hallway quivering. She seethed with anger, could feel it twisting and pulling at her organs. As the last ripples of her thunderous entry slowly faded from the apartment, she stood motionless, simply allowing herself to breathe and gather herself. Her mind was awash with sorrow after the revelations she had been forced to endure at the club. Half of her screamed to run to the bedroom and pack up what she could fit into a suitcase and drive away. She had emergency cash and bank accounts she could rely on to keep her going until she found somewhere new to settle. The killer didn't want her, he wanted Zeus. If she fled, disappeared into the vast expanse of the world, and lived out her immortality in peace, he would never find her, never hurt her. The other half of her pulled her back to her family and to Ares most of all. Hera adored the boy more than life itself. He was her perfect god with all his strength, ability, and rugged good looks. She didn't know if she could abandon him, and leave him to the mercy of some sick, twisted demigod without offering her support.

She knew she was no fighter, and that staying could mean the end of her life. In a confrontation she barely knew how to defend herself, even if Zeus was now allowing magic. Hera had always been a master of her own divine powers, but she used them to motivate others to fight, not to do the fighting.

The discourse racing through her mind was like an unstoppable wind blowing any semblance of reason into a violent whirlwind of chaos. She couldn't decide, couldn't even make herself feel. Everything hurt, every part of her ached with the knowledge that despite her best efforts, despite a marriage to a man she had grown to resent and despise, despite keeping the family living and working together, and clearing up every single mess that she found strewn at her feet, it had not been enough. Her family had fallen apart. One of her children was dead and the other was about to throw himself into a conflict that could very well kill him. The moment weighed heavy on her and eventually all Hera could do was slowly allow herself to fall back against the door and lower herself to the ground, her thick clothing keeping her softly cushioned as she found the polished floor.

Hera had never given up before, she had never allowed herself to fall and crumble, but in this moment, it was all her body would let her do. She wrapped her arms around her legs pulling them close to her chest, feeling the layers of clothing she wore bunch up. She rested her head on her knees and let the tears flow. She kept her eyes shut, thick droplets forcing themselves between her eyelids and splashing onto her hunched-up body. She tried to hold back sounds, but she couldn't, her body forcing out sobs and moans as she wept for the life she had failed to keep together. She had mourned the death of Demeter with her tears like any good sister, but now was different. She had permitted herself grief before, but now it consumed and controlled her. She was nothing but a puppet to her pain in this moment and she hated herself for it. Goddesses should not feel powerless, she told herself, as if to command the pain to vanish from her. It did not work.

Eventually Hera's tears began to dry. It was a slow process, she had no idea how long she had been curled up on the floor, a mass of fur and tears. She still couldn't move, still couldn't face the world. Light poured in around her, the day not over yet. She knew she had to make a decision, had to choose a path to take. She opened her eyes and allowed the sunlight to shimmer on her dark tearstained irises. She looked up at the art that surrounded her, the collection she had spent a lifetime building. Originals from every great artist filled her vision, colours surging towards her with charm and optimism.

Hera had always adored art and loved her wall of priceless portraits and landscapes. In her moment of grief, though, she found no charm in them. The dots and strokes, the abstract shapes and classical dark scenes brought forth no emotion. Everything but pain was locked away within her. In that moment she made her decision. She knew that she had been broken, that the final betrayal of a husband she had protected for millennia had been the thing to make the goddess stop caring. Her art meant nothing, her home was nothing more than a pen, and her family was broken. She knew she would miss Ares, but she had spent an eternity with her son, and he was bound to hurt her just like Zeus. Family loyalty had bound her to each and every one of them, and now she had been liberated. Her brother had finally pushed her too far.

Hera placed her hand down, running her fingers against the varnished surface of the floor, the smoothness feeling like glass at her touch. With a push she raised herself from her shameful hunched position and stood tall. If she was going to go, she would have to speak to her accountant and have her secret funds released as well as find transportation that wasn't a car she owned. She did not revel in the idea of public transport, but she knew she could afford at least a couple of first-class tickets on her way out. Hera had never run before, at least never alone.

Hera made her way to the bedroom. The lavishness of the room always amazed her. She may have lived on Olympus but the innovations in bedding and design made the heavenly mountain top look like a camping spot. A vast glittering chandelier descended from the ceiling, the thick crystal globules sending out reams of rainbow light that danced across every surface. The fourposter bed stood at the back wall, the layers of sheets neatly covering the soft mattress and sumptuous pillows. The thing looked so inviting that Hera had to restrain herself from lying down. The exhaustion of the day was taking its toll on her, making her yawn and rub at her already red and sore eyes. Hera managed to resist the call of her bed, the soft scent of lavender wafting effortlessly from the tranquil space, and made her way into the closet.

The space was larger than most rooms and was filled to the brim with class and decadence. Every rack was adorned with furs, velvets, cottons, and silk. Coats and jackets hung around her, their browns and blacks pulling in the light from the bedroom. Shelves were stacked with hats and shoes and draws sat silently, ready to burst with finery. Hera had offered to empty the closet to pay for the security the family needed after all their stock had been destroyed, but Zeus had refused. He had told her that selling their property would amount to failure. The damage to his reputation; the city seeing him pawning his wife's clothes would have started a turf war immediately. He would have lost everything. Hera ran her fingers over the sumptuous outfits, letting the soft fibres tickle at the tips. They had lost everything already, selling some coats could not have possibly made it worse.

Hera let out a sigh as she began rummaging through her possessions, pulling out anything of value. Jewellery was the first to fall into her bag: a cascade of creamy pearls and shimmering diamonds with sapphires, rubies, and emeralds. The gold and silver swam through the colours as jewellery box after jewellery box found itself upended. The base was lost beneath the hoarded wealth before Hera even looked at the clothes. She didn't bother to fold or neatly pack her items, instead she quickly pulled fistfuls of cloth from her wardrobe and let it cover the jewellery. She grabbed underwear and tops, anything light that could be squeezed in. Summer was still in full reign and she knew she could buy more of the finer, heavier items. She looked around the room, searching for anything she would need and then, content with what she had managed to pull together, she fastened the bag shut.

Lifting it was a challenge, but she managed to pull it up and make her way to the kitchen. The surfaces shone and the air was filled with the scents of lemon and cleaning fluid. The maid always came in the morning and kept the place immaculate. It also helped that Hera never ate at home. She always dined out, choosing to find ways to manipulate herself into the finest restaurants with month long waiting lists. It was the little game she had always chosen to play with the humans that swarmed New York.

Sharp clacks sounded, cutting through the silence of the empty kitchen as Hera walked forward. Kneeling down, she opened up a cupboard. A mess greeted her: cleaning supplies, empty tins, an assortment of kitchen detritus that had no real use or function but that had managed to find itself in this place. She pushed it all aside sending it sprawling across the black tiles, a sea of crap spiralling away from her. She pulled and pulled at the random assortment of objects until she knelt as an island amongst it. Tins and containers clanged and thudded as they fell, glass bottles, not able to break from the small fall, simply rolled away, their contents sloshing uselessly within. It didn't take her long to find what she was looking for.

Buried at the very back of the cupboard was a coffee pot, the dull metal container hiding deep in the darkness. Hera pulled it out and turned, rising as she did, to place the coffee can on the kitchen counter. She grabbed the top and released the small amount of magic she had imbued into it. Hera had been determined to keep her secrets and the only way to do this was to use her power. The magic of one god could never be broken by another and so this pathetic pot had become her impenetrable safe. The top popped off, releasing the lingering, heady smell of coffee grounds. Hera reached in to pull out the money she had stored there. Green bills emerged, tightly rolled to protect them, the sly eye of a long dead president looked out at her, shrewdly taking in her actions. Hera had never revealed this money. She had had faith in the family and their goals in Manhattan, but she would never be unprepared.

As Hera moved to put the money in her pocket, she looked up to see a man walk into the doorway. She narrowed her eyes at him, taking in his large build and dark eyes. His skin was almost ashen white, and his auburn hair had been cropped down to nothing but a fuzz that ran over the surface of his head. He leered at Hera as he walked through the doorway, his freckled skin wrinkling as he smiled at her with a sickening grin.

"Who are you?" Hera demanded of him, keeping her posture straight and her voice solid. She would not show any fear. "What are you doing in my home?"

She kept her eyes fixed on him as she spoke attempting to stare him down, but there was no success. The man did not reply, instead he continued to stalk forward.

"Tell me who you are now!" She demanded again, severity lacing her voice.

"Ah now dear" he responded, his voice dancing, the thick Irish accent seeming to sing every word that he uttered. "That's no way to treat a guest now is it? Your husband will be mighty mad when he finds out." He laughed as he continued his approach.

"You're not a guest in my home. You're an intruder."

"Did you hear that David, apparently we're intruders."

As he spoke another man followed through the doorway behind him. He was dwarfed by his ginger compatriot, his sharp and shrewd features fixed onto a head that looked too big for the scrawny body carrying it. His hair fell in long black strands and his eyes searched the room.

"We are intruders ya eejit." He responded equally as lyrically. "Now let's just grab the bitch and be done with it. Boss wants her back sharpish." He raised his gun to her as he spoke, the brawny ginger following suit. "Now dear you can come quietly, or we can hurt you and drag you there."

"I might just hurt yas anyway." The ginger man said taking another step forward.

Hera panicked, pushing herself back against the furthest countertop. She didn't know what to do. She knew these men couldn't kill her no matter how many holes they riddled her with, but she didn't have to think hard to figure out who their boss was, and she knew that he could kill her. She was determined to be free, determined to escape from all of this. She glanced at her bag, a source of hope, an opportunity for a life away from the curse of keeping Zeus' messes cleaned up. She would not let two slack jawed Irish men take that away from her.

She knew she couldn't fight them, they would be stronger than her by far. Centuries of living a mortal life had given their immortal bodies basic restrictions. She knew she couldn't pay them off. The killer had enough resources to take down the family, she doubted the small bundle of notes she had just pulled from the coffee can would compare to what they were normally paid. She needed to think quick. The brawny intruder was moving closer, stretching out his pale hand ready to grab the scruff of her clothing, ready to drag her kicking and screaming to her death. She could smell his cologne, the cheap odour hitting the back of her throat as he got closer, barely masking the smell of stale sweat that coated him.

"You don't want to do that." She said at him, sending out a wave of magic, letting her own mind push at his.

Zeus may be able to throw lightening from the sky, but she had her own tricks. Hera took in a deep breath as the man stopped, hand still outstretched, reaching towards her chest. He didn't move.

"Yes, I do." He replied, confusion visible across the squashed features of his face.

"No, you don't." Hera assured him, pushing against his mind. "You don't want to take me, and you definitely don't want to hurt me."

She nudged her words deep inside his thoughts, sending his mind spinning with contradictions, changing his motives from within him. She realised it had been too long since she had manipulated someone in this way. Her head began to ache as she concentrated on making her words true, on making him not want to hurt her. The attacker pulled his arm back, wobbling slightly as he stepped away. She let out a small sigh of relief, pleased to see her power was working.

"Jesus Christ, Seamus, what are ye doin? Get the bitch now." His friend demanded, his thin lips settling into a line of displeasure.

Seamus looked at Hera, his eyes almost pleading for her to give in and be taken. Hera felt her power, felt the goddess she had once been.

"Seamus you definitely don't want to hurt me, but you do want to hurt David there."

"What?" David barked.

Hera ignored him.

"He's never treated you right, never treated you like a friend."

She bombarded his mind with hatred and resentment, with cruelty and fear. Hera swarmed his consciousness with images of David dead, his body bleeding from bullet holes that had pierced through every limb and organ, and she made Seamus happy about it.

"He does nothing but bark orders and take the credit for your hard work. He doesn't deserve to live, he doesn't deserve to tell you what to do."

Hera didn't know if she was right, but in this moment everything she said felt like the absolute truth to Seamus. He turned and raised his gun at David, his hand shaking as his mind tried to reject Hera's manipulations. The man wasn't strong enough.

"What are ya doin Seamus?" The slender man screamed as the gun was raised to him. "Stop this. What kinda witch are ye?" He asked, staring at Hera, raising his own gun. "Stop it now or I'll shoot."

Hera didn't care, she didn't have time to focus on the little man waving the gun toward her face.

"Do it Seamus, take control like you've always wanted to, be the man you know you can be."

"Stop it!"

"A leader"

"I said stop it!"

"A champion"

"Shut up now ya witch!"

"A man that can look in the mirror with pride."

"STOP!"

"DO IT!"

A shot rang through the apartment, a sound that bellowed and cracked the air, sending pain searing through Hera's ears. She raised her hands and pushed them against the side of her head as a ringing noise settled in her skull. Infront of her the small David fell to the ground, the back of his head painted against the kitchen wall, blood swarming around him, his dark eyes wide open, staring into the abyss of Hades. Seamus looked down at his friend in horror, the intrusion of Hera's manipulation falling away as he fell to his knees, soaking his trousers in blood as he shook the lifeless body. Hera slowly moved forward and grabbed the gun Seamus had let fall to the floor. Smoke still rose from the barrel and whilst he was consumed by shame and grief, she aimed the pistol at the back of his head and pulled the trigger sending his corpse falling.

Thirty-two

Battle Begins

A res loved the smell before battle, loved the scent of rooms crowded with men, each one ready and willing to kill or die. His nose filled with the aroma of sweat and metal, with testosterone and adrenaline. He could feel the anticipation igniting the air, filling the cramped space with energy that made him feel alive once more. He looked back at the array of men following him, each one of them poised and ready to fight, not as well trained or well-equipped as an army but just as eager to spill blood. His gang was the toughest in New York and they knew it. He had found the street fighters and thugs that took pleasure in the beatings they administered to helpless by-passers and turned them into gangsters. His men had turned Manhattan from an island of squabbling crime bosses to an empire in under a year.

He had almost burnt the city to a cinder when some had left to work elsewhere or had refused to fight without pay. He had been their boss, the force that urged them to become mobsters of decent standing, that had made their life one of meaning rather than casual violence. He despised mercenaries; men who sought only money rather than the glory of battle. He thought he had done better, but he had been wrong. He hoped that the men following him now, pistols held steady, eyes sharp and focussed, were behind him because of their loyalty, but he had been able to pay them well. The night of poisoned drinks may have ruined their reputation but before customers started dying, they had spent dollars by the fistful, and every last red cent had found its way into his thugs' pocket. Manpower was needed now more than anything.

Ares couldn't help but feel smug as they made their way through the dirty underground that had been made within Harlem. For all of Zeus' connections and political manoeuvring, for all of Hera's involvement with the prohibitionists, for all of Athena's strategizing, they were left with a simple solution; fight and kill. Ares had always argued that anyone who opposed them should be crushed swiftly and brutally, but the others had tried to find a place in this modern civilisation of capitalist business and slide-of-hand politics. It had failed. For Ares there was one simple truth; take your enemy's head before they take yours. It was simple but it was fucking effective.

The escape tunnels had been made in the early days of the family when Harlem was more likely to be raided by the police and feds. Just because it was a black neighbourhood, they had taken liberties. Ares had never understood racism, a comrade was a comrade, and an enemy was an enemy. You fought for one and killed the other. The colour of their skin mattered extraordinarily little to him. In the darkness of the tunnel, it mattered little as well. He wished they had installed some lights but that would have been too expensive. The tunnels were a makeshift escape that led between a select few buildings, nothing that a few men with basic tools weren't able to put together. They were more of a connection of basements than an elaborate system - a collection of fake walls and hastily smashed through drywall. Dust still tainted the air, filling every nose with the scent of dampness and disuse.

Athena walked in front of him, her form barely visible in the weak torchlight. Ares had no idea where abouts in Harlem they were, but he could feel that they were close, could smell the impending fight. He had discarded his jacket and waistcoat, the clothing too fitting for a real fight. Instead he wore loose slacks and a shirt half opened at the front, he needed to be mobile, agile. Guns may have made close up fighting more difficult, but he knew his enemy would manage to get in close and he didn't want anything to hamper him dodging away from the scythe. He would not let himself fall like the rest of the family. He would win.

The parade of armed men stopped as Athena raised her hand to signal that they had reached their goal. The sound of weapons clicked behind him. Athena counted slowly and quietly, her voice barely audible in the dark chamber. She peered through a small hole in the wall, the faint light beyond illuminating her crystal blue eyes, making them shimmer. She turned to Ares and winked, pulling out her own gun and pushing her weight against the wall.

The secret door opened quicker than Ares expected. The sound of the wood frame grinding against the floor made him think it should open at a restrained pace, but in a blink, Athena had pushed the wall open sending light flooding through the passage. Ares briefly looked at his men, each one of them wearing looks of grim determination and joy for conflict. Ares sent out a wave of aggression, driving up their blood lust. He commanded them to fight with nothing more than his presence, and, following Athena, moved his bulk through the door into the space beyond.

They were in the storage room of a small tenement building that Casper was in the process of transforming. The space had belonged to the family long before Casper managed to get his grimy little hands on it, so they knew the place well. It had been a stroke of luck that Casper had decided to make this his base. After everything that had happened recently, Ares was happy to get all the luck that he could. As the fight started, he saw that Athena had begun her work early. There weren't many opponents in the small room, and she had dealt with two quickly. One lay dead on the floor, a bullet hole sending blood spilling from his lifeless form. Another sat against a box, screaming in horror and agony as his arms, now turned to snakes, bit at the rest of his body, pulling chunks of flesh from wherever they could find it.

Ares smiled at Athena's handiwork before beginning the battle in earnest. Men huddled behind boxes closest to the door that led into the rest of the building. They cowered, firing their revolvers blindly into the room, hoping to hit Ares or his men. The god of war moved swiftly behind some other crates, avoiding the bullets that flew through the air. The constant explosion of pistols sent a thrill through him. He loved the noise and chaos of battle.

He sent out feelings of decisiveness, of the need to watch the enemy bleed, to the men firing at them. He clouded their emotions with feelings of conquest and victory. As chips of wood were thrown into the air, and wall plaster puffed from bullet strikes, the men behind the crates emerged, their desire to kill face to face consuming them. Ares took the opportunity and, emerging from the safety of his hiding spot, fired three bullets, each one hitting the desired target.

The room settled into silence as men emerged from the passage into a room of smoke and dirt, to a floor coated with blood. They didn't care. They followed their bosses through the door and into the rest of the building. The plan was simple. Athena and Ares would act like a battering ram, moving through and killing everyone they could get find. Those that weren't killed would be corralled into the main bar space. When they realised that Ares and Athena had them cornered, they would flee into the street. There Zeus and Hera would be waiting with the rest of the men and they would gun them down like rats. Getting close to the killer was not an option until every single man was dead and his body was so riddled with bullets that he couldn't move. The family would have their revenge.

As they moved through the building Ares was surprised to find many of the rooms empty. Where there were people, they seemed to be ordinary workers rather than toughs or enforcers. He still gunned them down. Now was no time for mercy.

Before long they found themselves at the door to the bar. The men behind Ares were ready, their suits tight against tense muscles. Guns held aloft. Ares and Athena gave each other a nod and then rammed their shoulders into the door. It flew open and the gang stormed in. Empty darkness greeted them. Tables were strewn about the space and construction materials sat in piles or were propped up against the wall. There was silence all around them, an eerie and ominous absence of men or shooting. Ares told the boys to search every inch of the bar but there was still no sign of anyone. Athena looked just as confused, her stern features set into a scowl as her eyes moved across the room.

Her eyes widened in horror as she noticed the collection of tubs and crates set against the newly built stage.

"Run!" she bellowed into the room, making her way quickly toward the exit, reaching out and grabbing Ares, pulling him along with her. Ares had no idea why he should run but Athena rarely panicked unless it was warranted.

The stage erupted in flame. A great wave of fire burst forth, sending splinters of wood flying out towards them. The flames consumed the men closest to the stage, the intense orange light burning through their bodies, enveloping their screams with a thunderous roar. More men were thrown against the wall, their bodies crumpling into broken heaps as they collided with the solid bricks. Wood lacerated men who were not quick enough to shelter or hide, their skin ripping apart as the shards flew through them. Death filled the space and dark smoke billowed through the air in the wake of the fire.

Ares thought quick and, grabbing Athena, managed to use the mass of his body to shield her from direct contact. He threw them both through the door that led out of the building. The two of them fell to the ground in a heap, smoke and fire chasing them out of the door, rising into the air as a cloud of grey and black. Ares groaned, the pain of the scalds and lacerations searing at the back of his skin. He rolled away from Athena releasing her from the pressure of his body. The two of them lay there panting, listening to the screams of their men, hearing them beg and plead for help.

Athena was the first to rise. She had been the most protected from the inferno within the building and apart from a few singed edges of her clothing seemed to be untouched. She knelt over Ares checking his body for wounds. She gasped as she saw the state of his back. Charred skin and wooden shrapnel had turned the broad muscles and tough flesh into a chaotic patchwork. Every inch of his back looked tender and sore. Ares could feel the pain radiating in great waves across his body. It was so distracting that he barely noticed Athena move under his shoulder and lift him to his feet.

"What are you doing?" He asked through panted breaths. "Just leave me, you don't need to protect me."

"We've lost too many family members so far. I'm not letting you go." She replied, gritting her teeth as she struggled to hold up the weight of her behemoth brother. "Plus, you just saved me, and I can't be owing you one for all eternity."

She smiled up at him and together they slowly limped from the alleyway. The scene that greeted them was chaos.

Zeus' men had been ambushed almost as badly as they had. The street, bathed in the soft glow of the setting sun, was filled with men, some fist fighting, others shooting pistols and tommy guns towards their enemy. Ares looked around in horror, watching as more and more of his gang fell to the ground, giving way to the onslaught and barrage of bullets that surged toward them. The men were surrounded. On one side the police had gathered, their cars and vans sealing off the exit to the street, giving them cover as they fired endlessly into the gang members. On the other end Casper's boys were approaching, backed up by men in cheap dark suits. Ares recognised federal agents from a mile away. The street was a disaster zone. He couldn't believe they had been caught out like this, couldn't fathom how they had been so outplayed.

"Go help them." He mumbled to Athena, managing to speak through his pain.

"But you need me Ares."

"I'll be fine." He replied. "The key now is to save as many men as we can and get out. I'm too injured. I'll focus on healing whilst you round them up and we'll make our escape back through the building."

"Through the fire?" She looked at him as if he had gone insane.

"They'll never expect it."

"This is why I'm the tactician." She scoffed, smiling up at him. "Fine. I'll do what I can. I won't be long."

As Athena laid Ares against the wall, he groaned from the pain of rough brick pressing against his injuries. He gritted his teeth, trying to hide it from Athena, and watched as she ran out into the street. She ducked behind a parked car, shielding from bullets with the men. He couldn't hear what she was saying but he could see the command in her posture and read the respect on the face of the men she instructed. She strategized and soon enough the men began dashing to every other defensible position, passing along instructions. Ares sucked in raspy breaths. He knew his injuries wouldn't kill him, but they would take some time to heal. In the meantime, the agony was intense. He tried looking around for Zeus and Hera, but to no avail. He hoped beyond anything that they had not been killed, that they had not been slaughtered by the killer.

In the street Athena continued her instructions, allowing some of the gang to gain the upper hand. The police were acting like a barrier, but Athena had managed to find a spot where bullets could penetrate. Soon they started to drop. Athena used her powers, changing men in subtle ways to make fighting harder. Ares admired her commitment to transmutation. Watching as she gave men frail legs that snapped under their weight was a small piece of entertainment. Ares managed to look on with a ray of hope.

His senses pricked as he heard something to his other side. Turning his head, he looked up at the towering figure of a man dressed in black. William looked down at Ares, his expression grim and determined. He held the scythe in one hand, the curved, black blade pushed forward, as if he intended Ares to see how he would die.

The killer moved forward another step. Ares tried to shuffle away but the pain was too intense, every movement sent sharp stabs of agony through him. He wanted to lift his arm to swing, but he didn't have the strength. He tried to scream, to bellow his rage toward his enemy, but no sound escaped but a hoarse whimper, like a dying animal. The movement was swift, the scythe rising and swinging in one fluid motion. Ares' head fell with a thud to the cold ground of the alleyway.

The killer moved forward into the street. His dark clothes billowed in the wind that whipped through the battle around him. The smell of gunpowder, blood, and sweat swam through the air. Men fell, enemies and allies alike, giving way to the inevitable march of death. He didn't care about any of them. The humans around him were part of his plan, the tools, and agents of his revenge. If he could destroy everyone who had ever supported Zeus that would be a bonus, but for now all he wanted was the Olympian gods dead at his feet, with Zeus' head adorning them, like a crown. He moved down the street, his steps deliberate, a trail of blood following him, falling from the scythe.

He had been through such pains and trials to collect the weapon, but it had all been worth it. Only three monsters were left to be slain, only three needed their foul existences finally bringing to an end. He raised the scythe as he approached Athena, seeking to take her distraction as an opportunity. The woman was hunched behind a car, staring into the lines of federal agents. As she stared, awful things happened: bodies changed and contorted, becoming misshaped and uncoordinated, the men falling and stumbling over newly shrunken and exaggerated features. William's face screwed into an expression of disgust and he swung his weapon, aiming to embed the sharpened point into Athena's skull.

Athena rolled away, her body moving quickly out of the reach of the scythe. As she rolled, she reached to her side and pulled out a revolver. Her finger moved to the trigger, but William was fast. He ran toward her, reaching forward and pushing Athena's arm into the air. The pistol erupted with noise and smoke, sending its bullet flying into the orange sky. Athena twisted, escaping her enemy's clutch. She backed away. William followed, not allowing her to gain distance from him. She kept aiming her weapon at him, but he managed to get in close and mover her arm, destroying her ability to aim.

Athena kept up her attempts at distance, but William was too quick, and the goddess was tired. The energy it had taken to use that much magic in one go was draining. Her mind was foggy, and her body consumed by an aching weariness. She didn't know how long she could stay back. She gave up on trying to shoot, instead just trying to stay out of the reach of his weapon.

The two of them danced, William moving for a strike and Athena dodging just in time. She knew she couldn't keep it up, but she couldn't see an escape. As she fought, the enemy gained more ground, the police and agents gunning down more of her men, no longer distracted by her interventions. All around her, death swarmed. She moved one last time, but her ankle twisted, and she fell. The killer was upon her, using his weight to pin her to the ground. Athena struggled, using every move she knew, but it was all useless. As she panted and fought, twisting herself all she could, William managed to pull the scythe close to her. His strength was overwhelming and slowly the point of the scythe ran through the soft flesh of her neck, sending a torrent of blood out and ending the life of the goddess.

Thirty-three
Final Confrontation

Hera twisted and pulled to no avail. She struggled to release herself, but it was no good. Zeus clutched too tightly to her wrist, dragging her behind him, out of the car and into the depths and darkness of Club Olympus. She clawed at his brawny hand, her nails running through sweat, grime, flesh, and hair. He did not let her go or respond to her screams and cries. Nothing she did loosened his grip, not until they had descended the stairs and he had slammed the door shut behind her.

"I said let me go." She screamed at her husband.

He turned to her, his eyes cold and unforgiving. The piercing blue looked straight into her, commanding her silence. He finally released her wrist and walked over to the back room of the club. The small office space was a cramped nest of papers, empty bottles, and mismatched furniture.

"What are you doing in their Zeus? Why did we leave the fight? What's going on? Just answer me."

Hera's frustration started to boil within her, a swirling torrent of emotions that she no longer wished to control. Her confusion, her despair, and her anger were now all directed towards the man that ignored her, silently working away in the back office. She stormed forward and looked into the small space. Zeus was on his knees, pulling boxes away from the base of some shelfs.

"You said you'd put an emergency bag together." He stated not raising his head from his task. "We need to go back and get it. It's risky but should be fine. We won't have time to get my things but that doesn't matter. I can buy new clothes."

Hera was sure he was just speaking to himself now, never once looking in her direction as he spoke. She watched as Zeus pulled yet more junk from the lower shelf and finally emerged with a brown envelope engorged by its contents. Hera didn't even have to ask what was in the envelope, she recognised a secret cash storage when she saw one. Zeus rose from the ground and marched back into the bar, Hera stepping aside so he didn't knock her as he walk, his focus clearly elsewhere.

"Zeus?" Hera began. "What are you doing? Are we running away?"

He turned towards her and it was then that Hera truly noted the expression on his face. She saw the guilt and pain etched into the lines and creases that coated his tanned skin. She saw the weariness and despair in his eyes, which seemed sunken and lost in the shadow of his brow. Hera looked up at her husband, the god who had reigned over the birthplace of culture, who had defeated titans and monsters, and saw him broken, ready to flee for his life.

"We have to run Hera, we're the only two left and this killer is unstoppable. You saw what he did to Athena and Ares. We have to live and leaving is the only way to do that. We need to go far away and live a quiet existence that he can't possibly trace." Zeus spoke firmly, his voice strong, as if his announcement were somehow brave and well calculated rather than the act of a coward.

"I'm not going with you Zeus." Hera told him, walking forward as she spoke. Placing her hand on his chest, she looked up into the chiselled features and deep azure eyes. "I stayed with you to protect the family, to keep us all safe. You have destroyed my life. I came back for Ares." She almost whimpered and struggled to hold back her tears, the sight of her son: weak and helpless, falling dead with no fight left in him was traumatic. Zeus holding her back on that rooftop, not letting her save him was all too much for her. "But you let him die. Now I have nothing." She walked away.

"I didn't let him die." Zeus said, his voice hollow, filled with shame. "He died in battle. There was nothing I could do."

Hera didn't want to fight, she didn't know if she had the strength to argue with him anymore, but more than anything she was tired of his lies, tired of his failings.

"Really Zeus? I saw men transformed into monsters by Athena's power, men filled with confidence by Ares'. I even used my own magic to keep the police from advancing. I saw no lightening. You did nothing but watch as that monster and his men tore through the last remnants of our family, as he ripped apart my most beloved son."

She didn't turn to look at him, she just wanted him to know she saw his lies and his failure. Part of her wanted to scream at him more, about how all of this was his fault in the first place, but it would have been pointless, in the end she was going to leave and find a path for herself without him, if that was even possible.

"I couldn't." Zeus managed weakly. "I wanted to, but I couldn't. Summoning lightening without a conduit is dangerous and unpredictable. A storm would have hit Athena as well as the feds." Silence sat between them as Zeus confessed to his own weakness, the moment of actual truth holding Hera in place.

She knew she could argue, knew what he had once been capable of, the power he could twiddle around his fingers, but she had witnessed the killer cut through the other gods and had now lost her ability to care about Zeus' actions. She wouldn't argue. The reason why he did things didn't change that he did them: the motives, the desires, the greed, the hunger, and the lust all mattered so little now. They had resulted in everything she had feared. The Olympian family was gone, wiped from the face of the earth just as the cataclysm had wiped away the rest of the divine and magical beings of her home. She let out a sigh and continued walking toward the door.

"Hera don't go, we can survive together."

"I don't want to survive Zeus. I want to live." Hera replied, her voice quivering from the grief that sat like ice in the pit of her stomach.

"Then we have very different plans don't we."

The voice cut through Hera like a knife.

The shadowed recess of the doorway gave way to the tall, dark figure of William as he stepped forward, a grin smothered across his face, his dark eyes boring down at Hera. She stepped back, but he lurched forward quickly, dashing close to her, and grabbing her throat. He twisted her and pulled her against him, forcing her to look at Zeus, who watched the scene unfold with horror. William raised his scythe and placed the tip against Hera's temple. She could feel the cold, sharp steel on her flesh, ready to pierce through and kill her. Her eyes bulged in fear as she stared toward Zeus. She didn't want to die, despite everything, all the pain and loss, immortality was the last thing she possessed, she couldn't let it go, not to this man, not now.

"Let her go William." Zeus commanded, pulling his figure up straight, darkening his voice as he stared down his son.

"No, I don't think I will Zeus." I want you to watch as I slice open her skull, then I am going kill you. Finally, I'll do what needs to be done."

"If you kill her the last thing you will see is my living face as I choke the life from you." Zeus growled, like a caged animal desperate to tear at his prey.

"I've killed every other Olympian that's crossed my path Zeus, you will die too. I've lured them to my bed, tortured them as they lay helpless in a cage. I even came close to turning your own son against you. That would have been a nice twist of the knife in your back. I am the destroyer of Olympians."

"If you think you can compare me to the other Olympians then you are more of a fool than I thought."

Zeus took a step forward, pushing out his chest and straightening his back. Hera had almost forgotten how tall he was. He towered over her, even over the killer. His aged face was set into a scowl, the grey bristles of his beard trembling as his body shook with rage.

"Now let go of my wife and face me like a man."

The killer didn't move. Hera couldn't see him, but she could feel the tension in his body, every firm muscle and sinew ready to pounce, to kill her and move onto his next target. His odour clouded around her, the smell of blood coating him, overpowering his sweat and cologne, the metallic tang coating the back of her throat.

"Aren't you going to ask me then Zeus?"

"Ask you what?" Zeus sneered back.

"Ask me how I know you're a god, how I know how to kill you." His voice was laced with glee, a smug arrogance that he had managed to outsmart the gods themselves.

"I don't need to, we figured it out William."

"What?"

The shock was obvious. He had clearly wanted to reveal himself, to declare his true identity and finally have his revenge on a shocked and defeated Zeus. Hera had to admire, as much as she could with a hand around her throat, the man's flare for the dramatic. He would have fit in well with the demigods of old. He had certainly inherited the Olympian spirit, even if he was an insane and murderous brute. She tried to take advantage of his distraction and slither away, but she couldn't move. His grip was still firm, his body still tight and full of strength.

"You're my son." Zeus said, slowly taking a step towards the unstable man holding his wife. "Your mother was Mary, a young woman trapped in a squalid asylum. A woman I loved."

The killer's disbelief was apparent in his silence. He had no response. No part of his plan had accounted for them realising who he was.

"I can't for the life of me figure out why you hate me so much you would kill my entire family though."

"You can't?" William yelled, his voice echoing through the small space. "You broke her Zeus. You told her you loved her, that you would protect her, free her. You told my mother you would be with her and then you left her in a sanatorium to rot."

He breathed deeply, panting through his fury, the tip of his scythe pressing even more into Hera's temple. She held her breath, praying for the moment to end, praying that Zeus would be able to free her, or the killer would abandon her in order to attack him.

"I cared deeply for your mother." Zeus spoke softly and carefully. "We shared something special, but I had a family to protect, I had responsibilities."

"You had a responsibility to her."

"Not like this. Not like them." Zeus looked at Hera as he spoke. "I forged this family myself, kept it safe from everything that came before us. I couldn't abandon that no matter how much I loved Mary, no matter what she meant to me."

The killer tried to speak, to argue with Zeus, but the god ignored him.

"Think about it, William, you have never abandoned your family, no matter what, so how could you expect me to abandon mine. You tore through the city, killed gods, forged an alliance with a crime boss, just for your family. You have put death and destruction in your wake for her. Tell me we're not the same, boy."

As Zeus spoke, Hera could feel William's body relax, feel the doubts course through him. She took her opportunity. Moving swiftly, the goddess managed to pull his hand to her mouth and bit firmly on his flesh. She moved her foot, smashing the heel of her shoe onto his toes. The killer wailed in pain, loosening her even further and allowing her to pull herself away to fall in a heap on the sticky, alcohol-stained floor of the bar.

Zeus took the opening and launched himself at William. The time for discussion was over. The man who had killed her family had to die and Hera watched on as Zeus began an onslaught against him. Surging forward, the god gripped the attacker by his neck and, despite William's brawn and height, managed to lift him off the ground, throwing him against the wall. William hit with a thud, the force rippling through his body, sending the scythe to the floor in a clatter. William was shaken, not expecting the tide to turn against him so quickly. He struggled to pull himself upright, but Zeus came at him again, ramming him against the brick even harder, driving the air from his lungs.

William collapsed, winded, struggling for breath. Zeus gave him no opportunity to recover, sending his foot into William's gut. The man grunted from the force, groaning even louder as Zeus reached down to grab the scythe from the ground.

"You know, I used this castrate my own father. Now I will use it to kill my own son. I'm pretty sure there's irony in that but I'm not sure how."

Zeus raised the scythe and swung it down at William. It collided with the wall, pulling away drywall and brick dust, but no blood. William managed to roll out of the way and rise to his feet at Zeus' side. Despite the beating he had received, William gritted his teeth and raised his fist, throwing a punch toward Zeus. The god barely managed to dodge, moving out of reach just in time. William didn't stop, he came at Zeus with a barrage of jabs. Zeus was quick, but William seemed to move like air. He danced around his opponent, throwing his fists at him. Zeus swung back, using the scythe to try and put distance between them.

William was too good, moving in close, hammering Zeus with more and more blows. Zeus bellowed in frustration. As William came in close to land another hit, Zeus moved as if to strike with the scythe, In the last second of his movements he twisted his body, raising his leg and sending his boot squarely into William's chest. The attacker rose off of the ground, his dark figure flung against the bar. The wood cracked as the weight of the man collided with it. William looked up, pushing a sweaty mass of hair away from his face. Zeus charged at him, and again swung the scythe in a deadly blow. The blade made contact with wood, its sharpened point running into the grain and lodging in place.

Zeus turned in time to deflect William's next blows. The man was starting to slow down, exhaustion and pain getting the better of him. He slugged it out with Zeus, both men managing to strike blows on the other, ribs cracking as the two of them beat each other in a relentless onslaught of fury and pain. William went to deliver a kick of his own, but Zeus grabbed his ankle and swung him to the ground. William's skull let out a sickening sound as it collided with the firm ground, and a look of pain moved across his face. Zeus was on top of him, pinning him to the ground, his knees on William's wrists. He bore down on his son, his hands grasped round his throat, choking the very life from him.

Hera watched on as her husband showed his strength. Despite the punches that had assaulted him, despite the weapon that had killed his whole family being in the hands of his enemy, he had ended up winning. William struggled and writhed but Zeus had won. Slowly the man stopped moving, as the air left his body. There was nothing he could do and as he fell limp, Zeus rose, panting.

He looked towards Hera and allowed a small smile onto his face. She stared up at him as she steadily rose to her feet, shaking with every movement. Zeus staggered forward and wrapped his thick arms around Hera, pulling her close into his embrace. The two gods held each other, sharing in the pain and victory of the moment. Hera felt like she might never let him go.

The sound of metal cutting through flesh caused her eyes to snap open. Zeus weakened his grip on her. She felt his weight, the mass of his muscles pushing down on her. Looking up she saw the shock in his eyes and as he stumbled away, she saw William behind him, a surprised grin on him, his eyes full of elation. Zeus swayed and as he turned to look at his son, she saw the scythe in his back, rammed through his spine and into his heart.

"I did it. I killed Zeus." William declared to himself, victory dancing through his words.

Zeus fell to his knees. Hera could see him struggling to stay alive, his face contorting with pain. She wanted to yell, to scream, but she could only manage to stare on in horrified silence, her mouth agape, tears forming in her eyes. She never thought she would see the day that Zeus fell. William walked over to his father and rested a hand on his shoulder.

"Time to die old man" he sneered looking into Zeus' face.

"Not quite yet." Zeus said raising his own hand and touching the side of William's face. "I'd have been proud of you if you weren't insane. I won't let you hurt her."

With one final push of his will, with one great exertion that drained the last of the energy from his body, Zeus conjured lightning. For the first time in over one thousand years the god allowed himself to touch on the true power that was within him. His fingertips glowed with the brilliance of electricity that now, in a sudden and deadly jolt, surged into William. The man screamed as his organs cooked inside of him, the heat and pain too intense to bear. In his last moment he fell to the ground, smoking and charred.

Zeus collapsed to the side. All the energy in him gone, the wound in his back seeping blood. His breaths were ragged and strained, the last rattles of life catching in his throat. Hera dropped to her knees and crawled over to her husband. Tears fell in thick droplets, running down her face and dripping onto Zeus. She didn't blubber, determined to stay strong in her husband's final moments.

"Hera..."

"Don't speak Zeus. Save your energy."

"Save it for what? I'm a dead man." He coughed, blood and phlegm falling from his mouth, flecks spattering to the ground. "I need to confess something, to tell you the truth."

Hera listened in silence as, through ragged, shallow breaths, her husband spoke, and then, with tears consuming her, she watched Zeus, the king of Olympus, die.

Printed in Great Britain
by Amazon